The Best American
Mystery Stories 2018

GUEST EDITORS OF
THE BEST AMERICAN MYSTERY STORIES

The Best American Mystery Stories™ 2018

Edited and with an Introduction
by **Louise Penny**

Otto Penzler, Series Editor

A Mariner Original

HOUGHTON MIFFLIN HARCOURT

BOSTON • NEW YORK   2018

hmhco.com

ISSN 1094-8384 (print)   ISSN 2573-3907 (e-book)

ISBN 978-0-544-94909-6 (print)   ISBN 978-0-544-94922-5 (e-book)

Printed in the United States of America
DOC 10 9 8 7 6 5 4 3 2 1

Contents

Foreword

IT IS ENORMOUSLY gratifying and comforting to be reminded that readers continue to have affection for mystery fiction, a field in which I have found profound pleasure in both my personal and professional lives.

One recent bestseller list in the *New York Times* (generally regarded as the most important one, however flawed and suspect its methodology may be) placed eleven mystery/crime/suspense/thriller fiction titles in the top fifteen. For more than a quarter of a century, this distinguished genre has comprised at least half the titles on virtually every one of those lists.

We all became so used to seeing the most widely read mystery writers on the list that we would have been shocked or baffled to see a year pass without finding certain names in their customary spot at or near the top. The books by James Patterson, Sue Grafton, Dick Francis, Robert B. Parker, Harlan Coben, Mary Higgins Clark, Elizabeth George, P. D. James, John le Carré, Elmore Leonard, Lee Child, Jeffery Deaver, Nelson DeMille, Michael Connelly, John Grisham, Scott Turow, and many others continued to find a wide readership year after year, to the delight of their legions of fans.

What has recently surfaced as a surprise to me has been the evident resurrection of the mystery short story. It has been axiomatic in the publishing world that books of short stories, whether a collection (all stories written by one author) or an anthology (featuring stories by multiple authors), simply don't sell. These words of wisdom and warning were imparted to me at the very beginning of my career as a publisher.

Not being wise enough to heed the advice of professionals who knew what they were doing—which I quickly concede I did not—I started my own publishing company, the Mysterious Press, by publishing collections of short stories. Ross Macdonald, Cornell Woolrich, Donald E. Westlake, Patricia Highsmith, and Stanley Ellin were among the authors who allowed me to publish their stories. Those collections had some success and the Mysterious Press went on to publish novels by some of those outstanding authors, and that imprint remains happily alive today as part of Grove Atlantic.

Furthermore, as poorly as short story collections sell, I was assured that anthologies perform even worse. As an unrepentant lover of the short form, I need to point out that I have never had any difficulty in finding enough books to sate my appetite. An entire wall in my library, with a ceiling so high that I need a rolling ladder to reach the top shelves, is devoted exclusively to anthologies, and author collections number in excess of a thousand volumes. A large section of my bookshop is devoted to anthologies (not counting the shamelessly egotistical shelves devoted to those I edited).

How can all this publishing knowledge pertain when so many anthologies continue to be published? This series, *The Best American Mystery Stories,* is now twenty-two years old. Random House, under its Vintage imprint, has been publishing my series of Big books (*The Big Book of Christmas Mysteries, The Big Book of Sherlock Holmes Stories, The Big Book of Female Detectives,* etc.) annually for more than a decade. Is this just a display of generosity, of downright *charity,* on the part of publishing houses? Is the corporate mindset one that indicates it doesn't mind losing money on these publications because it is in the public interest to issue these profit-draining volumes?

This situation is being raised because I noticed this year that an astonishing number of anthologies have been published. Inevitably, a few have come from major houses, but a large number have come from small, even out-and-out tiny, publishers. Many are regional, where it seems that groups of mystery writers, almost certainly all known to each other in writing groups or other coteries, contribute stories to books, almost always in trade paperback form. These anthologies often have themes, sometimes outré, that elicit occasionally clever, creative stories that might not otherwise have found a home.

In 2017 more than forty such anthologies were published, at least half of which came from publishing houses that have never issued any other books. Whether they are one-and-done or the beginning of a lasting contribution to the mystery field remains to be seen. The literary genre described as "mystery" is large and inclusive. I define it liberally, to mean any work of fiction in which a crime, or the threat of a crime, is integral to the theme or plot, and you will find a great range of styles and subgenres in the present volume of *BAMS*.

A contributing factor to this cornucopia of crime is the ease with which individuals or groups can produce their own printed volumes at reasonable cost. It appears likely that the proliferation of independently produced books is a factor in the reduction of electronic magazines, which were growing in number as recently as a half-dozen years ago. Many of the best have fallen by the wayside, notably *Thuglit*, which had numerous stories selected among the fifty best of the year.

The person who reads all these e-zines and anthologies is my associate, Michele Slung, without whose extraordinary good taste and speed-reading skills these annual volumes would take three years to produce. Reading or at least partially reading more than three thousand stories a year, she passes along likely candidates for me to read, from which I cull the fifty best, which are then read by the guest editor, who selects the twenty that go into the book. All this dedication to the written word places me further in her debt, as has been the case for all twenty-two editions of this series.

Speaking of being in debt, words would be difficult to adequately describe my gratitude to Louise Penny, the guest editor for *BAMS 2018*. Best-selling writers are besieged relentlessly by demands on their time. Touring to promote a book—and not only in America—give a speech or a talk, read a manuscript in order to give it a blurb for the dust jacket, participate in a charitable event, write a story or article—the requests go on and on. And since authors are people too, dealing with their personal lives—cooking, shopping, doing laundry, paying bills, having time for family and friends—uses up still more of those precious twenty-four hours of the day. But Louise Penny agreed to be the guest editor as soon as I asked her.

As the author of thirteen novels in thirteen years, Louise Penny has enjoyed tremendous and well-deserved success with her series about Chief Inspector Armand Gamache, head of the homicide department of the Sureté de Quebec, a character heavily based on her husband of more than twenty years before his death in September 2016. She has been a bestseller for a decade and has won or been nominated for every major award in the mystery world, often many times. Set in her native Canada, her beautifully written books are among the rare few works reminiscent of the golden age of the British detective novel.

A debt of gratitude is also due to the previous guest editors, without whose generosity this series would not have had the success it happily enjoys, so sincere thanks to Robert B. Parker and Sue Grafton, who were followed by Ed McBain, Donald E. Westlake, Lawrence Block, James Ellroy, Michael Connelly, Nelson DeMille, Joyce Carol Oates, Scott Turow, Carl Hiaasen, George Pelecanos, Jeffery Deaver, Lee Child, Harlan Coben, Robert Crais, Lisa Scottoline, Laura Lippman, James Patterson, Elizabeth George, and John Sandford.

I would like to take a brief moment to mention the passing late last year of the mystery community's sweetheart, Sue Grafton, the author of the universally loved "alphabet series" featuring her series character Kinsey Millhone, and the guest editor for the second book in the *BAMS* series in 1998.

The hunt for stories for next year's edition has already begun. While Michele Slung and I engage in a relentless quest to locate and read every mystery/crime/suspense story published during the course of the year, I live in terror that I will miss a worthy story, so if you are an author, editor, or publisher, or care about one, please feel free to send a book, magazine, or tearsheet to me c/o The Mysterious Bookshop, 58 Warren Street, New York, NY 10007. If a story first appeared electronically, you must submit a hard copy. It is vital to include the author's contact information. No unpublished material will be considered, for what should be obvious reasons. No material will be returned. If you distrust the postal service, enclose a self-addressed, stamped postcard, on which I will happily acknowledge receipt of your story.

To be eligible, a story must have been written by an American or Canadian and first published in an American or Canadian publication in the calendar year 2018. The earlier in the year I receive the story, the more it is likely to warm my heart. For reasons known only to the dunderheads who wait until Christmas week to submit a story published the previous spring, this happens every year, causing severe irritability as I read a stack of stories while everyone else I know is busy celebrating the holiday season. It had better be a damned good story if you do this, because I already hate you. Due to the very tight production schedule for this book, the absolute firm deadline is December 31. If the story arrives two days later, it will not be read. Sorry.

O. P.

Introduction

I CANNOT WRITE short stories, any more than I can write poetry. I've tried, and the result, for both, is piles of something soft and smelly.

But oh, how I love to read them.

And how I admire both poets and those who can craft short stories. I think they come from the same taproot. A great short story is like a great poem. Crystalline in clarity. Each word with purpose. Lean, muscular, graceful.

Nothing wasted. A brilliant marriage of intellect, rational thought, and creativity.

I am in awe of those who can write short stories.

So when Otto Penzler asked me to be guest editor for this volume, I could not agree fast enough. To be honest, it's just possible he did not ask me but rather was (quite sensibly) asking me to suggest others who might be better placed to judge.

But I didn't care. I wanted to do it.

My love of the form started, as yours might have too, in infancy. With the stories read and reread at bedtime. While I was curled up, snug and warm and safe in bed, my mother would read, conjuring cowboys and princesses and untamed horses and wary piglets. Bringing whole worlds magically into the bedroom.

My first literary crush (I know I can trust you not to tell anyone) was Dr. Watson in the Sherlock Holmes stories. Not Holmes but Watson. I have tried not to spend too much time analyzing that.

Did you know that Arthur Conan Doyle first planned to call John Watson "Ormond Sacker"?

I have to wonder if I'd have fallen quite so hard for Ormond Sacker.

I devoured all the Conan Doyle stories, and was quite upset when Watson married Mary Morstan and sincerely tried to feel bad for his "own sad bereavement." But failed.

At university I spent a semester wearing a deerstalker. I began to question that fashion choice when I saw quite an attractive transvestite walking toward me, only to realize it was me in a mirror. After spending the semester date-free, I retired the deerstalker. But my love of all things Holmes (and Watson) remains to this day.

About that time I also met, figuratively speaking, Edgar Allan Poe, and while I did not develop a literary crush (nor did I repeat the deerstalker role-playing and have myself entombed prematurely—also bad for the love life), I have been haunted ever since by the horror of the telltale heart, the vivid images of the murders in the Rue Morgue, the house of Usher split apart by otherworldly forces. Poe's short stories are romantic, oddly sensual, deeply disturbing, and unforgettable.

Only later did I hear that the great cryptologist William Friedman had been inspired as a boy to study ciphers after reading Poe's "The Gold-Bug." Friedman was instrumental in cracking a key Japanese code during World War II. How about that? A short story won the war in the Pacific. Or at least helped.

The Canadian writer Alice Munro recently won the Nobel Prize for literature for her contributions to the short story discipline.

And discipline is, I believe, the word to use. That's what it takes to create a world, to breathe life into characters, to make us care about them. To give them flesh and blood, emotions and histories. All in a few well-chosen words.

A novel is a hundred thousand words, sometimes less, often more. But the works contained between these covers are only a few thousand. These writers are masters of the craft who, like Picasso and his sinuous line drawings, use a few short strokes to bring plot, characters, setting to life.

It takes creativity. Skill. Discipline. Knowledge of the form while not being formulaic. In a short story there is nowhere to hide. Each must be original, fresh, inspired.

And that's what you have here.

The stories in this collection have been chosen from the thousands published in the United States and Canada in the past twelve months. From all of those, twenty made the cut. You can imagine how good these are. Varied. Imaginative. Ingenious. But, oh, the misery in trying to get it down to twenty! Felt at times like gnawing off a limb. That might be a bit of an exaggeration, but it was painful.

I was far from alone in the task of choosing. Otto Penzler, the Godfather of the Short Story (I believe that is actually his official title), led the way. He is indeed a leader in promoting this literary field. Elevating it. Making sure short stories are recognized and given the respect they deserve and have earned.

Just as (to return to the poetry analogy) haiku is not the baby sister of the sonnet, so too the short story is not a lesser version of a novel. It is its own literary form. With rules made to be both followed and transcended. Done well, as they are here, short stories entertain, enthrall, amaze, haunt.

You will recognize some of the writers. Lee Child has been brilliant and generous in providing a near-novella. Michael Connelly's contribution is as smart and layered as you'd expect. The magnificent Joyce Carol Oates has a story that gets under the skin and into the marrow. And nests there.

Some of the writers will be new to you, as they were to me.

How thrilling it has been to discover new talent. To be a sentence, two, into a story and realize you're in the hands of a master. Then to look again at the name of the author and realize it's new to you. I think you'll have that experience more than once in this book.

If it's an exciting time to be a crime writer, it's an even better time for those of us who love reading crime fiction.

It has been a singular honor to be asked to be guest editor of this anthology. The only difficulty, and it was awful, was having to winnow the collection down.

If someone had told me as I wandered the halls of academe in my deerstalker, searching for clues as to why I wasn't being asked out, that one day I'd get to read all these marvelous short stories and guest-edit this volume, well, I'd never have believed it.

Not even Holmes could have predicted this. Now, my dear Dr. Watson . . .

LOUISE PENNY

The Best American
Mystery Stories 2018

LOUIS BAYARD

Banana Triangle Six

FROM *Ellery Queen Mystery Magazine*

FRIDAY LUNCHES WERE BOILED as a rule, and today's was no exception. With a feeling of numb resignation, Mr. Hank Crute guided his fork around the slab of corned beef, the bed of wild rice, the clutch of blanched green beans. His hand trembled just a hair as he let the fork drop to the table and pushed the plate away.

"Not hungry anyway," he announced, to no one in particular.

Some days, indeed, he ate so little he was amazed to find himself still alive. Some days the only reason to get out of bed was so they wouldn't come knocking for him. One of those stern Eritrean gals reminding him he had less than half an hour of breakfast left.

"Get a move on, Mr. Hank!"

For after breakfast, they would remind him, there was Morning Chairobics and a bus trip to CVS and the weekly meeting of the Card Club. And later on the Scrabble Club and the Scrapbooking Society and, still later, the Sing Along 'n Snacks Social and the ring toss and Twilight Walk with Miss Phyllis.

"Oh, and don't forget! Hair styling from Miss Desdemona!"

Never mind that Hank Crute had gone eighty-four years on God's earth without requiring a hair stylist. This was the kind of place that would foist activity on you whether you wanted it or not. As he sat staring at the ruin of his lunch, Hank grew a little dizzy thinking of all the places he was supposed to be or not supposed to be—the wheels that were already in motion on his behalf, ferrying him from one part of the Morning Has Broken facility to another without taking him anywhere.

He closed his eyes. Waited for some hard intention to contract out of the darkness.

My room, he thought.

Gripping the rim of the table, he edged his chair out and rocked himself to standing, only to see that another plate had materialized alongside the plate he had just pushed away. Almost identical, right down to the forked trails in the rice and the splayed green beans.

A prickle of terror climbed the back of his neck. Surely he hadn't actually gotten *two* plates for himself? Surely someone had joined him along the way. Someone whose name and face he had temporarily forgotten (as he was always doing). What other reason could there be for two plates of boiled food?

With a lurch, he took a step back and surveyed his surroundings. Among the semiambulatory and near-bedridden residents of Morning Has Broken, Hank took no small pride in being able to travel without walker or wheelchair, but that lonely eminence meant that sometimes he had to stand for upward of a minute orienting himself, and even after plunging forward, he might have no clear suspicion of where he was heading. As often as not, he would wait for something to rear up before him before concluding that this was the very thing toward which he had been tending.

In this manner, he came upon the elevator.

And concluded that yes, this was just where he'd been traveling. He was—he remembered now!—going back to his room. And once there, he would take a nap and forget all about corned beef and wild rice and lunch companions who slipped away when you weren't looking. It was a treacherous world.

He stabbed the Up button with his index finger, listened for the rumble of the car. A light flared above him, and the elevator doors exhaled open. So intent was he on bustling inside that he very nearly collided with a woman who was equally intent on leaving. For several seconds they stood regarding each other.

"Why, it's Mr. Hank," she said at last. "Good morning."

Her lips were dark and shrunken. Her walker rested on punctured tennis balls.

"It's afternoon," he said.

"So it is."

She wasn't moving.

"I'm Mrs. Sylvia," she said.

"I know who you are."

It was one of the curious things about this place that the residents only knew each other reliably by first name. Possibly Mrs. Sylvia had once divulged her last name, but that secret lay buried.

"You should come to the movie matinee today," she said. "It's a Stewart Granger movie."

"Who?"

"Stewart . . ." She had a flash of panic, wondering if she'd gotten it wrong. "Stewart *Granger.*"

"Little bushed," he mumbled.

"Nothing a fifteen-minute snooze wouldn't fix."

"Could be."

"Will I see you at dinner?" asked Mrs. Sylvia.

"That's as may be."

She was still watching him when the doors closed.

He let out a current of air and leaned back against the wood paneling. From somewhere in the not-distant past, a mocking voice (whose?) came curling back. "Man at your age, still able to walk. Why, you must be the rooster in the henhouse." He never felt less like a rooster than in the company of Mrs. Sylvia. Or any of the other widows who tried to cajole him into Bingo Night or wine, cheese, and crossword socials. He could remember some old crone flashing her aquamarine rings at him and crooning, "It's not right for a man to be alone. It's all right for a woman, but not for a man."

Well, it was all right for *this* man.

He must have dozed for a second, because when he next opened his eyes, the elevator doors were wide open and the gold-and-royal-green carpet of the ninth floor spread before him. Taking care to lift his sneakers clear of the shag, he traveled past the two wing chairs, past the vague seascape, turned the corner, and made his way to number 932, nearly at the end of the hall.

On the sconce alongside his door was a bud vase with a single white artificial carnation. Above the sconce an embossed nameplate: HENRY CRUTE. He had long ceased to notice it. The only nameplates he ever noticed were the ones that went away. Vanished overnight, some of them, leaving nothing but a rectangular outline on the wall.

Once inside, he stood for a moment gripping the door handle, then tottered toward his red corduroy armchair—collapsed into it with a despairing grunt. By habit his eyes swung toward his prescription-pill dispenser on his coffee table. Those seven small chambers with their soothing litany: M, T, W, TH, F, S, SU.

Pills, he thought. Had he taken his pills?

But his eyelids were already scrolling down, and in the grayness that swirled through him, not a single definite proposition could be entertained—until something that was not gray broke through, sharp and clear.

A voice.

Hank opened his eyes. A woman was standing over him.

That fact was so overladen with surprise that it very nearly mastered him. How had she gotten in? Had he left the door open? Had he been so unpardonably sloppy as that?

"Sorry to bother you, Mr. Hank," she said. "I was wondering if you had a moment."

He made to lever himself out of his chair, but even as she said, "Don't get up," he was already falling back.

"How are we doing today?" she said.

She was young. On the lower side of her thirties, he would have thought (though he could no longer trust himself on this score). She wore a smart lab coat, with a nametag pinned over her coat pocket and over her shoulder a leather satchel.

"I'm Dr. Landis," she said.

Next moment she was extending a clean, strong white hand, ringless. He held the hand briefly in his, felt the pulse of warmth beneath its lightly veined skin.

"If you say so," he said.

"I believe we had an appointment."

"We did?"

"I believe so."

"No one said anything to me."

"Um . . ." She slid some kind of phone contraption out of her coat pocket; her fingers gavotted across the screen. *Hank Crute . . . one o'clock to one fifteen . . . Yep, I got it right.*

She was smiling at him now. Nothing too gaudy, the lightest pearling of teeth.

"I've got loads of appointments," he said.

"Of course."

"Can't be bothered to write them all down. I'd be doing nothing else."

"Shall I sit here?" she asked, lowering herself decorously onto his bed. His face pinked, but just as he began to protest, he recalled there was nowhere else in the apartment for anyone to sit.

"We've met before," said Dr. Landis.

"I meet a lot of people."

"Well, to refresh your memory . . ." She gently dragged the coffee table into the space between them. "I'm the head clinician. And one of my jobs is to track the—the cognitive *function* among our residents."

"Why?"

"Because we want to make sure everyone at Morning Has Broken is healthy and happy and ready to roll." The words were chirpy, but the voice was cool, and the eyes were softly appraising. "So if it's all right, Mr. Hank, we're just going to run a few simple tests."

He said nothing.

"We'll be done before you know it," she said, "and you can get on with your afternoon."

"I hope so," he answered gruffly, wondering in the same breath how many times he had met this woman. How long had she even been working here? A month . . . a year . . .

"Mr. Hank? May we proceed?"

He curled his lip and folded his arms across his chest. "Get on with it."

She reached into her leather satchel, drew out three cards, and laid them on the coffee table.

"Now, Mr. Hank, each card has a word printed on it."

"I have eyes."

"Can you please read the words for me? Left to right."

"Banana. Triangle. Six."

"And again?"

"Oh, for . . . *Banana. Triangle. Six.*"

"Very good," she said, sweeping the cards back into the bag.

"That wasn't so hard," he muttered.

"No, it wasn't. Now in a few minutes I'm going to ask you to repeat them back to me, all right?"

"Fine."

Quickly and with minimum fuss, she took out a clipboard, lined with gridded paper, and uncapped a ballpoint pen.

"Mr. Hank, can you tell me what day it is today?"

"What do you mean, day?"

"Day of the week."

Normally the question would have panicked him, but it so happened that the smell of corned beef was still on his skin, and from there the inferential chain was startling in its efficiency. Corned beef was *boiled* beef. Boiled beef was boiled *food*. Boiled food was . . .

"Friday!"

He spit the word out with such force she actually drew back an inch. But the look of self-possession never wavered.

"That's correct. Now maybe you can tell me the date."

"Maybe I can."

"As in *month* and date."

"Let me think about that and get back to you."

"Okay."

Her hand sloped across the clipboard, leaving a trail of words in its wake.

"Do we do this every month?" he asked.

"Yes indeed."

"So the next time you come . . . that'll be Friday."

Pathetic, he knew. Clinging to his sole triumph.

"I'll be back on the twenty-fifth," she said. "Which will beee . . ." Her fingers once more set to dancing across her phone screen. *"Sun*day. But I take your point, Mr. Hank. Hey, can you tell me the name of our president?"

He blinked at her. "President?"

"Yes."

"Of what?"

"The United States."

"Ohh . . ." His mouth contracted to a point. "So many to choose from. I mean, there was Nixon and Reagan. Kennedy."

"That's true."

"What's to separate one from the other? They're all crooks."

The tiniest flutter on Dr. Landis's lips. "But only one of those crooks is currently our president."

"Well, you can . . ." His hands made a shooing motion. "You can take the whole lot, for all I care. And don't even ask me who my congressman is. I haven't voted in ten years. Bunch of shysters."

Dr. Landis's pen hovered gently over the paper.

"What state do you live in, Mr. Hank?"

"Virginia."

"What town?"

"Falls Church."

"I believe that's where you last lived."

"They may be calling it something else. I still call it Falls Church."

She contemplated him for a brief time, then set her pen down.

"Now, Mr. Hank. Just a few minutes ago I showed you three words. Can you tell me what they were?"

"Three words," he said noncommittally.

"That's right."

"I'm sure you said a lot more than three words."

"I didn't say them, Mr. Hank. I showed them to you."

"Sure you did."

"I'll give you the first word. It's *banana*."

"Banana," he said. "That's ridiculous. Why would you . . . there's not a banana in sight."

"I didn't show you an actual banana. I just showed you the word."

"Well, what good is a *word* if it—if it doesn't have a *thing* attached to it? That's just crazy talk."

He felt her dry, light, unsurprisable gaze. "The next word was *triangle*," she said.

"Well, I mean, these are not words I use in daily conversation. I mean, I don't eat *bananas*. I don't . . . I don't come into contact with *triangles*. I mean, if you'd said *rectangles* . . ."

He was conscious that every word that came out of his mouth dug him in deeper. Yet wouldn't silence do the same? His hands, for want of instruction, began to rake the arms of his chair, leaving little furrows in the corduroy.

"I'm kind of tired, you must know."

"Oh, I'm sure you are, Mr. Hank, and I do appreciate how hard you've been working. I just had one last question for you."

"Make it quick."

"What's your wife's name?"

"My . . ." His breath lodged just shy of his larynx. "My wife."

"That's right."

His hands spidered around his knees.

Very deliberately now, he angled his eyes away from her.

"Take your time," she said.

"I don't need to. I don't need to take my time. Asking me about my wife. That's goddamn rude is what it is. Why don't I ask you about your husband?"

"I'm not married, Mr. Hank."

"Well, there you are," he said, with an air of finality.

The silence fastened around them now like manacles.

"I *know* the name of my wife," he said. "I just don't care to share it with you."

"Do you know if she's alive or dead, Mr. Hank?"

"Well, she's not here, is she?"

That much he was sure of. If she were here, she'd be *here,* in this fifteen-by-fifteen square. But no matter where his eyes darted, there was no sign of another. He interrogated the remote control resting by his foot. The pair of reading glasses, slightly bent, on the bedside table. The row of tan Sansabelt slacks hanging in his closet. Over by the door, the pair of galoshes that sat waiting for him day after day (though he rarely went outside and never in the rain). Each object irretrievably and ruinously *his.*

Hank palmed his eyes shut. He thought, *If I concentrate hard enough, I can make this woman go away. I can make this whole thing stop. I can . . .*

"Silly me!"

Her voice in that moment was so different from what it had been — so sweet and disarming — that his eyes immediately sprang open, as if seeking reprieve. And there she was, smiling as sweetly as any woman had ever smiled.

"You didn't get a fighting chance, Mr. Hank."

"How . . . how's that?"

"You didn't take your meds."

Instinctively his gaze swerved back to the medication dispenser on the coffee table. There, in Friday's chamber, lay the usual troika: white, yellow, and blue. Untouched. Unconsumed.

"Well, Christ!" he shouted. "I could've told you that!"

Before she could stop him, he snatched the pills and dry-swallowed them. "There!" he cried, shoving the container away.

Dr. Landis had already averted her eyes, as if he had just started to undress himself. She was still looking away when she said, "Why don't we give it a few minutes to kick in?"

"Why the hell not?"

Here, he decided, was one benefit of getting old. You weren't obliged to make conversation. You could just sit in silence. Indeed, as the minutes passed, the only sound was the pattering of his Timex quartz on the bathroom washbasin. (Why hadn't he worn it?) If anything, it was the *light* that was making noise. Bright one moment, gray the next. He could've sworn he was nodding off, but every time he looked over at Dr. Landis, she was exactly as he had left her, patient and abiding.

"You don't remember me," she said at last.

"Sure I do."

"Then you remember what we talked about. The last time we talked."

"Naturally."

"Then you won't be surprised to learn how sorry I am."

His confusion registered now as a dull ache, rising up from his extremities and gathering in the joints.

"What've you got to be sorry for?" he demanded. "I'm the one ought to be—"

"When it comes to this part," she said, "I'm always sorry."

There was, in fact, a new warmth in her hazel eyes. A warmth too in her white hand, pressing on his.

"We only have a few minutes," she said.

For what? he was going to ask, but she was speeding straight on.

"Now if you promise not to get up or cry out, I'm going to show you a piece of paper. Is that all right with you?"

"Like I've got a choice," he grumbled.

"It's a piece of writing, okay?"

She drew out a sheet of taupe stationery, folded in half. With soft fingers, she spread it out on the coffee table.

"Hank, I'm going to ask if you recognize the handwriting."

But he misunderstood. He thought she was asking if he knew how to read. As if he could forget that! D. E. A. R. *Dear.* H. A. N. K. *Hank. Dear Hank.*

Why, it was a letter to him. Of course it was.

"You should keep reading," she said.

This is you talking, Hank. YOU.

He frowned down at the words. Noted the strange curlicue of

the *h*, the heavy dot over the *i*, the rather showy underswoop of the *y*. It was his own cursive, staring back at him.

"This . . . this doesn't . . ."

But as his fingers glided across the page, he realized they were moving in perfect synchronicity with each letter. Forming each word as it came.

With an inrush of air, he heaved his head back up. "I don't . . ."

"Keep reading, Mr. Hank."

You failed the test, Hank. Which means we're calling it a day, you and I.

I know this will be hard for you.

Living's a tough habit to kick, I get that. But long ago I—we—decided we didn't want to hang around past our due date. Not if it meant being a burden on the kids.

Kids. *Kids . . .*

You don't remember their names, I know. But the worst part is you don't remember HER name. And that's why it's come to this. Because long ago we decided that if we couldn't call her back anymore, life wasn't worth living.

Stop reading, he told himself. Stop.

But his eyes, without his volition, kept scanning, and his brain, that fevered contraption, kept interpreting, and the words rolled on. . . .

We gave it a good run, didn't we? We've got nothing to be ashamed of. And nothing to fear. It's just . . . quiet . . . from here on out. You won't even know we're gone.

And if we're lucky, if we're really lucky, we'll get to see her. Trust me. That would be nice.

Say goodbye . . .

His breath was growing ragged now as he raised his eyes to the woman on his bed.

"You . . . you don't work here at all."

She smiled softly, shook her head. "I work for an organization called Timely Endings. You don't remember, but you contacted us two years ago."

"But . . . but who gave you this letter? Who told you to—"

She pointed to the bottom of the page. There, like some child-ish prank, lay his own name, in his own hand.

Hank Crute

As real as anything could be. So real that everything around him grew more preposterous the more he contemplated it. Corned beef and Mrs. Sylvia and Stewart Granger. Bingo Night and hair styling with Miss Desdemona. The cord that bound him to Morning Has Broken, to waking and sleeping, had without another thought been severed. There was nothing to do now but drift.

From somewhere in the slipstream he could hear Dr. Landis's not-unsympathetic voice. ("We always make sure our clients write their own letters in advance. Just so they know it was their idea. It's *always* their idea.") He could see—just barely see—her soft white hands refolding the stationery, returning it to her leather satchel. ("Your account is paid in full, and there won't be any problem with medical examiners.") He could feel the air vibrating around her slender alabaster form as it rose. ("And of course your children will know nothing. We are the soul of discretion.") For a time she seemed to be floating away with the rest of his world, until suddenly, shockingly, she was kneeling beside him.

"Hank," she whispered. "This is what you wanted. When you still knew what you wanted."

"I didn't . . . I didn't . . ."

I didn't want this.

But what was *this*? What was *not* this? There was no way of sepa-rating one from the other.

"It's all right," she said, her breath stirring against his cheek. "I'll stay with you."

In that moment, how beautiful she loomed (though he could no longer see her, though he had forgotten her name). Her creamy white hands, pressed snugly over his. Her face, soft and plangent, parting now before another face. A face he recognized from the moment he saw it . . . parting now by the tiniest of fractions to emit a name . . .

Celia.

Dear God, it had been there all along. *Her* name. And with it a whole caravan of sensory data. A smell of sage. A crimson mouth. A drily tickled voice. Hair feathered across a pillow.

Celia. Celia.

If he could just speak it, he might yet stay tethered to the here and now. He might buy himself another month, another year. But his tongue had thickened into a slab, and his throat had dried to flint, and his lungs were crouching like beggars over their last remnants of air. So that when the end came for Mr. Hank Crute, his wife's name was nothing more than soundless drops, bathing his stilled brain.

Among the Morning Has Broken residents, no one took the news of Mr. Hank's death harder than Mrs. Sylvia. She told anyone who would listen that she and the late gentleman had enjoyed a special rapport. Only minutes before he died, he had promised to escort her to the Stewart Granger movie and then to dinner. How sad, and at the same time how fitting and beautiful, that hers should have been the last face he saw.

In the ensuing weeks Mrs. Sylvia went on at such length about Mr. Hank that one of her dinner cronies was moved to crack, "If he liked you so much, why didn't he put a ring on it?" Not long after that, Mrs. Sylvia's bridge club, weary of her exhibitions, replaced her with a less tiresome fourth and suggested she try her hand at blackjack or canasta. Mrs. Sylvia took the more dignified course of retreating to her room, where she sat in silence for hours at a time, conjuring memories of her departed lover, whose name and face were already blurring into something satisfyingly indeterminate.

In this pose she was interrupted one day by a visitor, who stood over her (had she forgotten to close the door?) with a leather satchel and an air of cool but not chilly professionalism.

"Mrs. Sylvia? I was wondering if you had a moment."

ANDREW BOURELLE

Y Is for Yangchuan Lizard

FROM *D Is for Dinosaur*

"WHAT'S THE Y stand for?"

We were staring at the package on Fender's glass coffee table, a quart-sized zip-lock bag full of gray-white powder. It looked like cocaine cut with fireplace ashes. There was a red sticker on the package with a black *Y* scrawled with a Sharpie.

"I'm not sure," Fender said. "That's just the street name."

Fender said it was the newest thing in Asia, some kind of opiate mixed with cocaine alkaloid and crushed dinosaur bones. Not just any dinosaur—one specific skeleton that was stolen from a Hong Kong museum. Fender couldn't remember the name of it. He said it was supposed to be like China's version of the Allosaurus, but I didn't know what the fuck that was either.

Because Y came from only one skeleton, that meant it was just short of impossible to get. Which is what made it attractive to Fender—who was a collector as much as he was a dealer.

"Have you tried it yet?" I said, but I could tell from the package that he hadn't touched it.

"Nope," he said. "I'm a businessman. Each snort is probably worth ten grand. But I am curious," he added.

Fender and I were sitting in the living room of his spacious penthouse apartment. He had a nice view of Lake Erie out his window. The sky was overcast, the water gray.

Collector guitars decorated the walls of Fender's apartment. An acoustic guitar reputedly owned by Johnny Cash. An electric from Eddie Van Halen. One with burn marks on it that was supposedly from that Great White concert where the pyrotechnics got out of control and killed a bunch of people.

Fender once joked that it was hard to know what was more valuable in this apartment, the guitars or the drugs. But I was as skeptical of the stories about the guitars as I was about the origins of Y.

We shared a joint and each had a bottle of beer, and talked about whether we thought the dinosaur-bone story had any truth to it. Fender said he believed there were real dinosaur bones in there—that much was probably true—but he doubted they contributed to the high.

"It's like a rhinoceros horn," he said. "People think it contains magical qualities, but that's all bullshit. The real rush is that you're snorting something rare. Exotic. We're talking about a supply so finite that it's practically nonexistent."

Fender was wearing a silk robe with silly leather slippers, and his shoulder-length hair was pulled back into a ponytail. He had a soul patch and hoop earrings and looked quite a bit different from the kid I shared a room with when we were freshmen in college.

I told him I didn't think the drug was going to go over well here. This was America. People here didn't believe in that crap about rhinoceros horns, and they wouldn't buy any mumbo-jumbo about mystical dinosaur-bone dust.

"I already got a buyer lined up," he said. "We're just haggling over price."

"Speaking of buying things, I need to get a move on."

He took me back to his study and unlocked the safe. I turned away so I wouldn't see the combination. It made me uncomfortable how leisurely he was about opening it in front of me. Did that mean he was like that with other people? I hoped not.

The safe was the size of a small refrigerator. A series of shelves lined the left side, some stacked with cash, others with every kind of drug you could think of. On the right side were guns: a shotgun, some kind of military rifle, a handgun. There was also a pearl-handled switchblade, which I'd seen Fender open lots of bags of drugs with.

Fender reached in and brought out a brick of marijuana.

I handed him a stack of bills.

I shoved the marijuana into my knapsack, and we headed back to the living room.

I excused myself to his restroom before I left. When I came back,

Fender and my backpack were sitting on the couch, but the bag of Y was gone.

"Why isn't there a Chinese symbol on the package instead of a Y?" I said.

At the bar I managed, I used rat poison that was from China— poison that I'm sure was illegal as hell here in the U.S. —and there were Chinese symbols all over the packaging. I would think that whether Y was the real thing or someone was just pretending it was an exotic Chinese drug, either way it would make sense to use a Chinese character instead of an English letter.

"Beats me, man. Maybe they're trying to Americanize it."

I smirked at Fender and shook my head.

"I think you've been had," I said. "Someone cremated a fucking dog and put it in a bag and you just paid God knows what for it."

"Ye of little faith," Fender said, clapping me on the back.

He opened the six deadbolts on his door, led me into the foyer, and opened the six deadbolts on the exterior door.

"See you," he said.

"Wouldn't want to be you," I said.

"Bullshit," he said, just like every time we said goodbye. "You wish like hell you were me."

I went directly to the bar to open up. It was important that I get there before Theresa because I had to clean up the dead rats before she arrived. She'd come in once before me and was gagging her whole shift.

Each night before I left, I'd set out the poison in the storage room. Each day when I came in to open, I'd find three or four dead rats. Today there were only two, which meant maybe I was finally making a dent in the population.

They were lying on the concrete, their bodies twisted into stiff, strangely contorted poses, like they'd been convulsing until their muscles finally locked up. Their tongues hung out of their mouths, clamped between their teeth, and a strange bloody foam spilled from their clenched jaws like dyed beer froth.

I always wondered if the rats ate the poison at the same time, or if they were so fucking stupid that they went ahead and ate it even after they could see that one of their brethren had died. I'd considered hooking up some kind of camera to watch, but that was too much effort. I didn't care that much.

I put the two dead rats in a plastic bag and was outside tossing it into the dumpster when Theresa came walking up.

"Hey, handsome," she said, and gave me a smile that was better than any drug.

"Hey," I said.

I wanted to call her beautiful or good-looking or something like that, but I couldn't bring myself to do it. I wasn't sure what Fender would think about me flirting with his kid sister, but I didn't figure he'd be too happy about it.

I was a decade older than her, for one thing. And I wasn't exactly what you'd call a good catch. My name was on the bar's deed, but it was really owned by Ramzen Akhmadov, the head of the Chechen mafia in Cleveland.

That's what happens when you borrow money from the mob for your drug problem. The vig is too steep. You get in over your head. Instead of getting your legs broken, you make a deal.

And then you're stuck. You can't walk away. Ever.

"Did you go see my brother today?" Theresa asked as she started taking chairs off the tables.

"Yep."

She grinned. If I saw Fender, that meant I had dope.

"You want to smoke a jay before we open?" she asked.

Theresa was a cute girl—how could I say no?

I didn't tap into the new brick of marijuana. I left that in my backpack behind the bar and went to the stash I kept in the freezer. I rolled a joint while Theresa finished setting up the chairs.

We sat at a table like a couple of regular customers and passed the joint back and forth. The funny thing about pot is that the best stuff in the country comes from Colorado, where it is legal. I figured it was just a matter of time before it was legal everywhere and my little side business would be defunct. I was trying to figure out a plan to get out from under Ramzen by then, but I hadn't come up with any ideas yet.

I'd been smoking so long now that smoking a joint was kind of like smoking a cigarette to me. I didn't get much of a buzz. Theresa had done some hard drugs in her day, but she didn't have as many years of smoking weed on her résumé as I did. Her eyes quickly turned glassy and she couldn't stop smiling.

Theresa had dirty-blond hair that wasn't nearly as well cared for as her brother's mane. She wore low-slung jeans, a tight T-shirt, and no bra underneath. Her breasts were small, but I liked looking at her nipples poking against the fabric.

I was sure she noticed.

I was sure she liked me looking.

It was just a matter of time before we hooked up. That would probably mess things up with Fender. And if I didn't have him supplying me anymore, then that would mess things up with Ramzen, who expected the cut I gave him every week and wouldn't like it if I went back to just being a bar manager.

In other words, hooking up with Theresa wouldn't just risk my oldest friendship. It might risk my life.

But I had a tendency to not think with my head. A younger version of me would have made my move already. Theresa and I would be fucking in the back room instead of sharing a joint up front.

But I was trying to be smarter these days.

Trying.

Two unusual things happened that night at the bar.

We were doing moderate business for a Tuesday night, enough that Theresa and I were busy but we could handle it ourselves. I worked behind the bar and she spent most of her time on the floor.

When customers came to the bar and ordered the special, I'd take them into the storage room and sell them however much pot they were looking for. I was always careful. I knew everyone I did business with.

The first surprise was that Ramzan Akhmadov and his henchman Zakir came in.

Ramzen never came himself. He always sent Zakir, or someone even lower on the food chain. So when Ramzen showed up, I got a knot in my stomach and started to sweat.

"Hello, Charlie," Ramzen said, sitting on a barstool across from me. "How's things?"

He and Zakir both had thick accents, like a couple of Russian terrorists in a bad action movie.

"Good," I said, wiping the bar off as if I was a character in such a movie.

Ramzen was in his fifties, with a face like a boxer who retired well past his prime, with lumpy, ruddy patches of skin and a mouth full of crooked teeth. He had a head full of silver hair and eyes that looked black in the bar's dim lighting. Zakir was in his thirties, maybe a few years older than me, and he was handsome, with slicked-back hair and a mouth full of straight white teeth. While Ramzen looked like a dock worker trying on a nice suit, Zakir looked the part of a gangster.

I made myself put the towel down and just stand and talk with the men. Stop pretending nothing was weird.

I asked Ramzen if he wanted anything, and he declined.

"You?" I said to Zakir.

Zakir always took single-barrel bourbon, and I would normally pour without asking, but with Ramzen here, he might not want to be seen drinking on the job, so I figured I better ask.

He shook his head no and came around the bar like he always did and went into the back to the cooler. There was a case of Budweiser that was always in the same place. There were twenty-three bottles of beer inside. In the one empty space was an envelope of cash that I kept up to date for these visits.

"Did you catch the game?" Ramzen asked, making small talk.

"No," I said. "I missed it."

I had no idea what he was talking about, not even what sport. It was summer, so that meant either the Indians or, if they were still in the playoffs, the Cavaliers. I didn't give a shit about professional sports, and I'm sure Ramzen didn't either, except for the betting that went along with it.

I figured the game, whatever game it was, had something to do with why he was here. Maybe he wanted me to start taking bets like a bookie.

I didn't want to do that. I didn't want to get any more involved with him than I already was.

"Have you seen your friend Fender lately?" he said.

"I saw him today," I said.

Honesty seemed the best policy here. I didn't want him to find out later that I was lying.

"And how was he?" Ramzen asked.

I shrugged. "Fine."

I was doing my best not to look over Ramzen's shoulder at Theresa out on the floor. As far as I knew, Ramzen didn't know that Fender's sister worked for me. She was just another cute waitress. I had a few of them. Call me sexist, but good-looking girls help with business.

"Did Fender tell you about a new drug he has?" Ramzen asked. "I think it is called Y."

Zakir came out from the back and sat next to Ramzen. Both of them stared at me.

"He mentioned something about it," I said, again choosing honesty. "Some new thing from China."

"Did you try it?"

"No," I said. "You know me. I stick with naturals—no pills, no powder."

Their eyebrows raised in unison, and that made me qualify my statement.

"No powder anymore," I said.

"This is from the bones of a prehistoric animal," Ramzen said. "What is more natural than that?"

I forced a laugh.

Zakir spoke up for the first time. "Did you see it?" he said. "The Y?"

Now I chose to lie.

"No," I said. "He knew I wouldn't be interested in something like that."

Now things were starting to make sense. Fender said he had a buyer lined up. They were just haggling about price.

Ramzen was his buyer.

Fender paid his cut to Ramzen just like everyone else. But he didn't work for Ramzen. He was never in debt, never needed Ramzen's money (unlike me), so he was able to operate more or less without any oversight.

Still, Fender needed to be careful.

Ramzen Akhmadov wasn't someone I would haggle with over a price. Fender had bigger balls than I did.

Ramzen and Zakir were boring into me with their stares. I could feel Theresa doing the same from across the room.

"If you find out anything you want to tell us," Ramzen said finally, "call this number."

He set a card on the counter. It was blank except for a handwritten number.

I frowned, hoping my expression would say, *I don't know what you're talking about.*

But I did, and they knew I did.

After they left, Theresa came over, her face full of worry.

"What was that all about?" she said.

"Do me a favor," I said. "Call your brother and see if he's okay."

That's when the second surprise of the night came: a police detective walked into the bar.

He was in street clothes, but I could tell he was a cop. For one, he had the air of scumbag smugness that cops have.

For another, he had a pistol strapped to his hip.

He came up to the bar, his eyes focused on Theresa, not me. He introduced himself as Detective Sean Williams.

"Are you Theresa Matthews?" he said.

She nodded, her eyes confused.

"And your brother is Glen Matthews?"

She nodded again, her eyes changing from confused to scared.

"I regret to inform you that your brother has been murdered."

I closed the bar, told all the remaining customers that their tabs were on the house tonight, and then Theresa sat down with Williams at the same table where she and I shared the joint a few hours ago. She was in shock. She hadn't cried yet. She had a dazed look on her face, a little like she was stoned but without the pretty smile that usually accompanied her highs.

Theresa asked if I could sit with them, and when I explained that Fender—i.e., Glen—was my college roommate and a long-time friend, Williams agreed.

He asked her questions about when she'd last seen Fender, if she was aware that he was a drug dealer. I knew which answers were lies and which were the truth.

When he came to me, I told him that I'd seen Fender earlier that day, that we'd each had a beer. I figured my fingerprints would be all over the place: the bottle, the bathroom faucet.

"What was the nature of your visit?" Williams asked.

"Just visiting," I said. "We're friends."

"And were *you* aware that your friend was one of the biggest drug dealers in the city?" he said.

"We didn't talk about that stuff," I said.

"What kind of stuff did you talk about?" he said.

"The girls we slept with in college," I said. "The time we stole a ceramic cow head from a fraternity party. Classes we failed. Stuff we did when we were eighteen and drunk and stupid."

This was all true. Fender and I had very little in common these days. I sold dope, and he sold it to me—and I gave his kid sister a job when she needed one—but that was pretty much it. Otherwise, we lived worlds apart. We talked about old times—*remember that one time?*—and that was usually it. Discussing his latest boutique drug purchase was out of the ordinary for us.

"Did he mention a drug called Y?" Williams asked.

"Look," I said, "Theresa and I don't know anything about what Fender did. We don't know what the hell is going on. What can you tell us?"

"The investigation is ongoing," he said bureaucratically.

"Cut the shit," I said. "Either you tell us what happened or we won't say another word until we get a lawyer."

Williams took a deep breath. He turned to Theresa.

"Your brother's throat was slashed," he said.

She gasped, bringing her hands to her face.

"But he was tortured first."

She started sobbing. Then she rose from the table and ran into the back room.

Williams turned his stare to me.

"His apartment was ransacked. His safe was emptied. His guitars smashed."

For some reason, that last bit hurt me the most. Fender loved those fucking guitars.

After the cop gave me his card and left, I found Theresa sitting in the cooler, her arms wrapped around her, covered in goose bumps. Her cheeks were streaked with tears, which had started to crystallize in the cold.

"I came in here because I wanted to feel some kind of pain besides what's inside of me," she said, her lips quivering, her teeth beginning to chatter.

"Come on," I said. "I'll walk you home."

I didn't bother to put out rat poison that night. Didn't balance the books. Didn't even take the tips out of the tip jar. I just grabbed my knapsack and locked the door.

On our walk, the warm summer air erased the goose bumps on Theresa's arms.

"What's this Y he was talking about?" Theresa asked.

"Some new drug," I said. "Your brother said it was super-rare."

"Do you think they killed him for it?"

"I don't know," I said, and I didn't ask her who she meant by "they."

She lived in a small one-bedroom. There wasn't much to it. A thrift-store futon that she used for a bed and a couch. An old box TV. She had some movie posters on her walls from back when she used to work at a theater.

Back in her heavy drug days.

Fender had introduced her to the hard stuff when she was a teenager, then paid for rehab when she was out of control. He asked me to hire her when she was out, told me to keep her away from anything stronger than pot. Since I didn't deal in chemicals—and because I'd been through something similar to her, back in my own dark days—he thought I was the right person for the job.

She sat down on her futon and pulled her legs up underneath her. She hugged herself like she had in the cooler even though her apartment was stuffy.

"Do you have anything stronger than pot?" she asked.

"No."

"Let's smoke a bowl then."

I opened up my backpack to get the new brick that Fender had sold me.

The bag of Y was inside.

I didn't tell Theresa the Y was there. I pretended like everything was normal. I pulled out a pinch of dope, packed her pipe, and passed it to her.

I took a couple hits, but that was just to give her the impression she wasn't smoking alone. My mind was reeling, reliving my last conversation with Fender.

Had he acted unusual in any way? Had he seemed scared?

No, he seemed perfectly normal. Yet when I went to take a piss, he slipped the Y into my backpack. It must have been an impulse move. He wouldn't have known I was going to pee before I left.

Still, he must have feared that someone would come looking for the stuff. I wondered if they'd tortured him for the combination to the safe, then killed him, only to find out that the safe didn't have what they were looking for. Or did they know the combination and torture him afterward when they didn't find what they were looking for?

They probably smashed every guitar looking for a secret hiding spot.

Theresa lay out on the futon and put her feet in my lap. I rubbed them. She had delicate feet, perfectly smooth, her nails painted an ugly purple color.

She groaned, "God, that feels good."

"I need to get going," I told her.

"No," she said. "Stay. I'm afraid of what I might do if I'm alone."

I was afraid of what I might do if I stayed. But I told her I would.

She sat up onto her knees and put one hand on my shoulder.

"This dope isn't strong enough," she said. "I need something else."

I stared at her, knowing what she was going to ask for.

"Make love to me, Charlie. I know you want to. The only thing stopping you was my brother."

"It doesn't feel right," I said.

She put her hand to my crotch, where my cock was hardening like quick-drying concrete.

"It feels right to me," she said.

We never bothered to fold the futon out. We spent the night curled together, cramped on the couch cushion. No sheets or blankets. Just our skin, clammy in the humid air. We talked for a long time. I knew she needed to be distracted, so I filled the silence with talk about my life and how I didn't know how I'd ended up where I was.

I should have been thankful, I guessed, that I kicked the coke that once brought me so close to ruin. But the cost was a partnership with the Chechen mob—a lifetime contract unless I could think of a way out.

"Why didn't you ask my brother for the money?" Theresa asked.

"Pride," I said. "Fender and I were friends back when we were nobodies. He was a somebody and I was back on track to becoming a bigger nobody than ever. Besides, Fender touched more drugs in one day than most people do in a lifetime, but he's never really been hooked on anything. The willpower that son of a bitch had. I was embarrassed to admit I needed help."

"I know the feeling," she said. "But I always hated him for introducing me to the stuff. What kind of brother does that?"

She was right: Fender was no saint. He was a narcissistic drug dealer.

But he was my friend.

When Theresa drifted off to sleep, I lay awake, staring at the water spots on the ceiling, listening to the sounds of the city coming in through the open window. Voices. Music. Sirens.

I felt antsy, unable to lie still. Finally I untangled myself from her and started to dress. Streetlights through the window illuminated her milk-white skin, her pink nipples, her lovely face, which looked incredibly young while she slept.

"Sorry, Fender," I whispered aloud.

Theresa's eyes opened a crack and she muttered in a dreamy voice, "Where are you going?"

"I've got a few things I need to do today," I said. "Go back to sleep. I'll call you later."

"I don't want you to go," she said, but she was already closing her eyes and drifting away.

"Theresa," I said. "Don't go anywhere. Don't trust anyone. Don't answer your door. Not until I call you."

"Okay," she said, but she seemed asleep already.

When I left, I locked the door handle but had no way of locking the deadbolt unless I woke her up to do it. I thought about it, and decided to let her sleep.

My apartment lived somewhere in the world between Fender's and Theresa's: not as shitty as hers, not nearly as nice as his. It was a modest two-bedroom with a nice TV and decent furniture.

I opened my backpack and put both bags of drugs on my wooden coffee table.

I stared at the Y.

Did Ramzen kill Fender?

Probably.

That meant the smart thing to do—smart for me but also smart for Theresa—was to hand the stuff over to him. That was the easiest way to stay safe, and to keep Theresa safe.

But Fender was my oldest friend, which pretty much made him my best friend. We didn't have much in common anymore, but I liked him more than most people.

And I was in love with his sister.

I admitted that to myself at that moment, with the dull dawn light coming in through the window making the powder in the Y bag look even more gray and ashen.

I told you before I often did stupid things, impulsive things. You could say sleeping with Theresa hours after her brother was killed might be one of them.

But there was an even dumber thing I felt like doing.

I wanted to try the Y.

I kept telling myself that I would be able to think better if I knew what I was dealing with. Was this some great revolutionary new drug? Or just ordinary coke with a made-up story to go with it?

I wasn't sure how knowing the answer would help me, but I felt like it would.

Or maybe I was just rationalizing. I wanted to try the Y, and so I convinced myself it was a good idea.

I got a drinking straw from the kitchen, cut off an inch section of it, and went back to the living room. When I opened the bag, there was a peculiar smell. Like a dusty book sitting on a shelf for a couple decades, with another underlying scent barely hidden — a rotten smell, like roadkill.

I stuck the straw into the bag, put the other end to my nose, and snorted a good, hard pull.

The effect was instantaneous.

It felt like I'd inhaled fire, and the flames spread through my skull and down into my limbs. I thought I was going to die, and then the pain turned into a soothing warmth. I sank back into the couch like I was falling into an ocean of pillows. I just kept sinking and sinking, my fingers and toes numb, the rest of my body nonexistent. I closed my eyes and began to dream.

I wasn't human. My heart was pounding, my breathing coming out in raspy, ragged bursts. I had big powerful legs and tiny little arms, and a long tail that balanced the weight of an enormous skull. I had a massive snout and teeth the size of kitchen knives. It felt natural to have this body, to have this balance.

I was running through a jungle of exotic plants. My sense of smell was stronger than any human's, and I inhaled rich, wild scents that I'd never experienced before.

It was intense, this dream, so lucid that I didn't want to open my eyes and risk dissolving it.

I don't know if it was the power of suggestion making me see what I was seeing and feel what I was feeling. Just knowing the story behind Y could have been enough to tell my brain what dream to have. Opiates can work that way.

But it didn't feel that way at the time. I felt like whatever was in the Y had transported me back — mentally, telepathically, supernaturally — to a time millions of years ago. When the world was embryonic and the animals were primal, instinctual, murderous. I could feel the stardust in my bones, the atoms that were once plants or animals or water. I was the world and the world was me.

In the dream I killed some smaller creature, a feathered, four-legged little dinosaur. I ripped it apart with my sharp teeth, and I woke up with the coppery taste of blood in my mouth.

I staggered to the bathroom, unsure how to walk without a tail. I slurped water from the sink and looked at myself in the mirror.

There was a little splotch of dried blood around my nostril.

I checked the time. Six hours had passed.

I rushed out the door and headed for the bar. Theresa and I were both scheduled to work tonight, and I needed to find people to cover for us. The employees' numbers were tacked up behind the bar. I didn't have them with me.

There was no way I was working, and I wasn't leaving Theresa alone either.

I didn't feel any closer to having a plan about what to do, and I wasn't sure if it was a good idea to tell Theresa how powerful the stuff was, given her drug history. But I felt like I should tell her. Her brother had died for this stuff. She had a right to have a say in what happened. And if I'm honest, I pictured us snorting the stuff together. It was that good.

I called her, but there was no answer.

When I walked into the alley behind the bar, Zakir's black BMW was sitting there idling.

His arm was sticking out the open window, holding a cigarette.

"Hey," I said, acting as if nothing out of the ordinary was happening.

"Where've you been?" he said. "You need to open soon."

"Having a rough morning," I said. "You heard about Fender?"

"Yeah," he said. "Tragic."

He said the words as unemotionally as if he was reporting on some crime on the other side of the planet.

He pitched his cigarette into the alley and followed me inside.

I poured him his single-barrel bourbon on the rocks, like always—when he wasn't accompanied by Ramzen, that is.

He threw it back and slurped it all down.

"Another?"

"No."

He reached into his sports jacket. I thought he was going to pull out a pistol, but instead he pulled out a switchblade.

The same pearl-handled one from Fender's safe.

He poked around in the ice of his glass. There was blood on the blade, and tendrils of red spread into the liquid remnants at the bottom of the glass.

He fished out a piece of ice and popped it into his mouth. He crunched on it like candy. Then he folded the knife and stuck it back in his coat. His hand came out with a plain white envelope.

"Open this after I leave," he said.

"What is it?"

"I'll be back when you close tonight," he said. "You give me what I want. I give you what you want."

I scrunched my nose to pretend that I didn't know what he was talking about.

As he walked toward the door, he called over his shoulder, "Don't get any smart ideas. Don't call the cops. Don't call Ramzen."

I said nothing. But I understood. He was going behind Ramzen's back.

When he was gone, I tore open the envelope. Inside was a small plastic sandwich bag, and inside that was a tiny severed toe.

With ugly purple paint on the nail.

I called in a waitress and a bartender, and I made them do most of the labor while I sat in my office. I let them each go an hour early, and then I told the few remaining customers that I needed to close early.

When Zakir came in with Theresa, I was sitting at the table she and I had used the day before, first to share a joint, then to talk to the cop.

Theresa was limping. She had on black Nike running shoes, and it looked like the toe area on one foot was wet.

Zakir shoved her roughly into a chair and sat down across from me.

His bourbon was already poured, sitting next to the bag of white powder.

"It looks like you opened it," Zakir said as he took his seat.

I nodded.

"And?"

"It gave me a bloody nose," I said. "It burned like a son of a bitch. But it was the best high I've ever had."

No need to lie about that.

He grinned widely. He picked up his bourbon and twirled it around, spiraling the ice cubes, which had started to melt while I waited.

"You didn't think of poisoning me, did you?"

"I thought about it," I said.

He laughed. Then he threw back the glass and slurped out the bourbon. Like before, he pulled out the switchblade and dug around in the glass. He fished out a piece of ice and crunched it in his teeth.

He left the switchblade sticking out of the glass, the tip bleeding into the puddle of bourbon at the bottom.

"So what happens now?" I said.

"What do you mean?" he said. "You get the girl. I get the Y."

"I mean with you and Ramzen. You trying to take over? Coup d'état?"

"Just a little side business," Zakir said. "You can keep your mouth shut, no?"

"Yes," I said.

"And you?" He looked at Theresa, his eyebrows arched.

"She can," I said.

"Good."

He grabbed the bag of powder and headed for the door.

"What do all these Chinese letters mean?" he said.

"I think it's supposed to be the name of the dinosaur whose bones are all busted up in there," I said.

He gave me a hard stare, and I wondered if he could see my pounding heart shaking my chest from where he was. His eyes drifted over to Theresa.

"You coming?" he said.

She looked at me, and in a second her demeanor changed from fear to a look of guilty pleasure. She gave me a smile that was part apology, part delight.

She stood and kissed me on the cheek.

"I did have fun," she whispered, and walked toward Zakir with no limp.

Zakir was grinning, his mouth full of white teeth, so pleased with himself that he couldn't contain his elation.

I glowered at Theresa. "You should have just taken it from me this morning after you fucked me."

She shrugged. "I was going to check to see if you had it with you. But you wouldn't fall asleep."

She turned to go and I didn't know what to say, so I blurted, "Your brother loved you."

She huffed and said, "My brother loved his stupid guitars."

They left and I sat alone in the bar for a long time. Then I collected the switchblade and my backpack and walked home. On the way I took a detour down to the lake's edge and tossed the baggie with the toe—whoever it belonged to—into the gray water.

I locked the door and spent the day with the switchblade in my hand, nodding in and out of sleep.

When evening came and no one had broken down my door, I went over to Theresa's apartment. The door was unlocked. She and Zakir were both there, Zakir doubled over on the futon, Theresa lying on the floor. The bodies were contorted, frozen in positions of agony. Their noses had hemorrhaged a pink foamy blood. Their eyes were bloodshot and bulging from their sockets, their faces locked in a rictus of pain. Theresa had bitten her tongue between her clenched teeth.

I had hoped that Zakir would go first and that Theresa would be smarter than the rats. But they must have done their lines together.

I took off Theresa's shoes just to be sure. She had all ten toes.

There was a framed photograph on the counter of Fender and Theresa. They were a few years younger, both smiling enthusiastically. I wondered if they were actually happy or just acting. I'd never really known Theresa at all.

"See you," I said to their smiling faces, my voice a hoarse, haunted whisper that I didn't recognize. "Wouldn't want to be you."

I called Detective Williams and spent the rest of the night at the police station answering questions.

"Turns out this drug called Y is nothing more than Chinese rat poison," he said.

He looked at me skeptically, wondering what I knew and wasn't telling him, but he seemed to be satisfied that the case was closed. He never searched my backpack.

I walked toward home, a zombie, in the early morning hours. I had hardly slept in three days. I'd lost my oldest friend and a girl I loved, even if only briefly, even if she never really existed. A fog rolled in and I stood at the edge of the lake, looking out into the smoky gray air, imagining a world on the other side with dinosaurs running around with eternity pulsing through their veins.

I called Ramzen.

"Zakir tried to blackmail me for the Y," I said. "He was going behind your back."

"You had the Y?"

"I gave him rat poison," I said. "He's dead."

Ramzen was quiet for a long moment, then he said, "Someone else will be making the collection next week."

"I figured."

"And what of the Y?" he asked. "Where is it?"

I knew the Y would buy my freedom. I had been looking for a way out for years, and this was it.

"I don't know," I said, and hung up.

In my apartment, I pulled out the bag of Y, opened it, breathed in its primordial scent.

I wanted to escape.

To disappear.

To go back in time to a prehistoric world where Fender hadn't died yet and Theresa hadn't revealed her true self.

I poked the knife, sticky with dried blood, into the Y and came out with a heap of bone dust on the blade. I lowered my nose to the tip and inhaled as quickly and deeply as I could.

T. C. BOYLE

The Designee

FROM *The Iowa Review*

The Boredom

WHAT HE COULDN'T have imagined, even in his bleakest as-
sessments of the future, was the boredom. He'd sat there in the
hospital while Jan lay dying, holding her hand after each of the
increasingly desperate procedures that had left her bald and ema-
ciated and looking like no one he'd ever known, thinking only of
the bagel with cream cheese he'd have for dinner and the identical
one he'd have for breakfast in the morning. If he allowed himself
to think beyond that, it was only of the empty space in the bed
beside him and of the practical concerns that kept everything else
at bay: the estate, the funeral, the cemetery, the first shovel of dirt
ringing on the lid of the coffin, closure. There was his daughter,
but she had no more experience of this kind of free fall than he,
and she had her own life and her own problems all the way across
the country in New York, which was where she retreated after the
funeral. A grief counselor came to the house and murmured in his
direction for an hour or two, people sent him cards, books, and
newspaper clippings in a great rolling wave that broke over him
and as quickly receded, but nobody addressed the boredom.

He got up at first light, as he always had. The house was silent.
He dressed, ate, washed up. Then he sat down with a book or the
newspaper, but his powers of concentration weren't what they
once were, and he wound up staring at the walls. The walls just
stood there. No dog barked, there was no sound of cars from the
street—even the leaky faucet in the downstairs bathroom seemed

to have fixed itself. He could have taken up golf, he supposed, but he hated golf. He could have played cards or gone down to the senior center, but he hated cards and he hated seniors, especially the old ladies, who came at you in a gabbling flock and couldn't begin to replace Jan anyway, not if there were ten thousand of them. The only time he was truly happy was when he was asleep, and even that was denied him half the time.

The walls just stood there. No dog barked. The water didn't even drip.

The Letter

The letter came out of nowhere, a thin sheet of paper in a standard envelope that bore a foreign stamp (England: Queen Elizabeth in brownish silhouette). It was buried in the usual avalanche of flyers, free offers, and coupons, and he very nearly tossed it in the recycling bin along with all the rest, but it was his luck that at the last minute it slipped free and drifted in a graceful fluttering arc to the pavement at his feet. He bent for it, noticing that it was addressed to him, using his full name—Mason Kenneth Alimonti—and that the return address was of a bank in London. Curious, he wedged the sheaf of ads under one arm and pried open the envelope right there in the driveway while the sun beat at the back of his neck and people drifted by like ghosts out on the street.

Dear Mr. Alimonti, the letter began, *kindly accept my sincere apologies for contacting you out of the blue like this, but something very urgent and important has come to our notice and we seek your consent for the mutual interest of all.*

His first thought was that this had something to do with the estate, with Jan's death, more paperwork, more *hassle,* as if they couldn't leave well enough alone, and he glanced up a moment, distracted. Suddenly—and this was odd, maybe even a portent of some sort—the morning seemed to buzz to life, each sound coming to him separately and yet blending in a whole, from the chittering of a squirrel in the branches overhead to a snatch of a child's laughter and the squall of a radio dopplering through the open window of a passing car. And more: every blade of grass, every leaf shone as if the color green had been created anew.

The letter was in his hand still, the junk mail still tucked under one arm. When Jan was alive, he'd bring the mail in to her where she'd be sitting at the kitchen table with her coffee and a book of crosswords, and now he was standing there motionless in his own driveway, hearing things, seeing things—and smelling things too, the grass, jasmine, a whiff of gasoline from the mower that suddenly started up next door. *I am Graham Shovelin,* the letter went on, *Operations & IT director, Yorkshire Bank PLC, and personal funds manager to the late Mr. Jing J. Kim, an American citizen. He died recently, along with his wife and only son, while holidaying in Kuala Lumpur, and was flown back to England for burial. In our last auditing, we discovered a dormant account of his with £38,886,000 in his name.*

This is a story, he was thinking, a made-up story, and what did it have to do with him? Still, and though he didn't have his glasses with him so that the letters seemed to bloat and fade on the page before him, he read on as if he couldn't help himself: *During our investigations, we discovered that he nominated his son as his next of kin. All efforts to trace his other relations have proved impossible. The account has been dormant for some time since his death. Therefore, we decided to contact you as an American citizen, to seek your consent to enable us to nominate you as the next of kin to the deceased and transfer the funds to you as the designated heir to the deceased.*

There was more—a proposed split of the proceeds, 60 percent for him, 38 percent for the bank, 2 percent to be set aside *for expenses both parties might incur (if any) during the transaction.* At the bottom of the page was a phone number and a request to contact the bank if the abovementioned transaction should be of interest, with a final admonition: *Please also contact me if you object to this proposal.* Object? Who could object? He did a quick calculation in his head, still good with numbers though he'd been retired from the college for fifteen years now: 60 percent of 38,886,000 was 23 million and something. Pounds, that is. And what was the conversion rate, one point two or three to the dollar?

It was a lot of money. Which he didn't need, or not desperately anyway, not the way most people needed it. While it was a sad fact that the bulk of what he'd set aside for retirement had been swallowed up in treatments for Jan the insurers had labeled "experimental" and thus nonreimbursable, he still had enough left, what with Social Security and his 401(k), to live at least modestly for as long as he lasted. This offer, this letter that had him standing stock-still in his own driveway as if he'd lost his bearings like half the other old men in the world, was too good to be true, he knew that. Or he felt it anyway.

But still. Thirty million dollars, give or take. Certainly there were places he'd like to visit—Iceland, for one, the Galápagos, for another—and it would be nice to leave his daughter and his grandson something more than a mortgaged house, funeral expenses, and a stack of bills. There were stranger things in this world—people won the lottery, got grants, prizes, estates went unclaimed all over the place, and it wasn't as if he was desperate. A voice warned him against it, but what did he have to lose? The cost of a phone call?

The Phone Call

The phone picked up on the third ring, and the first thing he heard was music, a soft trickle of music that was neither classical nor pop but something in between, and for a moment he thought he was being put on hold before the music cut off abruptly and a deep crisp voice—so deep it surprised him—swelled inside the receiver. "Yorkshire Bank, PLC, Graham Shovelin speaking. How may I help you?"

He'd rehearsed a little speech in his head, along the lines of establishing his authority as the person solicited rather than soliciting, but it deserted him now. "Um, I," he stuttered, "I, uh, received your letter?"

There was the faintest tick of hesitation, and then the voice came back at him, so deep he couldn't help thinking of Paul Robeson singing "Ol' Man River" on one of the old '78s his grandmother used to play for him when he was a boy. "Oh, yes, of course—delighted to hear from you. We have your number here on the computer screen, and it matches our records . . . Still, one can never be too careful. Would you be so kind as to identify yourself, please?"

"Mason Alimonti?"

"Mason *Kenneth* Alimonti?"

"Yes."

"Ah, well, wonderful. We'll need verification of your identity before we can proceed, of course, but for the moment, since we're just beginning to get acquainted, I am satisfied. Now, what do you think of our proposal?"

He was in the living room, sitting in the armchair under the reading lamp, using the old landline phone his daughter told him he ought to give up since the cell was all anybody needed these days and she really didn't know anyone, not a single soul, who still paid for a landline. But for something like this—an overseas call— he somehow felt better relying on the instrument he'd been using for thirty years and more. "I don't know," he said. "It sounds too good to be true—"

The man on the other end of the line let out a booming laugh, a laugh that scraped bottom and then sailed all the way up into the high register, a good-natured laugh, delighted, a laugh of assurance and joy that proclaimed all was right with the world. "Well, of course, it *is*," the man boomed, and here came the laugh again. "But sometimes we just have to accept the fact that luck has come our way—and be grateful, Mr. Alimonti, kick up our heels and embrace what life brings us, don't you think?"

For a moment he was confused. He felt as if he'd gone out of his body, everything before him—the loveseat, the houseplants, the blank TV screen—shifting on him so that it all seemed to be floating in air. The phone was in his hand. He was having a conversation. Somebody—the man on the other end of the line—wanted something from him.

"Mr. Alimonti—you there?"

"Yes," he heard himself say. There was something odd about the man's accent—it was British, proper British, Masterpiece Theatre British, but the syntax was off somehow. Or the rhythm, maybe it was the rhythm. "Why me?" he asked suddenly.

Another laugh, not quite so deep or pleased with itself as the last. "Because you've lived an unimpeachable life, because you pay your debts and you're as solid an American citizen as anyone could ever hope to find. Oh, rest assured we've vetted you thoroughly—as we have each of the nine other final candidates."

Nine other candidates? The receiver went heavy in his hand— molded plastic, but it might as well have been cast of iron.

"Am I hearing surprise on your end of the line, Mr. Alimonti? Of course, you understand, we must protect ourselves, in the event that our first choice doesn't wish to accept our offer for any reason—

and I can't really imagine that happening, can you?—but as you *are* the first on our list, the single most qualified individual we've examined to date, we have to say—*I* have to say—that we are delighted you've contacted us ahead of any of the others."

He felt a wave of relief sweep over him. The phone was just a phone again. He said, "What next?"

"Next?" the voice echoed. "Well, obviously we have to make certain that you're the man for us—and that we're the men for you too. Do you have any question about the figures I presented in my letter to you? You agree that a sixty/thirty-eight percent split is equable? You're content with that?"

He said nothing. He was back in himself, back in the moment, but he didn't know what to say—did the man want him to negotiate, to quibble over the way the money would be split?

"Again, let me anticipate you, Mr. Alimonti. You are wondering, no doubt, what's in it for us." The laugh again, but truncated now, all business. "Self-interest, pure and simple. If this account has not been claimed within a five-year period, the whole of it goes to the government and we receive nothing, though we've been the guardians of the late Mr. Kim's fortune for a quarter century now. We *need* you, Mr. Alimonti, and that is the bottom line. We need an American citizen in good standing, with an unblemished record and absolute probity, to be the designee for your fellow American, Mr. Kim." A pause. "Otherwise, none of us receives a shilling."

"What do I have to do?"

"Oh, nothing really, not for the moment. We'll need banking information, of course, in order to transfer the funds, and our solicitors will have to draw up a contract so as to be sure there are no misunderstandings, but all that can come in time—the only question now is, are you with us? Can we count on you? Can I hang up this phone and check the other nine names off my list?"

His heart was pounding in his chest, the way it did when he overexerted himself. His mouth was dry. The world seemed to be tipping under his feet, sliding away from him. *Thirty million dollars.* "Can I have some time to think it over?"

"Sadly, we have but two weeks before the government accounting office swoops in to confiscate this account—and you know how they are, the government, no different, I suppose than in your country, eh? A belly that's never full. Of course you can think it over, but for your sake—and mine—think quickly, Mr. Alimonti, think quickly."

A Night to Think It Over

The rest of the day he really couldn't do much more than sit—first in the armchair and then out on the deck in one of the twin recliners there—his mind working at double speed. He couldn't stop thinking about England, a country he'd visited only once, when he was in his twenties, along with Jan, in the year between grad school and the start of his first job, his daughter not yet even a speck on the horizon. They'd gone to Scotland too, to Edinburgh and where was it? Glasgow. He remembered he took to calling Jan "lassie," just for the fun of it, and how one day, leaving a fish and chips shop, she'd got ahead of him on the street and he cried out, "Wait up, lassie," and every woman's head turned. That was England. Or Scotland, anyway. Same difference. And they had banks there, of course they did, London the banking capital of Europe, though he couldn't remember actually having gone into one. He closed his eyes. Saw some sort of proud antique building, old, very old, with pillars and marble floors, brass fixtures, an elaborate worked-iron grate between customers and tellers, but here again, he realized, he was bringing up an image from one BBC drama or another, and what was that one called where they showed the lives not only of the lords and ladies but of the servants too? That had been Jan's favorite. She'd watch the episodes over and over, and sometimes, at breakfast, she'd address him as "my lord" and put on a fake accent. For the fun of it.

Yes, sure. And where was the fun in life now?

At some point, when the shadows began to thicken in the trees, he went into the house and clicked on the TV—sports, a blur of action, a ball sailing high against a sky crippled with the onset of night—but he couldn't concentrate on it, and really, what did it matter who won? Somebody had won before and somebody had lost and it would happen again. And again. Unless there was a tie— were there ties in baseball? He couldn't remember. He thought so. In fact, he distinctly remembered a tie once, but maybe that was only an exhibition game . . . or an all-star game, wasn't that it?

It was past eight by the time he remembered he ought to eat something, and he went to the refrigerator, extracted the stained pot there, and ladled out half a bowl of the vegetable-beef stew he'd made last week—or maybe it was the week before. No matter: he'd been rigorous about keeping it refrigerated, and in any case the microwave would kill anything, bacterial or otherwise, that might have tried to gain a foothold in the depths of the pot. The important thing was not to waste anything in a world of waste. He poured himself a glass of milk, scraped two suspicious spots from a slice of sourdough bread and put it in the toaster, then sat down to eat.

The walls just stood there. But the silence gave way to a sound from the other room, where the TV was, a long drawn-out cheer and the voice of an announcer unleashing his enthusiasm on the drama of the moment, and that was something at least. What was the time difference between here and England? Eight hours? Nine? Whatever it was, it was too early there to call yet. He was thinking he might like to endow a fellowship in Jan's name at the college—maybe in the art department; she'd always liked art— and if he gave enough they'd install a plaque, maybe even name a building after her. Or a wing. A wing at least. Maybe that was more practical, really. He saw her face then, not as it was in those last months, but her real face, her true face, fleshed out and beautiful even into her seventies, and he pushed himself up from the table, scraped his bowl over the trash can, and set it on the rack in the dishwasher, decided now, his mind clear, really clear, for the first time all day.

In the morning, after breakfast (no rush—he wouldn't want to come across as overeager), he would settle himself in the armchair, pick up the phone, and make the call.

The Second Phone Call

Of all days, this was the one he wound up oversleeping, so that it was past eight by the time he sat down with his morning coffee and punched in the bank's number with a forefinger that didn't seem to want to steady itself, as if this wasn't his finger at all but some stranger's that had been grafted on in the middle of the night. This time there was no music and the phone picked up on the first ring. He was all set to tell Mr. Shovelin— *Graham, can I call you Graham?*—that he'd found his man, that they'd grow rich together, though of course, as a bank employee, he didn't imagine that Mr. Shovelin would actually get any of the money, but a bonus maybe, there had to be that possibility, didn't there? Imagine his surprise then when it wasn't Shovelin, with his rich booming basso, who answered the phone, but a woman. "Yorkshire Bank, PLC, Chevette Afunu-Jones speaking," she said in a thin weary voice. "How may I help you?"

Again he drew a blank. This whole business made him nervous. The phone made him nervous. *London* made him nervous. "I was," he began, "I mean, I wanted to—is Mr. Shovelin there?"

A pause, the sound of a keyboard softly clicking. "Oh, Mr. Alimonti, forgive me," she said, her voice warming till you could have spread it on toast. "Mr. Shovelin, whom I am sorry to say is away from his desk at the moment, instructed me to anticipate your call. And let me say, from all the good things he's had to say about you, it is a real pleasure to hear your voice."

He didn't quite know how to respond to this, so he simply murmured, "Thank you," and left it at that. There was another pause, as if she were waiting for him to go on. "When do you expect him back?" he asked. "Because—well, it's urgent, you know? I have some news for him?"

"Well, I can only hope it's the good news all of us on Mr. Shovelin's staff have been waiting to hear," she said, her voice deepening, opening out to him in invitation. "Rest assured that Mr. Shovelin has given me full details and, in my capacity as his executive secretary, the authority to act on his behalf, though he's—well, he's indisposed today, poor man, and you can't begin to imagine what he's had to go through." Here she dropped her voice to a whisper: "Cancer."

This hit him like a blow out of nowhere. Jan's face was right there, hovering over him. "I'm sorry," he murmured.

"Believe me, the man is a lion, and he will fight this thing the way he has fought all his life—and when he returns from his treatment this afternoon, I know he will be lifted up by your good news, buoyed, that is . . ." Her voice had grown tearful. "I can't tell you how much he respects you," she whispered.

What he heard, though he wasn't really listening on an intuitive level, was an odd similarity to the accent or emphasis or whatever it was he'd detected in Shovelin's speech, and he wondered if somehow the two were related, not that it mattered, really, so long as they stayed the course and checked those other nine names off the list. He said, "Please tell him from me that I hope he's feeling better and, well, that I've decided to take him up on his offer—"

She clapped her hands together, one quick celebratory clap that reverberated through the phone like the cymbal that strikes up the band, before her voice was in his ear again: "Oh, I can't tell you how much this will mean to him, how much it means to us all here at the Yorkshire Bank PLC . . . Mr. Alimonti, you are a savior, you really are."

He was trying to picture her, this British woman all the way across the country and the sea too, a young woman by the sound of her voice, youngish anyway, and he saw her in business dress, with stockings and heels and legs as finely shaped as an athlete's. She was a runner, not simply a jogger but a runner, and he saw her pumping her arms and dashing through what, Hyde Park?, in the dewy mornings before coming to work with her high heels tucked in her purse. He felt warm. He felt good. He felt as if things were changing for the better.

"Now, Mr. Alimonti," she said, her voice low, almost a purr, "what we need you to do is this, just to get the ball rolling—officially, you understand?"

"Yes?"

"We will need your banking information so that we can begin transferring the funds—or at least cutting you a preliminary check—before the Royal Fiduciary Bureau for Unclaimed Accounts moves on this."

"But, but," he stammered, "what about the contract we were supposed to—?"

"Oh, don't you worry, darling—may I call you darling? Because you are, you really *are* darling—"

He gave a kind of shrug of assent, but nothing came out of his mouth.

"Don't you worry," she repeated. "Mr. Shovelin will take care of that."

The First Disbursement

Once the banking details were in place (within three working days, and he had to hand it to Shovelin for pulling strings and expediting things), he received his first disbursement check from the dormant account. It was in the amount of $20,000, and it came special delivery with a note from Shovelin, who called it "earnest money" and asked him to hold off for two weeks before depositing it in the new account, "because of red tape on this end, which is regrettable, but a simple fact of doing business in a banking arena as complex as this." The check was drawn on the Yorkshire Bank PLC, it bore the signature of Graham Shovelin, Operations Director, and it was printed on the sort of fine, high-grade paper you associated with stock certificates. When it came, when the doorbell rang and the mailman handed him the envelope, Mason accepted it with trembling hands, and for the longest time he just sat there in his armchair, admiring it. He was sitting down, yes, but inside he was doing cartwheels. This was the real deal. He was rich. The first thing he was going to do—and the idea came to him right then and there—was help out his daughter. Angelica, divorced two years now, with a son in high school and barely scraping by, was the pastry chef at a tony restaurant in Rye, New York; her dream was to open her own place on her own terms, with her own cuisine, and now he was going to be able to make it happen for her. Maybe she'd even name it after him. Mason's. That had a certain ring to it, didn't it?

That evening, just as he was ladling out his nightly bowl of stew, the phone rang. It was Shovelin, sounding none the worse for wear. "Mason?" he boomed. "May I call you Mason, that is, considering that we are now business partners?"

"Yes, yes, of course." He found that he was smiling. Alone there in his deserted house where the silence reigned supreme, he was smiling.

"Good, good, and please call me Graham . . . Now, the reason I'm calling is I want to know if you've received the disbursement."

"I have, yes, and thank you very much for that, but how *are* you? Your health, I mean? Because I know how hard it can be—I went through the same thing with Jan, with my wife . . ."

The voice on the other end seemed to deflate. "My health?"

"I'm sorry, I really don't want to stick my nose in, but your secretary told me you were, well, undergoing treatment?"

"Oh, that, yes. Very unfortunate. And I do wish she hadn't confided in you—but I assure you it won't affect our business relationship, not a whit, so don't you worry." There was a long pause. "Kidney," Shovelin said, his voice a murmur now. "Metastatic. They're giving me six months—"

"Six months?"

"Unless—well, unless I can qualify for an experimental treatment the insurance won't even begin to cover, which my physician tells me is almost a miracle, with something like a ninety percent remission rate . . . but really, forgive me, Mason—I didn't call you all the way from England to talk about my health problems. I'm a banker—and we have a transaction to discuss."

He didn't respond, but he was thinking of Jan, of course he was, because how can anybody—insurers, doctors, hospitals—put a price on the life of a human being?

"What I need you to do, Mason—Mason, are you there?"

"Yes, I'm here."

"Good. I need you to deposit twenty thousand dollars American in the account we've opened up at your bank, so as to cover the funds I've transferred to you until they clear. You see, I will need access to those funds in order to grease certain palms in the Royal Fiduciary Bureau—you have this expression, do you not? *Greasing* palms?"

"I don't—I mean, I'll have to make a withdrawal from my retirement, which might take a few days—"

"A few days?" Shovelin threw back at him in a tone of disbelief. "Don't you appreciate that time is of the essence here? Everyone in this world, sadly enough, is not as upright as you and I. I'm talking about graft, Mason, graft at the highest levels of government bureaucracy. We must grease the palms—or the wheels, isn't that how you say it?—to make certain that there are no hitches with the full disbursement of the funds."

There was a silence. He could hear the uncertain wash of the connection, as of the sea probing the shore. England was a long way off. "Okay," he heard himself say into the void.

But it wasn't a void: Shovelin was there still. "There are too few men of honor in this world," he said ruefully. "Do you know what they say of me in the banking industry? 'Shovelin's word is his honor and his honor is his word.'" He let out a sigh. "I only wish it were true for the unscrupulous bureaucrats we're dealing with here. The palm greasers." He let out a chuckle, deep and rolling and self-amused. "Or, to be more precise, the *greasees*."

A Problem with the Check

Two weeks later he was on the phone again, and if he was upset, he couldn't help himself.

"Yes, yes," Shovelin said dismissively. "I understand your concern, but let me assure you, Mason, we are on top of this matter."

"But the people at my bank? The Bank of America? They say there's a problem with the check—"

"A small matter. All I can say is that it's a good thing we used this as a test case, because think of the mess we'd be in if we'd deposited the whole sum of $30,558,780, which, by the way, is what our accountants have determined your share to be, exclusive of fees. If any."

He was seeing the scene at the bank all over again, the cold look of the teller, who seemed to think he was some sort of flimflam man—or worse, senile, useless, *old*. They'd sat him down at the desk of the bank manager, a full-figured young woman with plump butterfly lips and a pair of black eyes that bored right into you, and she'd explained that the check had been drawn on insufficient funds and was in effect worthless. Embarrassed—worse, humiliated—he'd shuffled out into the sunlight blinking as if he'd been locked up in a cave all this time.

"But what am I supposed to do?"

"Just what you—and I, and Miss Afunu-Jones—*have* been doing: exerting a little control, a little *patience*, Mason. The fact is, I am going to have to ask you to make another deposit. There is one man at the RFB standing in our way, a scoundrel, really—and I'll name him, why not? Richard Hyde-Jeffers. One of those men born with the gold spoon in his mouth but who is always greedy for more, as if that were the only subject they tutored him in at Oxford: greed."

"He wants a bribe?"

"Exactly."

"How much?'

"He wants twenty thousand more. Outrageous, I know. But you've — *we've* — already invested twenty thousand in him, the greedy pig, and we wouldn't want to see that go down the drain — do you use that expression, 'down the drain'? — or watch the deal of a lifetime wither on the vine right in front of our eyes."

Shovelin was silent a moment, allowing him to process all this. Which, he had to admit, was difficult, increasingly difficult. Nothing was as it seemed. The house slipped away from him again, everything in motion, as if an earthquake had struck. Spots drifted before his eyes. The phone was cast of iron.

"I promise you," Shovelin said, his voice gone deeper yet in a sort of croon, "as I live and breathe, *this* will be the end of it."

The Flight to Heathrow

He'd never been comfortable in the air, never liked the feeling of helplessness and mortal peril that came over him as the great metallic cage lifted off the tarmac and hurtled into the atmosphere, and over the years he'd made a point of flying as little as possible. His most memorable — and relaxing — vacations had been motor trips he and Jan had taken, usually to one national park or the other or just exploring little out-of-the way towns in Washington, Oregon, British Columbia. The last flight he'd been on — to Hawaii, with Jan, to celebrate their golden anniversary, or was it the silver? — had been nightmarishly bumpy, so much so he'd thought at one point the plane was going down and he'd wound up, embarrassingly, having to use the air-sickness bag. He couldn't help thinking about that as he found his way down the crowded aisle to his seat in economy, both his knees throbbing from his descent down the jetbridge and his lower back burning from the effort of lugging his oversized suitcase, which he'd randomly stuffed with far too many clothes and even an extra pair of shoes, though he was only staying two nights in London. At the expense — and insistence — of Yorkshire Bank PLC.

In the four months that had dragged by since he'd first received the letter, his expenses had mounted to the point at which he'd begun to question the whole business. That little voice again. It nagged him, told him he was a fool, being taken, and yet every time he protested, Graham—or sometimes Chevette—telephoned to mollify him. Yes, there was graft, and yes, part of the problem was Graham's health, which had kept him out of the office at crucial junctures in the negotiations with Mr. Hyde-Jeffers of the Royal Fiduciary Bureau, but he needed to have faith, not simply in the Yorkshire Bank PLC but in Graham Shovelin's word, which was his honor, as his honor was his word. Still, Mason had posted funds for fees, bribes, something Chevette called "vigorish," and beyond that to help defray Graham's medical expenses and even, once, to underwrite a graduation party for Chevette's niece, Evangeline, whose father had been run over by a bus and tragically killed the very week of his daughter's graduation (Mason had been presented with an itemized bill for the gown, corsage, limousine, and dinner at a Moroccan restaurant that had cost a staggering $1500). All to be reimbursed, of course, once the funds were released.

It was Graham who'd suggested he come to London to see for himself "how the land lies," as he put it. "After all this time, to tell me that you don't have absolute faith in me, my friend—my friend and partner—is to wound me deeply," Graham had said, pouring himself into the phone one late night in a conversation that must have gone on for an hour or more. "You hurt my reputation," he said in a wounded voice, "and worse than that, Mason, worse than that, you hurt my *pride*. And really, for a man in my condition, facing an uncertain future and the final accounting up above, what else is there for me to hold on to? Beyond love. Love and friendship, Mason." He'd let out a deep sigh. "I am sending you an airline ticket by overnight mail," he said. "You want your eyes opened? I will open them for you."

Two Days in London

If the walls just stood there back at home, he didn't know it. His life, the life of the widower, of the griever, of the terminally bored, had changed, and changed radically. Graham Shovelin himself took time off from work—and his chemo—to pick him up at the airport in a shining maroon Mercedes and bring him to his hotel, all expenses paid. Of course, there was a little contretemps at the airport: Mason, exhausted from a cramped and sleepless night and at eighty no steadier on his feet than he'd been at seventy-nine or expected to be at eighty-one, had mistaken this heavyset fortyish man with the shaved head and hands the size of baseball mitts for a porter and not the operations director of the Yorkshire Bank PLC. But then he hadn't expected him to be black. Not that he had any prejudices whatsoever—over the years he'd seen and worked with all types of students at the college and made a point of giving as much of himself as he could to each of them, no matter where they came from or what they looked like—but he just hadn't pictured Graham Shovelin this way. And that was his failing, of course. And maybe, he thought, that had to do with Masterpiece Theatre too, with the lords and ladies and the proper English butler and under-butler and all the rest. So Graham was black, that was all. Nothing wrong with that.

The hotel he took him to wasn't more than a twenty-minute drive from the airport, and it wasn't really a hotel, as far as Mason could see, but more one of these bed-and-breakfast sort of places, and the staff there was black too—and so were most of the people on the streets. But he was tired. Exhausted. Defeated before he even began. He found his bed in a back room and slept a full twelve hours, longer than he could ever remember having slept since he was a boy at home with his parents. In fact, when he finally did wake, he couldn't believe it was still dark outside and he had to tap the crystal of his watch to make sure it hadn't stopped.

He lay there for a long while after waking, in a big bed in a small room all the way on the other side of the world, feeling pleased with himself, proud of himself, having an *adventure*. He pushed himself up, fished through his suitcase for a pair of clean underwear and socks. Just then an ambrosial smell, something exotic, spicy, began seeping in under the door and seemed to take possession of the room, and he realized he was hungry, ravenous actually. Vaguely wondering if he was too late for breakfast—or too early—he eased open the door and found himself in a dim hallway that gave onto a brightly lit room from which the odor of food was emanating, a room he took to be the kitchen.

He heard a murmur of voices. His knees hurt. He could barely seem to lift his feet. But he made his way down the hall and paused at the door, not knowing what the protocol was in a bed-and-breakfast (he and Jan had always stayed in hotels or motor courts). He gave a light knock on the doorframe in the same instant that the room jumped to life: a gas stove, spotless, with a big aluminum pot set atop it; a table and chairs, oilcloth top, half a dozen beer bottles; and someone sitting at the table, a big man, black, in a white sleeveless T-shirt: Graham. It was Graham Shovelin himself, a newspaper spread before him and a beer clutched in one big hand.

The Explanation

"Really, Mason, you must forgive me for any misunderstanding or inconvenience regarding the accommodations, but I am only acting in your best interest—*our* best interest—in putting you here, in this quite reasonable bed-and-breakfast hotel rather than one of those drafty anonymous five-star places in the heart of the city, which is where Mr. Oliphant, president of the Yorkshire Bank PLC, had urged me to put you up. And why? To save our partnership any further out-of-pocket expense—*unnecessary* expense—until we are able to have the funds released in full. Tell me, have I done right?"

Mason was seated now at the table across from Shovelin, a bowl of stew that wasn't all that much different from what he ate at home steaming at his elbow while a woman who'd appeared out of nowhere provided bread and butter and poured him a glass of beer. She was black too, thin as a long-distance runner and dressed in a colorful wraparound garment of some sort. Her hair was piled atop her head in a massive bouffant and her feet were bare. She was very pretty, and for a moment Mason was so distracted by her he wasn't able to respond.

"Just tell me, Mason," Shovelin repeated. "If I've done wrong, let me know and I'll get in the car this minute and take you to the Savoy—or perhaps you prefer the Hilton?"

He wasn't tired, that wasn't it at all—just the opposite, he was excited. A new place, new people, new walls! And yet he couldn't quite focus on what Shovelin was saying, so he just shrugged.

"I take that to be accord, then?" Shovelin boomed. "Happily, happily!" he cried. "Let's toast to it!" and he raised his glass, tapped it against Mason's, and downed the contents in a gulp. His eyes reddened and he touched one massive fist to his breastbone, as if fighting down indigestion, then turned back to Mason. "Now," he

said, so abruptly it almost sounded like the sudden startled bark
of a dog, "let's get down to business. This lovely lady here, in the
event you haven't already divined her identity, is none other than
my executive secretary, Miss Afunu-Jones, who is taking time out
of her hectic schedule to devote herself to your comfort during
your brief stay. She has my full confidence, and anything you feel
you must say to me you can say to her and she can handle any and
all inquiries . . ." His voice trailed off. "In the event . . . well, in the
event I am, how shall I put it?, *indisposed.*"

Mason felt his heart clench. He could see the pain etched in the
younger man's face and he felt the sadness there, felt the shadow
of the mortality that had claimed Jan and would one day claim everyone alive, his daughter, his grandson, this man who'd reached
out across the ocean to him and become not only his friend but his
confidant.

Shovelin produced a handkerchief, wiped his eyes and blew his
nose. "Forgive me for injecting an element of what, *pathos,* into this
little party meant to welcome you to our land, and I know it's not
professional"—here he employed the handkerchief again—"but
I am only human." He looked up at the woman, who hovered behind them. "Chevette, perhaps you will take over for me and give
Mr. Alimonti—Mason—the explanation he's come for—"

Chevette, her eyes filled too, pulled up a chair and sat beside
Mason, so close their elbows were touching. She took her time,
buttering a slice of bread and handing it to him before taking a
sip of beer herself and looking him directly in the eye. "We will see
this business through to the end, believe me, Mason," she said, her
voice soft and hesitant. "We will not desert you. You have my word
on that."

"About tomorrow," Shovelin prompted.

Her eyes jumped to his and then back to Mason's. "Yes," she
said, "tomorrow. Tomorrow we will take you to the central office,
where you will meet with our president, Mr. Oliphant, and iron out
the final details to your satisfaction." She paused, touched a finger
to her lips. "I don't know that all this is necessary, but as you seem
to have lost faith in us—"

"Oh, no, no," he said, fastening on her eyes, beautiful eyes, really, eyes the color of the birch beer he used to relish as a boy on
family jaunts to Vermont.

"But the explanation is simple, it truly is. What I mean is, just look at us. We are not wealthy, we are not even accepted by many in white society, and I'm sorry to have to repeat it like a mantra, but we are diligent, Mr. Alimonti, diligent and faithful. The fact is, as my—as Mr. Shovelin—has told you, we are dealing with corruption, with thieves, and all the unconscionable holdup in this matter is to be laid at their feet, not ours, Mason, not ours." And here, whether conscious of it or not, she dropped a hand to his thigh and gave him the faintest squeeze of reassurance.

Unfortunate Circumstances

The next day, his last day, and not even a full day at that, as his plane was scheduled to depart at 6:45 in the evening, he was awakened from a dreamless sleep by Chevette, who stood at the foot of his bed, softly calling his name. She was dressed in the sort of business attire he'd envisioned when he'd first heard her voice over the phone, she was wearing lipstick and eyeshadow, and her hair had been brushed out over her shoulders. "Mr. Alimonti," she said, "Mason, wake up. I have some bad news."

He pushed himself up on his elbows, blinking at her. His knee throbbed. He seemed to have a headache. For a minute he didn't know where he was.

"Unfortunate circumstances have arisen," she was saying. "Graham has had a seizure and they've taken him to hospital—"

He fumbled to find the words. "Hospital? Is he—will he?—"

She made a wide sweeping gesture with one hand. "That is not for me to say. That"—her eyes hardened—"is in the hands of the insurers, who keep denying him the life-saving treatment he so desperately needs. And we, we are but humble bank employees and we are by no means rich, Mason, by no means. We've exhausted our savings . . . yes, *we,* because now I must confess to you what you must already have suspected—Graham is my husband. We didn't want to have to tell you for fear you might think us unprofessional, but the cat is out of the bag now." She caught her breath. Her eyes filled. "And I love him, I love him more than I could ever put into words—"

He was in his pajamas in a strange bed in a strange place, a strange woman was standing over him, and his heart was breaking.

"Please help us," she whispered. "Please?"

The Flight Back

He'd given her all he had on him—some $800 in cash he'd brought along for emergencies—and written her a check he'd be hard-pressed to cover when he got home. As the expenses had mounted, he'd taken out a second mortgage and depleted his retirement account so that things were going to get very difficult financially if the funds didn't come through soon. But they would, he was sure they would, every minute of every day pushing him closer to his goal. Chevette had tearfully assured him that Mr. Oliphant would see things through, whether her husband survived his emergency operation or not. "Truly," she told him, "he lies between this life and the next."

It wasn't until he'd buckled himself in and the plane was in the air that it occurred to him that he never had gotten to meet Mr. Oliphant, see what an English bank looked like from the inside, or even sign the agreement Graham had kept forgetting to produce, and now—he felt his heart seize again—might never be able to. He had two drinks on the plane, watched bits of three or four jumpy color-smeared movies, and fell off into a sleep that was a kind of waking and waking again, endlessly, till the wheels touched down and he was home at last.

Angelica Steps In

Three months later, after having missed four consecutive mortgage payments and receiving increasingly threatening letters from the bank, letters so depressing he could barely bring himself to open them, he telephoned his daughter to ask if she might be able to help him out with a small loan. He didn't mention Graham Shovelin, the Yorkshire Bank PLC, or the windfall he was expecting, because he didn't want to upset her, and, more than that, he didn't want her interfering. And, truthfully, he wasn't so sure of himself anymore, the little voice back in his head now and telling him he was a fool, that he'd been defrauded, that Graham Shovelin, whom he hadn't heard from in all this time, wasn't what he appeared to be. He had hope still, of course he did—he had to have hope—and he made up excuses to explain the silence, excuses for Graham, who for all he knew might be lying there in a coma. Or worse. He could be dead. But why then didn't anyone pick up the phone at the Yorkshire Bank PLC? Chevette, though she may have been grief-stricken, would certainly have had to be there, working, no matter what had befallen her husband, and then there was Mr. Oliphant and whatever secretaries and assistants he might have had.

At one point, despairing, after he'd called twenty times without response, he went online and found a home page for the Yorkshire Bank PLC, which didn't seem to list the names of the bank officers at any of their branches. He did find a general-purpose number and after having been put on hold for ten minutes spoke to a woman who claimed she'd never heard of a Mr. Oliphant, and of course he was unable to supply any specifics, not with regard to which branch Oliphant was affiliated with or even what his given name might be. He felt baffled, frustrated, hopeless. He called his daughter.

"Dad? Is that you? How are you? We've been worried about you—"

"Worried, why?"

"I've called and called, but you never seem to be home—what are you doing, spending all your time at dance clubs or what, the racetrack?" She let out a laugh. "Robbie's starting college in a month, did you know that? He got into his first-choice college, SUNY Potsdam, for music? The Crane School?"

He didn't respond. After a minute, when she paused for breath, he said flatly, "I need a loan."

"A loan? What on earth for? Don't you have everything you need?"

"For the mortgage. I—well, I got a little behind in my payments . . ."

It took a while, another five minutes of wrangling, but finally she got it out of him. When he'd told her the whole story, everything, the $30 million, the disbursement, the bribe money, Graham's treatments, even the two-day debacle in London, she was speechless. For a long moment he could hear her breathing over the phone and he could picture the expression she was wearing, her features compressed and her lips bunched in anger and disbelief, no different from the way Jan had looked when she was after him for one thing and another.

"I can't believe you," she said finally. "How could you be so stupid? You, of all people, a former professor, Dad, a math whiz, good with figures?"

He said nothing. He felt as if she'd stabbed him, as if she was twisting the knife inside him.

"It's a scam, Dad, it's all over the papers, the Internet, everywhere—the AARP newsletter Mom used to get. Don't you ever read it? Or listen to the news? The crooks even have a name for it, 419, after the Nigerian antifraud statute, as if it's all a big joke."

"It's not like that," he said.

"How much did you lose?"

"I don't know," he said.

"Jesus! You don't even know?" There was a clatter of pans or silverware. He could picture her stalking round her kitchen, her face clamped tight. "All right," she said. "Jesus! How much do you need?"

"I don't know—ten?"

"Ten what—thousand? Don't tell me ten thousand."

He was staring out the window on the back lawn and the burgundy leaves of the flowering plum he and Jan had planted when their daughter was born. It seemed far away. Miles. It was there, but it was shrinking before his eyes.

"I'm coming out there," she said.

"No," he said, "no, don't do that."

"You're eighty years old, Dad! Eighty!"

"No," he said, and he no longer knew what he was objecting to, whether it was his age or the money or his daughter coming here to discipline him and humble him and rearrange his life.

One More Phone Call

The house belonged to the bank now, all of it, everything, and his daughter and Robbie were there helping him pack up. He was leaving California whether he liked it or not, and he was going to be living, at least temporarily, in Robbie's soon-to-be-vacated bedroom in Rye, New York. Everything was chaos. Everything was black. He was sitting in his armchair, waiting for the moving van to take what hadn't been sold off in a succession of what Angelica called "estate sales" and haul it across the country to rot in her garage. In Rye, New York. For the moment all was quiet, the walls just stood there, no dog barked, no auto passed by on the street. He was thinking nothing. He couldn't even remember what Jan looked like anymore. He got to his feet because he had an urgent need to go fetch a particular thing before the movers got hold of it, but in the interval of rising, he'd already forgotten just what that particular thing was.

So he was standing there in the ruins of his former life, a high desperate sun poking through the blinds to ricochet off the barren floorboards, when the phone rang. Once, twice, and then he picked it up.

"Mason?"

"Yes?"

"Graham Shovelin here. How are you?"

Before he could answer, the deep voice rolled on, unstoppable, Old Man River itself: "I have good news, the best, capital news, in fact! The funds will be released tomorrow."

"You're"—he couldn't find the words—"you're okay? The, the treatment—?"

"Yes, yes, thanks to you, my friend, and don't think I'll ever forget it. I'm weak still, of course, which is why you haven't heard from me in some time now, and I do hope you'll understand . . . but listen, we're going to need one more *infusion* here, just to assure there are no glitches tomorrow when we all gather in Mr. Oliphant's office to sign the final release form—"

"How much?"

"Oh, not much, Mason, not much at all."

MICHAEL BRACKEN

Smoked

FROM *Noir at the Salad Bar*

WHEN BEAU JAMES raised the twin service-bay doors of the converted Conoco station at 11 a.m. Tuesday morning, he had already been smoking brisket and ribs for more than eight hours, just as he had six days a week since opening Quarryville Smokehouse twelve years earlier. Rain or shine, Tuesday through Sunday, he served a two-meat menu, offering a single side and no dessert, and closing when he had no brisket, ribs, or coleslaw remaining.

Beau worked the indirect-heat pit alone, not allowing anyone to learn his technique for preparing fall-off-the-bone beef ribs and moist brisket with dark peppery crust, and four days a week he also worked the counter alone. He only hired help—his girlfriend's teenage daughter, Amanda—on the weekends, when business typically doubled. The Quarryville Smokehouse lunch plate consisted of a choice between chopped brisket, sliced brisket, or beef ribs, accompanied by a scoop of coleslaw, four bread-and-butter pickle slices, a slice of sweet onion, two slices of Mrs Baird's Bread, and a twelve-ounce can of Dr Pepper. He offered no sauce and had been known to refuse service to anyone who requested it.

That Tuesday morning he wore his graying black hair in a ponytail that hung below his shoulders and a red paisley bandanna covered the expanding bald spot on the crown of his head. He had on an untucked black T-shirt that covered the tattoo on his left upper arm, faded blue jeans, and well-worn black harness motorcycle boots, a clothing selection that never varied and simplified dressing in the dark. He had gained a few pounds since opening the smokehouse, but at six foot two, he remained slender.

Like most mornings, Tommy Baldwin was sitting at one of the picnic tables beneath the canopy that had once sheltered the gasoline pumps. He had retired from Shell Oil after a lifetime spent as a roustabout, was living comfortably on his pension, and had nothing better to do each morning than read, eat barbecue, and visit with Beau. As the service-bay doors rolled up, Tommy stood and grabbed the popular state-named magazine he had been reading. He walked through the six picnic tables arranged in the service bays and into the former Conoco station's showroom, which had been transformed into the smokehouse's order and pickup counter.

"The usual?" Beau asked of the grizzled retiree.

Instead of answering, Tommy tossed the open magazine on the counter. "Have you seen this?"

Beau wasn't much of a reader, so he hadn't. He picked up the magazine and found himself reading a review of Quarryville Smokehouse, a review that referred to his place as "the best-kept secret in West Texas, certain to be a serious contender in the forthcoming roundup of the fifty best barbecue joints in the Lone Star State." Next to the review were a photograph of the chopped brisket lunch plate and another of him working behind the counter—a photograph for which he had not posed.

"Jesus H." He threw the magazine down and glared at Tommy. "When did you get this?"

"This morning's mail."

Beau swore again. He had been relocated to Quarryville thirteen years earlier so no one could find him. Without asking again if Tommy wanted his usual order, Beau scooped chopped brisket into a Styrofoam three-compartment takeout container, added coleslaw and accessories, and shoved the container across the counter, not realizing he'd gone heavy on the brisket, light on the coleslaw, and had completely forgotten the pickles. He slammed a cold can of Dr Pepper on the other side of the still-open magazine.

Tommy slid back exact change. "I thought you'd like the publicity, maybe get more business. You can't be making much from this place."

"I get by." Beau glared at his most reliable customer. "That's all I ever wanted."

"What about that girl of yours? You want to take care of Bethany, don't you? Her and her daughter?"

"What do they have to do with it?"

"I see the way she looks at you," Tommy said. "I've never had anybody look at me the way Bethany looks at you. I've seen you look at her the same way."

"So?"

"You can't live for yourself, Beau. You have to live for the people you love," Tommy explained. "I thought I could help, so about a year ago I sent a letter to the editor, telling her about your barbecue."

Beau stabbed at the magazine article with his forefinger. "This is your fault?"

"I suppose so." Tommy glanced at the magazine and the open Styrofoam container next to it. "You forgot my pickles."

"Fuck your pickles." Beau didn't bother with the serving spoon. He reached into the pickle jar, grabbed a handful of bread-and-butter pickle slices, and threw them on top of Tommy's chopped brisket lunch plate, flinging juice across the counter, the magazine, and Tommy.

The retiree shook his head, tucked the magazine under his arm, and carried his lunch to one of the picnic tables outside, where he adjusted the holster hidden at the small of his back and set aside most of the pickles before he began eating.

The lunch rush, such as it was, kept Beau busy for the next few hours. After he sold the last order of ribs, put the cash and checks —he didn't accept credit or debit cards—in the office safe, and shut everything down, he saw Tommy still reading his magazine. He rolled down the service-bay doors, carried two cold cans of Dr Pepper outside, and settled onto the picnic table bench opposite Tommy. "Don't you ever go home?"

Tommy looked up. "There's nothing there for me."

Beau put one Dr Pepper in front of Tommy and opened the other. After a long draw from the can, he said, "About earlier."

"Sorry for the surprise," Tommy replied. "I didn't think a little publicity would be a problem."

"You have no idea the world of hurt that's about to crash down on me," Beau said. He drained the last of the Dr Pepper. "There's no way you could know."

Beau had been one of the United States Marshals Service's easiest Witness Security Program relocations, a man without baggage. He had no family and no desire to drag any of several random female companions with him into a new life. The San Antonio office had recommended Quarryville, a dried-out scab of a town in West Texas that had once shipped granite east to Dallas. After the quarry closed in the early 1950s, the town began a long, slow slide into oblivion, and few people lived there by choice. With the U.S. Marshals Service's assistance and money from the Harley-Davidson he'd sold before disappearing into his new identity, Beau purchased and renovated a foreclosed home. On his own he later purchased the abandoned Conoco station he could see from his front window and turned it into Quarryville Smokehouse.

He mentioned none of this to Tommy as they sat in the afternoon heat watching traffic pass the smokehouse on the two-lane state highway. When they finished their drinks, Tommy excused himself to use the men's room around the back, leaving behind the magazine he'd been reading all morning.

Beau spun the magazine around, thumbed through the pages until he found the article about his smokehouse, and read it again. Had it not been for the accompanying photo capturing his face in three-quarter profile, nothing about the article would have bothered him. In fact, everything the author wrote was quite complimentary.

Beau lived on the other side of the railroad tracks that paralleled the state highway bisecting Quarryville, on a street that also paralleled the tracks, at the leading edge of a neighborhood of single-family homes constructed for quarry employees during the town's heyday. He waited until he was safely inside the living room of his two-bedroom bungalow before using his cell phone to call a phone number he had memorized years earlier.

A no-nonsense female voice answered. "United States Marshals Service."

"I want to talk to William Secrist."

"He retired nine months ago," said the voice. "May I help you?"

Beau paced in front of the gun cabinet containing his and Bethany's deer rifles. "This is Beau James. Secrist was my case officer."

"I'm his replacement, Deputy Marshal Sara Arquette. How may I help?"

"I've been outted," Beau said. He told her about the magazine article and accompanying photo.

"I should visit someday to see if your 'cue is as good as the writer says."

"You read the article?"

"I picked up a copy of the magazine yesterday."

"So everybody's seen it?"

"Not everybody," she said. "They don't read Texas magazines in Ohio."

Beau stopped pacing and stood at the front window, staring at his smokehouse and the other businesses on the far side of the railroad tracks and state highway. The storefronts along Main Street that weren't boarded up might as well have been. Only a pawnshop, the ubiquitous Dairy Queen, and a Texaco that still offered full service showed signs of life. "All it takes is one."

"What do you expect us to do?"

"Your job," Beau yelled into the phone. "Protect me. Relocate me. Express some concern for my health and well-being!"

"I'll reach out to the Columbus office and see if there's been any chatter about you," she said. "I'll let you know."

"You do that!" He could have slammed the receiver down if he'd phoned from the landline at the smokehouse. Instead he jabbed his finger against the disconnect button of his cell phone so hard he almost knocked it from his hand.

Beau ate barbecue for lunch every day and relied on his girlfriend to prepare dinner. That evening Bethany made deer stew, using meat from a white-tailed buck she'd killed the previous season. Beau had never hunted until he dated Bethany, and after many meals prepared using the game she brought home, he had learned to appreciate her marksmanship.

Bethany's teenage daughter, Amanda, had plans with one of her friends, so Beau and Bethany dined without her. They were nearly finished when Bethany said, "You've been quiet all evening. Is something wrong?"

Beau looked up from his last spoonful of stew. Bethany had not changed when she'd returned home from the veterinary clinic and still wore her blue scrubs. Six years his junior, she had the figure of a younger woman, but a lifetime in the Texas sun had weathered her. She wore her highlighted golden-brown hair cut in a stacked bob—short in the back but almost shoulder length in the front—and her pale blue eyes searched his for an answer to her question.

"I got some bad news today," Beau said. "I may have to leave you."

Stunned, Bethany asked, "Why?"

"Some people never forget the past, the rest of us try not to remember it," Beau explained, "and something I did a long time ago caught up to me today."

"You can't do this to me." Bethany dropped her spoon and leaned forward. Her hair had been tucked behind her ears as she ate and one lock fell free to swing against her cheek. "You can't do this to Amanda. Her father walked out on us when she was three. You promised us you would never—"

"It's for your own good."

"I don't believe you," Bethany said. "Where will you go?"

"I don't know."

"When are you leaving?"

"I don't know. It could be soon."

"What about the smokehouse?"

He shrugged.

"Don't you care about anything?"

"You," he said, "and Amanda."

"You can't care all that much if you're willing to walk away from us."

"It's because I care about you that I have to leave."

Bethany snorted with disgust, folded her arms under her breasts, and glared at Beau. "That's the worst line of crap I've ever heard. You don't know where you're going or when you're leaving, but you're doing it because you care about us?"

"I've done some bad things," Beau said. "The people I did them with might be coming for me."

"I thought we didn't have any secrets," Bethany said with equal parts anger and dismay. "Apparently I was wrong."

Beau did not know when—or even if—the U.S. Marshals Service would relocate him. "I'll say goodbye before I leave. If anything happens before I do, you call this number and ask for Sara Arquette."

As Beau recited the number, Bethany grabbed her smartphone to enter it into her contact list. He snatched the phone from her hands. "Don't put it in your phone. Don't write it down. Memorize it."

*

At 2 a.m. Wednesday morning, as he was dressing for the day and Bethany lightly snored on her side of the bed with her back to him, Beau heard the distinctive *potato-potato-potato* rumble of a lone Harley-Davidson motorcycle cruising along the state highway that bisected Quarryville. He kept a sawed-off double-barrel shotgun under the smokehouse's front counter, but he had grown complacent over the years and had long ago stopped carrying personal protection. The fading sound of the motorcycle haunted Beau until he unlocked the gun cabinet in the living room, removed and loaded his 9mm Glock, and tucked it into a worn leather holster at the small of his back. Then he relocked the gun cabinet and walked across the street, the train tracks, and the highway to the smokehouse, where he fired up the indirect-heat pit and prepped the brisket and ribs he would serve for lunch later that day.

Alone in the dark, in the fenced area beside the converted Conoco station where Beau smoked his meat away from the prying eyes of customers and competitors—though until the magazine article had appeared, he had never considered the possibility of competitors—Beau contemplated his actions during the coming days. He had more baggage than the first time he had been relocated, and he wondered how easy it would be to walk away this time.

Quarryville was a two-day ride from Columbus, a distance not much different than that from Columbus to North Dakota, a ride he had made several times with the Lords of Ohio to attend the annual Sturgis Motorcycle Rally. He likely had only a few days to decide where he wanted to go and who he wanted to be before the U.S. Marshals Service came for him. He was considering the Pacific Northwest when he finally rolled up the service-bay doors to find Tommy sitting at one of the picnic tables outside.

Tommy rose, tucked the magazine he'd been reading into his back pocket, and headed inside. He placed his usual order and added, "You aren't planning to throw pickles at me this morning, are you?"

"I should charge you extra for them," Beau said as he filled a Styrofoam three-compartment takeout container with Tommy's lunch order.

"Fat chance you could collect it."

Beau slid a cold can of Dr Pepper across the counter and Tommy slid back exact change.

There were no other customers in the smokehouse and none

approaching as far as Beau could see. "Yesterday you said there was nothing for you at home," he said, "but why do you keep coming here?"

"When I retired, I came home to care for my mother because she was all I had in the world," Tommy said. "She died a couple of years later, and I planted her in the Methodist cemetery, next to my father. I was spending every afternoon in the Watering Hole, drowning my sorry ass in cheap beer, before you opened this place."

"You chose brisket over beer?"

"You're better company than a bottle of Lone Star," Tommy said.

"What about your old friends, the people you grew up with?"

"The few that didn't move away are dead or as good as," Tommy said. "These days you're the closest thing to a friend I've got."

Unsure how to respond, Beau stared across the counter at his customer.

"I never hear you talk about your people."

"There's nothing to talk about," Beau said. "They're gone."

"That's a damn shame," Tommy said. "Good thing you found Bethany. When I had to put my mother's cat to sleep a couple of years ago, your Bethany held my hand. That's a good woman you have there. Worth fighting for, don't you think?"

Without waiting for a response, Tommy picked up his lunch and carried it outside. A lone biker drifted by on the highway, the *potato-potato-potato* sound echoing into the former showroom until the door swung closed. Beau stiffened.

Beau waited until he was in the privacy of his own home that afternoon before dialing the number he had memorized all those years earlier. After identifying himself to Deputy Marshal Arquette, Beau asked, "Have you heard anything?"

"Nothing," Arquette replied.

"Are you planning to relocate me?"

"Not at this time."

"I have people now."

"That complicates things."

"You have no idea."

"I'll be away from the office tomorrow and Friday," she said, "but my calls will be forwarded to my cell. Let me know if anything changes."

"Yeah," Beau said. "I'll call when I'm dead."

He stabbed the phone's disconnect switch with his finger and began pacing the living room. His first thought the previous day had been to abandon this life just as he had abandoned his previous life, but Bethany and Tommy had made him realize he had more to lose and nothing he wanted to leave behind.

He was sitting at the kitchen table nursing a bottle of Dos Equis when Bethany returned home from the veterinary clinic. He reached into the refrigerator behind him and brought out a second bottle. As he held it out to her, he said, "I'm sorry about last night."

"You should be." Bethany took the bottle and settled onto a chair on the other side of the table.

During preparation for relocation, William Secrist and other deputy marshals had promised that no one who followed their instructions had ever been hurt or killed while in the Witness Security Program under the protection of the U.S. Marshals Service. One of those rules was never, ever to divulge his prior identity, not even to a lover who entered his life after relocation. Too many relationships turn sour, and a spiteful ex who revealed his identity would endanger his life. Beau knew he had to risk that possibility.

"You know who I am," Beau said, "not who I was. I'm not that man anymore."

"Does this have something to do with your tattoo?"

Tattooed on Beau's left upper arm, usually covered by his shirt sleeve, was a skull with a crown of thorns and the phrase VENGEANCE IS MINE written in Old English script in a ribbon below the skull.

He nodded. "I was an enforcer for the Lords of Ohio."

She shook her head.

"Hell's Angels. Banditos," he said. "Like them, but a much smaller organization."

"Organization?" Bethany said. "You mean gang? You're in a motorcycle gang?"

"I was, a long time ago. I'm not now."

"So how do you quit? Do you just mail in a resignation letter?"

"I wish it were that easy." He told her about his arrest and the deal he'd made to roll over on his fellow Lords of Ohio. "The feds had me dead to rights," he said. "I was facing life in prison with no possibility of parole."

Bethany listened without interruption.

"The feds dropped all charges in return for my turning state's evidence, and they put me in the Witness Security Program, relocating me here when all the trials ended," Beau explained. "Eighteen members of the Lords of Ohio went to prison because of my testimony. Chainsaw Roberts must be out by now."

Chainsaw had not been convicted of any of the murders Beau had witnessed in his previous life, the evidence too circumstantial despite Beau's testimony, and had gone away for ten years on a combination of lesser charges. Beau told Bethany the big man used a chainsaw for easy disposal of bodies while leaving behind copious amounts of physical reminders attesting to the deceased's violent end to discourage the deceased's friends and family from pursuing matters further.

"Sweet Jesus," Bethany said under her breath. She opened her bottle of Dos Equis and downed half of it before she spoke again. "So you were just going to walk out on us?"

He told her about the magazine article and how he thought the photograph outed him.

"I thought if I left, you and Amanda would be safe." Beau didn't mention that the U.S. Marshals Service had not yet committed to relocating him. "I realized today that if I walk away, I leave behind everyone and everything I've ever loved. I couldn't leave without you knowing why."

"No," Bethany said. "You're staying. We'll get through this. Somehow, we'll get through this."

Amanda, a young woman who resembled photographs of Bethany at the same age, opened the back door and stepped into the kitchen. Her presence ended their conversation.

Tommy ordered his usual lunch on Thursday. As he paid, he said, "You didn't exist until you moved here, and you barely exist now."

"How's that?" Beau asked.

"I spent some time on the Internet yesterday. You're not on social media, don't have an email address I can find, and I've seen your cell phone. All it does is make calls."

"You have a problem with that?"

"A man has a right to privacy," Tommy said. "But your reaction to the magazine article got me to thinking."

"About?"

"About why a man might be hiding. About why a man might

have no past to speak of," Tommy said. "I worked in the oil fields with men like you. Quiet men. Just wanted the world to leave them alone."

"And?"

"Some were good men," he said. "Some weren't."

"And what do you think I am?"

Tommy smiled. "I haven't decided."

He took his food outside, and Beau watched Tommy through the front window until a pair of tellers from Quarryville Bank & Trust interrupted his contemplative observation with an order for seven lunch plates to go.

The rest of Beau's day was uneventful. Dinner that evening consisted of the last of the deer stew, and Bethany joined him in bed that night for a physical reminder of what he risked losing.

Friday was different from Thursday only because Beau received his weekly meat delivery at 10 a.m. and dinner that night came from the Dairy Queen because Bethany was too tired to cook.

Saturday brought a slew of unfamiliar faces to the smokehouse counter, people who had seen the magazine article and had ventured out of their way to experience Quarryville Smokehouse's limited menu. The phone also rang more than usual, with people phoning for directions or asking questions. Amanda answered most of the calls.

Just before 2 p.m., after they had sold out of ribs but still had brisket and coleslaw, Amanda picked up the ringing phone, listened for a moment, and then said, "There's no one here by that name."

After she hung up, Beau asked, "What was that about?"

"Some guy wanted to speak to 'Stick.'"

Beau looked out the window, saw nothing unusual, and then told his girlfriend's daughter, "You should head home."

"But you still have brisket."

"Not much," he said. "I can handle the last few sales."

Amanda removed her apron, hung it by the office door, and was on her smartphone to one of her friends before she stepped outside. She turned back just long enough to wave her fingers before sashaying down the street toward the Dairy Queen, where her best friend had yet to master the art of making dip cones.

Beau watched her walk away, glanced at Tommy sitting at one of the picnic tables outside, his nose buried in yet another magazine, and examined the other remaining customers—a young couple outside making goo-goo eyes at one another over a single lunch order of chopped brisket, and a somewhat older couple wrangling two young children at a table in the service bays.

Deputy Marshal Arquette had been in Midland Thursday and Friday and was returning to the San Antonio office when she decided to take a slight detour to check in on Beau James and taste his brisket. Her unmarked black SUV entered Quarryville from the north, avoiding the east-west state highway that bisected the town. In a rush, she parked behind the Quarryville Smokehouse, climbed out, and hurried into the women's restroom.

The veterinary clinic closed at 2 p.m. that day, and Bethany was almost home when she saw a dozen motorcycles pulling into the Quarryville Smokehouse parking lot. The colors affixed to the backs of the bikers' jackets matched the tattoo on Beau's arm.

As the bikers parked and silenced their motorcycles, Beau stepped out of the former showroom and suggested the couple with children clear out. They didn't hesitate. The couple at the outside table also wrapped up their things and slipped away. Tommy Baldwin closed the magazine he'd been reading and watched as the bikers dismounted. None of the bikers paid attention to him as he slid the pistol from the holster at the small of his back.

As Bethany pulled her pickup into the driveway at home, she retrieved her smartphone from her purse and dialed the number Beau had made her memorize.

The roar of the motorcycles brought Amanda and her friend out of the Dairy Queen, and they captured the scene with their smartphones.

Two of the bikers entered the showroom, where Beau stood behind the counter. The others began overturning the tables in the service bays and tearing apart the limited decorations.

Bethany ran into the home she shared with Beau and shoved her smartphone into her pocket before she unlocked the gun cabinet and retrieved her deer rifle. She loaded it as she ran back outside and braced her arm on the hood of her pickup. She peered through the scope at the two men inside the showroom with her boyfriend. Both were armed. Beau had one hand beneath the counter.

"Been a long time, Stick," Chainsaw said. "You've put on weight."
Though they were of similar height, Chainsaw weighed more than twice what Beau weighed, heavy muscle hidden beneath rolls of fat. He wore a sleeveless jean jacket revealing arms liberally decorated with violent tattoos, and a crown of thorns was tattooed on his bald head. A chainsaw hung from his left hand, a .38 from his right.

Beau replied, "Not long enough."

Chainsaw glanced around. "Looks like this here's your last supper."

The deputy marshal in the women's restroom looked down at her cell phone when it rang. A call was being forwarded from the office.

Chainsaw raised the .38 he carried in his right hand and aimed it at Beau.

Bethany had Chainsaw's head squarely in her crosshairs. When he pointed his revolver at Beau, she squeezed the trigger, hoping the window separating them would not deflect her shot.

Before Arquette could answer her phone, she heard gunfire through the concrete wall. Then she heard the roar of a shotgun.

At the sound of the first shot, the ten bikers tearing apart the seating area in the former service bays drew their weapons.

The sounds catapulted Arquette, her sidearm drawn, from the restroom and around the building into a firefight involving a gang of bikers hiding behind overturned picnic tables in the former service bays, Beau James behind the smokehouse's counter, and an old man hiding behind one of the pillars supporting the canopy outside. What she didn't see was the woman on the far side of the railroad tracks using a deer rifle to pick off bikers.

The bikers had superior firepower, including automatic weapons, but expecting no resistance they had trapped themselves in a box. The entire melee lasted less than ten minutes and left the Quarryville Smokehouse riddled with bullet holes and every biker dead or dying. Sorting out the chain of events took much, much longer and involved the use of video provided by Amanda and her friend.

The coroner was unable to determine if Chainsaw was killed by the single shot to the head or by the dual shotgun blasts to the abdomen. Slugs retrieved from the other bodies also came from more than one weapon.

No charges were brought against Bethany or Tommy, and after intervention from the U.S. Marshals Service, the U.S. attorney's office declined to pursue charges against Beau for possession of a sawed-off shotgun without proper tax-paid registration.

When the smoke cleared, Beau James refused the U.S. Marshals Service's offer to relocate him. He had survived being outed, and the Lords of Ohio had disbanded, the few remaining members in Columbus absorbed into the local Hell's Angels chapter.

At Bethany's insistence, Beau did not patch any of the bullet holes before reopening the smokehouse. A significant increase in business followed, not just from being named the ninth best barbeque joint in the Lone Star State, but also from the notorious reputation the smokehouse had gained from the shootout.

The smokehouse had been highly rated for the quality of its brisket and ribs but lost points for the limited menu. So Beau added two sides—macaroni and cheese, made from Bethany's recipe, and potato salad made from Tommy's mother's recipe.

Business increased so much that Beau could no longer handle it all himself. Each morning at eleven, Tommy rolled up the service-bay doors and worked behind the counter with him until closing. On weekends Amanda and two of her high school friends waited tables.

And at the end of every day Beau returned home to his new wife, Bethany. She still knew him only as Beau James, the man he was, and not the man he had been.

The Wild Side of Life

FROM *The Southern Review*

THE CLUB WHERE the oil-field people hung out was called the Hungry Gator. It stood on pilings by a long green humped levee in the Atchafalaya Basin, a gigantic stretch of bayous and quicksand and brackish bays and flooded cypress and tupelos that looked like a forgotten piece of Creation before fish worked their way up on the land and formed feet. There were no clocks inside the Gator, no last names, sometimes not even first ones, just initials. By choice most of us lived on the rim. Of everything. Get my drift?

I liked the rim. You could pretend there was no before or after; there was just *now*, a deadness in the sky on a summer evening, maybe a solitary black cloud breaking apart like ink in clear water, while thousands of tree frogs sang. It was a place I didn't have to make comparisons or study on dreams and memories that would come flickering behind my eyelids five seconds into sleep.

I worked on a seismograph rig, ten days on and five days off; on land, I sometimes played drums and mandolin at the club and even did a few vocals. My big pleasure was looking at the girls from the bandstand, secretly thinking of myself as their protector, a guy who'd been around but didn't try to use people. The truth is I was a mess with women and about as clever in a social situation as the scribbles on the washroom wall.

I'd blank out in the middle of conversations. Or go away someplace inside my head and not get back for a few hours. People thought it was because I was at Pork Chop Hill. Not so. I was never ashamed of what we did at Pork Chop.

I was thinking on this and half in the bag when a woman at the bar touched my cheek and looked at me in a sad way, probably because she was half jacked on flak juice too, even though it was only two in the afternoon. "You got that in Korea?" she said.

"My daddy made whiskey," I replied. "Stills blow up sometimes."

Her eyes floated away from me. "You don't have to act smart."

I tried to grin, the scarred skin below my eye crinkling. "It wasn't a big deal. On my face it's probably an improvement."

She gazed at herself in the mirror behind the liquor counter. I waited for her to speak, but she didn't.

"Buy you a drink?" I said.

She lifted her left hand so I could see her ring. "He's nothing to brag on, but he's the only one I got."

"I admire principle," I said.

"That's why you hang out in here?"

"There's worse."

"Where?"

I didn't have an answer. She picked the cherry out of her vodka collins and sucked on it. "It's not polite to stare."

"Sorry."

"I get the blues, that's all," she said.

"I know what you mean," I replied.

I couldn't tell if she heard me or not. Kitty Wells was singing on the jukebox.

"Will you dance with me?" I said.

"Another time."

Through the screen door the sun was bright and hot, and heat waves were bouncing on the bay. The electric fan on the wall feathered her hair against her cheeks. She had a sweet face and amber eyes, with a shine in them like beer glass. There was no pack of cigarettes or an ashtray in front of her. She bent slightly forward, and I saw the shine on the tops of her breasts. I didn't think it was intentional on her part.

"I played piano for Ernie Suarez and Warren Storm at the Top Hat in Lafayette," she said.

"Looking for a job?"

"My husband doesn't like me hanging in juke joints."

"What's he do?"

"He comes and goes."

"What's that mean?"

"Not what you're thinking. He flies a plane out to the rigs."

"How'd you know I was in Korea?"

"The bartender."

Her face colored, as though she realized I knew she'd been asking about me. "My name is Loreen Walters."

"How you do, Miss Loreen?"

"Where'd you get the accent?" she asked.

"East Kentucky."

She put her wallet in her drawstring bag. The leather was braided around the edges and incised with a rearing horse ridden by a naked woman. It was a strange wallet for a woman to carry. I glanced at Loreen. She seemed to be one of those people whose faces change constantly in the light, so you never know who they actually are.

"Are you fixing to leave?" I said.

"There's nothing wrong in talking, is there?" she said.

"No, ma'am, not at all."

I could see myself close to her, next to the jukebox, my face buried in her hair, breathing her perfume and the coolness of her skin. I felt my throat catch.

"Then, again, why borrow trouble?" she said. "See you, sweetie. Look me up in our next incarnation. Far as I'm concerned, this one stinks."

I went back on my seismograph barge early the next day. The sun was red and streaked with dust blowing out of the cane fields, the steel plates on the pilothouse dripping with drops of moisture as big as silver dollars.

The lowest and hardest job in the oil business was building board roads through swamps and marshland; the second lowest was "doodlebugging," stringing underwater cable off a jug boat, sometimes carrying it on a spool along with the seismic jugs through a flooded woods thick with cottonmouths and mosquitoes. We'd drop eighteen dynamite cans screwed end-to-end down a drill hole and teach the earth who was running things. The detonation was so great it jolted the barge on its pilings and blew fish as fat as logs to the surface and filled the air with a sulfurous yellow cloud that would burn the inside of your head if you breathed it.

Lizard was the driller. His skin looked like leather stretched on a skeleton. At age twenty he already had chain-gang scars on his ankles and whip marks from the Black Betty on his back. He whistled and sang while he worked, and bragged on his conquests in five-dollar brothels. I was jealous of his peace of mind. He knew about what happened on our drill site down in South America, but he slept like he'd just gotten it on with Esther Williams. I had nightmares that caused me to sit on the side of my bunk until the cook clanged the breakfast bell.

My first day back on the quarter boat, Lizard sat down across from me at supper. He speared a steak off the platter and scooped potatoes and poured milk gravy on it and sliced it up, and started eating like he was stuffing garbage down a drain hole. "Word to the wise, Elmore," he said.

"What's that, Lizard?" I asked.

"Don't be milking through the wrong fence."

"Who says I am?"

"Saw you with Miss Loreen at the Gator."

"Then you didn't see very much."

He worked a piece of steak loose from his teeth. "Know who her old man is?"

"No, and I don't care, because I haven't done anything wrong," I said.

"Except not listen to the wisdom of your betters."

"How'd you like your food pushed in your face?"

"Where's that shithole you grew up in?"

"The Upper South."

"Much inbreeding thereabouts, retardation and such?"

My dreams were in Technicolor, full of murmurs and engine noise and occasionally the sundering of the earth. A man caught by a flamethrower makes a sound like a mewing kitten. A shower of potato mashers is preceded by the enemy clanging their grenades on their helmets before lobbing them into our foxholes. A toppling round becomes a hummingbird brushing by your ear. The canned dynamite we slide down our drill pipe kills big creatures stone dead and belly-up, somehow assuring us we are the dispatchers of death and not its recipient. Sometimes I heard a baby crying.

I once used a boat hook to kill a moccasin that was trapped in the current. I threw it up on the deck to scare Lizard. I don't know why. Later I felt ashamed and told a prostitute in a Morgan City bar what I'd done. She tapped her cigarette ash in a beer can.

"My stories are a little weird?" I said.

"I think you're in the wrong bar," she replied.

Every memory in my head seemed like a piece of glass. I woke the second day on the hitch to a single-engine, canary-yellow pontoon plane coming in above the trees, swooping right over the upper deck. Ten minutes later, down in the galley, I saw the plane touch the water and taxi to the bow of the quarter boat. The pilot was Hamp Rieber, a geologist with degrees from the University of Texas and MIT. His hair was mahogany-colored and wavy, combed straight back with Brylcreem. He liked to wear polo shirts and jodhpurs and tight, ventilated leather gloves, and always buzzed us when he visited the quarter boat or the drill barge. One time Lizard climbed on the pilothouse and flung a wrench at him. He missed the prop by less than a foot.

Hamp was sent to check on us by the Houston office. Sometimes he went to a brothel in Port Arthur with the crew, although I couldn't figure out why. He was rich and lived with a handsome wife in an old plantation house south of Lake Charles.

He came in and started eating scrambled eggs and bacon and pancakes across from me. Lizard was three places down. A big window fan drew a cool breeze through the room. It was a fine time of day, before the sun started to flare on the water and the smell of carrion rose out of the swamp. Hamp's face was full of self-satisfaction while he talked. I wished Lizard had parked that wrench in his mouth.

"You look thoughtful, Elmore," he said.

"I'm philosophically inclined."

"Been reading your thesaurus?"

"I go my own way and don't have truck with those who don't like it," I said.

"You're a mystery man, all right," he said, reaching for the grits. "I always get the feeling you're looking at me when my back is turned. Why is that?"

"Search me."

"Yes, sir, a regular mystery man."

I got up with my plate and coffee mug and finished eating in a shady spot on the deck. I wished I could float away to a palm-dotted island beyond the horizon, a place where machines had never been invented, where people drank out of coconut husks and ate shellfish they harvested from the surf with their hands.

*

The real reason I didn't like Hamp was because of what happened down in Latin America. At first the Indians were curious about our seismograph soundings, but eventually they lost interest and disappeared back into trees that clicked and rattled with animal bones. Hamp selected a drill site in the jungle and we started clearing the earth with a dozer, piling greenery as high as a house, soaking and burning it with kerosene and turning the sun into an orange wafer. The soil was soggy, with thousands of years of detritus in it. When it was compressed under the weight of the dozer, the severed root systems twitched like they were alive.

We put up the derrick and starting drilling twenty-four hours a day, using three crews, tying canvas on the spars when monsoon amounts of rain swept through the jungle. After we punched into a pay sand, the driller ignited the flare line to bleed off the gas, and a flame roared two hundred feet into the sky. The sludge pit caught fire and blew a long flume of thick, black, lung-choking smoke all the way to the horizon. It hung over the jungle like a serpent until morning.

The next night the Indians showered us with arrows.

The company built a wooden shell around the rig. It must have been 120 degrees inside. By noon the floor men were puking in a bucket and pouring water on their heads to keep from passing out. But at least we'd stymied the Indians, we thought. Then an Indian shot a blowgun from the trees at one of our supply trucks coming up the road. A kid from Lufkin got it in the cheek and almost died.

"This shit ends," Hamp said.

He'd flown a spotter plane in Korea and bragged he'd shot down Bed Check Charlie with a .45.

"What are you aiming to do?" I asked.

"Know who Alfred Nobel was?"

"The man who invented dynamite."

"Nobody is going to catch flies on you."

At sunset Hamp and another guy flew away in a two-cockpit biplane. About ten minutes later we heard a dull boom and felt a tremor under our feet and saw birds lift from the canopy in the jungle. A minute later there was a second boom, this one much stronger, then we heard the drone of the plane's engine headed back toward us. Lizard was standing next to me, bare-chested, staring at the smoke rising from the trees and the sparks churning inside it. He poured mosquito repellent on his palm and rubbed it on his neck and face. "Satchel charges," he said.

"What?" I said.

"He brought them from town a couple of days ago. He was just waiting on the excuse." He looked at my expression. "You keep them damn thoughts out of your head."

"What thoughts?"

"The kind a water walker has. It's their misfortune and none of our own. Stay the hell out of it."

I looked around at the other men on the crew. They had come out of the bunkhouse, some of them with GI mess kits in their hands. None of them seemed to know what they should say. The tool pusher, a big man who always wore khaki trousers and a straw hat and a Lima watch fob and long-sleeve shirts buttoned at the wrists, looked at the red glow in the jungle. You could hear the wind rustling the trees and smell an odor like the chimney on a rendering plant. "I don't know about y'all, but I got to see a man about a dog," he said.

The others laughed as he unzipped his fly and urinated into the dark.

In the morning the tool pusher told me to take a supply truck to the port twenty miles away and pick up a load of center cutters for the ditching machine. I tried to convince myself that Hamp had frightened the Indians out of the village before he dropped the satchel charges, that he meant to scare people and not kill them. My head was coming off as we drove down the dirt road that skirted the jungle. It was raining and the sun was shining, and a rainbow curved out of the clouds into almost the exact spot where the fire had burned out during the night.

I told the driver to stop.

"What for?" he said.

"I got dysentery. I'll walk back." I took the first-aid kit and a roll of toilet paper from under the seat.

The gearshift knob was throbbing in his palm. "You sure you know what you're doing, Elmore?"

"Some Tums and salt tablets and I'll be right as rain."

The huts in the village had been made from thatch and scrap lumber and corrugated tin the Indians stole from construction sites.

The satchel charges had blown them apart and set fire to most everything inside. I counted nine dead in the ashes, their eyes starting to sink in the sockets like they were drifting off to sleep. I took some alcohol out of the first-aid kit and poured it on my bandanna and tied it across my nose and mouth, and tried not to breathe too deeply.

There was not a living creature in the village, not even a bird or insects. The only sound came from the cry of a small child, the kind that says the child is helpless, unfed, and thirsty, its diaper soaked and dirty and raw on the skin.

I followed a path along a stream that had overflowed its banks. The ground was carpeted with leaves and broken twigs. Then I started to see more bodies. There were nails embedded in some of the trees, blood drags where people had tried to reach the water, pieces of hair and human pulp on the rocks by the stream. The child was lying on its back next to a woman who looked made out of sticks. One of her breasts was exposed. She wore old tennis shoes without socks and a wooden cross on a cord around her neck. A tear was sealed in one eye.

I could see branches that were broken farther down the path. The air was sweet from the spray on the rocks in the stream, the rain pattering on huge tropical plants that had heart-shaped leaves. I cleaned the child and pulled the shirt off a dead man and wrapped the child's thighs and genitals and bottom inside it, and tied the first-aid kit on my belt and started walking. My passenger was a little boy. I had never married and had always wanted to have a little boy, or a little girl, it didn't matter, and it felt funny walking with him curled inside my arms, like I was back in the infantry, except this time I wasn't humping a BAR.

I walked until high noon, when I saw the edge of the jungle thin into full sunlight. Farther down the dirt road I could see a stucco farmhouse, with a deuce-and-a-half army truck parked in front and a canvas tarp on poles where people were lying on blankets in the shade. I looked down at my little passenger. His eyes were closed, the redness gone from his face, his nostrils so tiny I wanted to touch them to make sure he was all right.

"*¿Qué quieres?*" a soldier said.

"What does it look like?" I said.

"*No entiendo. ¿Qué haces aquí?*"

He wore a dirty khaki uniform and a Sam Browne belt and a

stiff cap with a lacquered bill, a bandolier full of M1 clips strapped around his waist. His armpits were looped with sweat, his shirt unbuttoned, his chest shiny. He kept swiping at a fly, his eyes never leaving my face. There were other soldiers standing around, as though their role was just to be there. The Indians lying on the ground in the shade of the tarp looked frightened, afraid to speak. A nun in a soiled white habit was giving water to a woman out of a canteen.

"I've got to get the child to a hospital," I said. "Where's the hospital?"

"*Está aquí, hombre.*" He pointed to the child in my arms. "Put down."

"No."

"Yes, you put down."

I stepped back from him.

"You don't hear, *gringo?* " he said.

"Stay away from me."

He gestured to one of his men. The nun stepped between them and me and took the child from my arms.

"See, everything gonna be okay, man," the soldier in the cap said.

"No, it isn't. A plane bombed the village."

"You ain't got to say nothing, man. Go back to where you come from. All is taken care of."

"You're not going to do anything about it?"

"Go back with your people, *gringo.*"

"Where's the *jefe?* "

"I'm the *jefe.* You want to be my friend? Tell me now. If you ain't our friend, I got to take you back to town, give you a place to stay for a while, let you get to know some guys you ain't gonna like."

The wind was hot, the tarp popping in the silence, the sky filled with an eye-watering brilliance.

"You don't look too good," he said. "Sit down and have some pulque. I'm gonna give you some food. See, it's cool here in the shade."

"What are you going to do with the child?"

"What you think? *Está muerto.* You been in the jungle too long, man."

Now back to the present. When I got off the hitch, I headed straight for the Hungry Gator and went to work on an ice-cold bottle of Jax and four fingers of Jack Daniel's. I heard somebody drop a nickel in the jukebox and play Kitty Wells's "It Wasn't God Who Made Honky Tonk Angels." Somehow I knew who was playing that song. I also knew the kind of trouble I might get into drinking B-52s. She sat down next to me, wearing a white skirt and blouse and thin black belt and earrings with red stones in them. She smelled like a garden full of flowers.

"I thought I might have scared you off," she said.

"You're not the kind that scares people, Miss Loreen," I said.

"Still want to buy me a drink?"

Warning bells were clanging and red lights flashing. An oscillating fan fluttered the pages of a wall calendar in a white blur. "Anytime," I replied.

She ordered a small Schlitz. The bartender put the bottle and a glass in front of her. She poured it into the glass and put salt in it and watched the foam rise. "I'm trying to take it easy today."

"You have a taste for it?"

"You could call it that." She took a sip. "I was going to ask your bandleader if he could use a piano player."

"He's not around today. He plays weekends."

"Oh," she said, her disappointment obvious.

"You okay?"

"Sure." She kept her face turned to one side, away from the sunlight blazing on the shell parking lot.

"Look at me, Miss Loreen."

"What for?"

"Somebody hurt you?"

"He was drunk."

"Your husband?"

"Who else?"

"A man who hits a woman is a coward."

"He takes the fall for other people and resents himself. You never do that?"

"Not if I can help it."

"Lucky you." She ordered a whiskey sour.

"Miss Loreen, they say if you think you've got a problem with it, you probably do."

"Too late, sailor."

She watched the bartender make her drink in the blender and pour it into a glass. She drank it half empty, her eyes closed, her face at peace. "Did you know that song was banned from the Grand Ole Opry?"

"No."

"It's the female answer to 'The Wild Side of Life,'" she said.

"You know a lot about country music."

"I got news for you," she said.

"What's that?"

"I don't know shit about anything."

"You shouldn't talk rough like that."

"Yeah?"

"I think you put on an act. You're a nice lady."

She stared into the gloom, her eyes sleepy. The wall calendar had a glossy picture on it; a cowboy on a horse was looking into the distance at purple mountains, snow on the peaks.

"I went to a powwow once in Montana," I said. "Hundreds of Indian children were dancing in jingle shirts, all of them bouncing up and down. You should have heard the noise."

"Why are you talking about Indians?"

"Whenever I'm down about something, I think about those Indian kids dancing, the drums pounding away."

"You're not a regular guy, I mean, not like you meet in this place."

Her bag lay open on the bar. I could see the steel frame and checkered grips of a revolver inside. I touched the bag with one finger. "What you've got in there can get a person in trouble."

She turned her face so I could see her bruise more clearly. "Like I'm not already?"

"Why do somebody else's time?"

"It beats the graveyard." She licked the rim of her glass. "You know where this is going to end."

"What's going to end?"

"You got a place?"

When I didn't reply, she lowered her hand until it was under the bar and put it in mine. "Did you hear me?"

Don't answer. Say goodbye. Walk into the sunlight and get in the truck. It's never too late. "The Teche Motel in New Iberia," I said. "It's on the bayou. When the sun sets behind the oaks, you'd think it was the last day on earth."

She squeezed my hand, hard.

*

When I woke up the next morning, she was sitting at the table by the window shade in her panties and bra, writing on a piece of stationery, an empty bottle of Cold Duck on the floor.

"You were talking about the Indian dancers in your sleep," she said.

"What'd I say?"

"They're happy. The way kids ought to be."

I sat on the edge of the bed in my skivvies. Between the curtains I could see a shrimp boat passing on Bayou Teche; the wake, yellow and frothy, slapped the oak and cypress trees along the bank.

"My husband says Indians are no good," she said.

"What's he know about Indians?"

"He's an expert on everything."

"Did he give you your wallet?"

"For Christmas. With a naked woman on it."

I didn't speak.

"Why'd you ask?" she asked.

"Was he in the pen?"

"His brother is a guard in Huntsville. The whole family works in prisons. If they weren't herding convicts, they'd be doing time themselves."

"Were you writing me a Dear John?"

"I was going to tell you last night didn't happen."

"That's how you feel about it?"

"My feelings don't matter."

"To me they do. Tear it up."

"You've never messed around, have you?"

"Not with a married woman, if that's what you mean."

"You know what that just did to my stomach?"

"Way I see it, a man who hits his wife doesn't have claim."

"Tell the state of Louisiana that," she said. "Tell my in-laws."

Ten minutes later the owner knocked on the door and told me I had a phone call. "A man named Lizard," he added.

"She with you?" he said.

"Who?"

"The one whose husband I warned you about and who's looking for you now," he said.

"He's headed here?"

"I told him you hung out in the French Quarter."

"Who is this guy?"

"The same guy who liked to throw satchel charges out of a plane with his buddy Hamp Rieber. You know how to pick them, Elmo."

I said nothing to Loreen and showered and shaved and took my time doing it, pretending I didn't care about the bear trap I had stepped in. Then I threw my duffel bag in the back of the truck and told her to hop in.

She was pinning back her hair with both hands, her bare arms as big as a man's. "Where we going?" she said.

"The beach in Biloxi is beautiful this time of year," I replied.

The storm was way out in the Gulf and not a hurricane yet, but you could feel the barometer dropping and see horsetails of purple rain to the south and hundreds of breakers forming and disappearing on the horizon. When we checked into the motel the waves were sliding over the jetties and sucking backward into the Gulf, scooping truckloads of sand and shellfish with them. The air smelled like brass and iodine and seaweed full of tiny creatures that had died on the beach, the way it smells when you know a hard one is coming.

I opened the windows in our room. Up on the boulevards the fronds of the palm trees were straightening in the wind. I told Loreen what Lizard had said. She sat down on the edge of the bed, her face white. "Does he know where we are?"

"I don't see how."

"His whole family are cops and prison guards. They know everybody. They all work together."

"It's not against the law to check into a motel."

"This is Mississippi. The law is what some redneck says it is."

"He's just a man, nothing more."

But she wasn't listening. She seemed to be looking at an image painted on the air.

"He's buds with Hamp Rieber?" I said.

"Who?"

"A pilot. Rieber and another guy killed a bunch of Indians on a job in South America. They dropped explosive charges on their village. Maybe the other guy was your husband."

"Charles is an asshole but he wouldn't do that."

"His name isn't Charlie? I think a guy like that would be called Charlie."

"Who told you this about Charles?"

"Nobody had to tell me anything. I was there when it happened."

"Why didn't we hear about it? It would have been in the paper or on television."

I looked at the confusion and alarm in her face. "You want a drink?"

"See? You can't answer my question. It wasn't in the news because it didn't happen."

"I carried an infant for miles to a first-aid station. He was dead when I arrived."

Her eyes were too large for her face. "I need to sit down. This isn't our business. We have to think about ourselves. You didn't tell anybody where we were going?"

"Give me the gun."

"What for?"

"We've got each other. Right?"

She stared at me, her upper lip perspiring, her pulse jumping in her neck.

I had acted indifferent about taking off with a married woman. It wasn't the way I felt. My father was a pacifist who made and sold moonshine, and my mother a minister in the Free Will Baptist Church. They gave me a good upbringing, and I felt I'd flushed it down the commode.

While Loreen slept off her hangover, I sat on a bench by the surf and played my mandolin. I could hear a buoy clanging and electricity crackling across the sky. The beach was empty, the sand damp and biscuit-colored, a towel with Donald Duck on it blowing end over end past my foot. I wondered how long it would take for Loreen's husband and in-laws to catch up with me.

Southern culture is tribal. They might holler and shout in their church houses, but they want blood for blood, and at the bottom of it is sex. The kind of mutilation the KKK visits on its lynch victims isn't coincidental. The system wasn't aimed at just people of color, either. Guys I knew who'd done time in Angola said there were over one hundred convicts buried in the levee, and the iron sweatboxes on Camp A that had been bulldozed out in '52 were a horror story the details of which no newspaper would touch.

Thinking about these things made my eyes go out of focus.

The next day Loreen was drunk again and told me she was taking the bus to Lafayette to stay with her sister. "Give me back the gun," she said.

"Bad idea."

"It's my goddamn gun. Give it to me."

I took the revolver from my duffel bag and flipped the cylinder out of the frame. I noticed that only five chambers were loaded.

"Where'd you learn to set the hammer on an empty chamber?"

"I don't know what you mean. You squeeze them on one end and a bullet comes out the other."

I shook the bullets into my palm and dropped them in my pocket. I tossed the revolver on the bed. "I'll drive you to the depot."

I decided to stay clear of the Teche Motel in case Loreen or her husband came looking for me. I drove to Lizard's trailer outside Morgan City and asked if I could stay with him. In two more days I'd be back on the quarter boat, maybe back to a regular life. Lizard stood in the doorway, wearing only swim trunks and cowboy boots, gazing at the palmettos and palm and persimmon trees. "You threw a rock at a beehive," he said.

"You don't have to tell me."

"Did she go back to him?"

"They usually do."

"You got played, son."

"By who?"

"She's one of those who digs badasses and taking chances. She'll have you sticking a gun in your mouth."

"She's scared to death," I said.

"That's how she gets off." He tapped his fist against the jamb. "For a man who spends a lot of time in libraries, you're sure dumb. Come inside."

We listened to the weather reports and read his collection of *Saga* and *Argosy* and *True West* magazines, and went to a beer garden in town and ate boiled crawfish and crabs. The storm we'd worried about had disappeared, although another one had developed unexpectedly out of a tropical swell in the Bay of Campeche and was headed toward the central Gulf Coast.

Lizard sucked the fat out of a crawfish shell and threw the shell in a trash barrel. "They try to keep everybody scared and tuned to the radio. That's how they sell more products."

"I don't think the United States Weather Bureau is involved in a plot," I said.

"Like Roosevelt didn't know the Japs was fixing to bomb Pearl Harbor. You're a card."

I tried to keep in mind that after being thrown out of a road-house in Maringouin, Lizard got in the welding truck and drove it through the front wall and onto the dance floor, blowing his horn for a drink. The bouncers almost killed him.

I wanted to believe my problems would pass. The Japanese lanterns were swaying in a light breeze; a solitary raindrop touched my face. I watched a shooting star slip down the side of the sky.

"You're a good guy, Lizard."

His expression was as blank as a breadboard.

We paid the check and walked out to his beloved cherry-red pickup, a little lighthearted, feeling younger than our years. Two men were eating cracklings out of a paper bag in a patrol car. The car was old, salt-eaten around the fenders, the white star on the door streaked with mud. The two men got out of the car. They were big and wore slacks and short-sleeve tropical shirts. One wore a straw cowboy hat; the other had a baton that hung from a lanyard on his wrist. Their eyes passed over me and locked on Lizard.

"That your truck?" the man with the baton said.

"Yes, sir," Lizard said.

"My name is Detective Benoit. I saw this vehicle run a red light." He adjusted the mirror on the driver's door and examined his face as though looking for a razor nick. Then he hammered the mirror loose from the door, tearing the screws out of the metal. "Your tail-lights working?"

Lizard's face turned gray. "Why y'all bracing me?"

Benoit walked to the back of the pickup. "Looks like they're busted, all right."

He broke out both taillights, then tapped the fragments off the baton.

Neither man seemed to take interest in me.

"I ain't caused y'all no trouble," Lizard said.

"We've seen your jacket," the man in the hat said. A white scar hung from one eye, like a piece of string. "You're here on interstate parole. You shouldn't have been drinking."

"I ain't on parole," Lizard said.

"It's me they're after," I said.

Neither cop looked at me. They turned Lizard around and pushed him against the truck, then cuffed his wrists behind him, snicking them tight into the skin. The man in the hat pushed him into the back seat of the patrol car.

I felt like I was standing by while my best friend drowned.

The car drove away, with Lizard looking out the back window. A group in the beer garden was singing "You Are My Sunshine." At the end they clapped and shouted.

I walked back to the highway and hitched a ride to the trailer court. The door to Lizard's trailer hung on one hinge. The inside was a wreck. Most of my clothes had been taken from my duffel bag and stuffed in the toilet and pissed on. My mandolin had been smashed into kindling.

The cops were partly right. Lizard had finished his parole time in Georgia, but he had a minor bench warrant in Florida. The cops put him in a can down by Plaquemines Parish, the kind of place where people thought habeas corpus was a Yankee name for a disease.

In the oil patch there were no second chances. If you were wired, you were fired. Lizard wasn't wired, but he got fired just the same.

I went back to the Teche Motel in New Iberia. That's where she found me, and didn't even bother to turn off her engine when she knocked on the door. When I opened it she was breathing hard through her nose, a clot of blood in one nostril, her little fist knotted on her drawstring bag. "You've got to help me."

"What did he hit you with?"

"A belt. Can I come in?"

There was no one in the long, tree-shaded driveway that separated the two rows of cottages. Chickens were pecking on the lawns. "Park the car behind the building," I said.

She came back a minute later and closed the door after her. She tried to hand me her car keys.

"You can't stay, Loreen."

"He's going to kill me."

"Call the cops. Show them what he did."

"He saw me look at the phone and asked me how I'd like to dial it with broken fingers. Then he said he was just kidding and poured me a drink. He's crazy."

"I've got a couple of hundred dollars. That'll get you to Los Angeles. A friend of mine owns a hillbilly nightclub in Anaheim. I can probably get you a job there."

"I asked him about this Hamp Rieber guy."

"What about him?"

"Charles said Hamp was going to take care of you. Charles says you bug him."

"Say that again?"

"He said something happened in South America. I pretended not to know what he was talking about. He said Hamp knows people who can shut you up. Hamp told Charles somebody should have done it a long time ago."

She took the revolver out of her bag and set it heavily on the nightstand. Her mouth was a tight line. "You still have the bullets?"

"I don't want it."

"Throw it in the bayou. It's your life. Charles says if he has his way he's going to put something of yours in a pickle jar."

She went out on the stoop. I followed her. "Take the two hundred anyway."

Her hair was blowing in the wind. It was thick and auburn, and almost hid the stripes and lumps on her face. "We could have had fun, you and me."

Lizard said I was being played. Maybe he was right, maybe not. It didn't matter. Hamp Rieber was in the mix. He knew I knew what he had done down in the tropics, and I suspected it had probably eaten a hole in his stomach.

I still had the rounds for the revolver. It was a .38 Special, blue-black and snub-nosed, the serial numbers burned off. I sat in a chair by the front window and dropped the shells one by one into the cylinder. The bayou was chained with rain rings, the light in the trees turning to gold needles. I remembered the words to a song my mother's congregation used to sing:

Gonna lay down my sword and shield,
Down by the riverside,
I ain't gonna study war no more.

I wanted to crawl inside the lyrics and never come out. Instead I drove to Lake Charles and found the antebellum home of Hamp

Rieber, where he lived in the middle of wetlands with a rainbow arching overhead. The rainbow reminded me of the one that seemed to fall on the village Hamp had bombed.

No one in my acquaintance thought me capable of wicked acts. I knew different. If people asked me how my face came to be burned, I would make a joke about whiskey stills or if pressed mention Pork Chop Hill or for fun say "friendly fire."

I pulled the tanks from the back of a corporal who had caught one right through his steel pot, and went straight up the hill and jammed the igniter head into the slit of a North Korean pillbox. I had never pulled the trigger on a flamethrower. The blowback cooked half my face. What it did to the men inside I won't try to describe.

I parked my pickup behind an old Hadacol billboard on a dirt road and entered the back of Hamp's property through a pecan orchard. The house was a two-story antebellum, with twin chimneys and a veranda, and from behind the stable I could hear people in the side yard. I had the pistol stuck in the back of my khakis, the barrel cutting into my skin.

What were my plans?

I had none. Or none I would admit.

I began walking across the lawn toward the side yard, sweating, a warm wind on my face, my pulse beating in my wrists. I saw not only Hamp Rieber and his wife but the man who I used to see with him, the man who was probably Charles Walters. Three children were hitting croquet balls on the lawn.

I had never shot an unarmed man. I had seen it happen, but I never did it. I saw F-8os strafe roads choked with civilians and wood carts and draft animals because intelligence said the refugee columns streaming south had been infiltrated by the Chinese. But I had not let these things lay claim on me.

Walters had sun-browned skin, pale eyes, the military posture of a man who is constantly aware of himself, and coarse, large hands that swallowed the small paper plate and plastic fork he was using to eat a piece of pie. As I gazed at the emptiness in his face, I realized that he was not a man I would ever take seriously. He was a wife-beater. I never saw one of them who wouldn't cut bait when you called him out. The issue was Hamp. It had always been Hamp.

I grew up on a ridge above a place called Snaky Hollow. I knew children who lived in dirt-floor cabins and went barefoot in the snow and wore clothes made from Purina feed sacks. When I looked at Hamp, I saw those children. Call me a communist.

I wanted him to pick up a cake knife and cut me, or come at me with a shotgun. I was ready to go out smoking, as long as I could sling his blood on the shrubbery with a clear conscience.

But under my hatred I knew the real problem was the fact I had never been to the company about him or reported him to the authorities. I told myself it was a waste of time and I would lose my job for no purpose. But the words *I didn't try* wouldn't go out of my head.

He sighed. "Tired of being a spectator?"

"That's close."

"And thought you'd roll the dice."

"You're a mind reader, Hamp."

His eyes traveled up and down my person. "You packing, kid?"

"You never know."

"Let's talk out by the gazebo."

"Right here is okay," I said.

"No, it isn't," he replied.

My hands were at my sides. "Why'd you do it?"

"Do what?" he asked.

"You know. Down *there.*"

"I didn't do anything there except do my job."

"Our man Charles here didn't do anything either?" I said.

"Ask him."

"What about it, Charles?" I said. "Did you fling the charges or just fly the plane?"

"Let's go out to the stable," Charles replied. "I'll show you Hamp's horses."

"I toted a child out of the jungle and never knew he died," I said.

"Lower your voice, please," Hamp said.

"Sorry. I have a hard time sleeping at night. It reduces my powers of judgment."

"Try a glass of warm milk," Hamp said.

Then I felt myself slipping loose from my tether, a red bubble swelling inside my brain. I saw myself pulling the snub-nose from my belt and squeezing off a round in Hamp's throat, then a second one in Walters's forehead before he knew what hit him. I wet my lips and swallowed.

"Are you going to get sick on us?" Hamp said.

"No, sir," I said. "I just want to say I'm sorry to do this."

I arched an imaginary crick out of my back and let my right hand drift to the butt of the revolver, my fingertips touching the grips. I saw Hamp's wife pick up a little girl and heft her on her hip. The little girl's face was like a flower turning into the sunlight. "Daddy! Come back and play with us," she said, extending her arms.

"I'll be right there, hon," he said.

I stepped backward and hooked the thumb of my right hand on my pocket.

"You got something else to say?" Hamp asked.

"Y'all or somebody y'all hired busted my mandolin. I wish you hadn't done that."

"You need to give your listeners a decoder, Elmore," Hamp said.

"See y'all down the track," I said. I looked at his wife. "Forgive me for breaking in on y'all's party, ma'am."

I walked backward until I was clear of the picket gate, then went to my pickup, my hands shaking so badly I could hardly start the engine.

I drove to town along the edge of the lake, the palm trees bending, waves scudding, and went into a stationery store and bought a writing tablet and a small shipping box and a pencil and a ball of string. Then I drove to a park and sat at a picnic table and wrote the following note:

> This gun belongs to a pilot in Golden Meadow, Louisiana, named Charles Walters. The acid-burned numbers tell me the gun has been used in a crime or as a drop by corrupt cops. Walters and a geologist named Hamp Rieber killed many Indians with satchel charges thrown from their airplane.

I wrote down the place and date of the bombing and the name of the company we all served. Then I added:

> My name is Elmore Caudill. I live out of a duffel bag and a pickup truck. My mailing address is the Hungry Gator in the Atchafalaya Swamp.

I unloaded the revolver and placed it in the box, and wrote *FBI* across the top, and tied the box with string, and stopped long enough at the post office to drop it in the mailbox outside.

I was fired from my job. Lizard was sprung from the can. A federal agent interviewed me at the Teche Motel. Loreen dumped her husband, opened a bakery in Lafayette, and asked me to marry her. My attempt at telling the world of our misdeeds in the tropics changed nothing. In fact, I think my account had all the weight of an asterisk.

The big news of that summer was Hurricane Audrey. The tidal surge curled like a huge fist over Cameron, Louisiana, and killed hundreds of people. I worked a minimum-wage cleanup job pulling bodies out of the Calcasieu River. Over in the Atchafalaya Swamp I saw every type of animal in the wetlands starve or drown on the tops of flooded trees and floating piles of trash. I smelled more death in the aftermath of the storm than I did in war.

Hamp Rieber died trying to rescue people on a rooftop with his pontoon plane. Charles Walters became a drunk who worked the gate at Angola because he was too fat to sit on a horse and too scared to walk among the inmates. I started my own company and drilled for oil in eastern Montana and hit four dusters in a row, and, dead broke, headed over to Lame Deer and put on a jingle shirt and danced among the Cheyenne children. What a noise we made.

LEE CHILD

Too Much Time

FROM *No Middle Name*

SIXTY SECONDS IN a minute, sixty minutes in an hour, twenty-four hours in a day, seven days in a week, fifty-two weeks in a year. Reacher ballparked the calculation in his head and came up with a little more than 30 million seconds in any twelve-month span. During which time nearly 10 million significant crimes would be committed in the United States alone. Roughly one every three seconds. Not rare. To see one actually take place, right in front of you, up close and personal, was not inherently unlikely. Location mattered, of course. Crime went where people went. Odds were better in the center of a city than in the middle of a meadow.

Reacher was in a hollowed-out town in Maine. Not near a lake. Not on the coast. Nothing to do with lobsters. But once upon a time it had been good for something. That was clear. The streets were wide, and the buildings were brick. There was an air of long-gone prosperity. What might once have been grand boutiques were now dollar stores. But it wasn't all doom and gloom. Those dollar stores were at least doing some business. There was a coffee franchise. There were tables out. The streets were almost crowded. The weather helped. The first day of spring, and the sun was shining.

Reacher turned in to a street so wide it had been closed to traffic and called a plaza. There were café tables in front of blunt red buildings either side, and maybe thirty people meandering in the space between. Reacher first saw the scene head-on, with the people in front of him, randomly scattered. Later he realized the ones that mattered most had made a perfect shape, like a capital letter *T*.

He was at its base, looking upward, and forty yards in the distance, on the crossbar of the *T,* was a young woman, walking at right angles through his field of view, from right to left ahead of him, across the wide street direct from one sidewalk to the other. She had a canvas tote bag hooked over her shoulder. The canvas looked to be medium weight, and it was a natural color, pale against her dark shirt. She was maybe twenty years old. Or even younger. She could have been as young as eighteen. She was walking slow, looking up, liking the sun on her face.

Then from the left-hand end of the crossbar, and much faster, came a kid running, head-on toward her. Same kind of age. Sneakers on his feet, tight black pants, sweatshirt with a hood on it. He grabbed the woman's bag and tore it off her shoulder. She was sent sprawling, her mouth open in some kind of a breathless exclamation. The kid in the hood tucked the bag under his arm like a football, and he jinked to his right, and he set off running down the stem of the *T,* directly toward Reacher at its base.

Then from the right-hand end of the crossbar came two men in suits, walking the same sidewalk-to-sidewalk direction the woman had used. They were about twenty yards behind her. The crime happened right in front of them. They reacted the same way most people do. They froze for the first split second, and then they turned and watched the guy run away, and they raised their arms in a spirited but incoherent fashion, and they shouted something that might have been *Hey!*

Then they set out in pursuit. Like a starting gun had gone off. They ran hard, knees pumping, coattails flapping. Cops, Reacher thought. Had to be. Because of the unspoken unison. They hadn't even glanced at each other. Who else would react like that?

Forty yards in the distance the young woman scrambled back to her feet and ran away.

The cops kept on coming. But the kid in the black sweatshirt was ten yards ahead of them and running much faster. They were not going to catch him. No way. Their relative numbers were negative.

Now the kid was twenty yards from Reacher, dipping left, dipping right, running through the broken field. About three seconds away. With one obvious gap ahead of him. One clear path. Now two seconds away. Reacher stepped right, one pace. Now one second away. Another step. Reacher bounced the kid off his hip and sent him down in a sliding tangle of arms and legs. The canvas bag sailed up in the air and the kid scraped and rolled about ten more feet, and then the men in the suits arrived and were on him. A small crowd pressed close. The canvas bag had fallen to earth about a yard from Reacher's feet. It had a zipper across the top, closed tight. Reacher ducked down to pick it up, but then he thought better of it. Better to leave the evidence undisturbed, such as it was. He backed away a step. More onlookers gathered at his shoulder.

The cops got the kid sitting up, dazed, and they cuffed his hands behind him. One cop stood guard and the other stepped over and picked up the canvas bag. It looked flat and weightless and empty. Kind of collapsed. Like there was nothing in it. The cop scanned the faces all around him and fixed on Reacher. He took a wallet from his hip pocket and opened it with a practiced flick. There was a photo ID behind a milky plastic window. Detective Ramsey Aaron, county police department. The picture was the same guy, a little younger and a lot less out of breath.

Aaron said, "Thank you very much for helping us out with that."

Reacher said, "You're welcome."

"Did you see exactly what happened?"

"Pretty much."

"Then I'll need you to sign a witness statement."

"Did you see the victim ran away afterward?"

"No, I didn't see that."

"She seemed okay."

"Good to know," Aaron said. "But we'll still need you to sign a statement."

"You were closer to it all than I was," Reacher said. "It happened right in front of you. Sign your own statement."

"Frankly, sir, it would mean more coming from a regular person. A member of the public, I mean. Juries don't always like police testimony. Sign of the times."

Reacher said, "I was a cop once."

"Where?"

"In the army."

"Then you're even better than a regular person."

"I can't stick around for a trial," Reacher said. "I'm just passing through. I need to move on."

"There won't be a trial," Aaron said. "If we have an eyewitness on the record, who is also a military veteran with law enforcement experience, then the defense will plead it out. Simple arithmetic.

Pluses and minuses. Like your credit score. That's how it works
now."

Reacher said nothing.

"Ten minutes of your time," Aaron said. "You saw what you saw.
What's the worst thing could happen?"

"Okay," Reacher said.

It was longer than ten minutes, even at first. They hung around and
waited for a black-and-white to come haul the kid to the police station. Which showed up eventually, accompanied by an EMS truck
from the firehouse, to check the kid's vital signs. To pass him fit
for processing. To avoid an unexplained death in custody. Which
all took time. But in the end the kid went in the back seat and the
uniforms in the front, and the car drove away. The rubberneck-
ers went back to meandering. Reacher and the two cops were left
standing alone.

The second cop said his name was Bush. No relation to the
Bushes of Kennebunkport. Also a detective with the county. He
said their car was parked on the street beyond the far corner of the
plaza. He pointed. Up where their intended stroll in the sun had
begun. They all set out walking in that direction. Up the stem of
the *T*, then a right turn along the crossbar, the cops retracing their
earlier steps, Reacher following the cops.

Reacher said, "Why did the victim run?"

Aaron said, "I guess that's something we'll have to figure out."

Their car was an old Crown Vic, worn but not sagging. Clean
but not shiny. Reacher got in the back, which he didn't mind, because it was a regular sedan. No bulletproof divider. No implica-
tions. And the best legroom of all, sitting sideways, with his back
against the door, which he was happy to do, because he figured the
rear compartment of a cop car was very unlikely to spontaneously
burst open from gentle internal pressure. He felt sure the design-
ers would have thought of that consideration.

The ride was short, to a dismal low-built concrete structure on
the edge of town. There were tall antennas and satellite dishes on
its roof. It had a parking lot with three unmarked sedans and a lone
black-and-white cruiser all parked in a line, plus about ten more
empty spaces and the stove-in wreck of a blue SUV in one far corner. Detective Bush drove in and parked in a slot marked D2. They
all got out. The weak spring sun was still hanging in there.

"Just so you understand," Aaron said. "The less money we put in our buildings, the more we can put in catching the bad guys. It's about priorities."

"You sound like the mayor," Reacher said.

"Good guess. It was a selectman, making a speech. Word for word."

They went inside. The place wasn't so bad. Reacher had been in and out of government buildings all his life. Not the elegant marble palaces of D.C., necessarily, but the grimy beat-up places where government actually happened. And the county cops were about halfway up the scale when it came to luxurious surroundings. Their main problem was a low ceiling. Which was simple bad luck. Even government architects succumbed to fashion sometimes, and back when *atomic* was a big word they briefly favored brutalist structures made of thick concrete, as if the 1950s public would feel reassured the forces of order were protected by apparently nuclear-resistant structures. But whatever the reason, the bunkerlike mentality too often spread inside, with cramped airless spaces. Which was the county police department's only real problem. The rest was pretty good. Basic, maybe, but a smart guy wouldn't want it much more complicated. It looked like an okay place to work.

Aaron and Bush led Reacher to an interview room on a corridor parallel to the detectives' pen. Reacher said, "We're not doing this at your desk?"

"Like on the TV shows?" Aaron said. "Not allowed. Not anymore. Not since 9/11. No unauthorized access to operational areas. You're not authorized until your name appears as a cooperating witness in an official printed file. Which yours hasn't yet, obviously. Plus our insurance works best in here. Sign of the times. If you were to slip and fall, we'd rather there was a camera in the room, to prove we were nowhere near you at the time."

"Understood," Reacher said.

They went in. It was a standard facility, perhaps made even more oppressive by a compressed, hunkered-down feeling, coming from the obvious thousands of tons of concrete all around. The inside face was unfinished, but painted so many times it was smooth and slick. The color was a pale government green, not helped by ecological bulbs in the fixtures. The air looked seasick. There was a large mirror on the end wall. Without doubt a one-way window.

Reacher sat down facing it, on the bad-guy side of a crossways table, opposite Aaron and Bush, who had pads of paper and fistfuls of pens. First Aaron warned Reacher that both audio and video recording were taking place. Then Aaron asked Reacher for his full name, and his date of birth, and his Social Security number, all of which Reacher supplied truthfully, because why not? Then Aaron asked for his current address, which started a whole big debate.

Reacher said, "No fixed abode."

Aaron said, "What does that mean?"

"What it says. It's a well-known form of words."

"You don't live anywhere?"

"I live plenty of places. One night at a time."

"Like in an RV? Are you retired?"

"No RV," Reacher said.

Aaron said, "In other words you're homeless."

"But voluntarily."

"What does that mean?"

"I move from place to place. A day here, a day there."

"Why?"

"Because I like to."

"Like a tourist?"

"I suppose."

"Where's your luggage?"

"I don't use any."

"You have no stuff?"

"I saw a little book in a store at the airport. Apparently we're supposed to get rid of whatever doesn't bring us joy."

"So you junked your stuff?"

"I already had no stuff. I figured that part out years ago."

Aaron stared down at his pad of paper, unsure. He said, "So what would be the best word for you? Vagrant?"

Reacher said, "Itinerant. Distributed. Transient. Episodic."

"Were you discharged from the military with any kind of diagnosis?"

"Would that hurt my credibility as a witness?"

"I told you, it's like a credit score. No fixed address is a bad thing. PTSD would be worse. Defense counsel might speculate about your potential reliability on the stand. They might knock you down a point or two."

"I was in the 110th MP," Reacher said. "I'm not scared of PTSD. PTSD is scared of me."

"What was the 110th MP?"

"An elite unit."

"How long have you been out?"

"Longer than I was in."

"Okay," Aaron said. "But this is not my call. It's about the numbers now, pure and simple. Trials happen inside laptop computers. Special software. Ten thousand simulations. The majority trend. A couple of points either way could be crucial. No fixed address isn't ideal, even without anything else."

"Take it or leave it," Reacher said.

They took it, like Reacher knew they would. They could never have too much. They could always lose some of it later. Perfectly normal. Plenty of good work got wasted, even on slam-dunk successful cases. So he ran through what he had seen, carefully, coherently, completely, beginning to end, left to right, near to far, and afterward they all agreed that must have been about all of it. Aaron sent Bush to get the audio typed and printed, ready for Reacher's signature. Bush left the room, and Aaron said, "Thank you again."

"You're welcome again," Reacher said. "Now tell me your interest."

"Like you saw, it happened right in front of us."

"Which I'm beginning to think is the interesting part. I mean, what were the odds? Detective Bush parked in the D2 slot. Which means he's number two on the detective squad. But he drove the car and now he's doing your fetching and carrying. Which means you're number one on the detective squad. Which means the two biggest names in the most glamorous division in the whole county police department just happened to be taking a stroll in the sun twenty yards behind a girl who just happened to get robbed."

"Coincidence," Aaron said.

Reacher said, "I think you were following her."

"Why do you think that?"

"Because you don't seem to care what happened to her afterward. Possibly because you know who she is. You know she'll be back soon, to tell you all about it. Or you know where to find her. Because you're blackmailing her. Or she's a double agent. Or maybe she's one of your own, working undercover. Whichever, you trust her to look out for herself. You're not worried about her. It's the bag you're interested in. She was violently robbed, but you followed the bag, not her. Maybe the bag is important. Although I don't see how. It looked empty to me."

"Sounds like a real big conspiracy going on, doesn't it?"

"It was your choice of words," Reacher said. "You thanked me for my help. My help in what exactly? A spontaneous split-second emergency? I don't think you would have used that phrase. You would have said, *Wow, that was something, huh?* Or an equivalent. Or just a raised eyebrow. As a bond, or an icebreaker. Like we're just two guys, shooting the shit. But instead you thanked me quite formally. You said, *Thank you very much for helping us out with that.*"

Aaron said, "I was trying to be polite."

Reacher said, "But I think that kind of formality needs a longer incubation. And you said *with that.* With what? For you to internalize something as *that,* I think it would need to be a little older than a split second. It would need to be previously established. And you used a continuous tense. You said I was *helping you out.* Which implies something ongoing. Something that existed before the kid snatched the bag and will continue afterward. And you used the plural pronoun. You said thanks for helping *us* out. You and Bush. With something you already own, with something you're already running, and it just came off the rails a little bit, but ultimately the damage wasn't too bad. I think it was that kind of help you were thanking me for. Because you were extremely relieved. It could have been much worse, if the kid had gotten away, maybe. Which is why you said thank you *very much.* Which was way too heartfelt for a trivial mugging. It seemed more important to you."

"I was being polite."

"And I think my witness statement is mostly for the chief of police and the selectmen, not a computer game. To show them how it wasn't your fault. To show them how it wasn't you who just nearly screwed up some kind of a long-running operation. That's why you wanted a regular person. Any third party would do. Otherwise all you would have is your own testimony, on your own behalf. You and Bush, watching each other's back."

"We were taking a stroll."

"You didn't even glance at each other. Not a second thought. You just chased after that bag. You'd been thinking about that bag all day. Or all week."

Aaron didn't answer, and got no more opportunity to discuss it, because at that moment the door opened and a different head stuck in. It gestured Aaron out for a word. Aaron left and the door snicked shut behind him. But before Reacher could get around to worrying about whether it was locked or not, it opened up again, and Aaron stuck his head back in and said, "The rest of the interview will be conducted by different detectives."

The door closed again.

Opened again.

The guy who had stuck his head in the first time led the way. He had a similar guy behind him. Both looked like classic New England characters from historic black-and-white photographs. The product of many generations of hard work and stern self-denial. Both were lean and wiry, all cords and ligaments, almost gaunt. They were wearing chino pants, with checked shirts under blue sport coats. They had buzzed haircuts. No attempt at style. Pure function. They said they worked for the Maine Drug Enforcement Agency. A statewide organization. They said state-level inquiries outbid county-level inquiries. Hence the hijacked interview. They said they had questions about what Reacher had seen.

They sat in the chairs Aaron and Bush had vacated. The one on the left said his name was Cook, and the one on the right said his name was Delaney. It looked like he was the team leader. He looked set to do all the talking. About what Reacher had seen, he said again. Nothing more. Nothing to be concerned about.

But then he said, "First we need more information on one particular aspect. We think our county colleagues went a little light on it. They glossed right over it, perhaps understandably."

Reacher said, "Glossed over what?"

"What exactly was your state of mind, in terms of intention, at the moment you knocked the kid down?"

"Seriously?"

"In your own words."

"How many?"

"As many as you need."

"I was helping the cops."

"Nothing more?"

"I saw the crime. The perpetrator was fleeing straight toward me. He was outrunning his pursuers. I had no doubt about his guilt or innocence. So I got in his way. He wasn't even hurt bad."

"How did you know the two men were cops?"

"First impressions. Was I right or wrong?"

Delaney paused a beat.

Then he said, "Now tell me what you saw."

"I'm sure you were listening in the first time around."

"We were," Delaney said. "Also to your continued conversation afterward, with Detective Aaron. After Detective Bush left the room. It seems you saw more than you put in your witness statement. It seems you saw something about a long-running operation."

"That was speculation," Reacher said. "It didn't belong in a witness statement."

"As an ethical matter?"

"I suppose."

"Are you an ethical man, Mr. Reacher?"

"I do my best."

"But now you can knock yourself out. The statement is done. Now you can speculate to your heart's content. What did you see?"

"Why ask me?"

"We might have a problem. You might be able to help."

"How could I help?"

"You were a military policeman. You know how this stuff works. Big picture. What did you see?"

Reacher said, "I guess I saw Aaron and Bush following the girl with the bag. Some kind of surveillance operation. Surveillance of the bag, principally. When the thing happened they ignored the girl completely. Best guess, maybe the girl was due to hand the bag off to an as-yet-unknown suspect. At a later stage. In a different place. Like a delivery or a payment. Maybe it was important to eyeball the exchange itself. Maybe the unknown suspect is the last link in the chain. Hence the high-status eyewitnesses. Or whatever. Except the plan failed because fate intervened in the form of a random purse-snatcher. Sheer bad luck. Happens to the best of us. And really no big deal. They can run it again tomorrow."

Delaney shook his head. "We're in murky waters. People like we're dealing with here, if you miss a rendezvous, you're dead to them. This thing is over."

"Then I'm sorry," Reacher said. "But shit happens. Best bet would be get over it."

"Easy for you to say."

"Not my monkeys," Reacher said. "Not my circus. I'm just a guy passing by."

"We need a word about that too. How could we get ahold of you if we needed to? Do you carry a cell phone?"

"No."

"Then how do folks get ahold of you?"

"They don't."

"Not even family and friends?"

"No family left."

"No friends either?"

"Not the kind you call on the phone every five minutes."

"So who even knows where you are?"

"I do," Reacher said. "That's enough."

"You sure?"

"I haven't needed rescuing yet."

Delaney nodded. Said, "Let's go back to what you saw."

"What part?"

"All of it. Maybe it ain't over yet. Could there be another interpretation?"

"Anything's possible," Reacher said.

"What kind of thing would be possible?"

"I used to get paid for this kind of discussion."

"We could trade you a cup of county coffee."

"Deal," Reacher said. "Black, no sugar."

Cook went to get it, and when he got back Reacher took a sip and said, "Thank you. But on balance I think it was probably just a random event."

Delaney said, "Use your imagination."

Reacher said, "Use yours."

"Okay," Delaney said. "Let's assume Aaron and Bush didn't know where or when or who or how, but eventually they were expecting to see the bag transferred into someone else's custody."

Reacher said, "Okay, let's assume."

"And maybe that's exactly what they saw. Just a little earlier than anticipated."

"Anything's possible," Reacher said again.

"We have to assume secrecy and clandestine measures on the bad guys' part. Maybe they gave a decoy rendezvous and planned to snatch the bag along the way. For the sake of surprise and unpredictability. Which is always the best way to beat surveillance. Maybe it was even rehearsed. According to you, the girl gave it up pretty

easily. You said she went down on her butt and then she sprang
back up and ran away."

Reacher nodded. "Which means you would say the kid in the
black sweatshirt was the unknown suspect. You would say he was
due to receive the bag all along."

Delaney nodded. "And we got him, and therefore the operation
was in fact a total success."

"Easy for you to say. Also very convenient."

Delaney didn't answer.

Reacher asked, "Where is the kid now?"

Delaney pointed to the door. "Two rooms away. We're taking
him to Bangor soon."

"Is he talking?"

"Not so far. He's being a good little soldier."

"Unless he isn't a soldier at all."

"We think he is. And we think he'll talk, when he comes to appreciate the full extent of his jeopardy."

"One other major problem," Reacher said.

"Which is?"

"The bag looked empty to me. What kind of a delivery or a payment would that be? You won't get a conviction for following an
empty bag around."

"The bag wasn't empty," Delaney said. "At least not originally."

"What was in it?"

"We'll get to that. But first we need to loop back around. To what
I asked you at the very beginning. To make sure. About your state
of mind."

"I was helping the cops."

"Were you?"

"You worried about liability? If I was a civilian rendering assistance, I get the same immunity law enforcement gets. Plus the kid
wasn't hurt anyway. Couple of bruises, maybe. Maybe a scrape on
his knee. No problem. Unless you got some really weird judges
here."

"Our judges are okay. When they understand the context."

"What else could the context be? I witnessed a felony. There was
a clear desire on the part of the police department to apprehend
the perpetrator. I helped them. Are you saying you've got an issue
with that?"

Delaney said, "Would you excuse us for a moment?"

Reacher didn't answer. Cook and Delaney got up and shuffled out from behind the crossways table. They stepped to the door and left the room. The door snicked shut behind them. This time Reacher was pretty sure it locked. He glanced at the mirror. Saw nothing but his reflection, gray tinged with green.

Ten minutes of your time. What's the worst thing could happen?

Nothing happened. Not for three long minutes. Then Cook and Delaney came back in. They sat down again, Cook on the left and Delaney on the right.

Delaney said, "You claim you were rendering assistance to law enforcement."

Reacher said, "Correct."

"Would you like to revisit that statement?"

"No."

"Are you sure?"

"Aren't you?"

"No," Delaney said.

"Why not?"

"We think the truth was very different."

"How so?"

"We think you were taking the bag from the kid. The same way he took it from the girl. We think you were a second surprising and unpredictable cutout."

"The bag fell on the ground."

"We have witnesses who saw you bend down to pick it up."

"I thought better of it. I left it there. Aaron picked it up."

Delaney nodded. "And by then it was empty."

"Want to search my pockets?"

"We think you extracted the contents of the bag and handed them off to someone in the crowd."

"What?"

"If you were a second cutout, why wouldn't there be a third?"

"Bullshit," Reacher said.

Delaney said, "Jack-none-Reacher, you are under arrest for felonious involvement with a racketeer-influenced corrupt organization. You have the right to remain silent. Anything you say can be used against you in a court of law. You have the right to the presence of an attorney before further questioning. If you cannot afford an attorney, then one will be appointed for you, on the tax-payers' dime."

Four county cops came in, three with handguns drawn and the fourth with a shotgun held at port arms across his body. Across the table Cook and Delaney merely peeled back their lapels to show off Glock 17s in shoulder holsters. Reacher sat still. Six against one. Too many. Dumb odds. Plus nervous tension in the air, plus trigger fingers, plus a completely unknown level of training, expertise, and experience.

Mistakes might be made.

Reacher sat still.

He said, "I want the public defender."

After that he said nothing at all.

They handcuffed his wrists behind his back and led him out to the corridor, and around two dogleg corners, and through a locked steel door in a concrete frame, into the station's holding area, which was a miniature cell block with three empty billets on a narrow corridor, all ahead of a booking table that was currently unoccupied. One of the county cops holstered his weapon and stepped around. Reacher's handcuffs were removed. He gave up his passport, his ATM card, his toothbrush, seventy bucks in bills, seventy-five cents in quarters, and his shoelaces. In exchange he got a shove in the back and sole occupancy of the first cell in line. The door clanged shut, and the lock tripped like a hammer hitting a railroad spike. The cops looked in for a second more, like people at the zoo, and then they about-turned and walked back past the booking table and out of the room, one after the other. Reacher heard the steel door close after the last of them. He heard it lock.

He waited. He was good at waiting. He was a patient man. He had nowhere to go and all the time in the world to get there. He sat on the bed, which was a cast concrete structure, as was a little desk with an integral stool. The stool had a little round pad, made of the same thin vinyl-covered foam as the mattress on the bed. The toilet was steel, with a dished-in top to act as a basin. Cold water only. Like the world's lousiest motel room, further stripped back to the unavoidable minimum requirements and then reduced in size to the barely bearable. The old-time architects had used even more concrete than elsewhere. As if prisoners trying to escape might exert more force than atom bombs.

Reacher kept track of time in his head. Two hours ticked by, and part of a third, and then the youngest of the county uniforms came by for a status check. He looked in the bars and said, "You okay?"

"I'm fine," Reacher said. "A little hungry, maybe. It's past lunchtime."

"There's a problem with that."

"Is the chef out sick?"

"We don't have a chef. We send out. To the diner down the block. Lunch is authorized up to four dollars. But that's the county rate. You're a state prisoner. We don't know what they pay for lunch."

"More, I hope."

"But we need to know for sure. Otherwise we could get stuck with it."

"Doesn't Delaney know? Or Cook?"

"They left. They took their other suspect back to their HQ in Bangor."

"How much do you spend on dinner?"

"Six and a half."

"Breakfast?"

"You won't be here for breakfast. You're a state prisoner. Like the other guy. They'll come get you tonight."

An hour later the young cop came back again with a grilled cheese sandwich and a foam cup of Coke. Three bucks and change. Apparently Detective Aaron had said if the state paid less than that, he would cover the difference personally.

"Tell him thanks," Reacher said. "And tell him to be careful. One favor for another."

"Careful about what?"

"Which mast he nails his colors to."

"What does that mean?"

"Either he'll understand or he won't."

"You saying you didn't do it?"

Reacher smiled. "I guess you heard that before."

The young cop nodded. "Everyone says it. None of you ever did a damn thing. It's what we expect."

Then the guy walked away, and Reacher ate his meal and went back to waiting.

Another two hours later the young cop came back for the third time. He said, "The public defender is here. She's going through the case on the phone with the state guys. They're still in Bangor. They're talking right now. She'll be with you soon."

Reacher said, "What's she like?"

"She's okay. One time my car got stole and she helped me out with the insurance company. She was in my sister's class in high school."

"How old is your sister?"

"Three years older than me."

"And how old are you?"

"Twenty-four."

"Did you get your money back for your car?"

"Some of it."

Then the guy went and sat on the stool behind the booking table. To give the impression of proper prisoner care, Reacher supposed, while his lawyer was in the house. Reacher stayed where he was, on the bed. Just waiting.

Thirty minutes later the lawyer came in. She said hello to the cop at the desk, in a friendly way, like a person would, to an old high school classmate's kid brother. Then she said something else, lawyerlike and quietly, about client confidentiality, and the guy got up and left the room. He closed the steel door behind him. The cell block went quiet. The lawyer looked in the bars at Reacher. Like a person at the zoo. Maybe at the gorilla house. She was medium height and medium weight, and she was wearing a black skirt suit. She had short brown hair with lighter streaks, and brown eyes, and a round face with a downturned mouth. Like an upside-down smile. As if she had suffered many disappointments in her life. She was carrying a leather briefcase too fat to zip. There was a yellow legal pad poking out the top. It was covered with handwritten notes.

She left the briefcase on the floor and went back and dragged the stool out from behind the booking table. She positioned it outside Reacher's cage and climbed up on it and got comfortable, with her knees pressed tight together and the heels of her shoes hooked over the rail. Like a regular client meeting, one person either side of a desk or a table, except there was no desk or table. Just a wall of thick steel bars, closely spaced.

She said, "My name is Cathy Clark."

Reacher said nothing.

She said, "I'm sorry I took so long to get here. I had a closing scheduled."

Reacher said, "You do real estate too?"

"Most of the time."

"How many criminal cases have you done?"

"One or two."

"There's a large percentage difference between one and two. How many exactly?"

"One."

"Did you win?"

"No."

Reacher said nothing.

She said, "You get who you get. That's how it works. There's a list. I was at the top today. Like the cab line at the airport."

"Why aren't we doing this in a conference room?"

She didn't answer. Reacher got the impression she liked the bars. He got the impression she liked the separation. As if it made her safer.

He said, "Do you think I'm guilty?"

"Doesn't matter what I think. It matters what I can do."

"Which is?"

"Let's talk," she said. "You need to explain why you were there."

"I have to be somewhere. They need to explain why I would have given up my co-conspirator. I delivered him right to them."

"They think you were clumsy. You intended merely to grab the bag, and you knocked him over by mistake. They think he intended to keep on running."

"Why were county detectives involved in a state operation?"

"Budgets," she said. "Also sharing the credit, to keep everyone sweet."

"I didn't grab the bag."

"They have four witnesses who say you bent down to it."

Reacher said nothing.

She said, "Why were you there?"

"There were thirty people in that plaza. Why were any of them there?"

"The evidence shows the boy ran straight toward you. Not toward them."

"Didn't happen that way. I stepped into his path."

"Exactly."

"You think I'm guilty."

"Doesn't matter what I think," she said again.

"What do they claim was in the bag?"

"They're not saying yet."

"Is that legal? Shouldn't I know what I'm accused of?"

"I think it's legal for the time being."

"You think? I need more than that."

"If you want a different lawyer, go right ahead and pay for one."

Reacher said, "Is the kid in the sweatshirt talking yet?"

"He claims it was a simple robbery. He claims he thought the girl was using the bag as a purse. He claims he was hoping to get cash and credit cards. Maybe a cell phone. The state agents see that as a rehearsed cover story, just in case."

"Why do they think I didn't run too? Why would I stick around afterward?"

"Same thing," she said. "A rehearsed cover story. As soon as it all went wrong. You saw them grab your pal, so you both switched to plan B, instantly. He was a mugger, you were helping law enforcement. He would get a trivial sentence, you would get a pat on the head. They anticipate a certain level of sophistication from both of you. Apparently this is a big deal."

Reacher nodded. "How big of a deal, do you think?"

"It's a major investigation. It's been running a long time."

"Expensive, do you think?"

"I imagine so."

"At a time when budgets seem to be an issue."

"Budgets are always an issue."

"As are egos and reputations and performance reviews. Think about Delaney and Cook. Put yourself in their shoes. A long-running and expensive investigation falls apart due to random chance. They're back to square one. Maybe worse than that. Maybe there's no way back in. Lots of red faces all around. So what happens next?"

"I don't know."

"Human nature," Reacher said. "First they shouted and cussed and punched the wall. Then their survival instinct kicked in. They looked for ways to cover their ass. They looked for ways to claim the operation was in fact a success all along. Agent Delaney said exactly that. They dreamed up the idea the kid was a part of the scam. Then they listened in when Aaron was talking to me. They heard me say I don't live anywhere. I'm a vagrant, in Aaron's own words. Which gave them an even better idea. They could make it a twofer. They could claim they bagged two guys and ripped the heart out of the whole damn thing. They could get pats on the back and letters of commendation after all."

"You're saying their case is invented."

"I know it is."

"That's a stretch."

"They double-checked with me. They made sure. They confirmed I don't carry a cell phone. They confirmed no one keeps track of where I am. They confirmed I'm the perfect patsy."

"You agreed with the idea the kid was more than a mugger."

"As a hypothetical," Reacher said. "And not very enthusiastically. Part of a professional discussion. They flattered me into it. They said I know how this stuff works. I was humoring them. They were making shit up, to cover their ass. I was being polite, I guess."

"You said it was possible."

"Why would I say that if I was involved?"

"They think it was a double bluff."

"I'm not that smart," Reacher said.

"They think you are. You were in an elite MP unit."

"Wouldn't that put me on their side?"

The lawyer said nothing. Just squirmed on her stool a little. Uneasiness, Reacher figured. Lack of sympathy. Distrust. Even revulsion, maybe. A desire to get away. Human nature. He knew how this stuff worked.

He said, "Check the timing on the tape. They heard me say I have no address, and the mental cogs started turning, and pretty soon after that they had hijacked the interview and were in the room with me. Then they left again later, just for a minute. For a private chat. They were confirming with each other whether they had enough. Whether they could make it work. They decided to go for it. They came back in and arrested me."

"I can't take that to court."

"What can you take?"

"Nothing," she said. "Best I can do is try for a plea bargain."

"Are you serious?"

"Completely. You're going to be charged with a very serious offense. They're going to present a working theory to the court, and they're going to back it up with eyewitness testimony from regular Maine folk, all of whom are either literally or figuratively friends and neighbors of the jury members. You're an outsider with an incomprehensible lifestyle. I mean, where are you even from?"

"Nowhere in particular."

"Where were you born?"

"West Berlin."

"Are you German?"

"No, my father was a Marine. Born in New Hampshire. West Berlin was his duty station at the time."

"So you've always been military?"

"Man and boy."

"Not good. People thank you for your service, but deep down they think you're all screwed up with trauma. There's a substantial risk you'll be convicted, and if you are, you'll get a long custodial sentence. It will be far safer to plead guilty to a lesser offense. You'd be saving them the time and expense of a contested trial. That counts for a lot. It could be the difference between five years and twenty. As your lawyer I would be delinquent in my duty if I didn't recommend it."

"You're recommending I do five years for an offense I didn't commit?"

"Everyone says they're innocent. Juries know that."

"And lawyers?"

"Clients lie all the time."

Reacher said nothing.

His lawyer said, "They want to move you to Warren tonight."

"What's in Warren?"

"The state pen."

"Terrific."

"I petitioned to have you kept here a day or two. More convenient for me."

"And?"

"They refused."

Reacher said nothing.

His lawyer said, "They'll bring you back tomorrow morning for the arraignment. The courthouse is in this building."

"So I'm going there and back in less than twelve hours? That's not very efficient. I should stay here."

"You're in the system now. That's how it works. Nothing will make sense ever again. Get used to it. We'll discuss your plea in the morning. I suggest you think about it very seriously overnight."

"What about bail?"

"How much can you pay?"

"About seventy bucks and change."

"The court would regard that as an insult," she said. "Better not to apply at all."

Then she slid down off her stool and picked up her overstuffed bag and walked out of the room. Reacher heard the steel door open and close. The cell block went quiet again.

Ten minutes of your time. What's the worst thing could happen?

Another hour went by, and then the young cop came back in. He said the state had authorized the same six dollars and fifty cents for dinner that the county would have spent. He said that would get most anything on the diner's menu. He recited a list of possibilities, which was extensive. Reacher thought about it for a moment. Chicken pot pie, maybe. Or pasta. Or an egg salad. He mused out loud between those three alternatives. The cop recommended the chicken pie. He said it was good. Reacher took his word for it. Plus coffee, he added. Lots of it, he emphasized, a really serious quantity, in a flask to keep it warm. With a proper china cup and saucer. No cream, no sugar. The cop wrote it all down on a slip of paper with a stub of a pencil.

Then he said, "Was the public defender okay?"

"Sure," Reacher said. "She seemed like a nice lady. Smart, too. She figures it's all a bit of a misunderstanding. She figures those state guys get a bit overenthusiastic from time to time. Not like you county people. No common sense."

The young cop nodded. "I guess it can be like that sometimes."

"She says I'll be out tomorrow, most likely. She says I should sit tight and trust the system."

"That's usually the best way," the kid said. He tucked the slip of paper in his shirt pocket, and then he left the room.

Reacher stayed on his bed. He waited. He sensed the building grow quieter as the day watch went home and the night watch came in. Fewer people. Budgets. A rural county in an underpopulated part of the state. Then eventually the young cop came back with the food. His last duty of the day, almost certainly. He was carrying a tray with a china plate with a metal cover, and a white fluted fat-bellied plastic coffee flask, and a saucer topped with an upside-down cup, and a knife and a fork wrapped in a paper napkin.

The plastic flask was the key component. It made the whole assemblage too tall to fit through the horizontal pass-through slot in the bars. The kid couldn't lay the flask down on its side on the tray. It would roll around and the coffee would spill out all over the pie. He couldn't pass it upright on its own through a regular part of the bars because they were too close together for its fat-bellied shape.

The kid paused, unsure.

Twenty-four years old. A rookie. A guy who knew Reacher as nothing worse than a placid old man who spent all his time on his bed, apparently relaxed and resigned. No shouting, no yelling. No complaints. No bad temper.

Trusting the system.

No danger.

He would balance the tray one-handed on steepled fingers, like a regular waiter. He would take his keys off his belt. He would unlock the gate and slide it open with his toe. His holster was empty. No gun. Standard practice everywhere in the world. No prison guard was ever armed. To carry a loaded weapon among locked-up prisoners would be just asking for trouble. He would step into the cell. He would hook his keys back on his belt and juggle the tray back into two hands. He would turn away, toward the concrete desk.

Which relative positioning would offer a number of different opportunities.

Reacher waited.

But no.

The kid was the kind of rookie who got his car stolen, but he wasn't totally dumb. He put the tray on the floor outside the cell, just temporarily, and he took the coffee pot off it, and the cup and saucer, and he placed them all on the tile on the wrong side of the bars, and then he picked up the tray again and fed it through the slot. Reacher took it. To get a drink, he would have to put his wrists between the bars and pour on the outside. The cup would fit back through. Maybe not on its saucer, but then, he wasn't dining at the Ritz.

The kid said, "There you go."

Not totally dumb.

"Thanks," Reacher said anyway. "I appreciate it."

The kid said, "Enjoy."

Reacher didn't. The pie was bad and the coffee was weak.

An hour later a different uniform came by to collect the empties. The night watch. Reacher said, "I need to see Detective Aaron."

The new guy said, "He isn't here. He went home."

"Get him back. Right now. It's important."

The guy didn't answer.

Reacher said, "If he finds out I asked but you didn't call him, he'll kick your ass. Or take your shield. I hear there are budget issues. My advice would be don't give him an excuse."

"What's this all about?"

"A notch on his belt."

"You going to confess?"

"Maybe."

"You're a state prisoner. We're county. We don't care what you did."

"Call him anyway."

The guy didn't answer. Just carried the tray away and closed the steel door behind him.

The guy must have made the call, because Aaron showed up ninety minutes later. About halfway through the evening. He was wearing the same suit. He looked neither eager nor annoyed. Just neutral. Maybe a little curious. He looked in through the bars.

He said, "What do you want?"

Reacher said, "To talk about the case."

"It's a state matter."

"Not if it was a simple mugging."

"It wasn't."

"You believe that?"

"It was a credible way to beat surveillance."

"What about me as the second secret ingredient?"

"That's credible too."

"It would have been a miracle of coordination. Wouldn't it? Exactly the right place at exactly the right time."

"You could have been waiting there for hours."

"But was I? What do your witnesses say?"

Aaron didn't reply.

Reacher said, "Check the timing on the tape. You and me talking. Picture the sequence. Delaney got a hard-on for me because of something he heard."

Aaron nodded. "Your lawyer already passed that on. The homeless patsy. Didn't convince me then, doesn't convince me now."

"Beyond a reasonable doubt?" Reacher asked.

"I'm a detective. Reasonable doubt is for the jury."

"You happy for an innocent man to go to prison?"

"Guilt and innocence is for the jury."

"Suppose I get acquitted? You happy to see your case go down in flames?"

"Not my case. It's a state matter."

Reacher said, "Listen to the tape again. Time it out."

"I can't," Aaron said. "There is no tape."

"You told me there was."

"We're the county police. We can't record a state interview. Not our jurisdiction. So the recording was discontinued."

"It was before that. When you and I were talking."

"That part got screwed up. The previous stuff got erased when the recording was stopped."

"It got?"

"Accidents happen."

"Who pressed the stop button?"

Aaron didn't answer.

"Who was it?" Reacher said.

"Delaney," Aaron said. "When he took over from me. He apologized. He said he wasn't familiar with our equipment."

"You believed him?"

"Why wouldn't I?"

Reacher said nothing.

"Accidents happen," Aaron said again.

"You sure it was an accident? You sure they weren't making a silk purse out of a pig's ear? You sure they weren't covering their tracks?"

Aaron said nothing.

Reacher said, "You never saw such a thing happen?"

"What do you want me to say? He's a fellow cop."

"So am I."

"You were, once upon a time. Now you're just a guy passing by."

"One day you will be too. You want all these years to count for nothing?"

Aaron didn't answer.

Reacher said, "Right back at the beginning you told me juries don't always like police testimony. Why would that be? Are those juries always wrong?"

No response.

Reacher said, "Can't you remember what we said on the tape?"

"Even if I could, it would be my word against the state. And it ain't exactly a smoking gun, is it?"

Reacher said nothing. Aaron gazed through the bars a minute more, and then he left again.

Reacher lay on his back on the narrow bed with one elbow jammed against the wall and his head resting on his cupped hand. *Check the timing on the tape,* he had said. He ran through what he remembered of his first conversation with Aaron. In the green bunkerlike room. The witness statement. The preamble. Name, date of birth, Social Security number. Then his address. No fixed abode, and so on and so forth. He pictured Delaney listening in. A tinny loudspeaker in another room. *In other words you're homeless,* Aaron had said. Delaney had heard him say it. Loud and clear. How long did he take to spot his opportunity and come barging in?

Too long, Reacher thought.

There had been the bravura bullshit about PTSD and the 110th, and some lengthy dickering from Aaron about whether his testimony would be helpful or hurtful, and then the testimony itself, careful, composed, coherent, detailed, clear, and slow. Then the private chat afterward. After Bush had left the room. The speculation, and the semantic analysis backing it up. *You said thank you very much for helping us out with that.* And so on. All that stuff. Altogether seven minutes, maybe. Or eight, or nine.

Or ten.

Too much time.

Delaney had reacted to something else.
Something he heard later.

At ten o'clock in Reacher's head there was the heavy tramp of foot-steps in the corridor outside the steel door. The door opened and people came in. Six of them. Different uniforms. State police. Prisoner escorts. They had Mace and pepper spray and Tasers on their belts. Handcuffs and shackles and thin metal chains. They knew what they were doing. They made Reacher back up against the bars and stick his hands out behind him, through the meal slot. They cuffed his wrists, and held tight to the link, and squatted down and put their hands in through the bars, the same way he had poured his coffee but in reverse. They put shackles around his ankles and linked them together, and ran a chain up to his handcuffs. Then they unlocked his gate and slid it open. He shuffled out, small clinking steps, and they stopped him at the booking desk, where they retrieved his possessions from a drawer. His passport, his ATM card, his toothbrush, his seventy bucks in bills, his seventy-five cents in quarters, and his shoelaces. They put them all in a khaki envelope and sealed the flap. Then they escorted him out of the cell block, three ahead, three behind. They walked him around the dogleg corners, under the low concrete ceilings, and out to the lot. There was a gray-painted school bus with wire on the windows parked next to the wrecked SUV in the far corner. They pushed him inside and planted him on a bench seat in back. There were no other passengers. One guy drove and the other five sat close together up front.

They got to Warren just before midnight. The prison was visible from a mile away, with bright pools of arc light showing through the mist. The bus waited at the gate, idling with a heavy diesel clatter, and spotlights played over it, and the gate ground open, and the bus drove inside. It waited again for a second gate and then shut down in a brightly lit space near an iron door marked PRIS-ONER INTAKE. Reacher was led through it and down the right-hand spur of a *Y*-shaped junction to the holding pen for inmates as yet unconvicted. His cuffs and chains and shackles were removed. His possessions in their khaki envelope were filed away, and he was issued with a white jumpsuit uniform and blue shower shoes. He was led to a cell more or less identical to the one he had just left.

The gate was slid shut and the key was turned. His escort left, and a minute later the light clicked off and the block was plunged into noisy and restless darkness.

The lights came back on at six in the morning. Reacher heard a guard in the corridor, unlocking one gate after another. Eventually the guy showed up at Reacher's door. He was a mean-looking man about thirty. He said, "Go get your breakfast now."

Breakfast was in a large low room that smelled of boiled food and disinfectant. Reacher lined up with about twelve other guys. The kid in the black sweatshirt was not among them. Still in Bangor, Reacher figured, at the state DEA's HQ. Maybe talking, maybe not. Reacher arrived at the serving station and got a spoonful of bright yellow mush that might have been scrambled eggs, served on a slice of what might have been white bread, with a melamine mug half full of what might have been coffee. Or the water left over from washing the previous night's dishes. He sat on a bench at an empty table and ate. The inmates all around him were a mixed bunch, mostly squirrelly and furtive. The back part of Reacher's brain ran an automatic threat assessment and found nothing much to worry about, unless tooth decay was contagious.

When breakfast was over they were all corralled out for a compulsory hour of early-morning exercise. The jail part of the installation was much smaller than the prison part, and therefore it had a correspondingly smaller yard, about the size of a basketball court, separated from the general population by a high wire fence. The fence had a gate with a bolt but no lock. The guard who had led them out took up station in front of it. Beyond him a wan spring dawn was coming up in the sky.

The bigger part of the yard was full of men in jumpsuits of a different color. Hundreds of them. They were milling about in groups. Some of them looked like desperate characters. One of them was a huge guy about six-seven and three hundred pounds. Like a caricature of an old Maine lumberjack. All he needed was a plaid wool shirt and a two-headed ax. He was bigger than Reacher, which was a statistical rarity. He was twenty feet away, looking in through the wire. Looking at Reacher. Reacher looked back. Eye to eye. The guy came closer. Reacher kept on looking. Dangerous etiquette, in prison. But looking away was a slippery slope. Too submissive. Better to get any kind of hierarchy issues straightened out right from the get-go. Human nature. Reacher knew how these things worked.

The guy stepped close to the fence.

He said, "What are you looking at?"

A standard gambit. Old as the hills. Reacher was supposed to get all intimidated and say, *Nothing.* Whereupon the guy would say, *You calling me nothing?* Whereupon things would go from bad to worse. Best avoided.

So Reacher said, "I'm looking at you, asshole."

"What did you call me?"

"An asshole."

"You're dead."

"Not yet," Reacher said. "Not the last time I checked."

At which exact moment a big commotion started up in the far corner of the big yard. Later Reacher realized it was precisely timed. Whispers and signals had been passed through the population, diagonally, man to man. There was distant shouting and yelling and fighting. Searchlights sparked up in the towers and swung in that direction. Radios crackled. Everyone rushed over. Including the guards. Including the guard at the small yard's gate. He slipped through and ran into the crowd.

Whereupon the big guy moved the opposite way. In through the unattended gate. Into the smaller yard. Straight toward Reacher. Not a pretty sight. Black shower shoes, no socks, an orange jumpsuit stretched tight over bulging muscles.

Then it got worse.

The guy snapped his arm like a whip and a weapon appeared in his hand. From up his sleeve. A prison shiv. Clear plastic. Maybe a toothbrush handle sharpened on a stone, maybe six inches long. Like a stiletto. A third of its length was wrapped with surgical tape. For grip. Not good.

Reacher kicked off his shower shoes.

The big guy did the same.

Reacher said, "All my life I've had a rule. You pull a knife on me, I break your arms."

The big guy said nothing.

Reacher said, "It's completely inflexible, I'm afraid. I can't make an exception just because you're a moron."

The big guy stepped closer.

The other men in the yard stepped back. Reacher heard the

fence clink as they pressed up tight against it. He heard the distant riot still happening. Manufactured, therefore a little halfhearted. Couldn't last forever. The searchlights would soon swing back. The guards would regroup and return. All he had to do was wait.

Not his way.

"Last chance," he said. "Drop the weapon and get down on the ground. Or I'll hurt you real bad."

He used his MP voice, honed over the years to a thing of chill and dread, all floating on the unhinged psycho menace he had been as a kid, brawling in back streets all over the world. He saw a flicker of something in the big guy's eyes. But nothing more. Wasn't going to work. He was going to have to fight it out.

Which he was suddenly very happy about.

Because now he knew.

Ten minutes of your time. You saw what you saw.

He didn't like knives.

He said, "Come on, fat boy. Show me what you got."

The guy stepped in, rotating on the way, leading with the shiv. Reacher feinted to his left, and the shiv jerked in that direction, so Reacher swayed back to his right, inside the trajectory, and aimed his left hand inside out for the guy's wrist, but mistimed it a little and caught the guy's hand instead, which was like gripping a softball, and he pulled on it, which turned the guy more, and he slammed a triple right jab to the guy's face, *bang bang bang,* a blur, all the while crushing the guy's right hand as hard as possible, shiv and all. The guy pulled back, and the sweat on Reacher's palm greased his exit, until Reacher had nothing but the shiv in his grip, which was okay, because it was a pick, not a blade, sharp only at the point, and it was plastic, so Reacher put the ball of his thumb where the tape ended and snapped it like turning a door handle.

So far so good. At that point, about three seconds in, Reacher saw his main problem as how the hell he was going to make good on his promise to break the guy's arms. They were huge. They were thicker than most people's legs. They were sheathed and knotted with slabs of muscle.

Then it got worse again.

The guy was bleeding from the nose and the mouth, but the damage seemed only to energize him. He braced and roared like the kind of guy Reacher had seen on strongman shows on afternoon cable in motel rooms. Like he was psyching himself up to pull a semi truck in a harness or lift up a rock the size of a Volkswagen. He was going to charge like a water buffalo. He was going to knock Reacher down and pummel him on the ground.

The lack of shoes didn't help. Kicking barefoot was strictly for the health club or the Olympic Games. Rubbery shower shoes were worse than none at all. Which Reacher supposed was the point of making prisoners wear them. So kicking the guy was off the menu. Which was a sad limitation. But knees would still work, and elbows.

The guy charged, roaring, arms wide as if he wanted to catch Reacher in a bear hug. So Reacher charged too. Straight back at him. It was the only real alternative. A collision could be a wonderful thing. Depending on what hit who first. In this case the answers were Reacher's forearm and the big guy's upper lip. Like a wreck on the highway. Like two trucks crashing head-on. Like getting the guy to punch himself in the head.

The prison sirens went off.

Big picture. What did you see?

The searchlights swung back. The riot was over. The prison yard went suddenly quiet. The big guy couldn't resist. Human nature. He wanted to look. He wanted to know. He turned his head. Just a tiny spasm. An instinct, instantly crushed.

But enough. Reacher hit him on the ear. All the time in the world. Like hitting a speed ball hanging down from a tree. And no one has muscles on his ear. All ears are pretty much equal. The smallest bones in the body are right there. Plus all kinds of mechanisms for maintaining balance. Without which you fall over.

The guy went down hard.

The searchlights hit the fence.

Reacher took the big guy's hand. As if to help him up. But no. Then as if to shake respectfully and congratulate him warmly on a valiant defeat.

Not that either.

Reacher drove the broken shiv through the guy's palm and left it sticking out both sides, and then he stepped away and mingled with the others by the door. A second later a searchlight beam came to rest on the guy. The sirens changed their note, to lockdown.

Reacher waited in his cell. He expected the wait to be short. He was the obvious suspect. The others from the small yard were half the big guy's size. So the guards would come to him first. Probably.

Which could be a problem. Because technically a crime had been committed. Some would say. Others would say offense was the best kind of self-defense, which was still mostly legal. Purely a question of interpretation.

It would be a delicate argument to make.

What's the worst thing could happen?

He waited.

He heard boots in the corridor. Two guards came straight to his cell. Mace and pepper spray and Tasers on their belts. Handcuffs and shackles and thin metal chains.

One said, "Stand by to turn around on command and stick your wrists out through the meal slot."

Reacher said, "Where are we going?"

"You'll find out."

"I'd appreciate sooner rather than later."

"And I'd appreciate half a chance to use my Taser. Which one of us is going to get what he wants today?"

Reacher said, "I guess neither would be best for both of us."

"I agree," the guy said. "Let's work hard to keep it that way."

"I still want to know."

The guy said, "You're going back where you came from. You have your arraignment this morning. You have half an hour with your lawyer beforehand. So put your street clothes on. You're innocent until you're proven guilty. You're supposed to look the part. Or we ain't being constitutional. Or some such thing. They say jail uniforms look like you're already guilty. That's where prejudice comes from, you know. The judicial system. It's right there in the word."

He led Reacher out of the cell, small clinking steps, and his partner crowded in from behind, and they met a team of two state prisoner escorts in an airlock lobby, halfway in and halfway out of the place, where responsibility was handed over from one team to the other, who then led Reacher onward, out to a gray prison bus, the same kind of thing he had ridden in on. He was pushed down the aisle and dumped on the rearmost bench. One of the escorts got in behind the wheel to drive, and the other sat sideways behind him with a shotgun in his lap.

They retraced the journey Reacher had made in the opposite direction less than twelve hours previously. They covered every yard of the same pavement. The two escorts talked all the way. Reacher heard some of the conversation. It depended on the engine note.

Some of the words were lost. But he got plenty of gossip about the big guy found knocked down in the small yard that morning. No one was yet implicated in the incident. Because no one could understand it. The big guy was a month away from his first parole hearing. Why would he fight? And if he didn't fight, who would fight him? Who would fight him and win and drag him back to the small yard like some kind of trophy?

They shook their heads.

Reacher said nothing.

The drive back took the same duration, just shy of two hours, the same night and day, because their speed was not limited by visibility or traffic but by a slow-revving engine and a short gearbox, good for stopping and starting in cities and towns but not so good for the open road. But eventually they pulled into the lot Reacher recognized, next to the stove-in wreck of the blue SUV, and Reacher was beckoned down the aisle and off the bus and in through the same concrete door he had come out of. Inside was a lobby, lockable both ends, where his chains and cuffs were taken off, and where he was handed over to a two-person welcoming committee.

One person was Detective Bush.

The other person was the public defender, Cathy Clark.

The two prisoner escorts turned around and left double-quick. Anxious to get going. Back later. Couldn't keep a bus standing idle. They gave the impression they had many different jobs that day. Many bits and pieces. Maybe they did. Or maybe they liked a long lazy lunch. Maybe they knew somewhere good to go.

Reacher was left alone with Bush and the lawyer.

Just for a second.

He thought, *You got to be kidding me.*

He tapped Bush high on the chest, just a polite warning to the solar plexus, like a wake-up call, enough to cause a helpless buzzing in all kinds of retaliatory muscles but no real pain anywhere else. Reacher stuck his hand in Bush's pocket and came out with car keys. He put them in his own pocket and shoved the guy in the chest, quite gently, as considerately as possible, just enough to send him staggering backward a pace or two.

Reacher didn't touch the lawyer at all. Just pushed past her and walked away, head up and confident, under the low ceilings, through the dogleg corridors, and out through the front door. He went straight to Bush's car, in the D2 slot. The Crown Vic. Worn but not sagging, clean but not shiny. It started first time. It was already warmed up. The prisoner escorts were already beyond it. They were on their way to their bus. They didn't look back.

Reacher took off, just as the first few *wait a damn minute* faces started showing at doors and windows. He turned right and left and left again, on random streets, aiming at first for what passed for downtown. The first squad car was more than two whole minutes behind him. Starting out from the stationhouse itself. A disgrace. Others were worse. It was not the county police department's finest five minutes.

They didn't find him.

Reacher called on the phone, just before lunch. From a pay phone. The town still had plenty. Cell reception was poor. Reacher had quarters, from under café tables. Always a few. Enough for local calls at least. He had the number, from a business card pinned up behind the register in a five-and-dime even cheaper than the dollar stores. The card was one of many, as if together they made a defensive shield. It was from Detective Ramsey Aaron, of the county police department. With a phone number and an email address. Maybe some kind of neighborhood outreach. Modern police did all kinds of new things.

Evidently the number on the card rang through to Aaron's desk. He answered first ring.

He said, "This is Aaron."

Reacher said, "This is Reacher."

"Why are you calling me?"

"To tell you two things."

"But why me?"

"Because you might listen."

"Where are you?"

"I'm a long way out of town by now. You're never going to see me again. I'm afraid your uniformed division let you down badly."

"You should give yourself up, man."

"That was the first thing," Reacher said. "That ain't going to happen. We need to get that straight from the get-go. Or we'll waste a lot of energy on the back-and-forth. You'll never find me. So don't even try. Just give it up gracefully. Spend your time on the second thing instead."

"Was that you at the prison? With the parolee that got beat up?"

"Why would a parolee be in prison?"

"What's the second thing?"

"You need to find out exactly who the girl with the bag was and exactly who the kid in the sweatshirt was. Names and histories. And exactly what was in the bag."

"Why?"

"Because before you tell me, I'm going to tell you. When you see I'm right, maybe you'll start paying attention."

"Who are they?"

Reacher said, "I'll call again later."

He was in the diner down the block. Where his lunch and his dinner had come from. The safest place to be, amid all the panic. No one in there had ever seen him before. No cop was going to come in for a coffee break. Not right then. Out of the question. And the police station was the eye of the storm, which meant for a block all around the squad cars were either accelerating hard to get away and go search some other distant place or braking hard as they came back in again, all negative and disappointed and frustrated. In other words there was visual drama and emotion, but therefore not very much patient looking out through the car windows at the immediate neighborhood surroundings.

The phone was on the wall of a corridor in the back of the diner, with restrooms left and right and a fire door at the end. Reacher hung up and walked back to his table. He was one of six people sitting alone in the shadows. No one paid him attention. He got the feeling strangers were not rare. At least as a concept. There were old photographs on the wall. Plus old-time artifacts hung up on display. The town had been in the lumber business. Fortunes had been made. People had been in and out constantly for a hundred years, hauling loads, selling tools, putting on all kinds of mock outrage about prices.

Maybe some part of the town was still working. A lone sawmill here or there. Maybe some people were still coming by. Not many, but enough. Certainly no one stared in the diner. No one hid behind a newspaper and surreptitiously dialed a phone.

Reacher waited.

He called again, a random number of minutes after the first hour had gone by. He cupped his hand over his mouth so the background noise wouldn't sound the same twice. He wanted them to think he was always on the move. If they thought he wasn't, they would start to ask themselves where he was holed up, and Aaron seemed a smart enough guy to figure it out. He could step right in and pull up a chair.

The phone was answered on the first ring.

Aaron said, "This is Aaron."

Reacher said, "You need to ask yourself a transportation question. Six guys took me to Warren last night. But only two guys brought me back this morning. Six guys was a lot of overtime in one evening. Overkill, some might say, for one prisoner in a bus. Especially when budgets are an issue. So why did it happen that way?"

"You were an unknown quantity. Better safe than sorry."

"Then why didn't I get the same six guys again this morning? They don't know me any better now than they did last night."

Aaron said, "I'm sure you're going to tell me why."

"Two possibilities. Not really competing. Kind of interlinked."

"Show me."

"They really, really wanted to get me there last night. It was important I went. My lawyer put in a reasonable request. They said no. They signed off on an unnecessary round trip that did nothing but waste gas and man-hours. They assigned six guys to make sure I got there safe and sound."

"And?"

"They didn't expect me to leave again this morning. So they didn't assign escorts. So when it came to it they had to scramble an odd-job crew who already had a bunch of other stuff to do today."

"That doesn't make sense. Everyone expected you to leave again this morning. For the arraignment. Standard procedure. Common knowledge."

"So why the scramble?

"I don't know."

"They weren't expecting me to leave."

"They knew you had to."

"Not if I was in a coma in the hospital. Or dead in the morgue. Which normally would be a surprise event. But they knew well in advance. They didn't arrange round-trip transportation."

Aaron paused a beat.

He said, "It was you up at the prison."

Reacher said, "The guy didn't even know me. We had never crossed paths before. Yet he came straight for me. While his pals staged a diversion far away. He was coming up for parole. My guess is Delaney was the guy who busted him, way back in the day. Am I right?"

"Yes, as it happens."

"So they made a deal. If the big guy took care of me, under the radar, then Delaney would speak up for him at his parole board hearing. He would say he was a reformed character. Who better to know than the arresting officer? People assume some kind of a mystical connection. Parole boards love all that shit. The guy would have walked. Except he didn't get the job done. He underestimated his opponent. Possibly he was badly briefed."

"You're admitting felony assault."

"You'll never find me. I could be in California tomorrow."

Aaron said, "Tell me who the girl was. And the boy in the sweatshirt. Show me you know what you're talking about here."

"The boy and the girl were both stooges. Both blackmailed into playing a part. Probably the girl had just gotten busted. Maybe her second time. Maybe even her first. By the state DEA. By Delaney. She thinks he's making up his mind about whether to drop it. He proposes a deal. All she has to do is carry a bag. He proposes a similar deal to the boy. A minor bust could go away. He could get back to Yale or Harvard or wherever he's from with his record unblemished. Daddy need never know. All he has to do is run a little and grab a bag. The boy and the girl don't know each other. They're from different cases. Am I right so far?"

Aaron said, "What was in the bag?"

"I'm sure the official report says it was either meth or Oxycontin or money. One or the other. A delivery, or a payment."

"It was money," Aaron said. "It was a payment."

"How much?"

"Thirty thousand dollars."

"Except it wasn't. Think about it. What makes me exactly the same as the boy and the girl, and what makes me completely different?"

"I'm sure you're going to tell me."

"Three people in the world could testify that bag was empty all along. The girl and the boy, because they had to carry it, so they knew it was light as a feather, and then later me, because it sailed up in the air a yard from my face, and I could see there was nothing in it. It was obvious."

"How are you different?"

"He controls the boy and the girl. But he doesn't control me. I'm a wild card running around in public saying the bag was empty. That's what he heard. On the tape. That's what he reacted to. He couldn't let me say that. No one else was supposed to know the bag was empty. It could ruin everything. So he deleted the tape and then he tried to delete me."

"You're arguing ahead of the facts."

"That's why he asked how people get ahold of me. He found out he could put me in a potters' field and no one would ever know."

"You're speculating."

"There's only one way this thing works. Delaney stole the thirty grand. He knew it was coming through. He's DEA. He thought he could get away with it if he staged a freak accident. I mean, accidents happen, right? Like if your house sets on fire and the money is all in the sofa. It's an operating loss. It's a rounding error. It's the cost of doing business for these guys. They don't trust their mothers, but they know that shit happens eventually. One time I read in the paper where some guy lost nearly a million dollars, all eaten up by mice in his basement. So Delaney figured he could get away with it. Without getting his legs broken. All he had to do was put on a bold face and stick to his story."

"Wait," Aaron said. "None of that makes sense."

"Unless."

"That's ridiculous."

"Say it out loud. See how ridiculous it sounds."

"None of that makes sense, because okay, Delaney might know thirty grand is coming through, but how does he get access to it? How does he dictate who carries what in a bag? And when and where and by which route?"

"Unless," Reacher said again.

"This is crazy."

"Say it."

"Unless Delaney is walking on the dark side of the street."

"Don't hide behind flowery language. Say it out loud."

"Unless Delaney is himself a link in the chain."

"Still kind of flowery."

"Unless Delaney is secretly a drug dealer as well as a DEA agent."

"Thirty grand might be about right for the kind of franchise fee he has to pay. For the kind of dealer he is. Which is not big. But not small-time either. Probably medium-sized, with a relatively civilized clientele. The work is easy. He's well placed to help himself out with legal problems. He makes a decent living from it. Better than his pension is going to be. It was all good. But even so, he started to get greedy. This time he wanted to keep all the money for himself. He only pretended to pass along his boss's share. The bag was empty from the get-go. But no one would know that. The police report would list thirty grand missing. Any gossip about what eyewitnesses saw would make it sound exactly like a freak robbery. His boss might write it off as genuine. Maybe Delaney planned to do it once a year. Kind of randomly. As an extra little margin."

"Still makes no sense," Aaron said. "Why would the bag be empty? He would have used a wad of cut-up newspaper."

"I don't think so," Reacher said. "Suppose the kid had blown it? Suppose he missed the tackle? Or chickened out beforehand. The girl might have gotten all the way through. The real people might have taken the bag. Newspaper would be hard to explain. It's the kind of thing that could sour a relationship. Whereas an empty bag could be claimed as reconnaissance. A dry run, looking for surveillance. An excess of caution. The bad guys couldn't complain about that. Maybe they even expect it. Like employee-of-the-month competitions."

Aaron said nothing.

Reacher said, "I'll call again soon," and he hung up the phone.

This time he moved on. He went out the back of the diner and across one exposed street corner and into an alley between what might once have been elegant furniture showrooms. He scouted out a phone on the back wall of a franchise tire shop. Maybe where you called a cab, if the shop didn't have the right tires.

He backed into a doorway and waited. The police station was now two blocks away. He could still hear cars driving in and out. Speed and urgency. He gave it thirty more minutes. Then he headed for the tire shop. For the phone on the wall. But before he got there a guy came out the back of the building. From where the customers waited for their cars, on mismatched chairs, with a pay machine for coffee. The guy had buzzed hair and a blue sport coat over a checked shirt, with tan chino pants below.

The guy had a Glock in his hand.

From his shoulder holster.

Delaney.

Who pointed the gun and said, "Stop walking."

Reacher stopped walking.

Delaney said, "You're not as smart as you think."

Reacher said nothing.

Delaney said, "You were in the police station. You saw how basic it was. You gambled they couldn't trace a pay-phone location in real time. So you talked as long as you wanted."

"Was I right?"

"The county can't do it. But the state can. I knew where you were. From the start. You made a mistake."

"That's always a theoretical possibility."

"You made one mistake after another."

"Or did I? Because think about it for a minute. From my point of view. First I told you where I was, and then I gave you time to get here. I had to hang around for hours. But never mind. Because here you are. Finally. Maybe I'm exactly as smart as I think."

"You wanted me here?"

"Face-to-face is always better."

"You know I'm going to shoot you."

"But not yet. First you need to know what I said to Aaron. Because I gambled again. I figured you would know where the phone was, but I figured you couldn't tap in and listen. Not instantly and randomly anywhere in the state. Not without warrants and subpoenas. You don't have that kind of power. Not yet. So you knew about the call but you didn't hear the conversation. Now you need to know how much more damage control will be necessary. You hope none at all. Because getting rid of Aaron will be a lot harder than me. You'd rather not do it. But you need to know."

"Well?"

Reacher said, "Let's talk about county police technology. Just for a moment. I was safe as long as I was talking. They're basic, but it's not exactly the Stone Age in there. At least they can get the number after the call is over. Surely. They can find out who owns it. Maybe they even recognize it. I know they call that diner from time to time."

"So?"

"So my guess is Aaron knew where I was pretty early. But he's a

smart guy. He knows why I'm yapping. He knows how long it takes
to drive from Bangor. So he sits tight for an hour or two, just to see
what comes out of the woodwork. Why not? What's he got to lose?
What's the worst thing could happen? And then you show up. A
crazy theory is proved right."

"You saying you got reinforcements here? I don't see any."

"Aaron knew I was in the diner. Now he knows I'm a block or two
away. It's all about where the pay phones are. I'm sure he figured
that out pretty early. My guess is he's watching us right now. His
whole squad is watching us, probably. Lots of people. It's not just
you and me, Delaney. There are lots of people here."

"What is this? Some kind of psy-ops bullshit?"

"It's what you said. It's a gamble. Aaron is a smart guy. He could
have picked me up hours ago. But he didn't. Because he wanted to
see what would happen next. He's been watching for hours. He's
watching right now. Or maybe he isn't. Because maybe he's actually
a dumb guy all along. Except did he look dumb to you? That's the
gamble. I have to tell you, personally, I'm betting on smart. My
professional advice would be close your mouth and lie down on the
ground. There are witnesses everywhere."

Delaney glanced left, at the back of the tire shop. Then right, at
the derelict showroom. Ahead, at the narrow alley between. Doors
and windows all around, and shadows.

He said, "There's no one here."

Reacher said, "Only one way to be sure."

"Which is?"

"Back up to one of the windows and see if someone grabs you."

"I ain't doing that."

"Why not? You said no one is here."

Delaney didn't answer.

"Time to cast your vote," Reacher said. "Is Aaron smart or
dumb?"

"He's going to see me shoot a fugitive. Doesn't matter if he's
smart or dumb. As long as he spells my name right, I'll get a medal."

"I'm not a fugitive. He sent Bush and the lawyer to meet me. It
was an invitation. No one chased after me. He wanted me gone. He
wanted some bait in the water."

Delaney paused a beat.

He glanced left. Glanced right.

He said, "You're full of shit."

"That's always a theoretical possibility."

Reacher said nothing more. Delaney glanced all around. Old brick, gone rotten from soot and rain. Doorways. And windows. Some glassed and whole, some punched out and ragged, some just blind holes in the wall, with no frames left at all.

One such was on the ground floor of the nearby derelict showroom. Chest-high above the sidewalk. About nine feet away. A little behind Delaney's left shoulder. It was a textbook position. The infantry would love it. It commanded most of the block.

Delaney glanced back at it.

He edged toward it, crabwise, his gun still on Reacher, but looking back over his shoulder. He got close, and he sidled the last short distance diagonally, craning backward, trying to keep an eye on Reacher, trying to catch a glimpse inside the room, both at once.

He arrived at the window. Still facing Reacher. Backing up. Glancing over his shoulders, left and right. Seeing nothing.

He turned around. Fast, like the start of a quick there-and-back glance. For a second he was face-on to the building. He went up on his toes and he put his palms on the sill, Glock and all, temporarily awkward, and he levered himself up as high as he could and he bent forward and stuck his head inside for a look.

A long arm grabbed him by the neck and reeled him in. A second arm grabbed his gun hand. A third arm grabbed his coat collar and tumbled him over the sill into the darkness inside.

Reacher waited in the diner, with coffee and pie all paid for by the county police department. Two hours later the rookie uniform came in. He had driven to Warren to get the khaki envelope with Reacher's stuff in it. His passport, his ATM card, his toothbrush, his seventy bucks in bills, his seventy-five cents in quarters, and his shoelaces. The kid accounted for it all and handed it over.

Then he said, "They found the thirty grand. It was in Delaney's freezer at home. Wrapped up in aluminum foil and labeled steak."

Then he left, and Reacher laced his shoes again and tied them off. He put his stuff in his pockets and drained his cup and stood up to go.

Aaron came in the door.

He said, "Are you leaving?"

Reacher said yes, he was.

"Where are you going?"

Reacher said he had no idea at all.

"Will you sign a witness statement?"

Reacher said no, he wouldn't.

"Even if I ask you nicely?"

Reacher said no, not even then.

Then Aaron asked, "What would you have done if I hadn't put guys in that window?"

Reacher said, "He was nervous by that point. He was about to make mistakes. Opportunities would have presented themselves. I'm sure I would have thought of something."

"In other words you had nothing. You were gambling everything on me being a good cop."

"Don't make a whole big thing out of it," Reacher said. "Truth is, I figured it would be about fifty-fifty at best."

He walked out of the diner, away from town, to a left-right choice on a county road, north or south, Canada one way and New Hampshire the other. He chose New Hampshire and stuck out his thumb. Eight minutes later he was in a Subaru, listening to a guy talk about the pills he got to ease his back. Nothing like them. Best thing ever, the guy said.

MICHAEL CONNELLY

The Third Panel

FROM *Alive in Shape and Color*

DETECTIVE NICHOLAS ZELINSKY was with the first body when the captain called for him to come outside the house. He stepped out and pulled the breathing mask down under his chin. Captain Dale Henry was under the canopy tent, trying to protect himself from the desert sun. He gestured toward the horizon and Zelinsky saw the black helicopter coming in low under the sun and over the open scrubland. It banked and he could see *FBI* in white letters on the side door. The craft circled the house as if looking for a place to land in tight circumstances. But the house stood alone in a gridwork of dirt streets where the planned housing development was never built after the big bust a decade earlier. They were in the middle of nowhere seven miles out of Lancaster, which in turn was seventy miles out of L.A.

"I thought you said they were driving out," Zelinsky called above the sound of the chopper.

"The guy I talked to—Dixon—said they were," Henry called back. "Probably realized that would take them half the day driving up here and back."

The helicopter finally picked a landing spot and came down, kicking up a dust cloud with its rotor wash.

"Dumb shit," Henry said. "He lands upwind from us."

One man got out of the chopper as the pilot killed the turbine and the rotor started free-spinning. The man wore a suit and dark aviator glasses. With one hand he held a white handkerchief over his mouth and nose to filter the dust. With the other he carried a tube used to carry blueprints or artwork. He trotted toward the canopy.

"Typical fed," Henry said. "Wears a suit to a multiple-murder scene."

The man in the suit made it to the canopy. He put the tube under one arm so he could shake hands and still keep his handkerchief over his mouth and nose.

"Agent Dixon?" Henry asked.

"Yes, sir," Dixon said. "Sorry about the dust."

They shook hands.

"That's what happens when you land upwind from a crime scene," Henry said. "I'm Captain Henry, L.A. County Sheriff's Department. We spoke on the phone. And this is our lead detective on the case, Nick Zelinsky."

Dixon shook Zelinsky's hand.

"Do you mind?" Dixon said.

He pointed to a cardboard dispenser on one of the equipment tables containing breathing masks.

"Be our guest," Henry said. "You might want to put on the booties and a spacesuit along with the mask. A lot of chemicals floating around in the house."

"Thank you," Dixon replied.

He went to the table and put the tube down as he swapped his handkerchief for a breathing mask. He then took off his jacket and pulled on one of the white plastic protection suits, followed by the paper booties and latex gloves. He pulled the suit's hood up over his head as well.

"I thought you were driving out," Henry said.

"We were, but then I got a window on the chopper," Dixon said. "But it's a short window. They need it this afternoon for a dignitary surveillance. So should we go in, see what you've got?"

Henry gestured toward the open door of the house.

"Nick, give him the grand tour," he said. "I'll be out here."

Dixon stepped through the threshold into a small entranceway that had been remodeled as a mantrap with fortified doors on either end. It was typical of most drug houses. Zelinsky stepped in behind him.

"I assume the captain filled you in on the basics when you talked," Zelinsky said.

"Let's not assume anything, Detective," Dixon said. "I'd rather get the rundown from the case lead than the captain."

"Okay, then. This place was a sample house built before the

crash in '08. Nothing else was ever built out here. Made it perfect for cooking meth."

"Got it."

"Inside we have four victims—all in different parts of the house. Three cooks and a guy you would call the house security man. There are several weapons in the house, but it looks like nobody got off a defensive shot. It looks like they were taken out by fucking ninjas, to tell you the truth. All four are heart-shot with arrows. Short arrows."

"Crossbow?"

"Most likely."

"Motive?"

"It doesn't appear to be robbery, because there are bags and full pans of product in all the rooms and all of it readily visible for the taking. It just looks like a hit-and-run. And there is something else we didn't put out on the bulletin that I think you'll want to see."

"On the phone I think the captain mentioned this is a Saints and Sinners operation."

"That's right. Lancaster and Palmdale is their territory and this is their place, so it's not looking like a turf thing either."

"Okay, let's see the rest."

"First, your turn. What made the FBI jump on the bulletin we sent out?"

"The arrows. The crossbow. If it connects to something else we have working, I will tell you once I confirm it."

Dixon stepped through the second door and paused to look at the front room of the house. It was furnished like a normal living room with two leather couches, two other stuffed chairs, a coffee table, and large flat-screen television on the wall. There was an-other, smaller screen on the coffee table and it was quadded into four camera views of the scrubland and desert surrounding the house.

There was a dead man sitting on the couch in front of the se-curity screen, his body turned to the left, his right arm reaching across his body toward a side table where a sawed-off shotgun waited. He never got to it. A black graphite arrow had pierced his torso back to front, a heart shot, as Zelinsky had said, penetrating the leather vest he wore with the Saints & Sinners motorcycle club logo—the grinning skull with devil horns and angel halo tilted at a rakish angle. There was very little blood because the arrow had

struck with such high velocity that the entrance and exit wounds
sealed around its shaft.

"We have this guy as victim number one," Zelinsky said. "Name
is Aiden Vance, multiple arrests for drugs and acts of violence—
ADWs and attempted murders. Did a nickel up in Corcoran. Your
basic motorcycle gang enforcer. But it looks like they got the drop
on him here. He apparently didn't see them coming on the monitors, didn't hear them pick the lock or come through the mantrap.
Until it was too late."

"Neat trick," Dixon said.

"Like I said, ninjas."

"Ninjas? More than one?"

"Doesn't feel like a one-man op, you ask me."

"The cameras—are there digitized recordings?"

"No such luck. Purely for live monitoring. I guess they didn't
want digital evidence of their own goings and comings here. It
could have put them away."

"Right."

They proceeded further into the house. There were several
evidence technicians, photographers, and detectives working
throughout. Yellow evidence markers were placed on the floor, on
furniture, and on walls everywhere Dixon looked. The place had
been used as a cook house for crystal meth, which was the main
income stream for the Saints & Sinners. Zelinsky explained that
this was only one of several such houses operated by the group
and scattered through the desert northeast of Los Angeles, where
the finished product was shipped to and distributed to dealers and
then to the hapless victims of the devastatingly addictive drug.

"The starting point," Dixon said.

"Starting point of what?" Zelinsky asked.

"The trail of human misery. What was cooked in this house destroyed lives."

"Yeah, you could say that. A place like this—it was probably producing seventy, eighty pounds a week."

"Makes it hard to feel sorry for these people."

It was a three-bedroom house, and each bedroom was a separate
cook room that was probably in operation twenty-four hours a day,
with two or three shifts of cooks and security men. In each cook
room there was another body pierced by an arrow and sprawled on
the floor. Each one a man in a protection suit and wearing a breath-

ing mask. No blood, just a clean heart shot each time. Zelinsky gave Dixon their names and criminal pedigrees as part of the tour.

Dixon didn't seem to care who they were, just how they died. He squatted down and studied the arrows protruding from each of the bodies, seemingly attempting to find some clue or confirm something from the markings on each shaft.

Zelinsky took Dixon into the master bedroom last because here was the only anomaly and the only visible blood. The victim here was on the floor on his left side. The sleeve of his protection suit had been pulled back and the right hand was cleanly severed at the wrist.

"Guys," Zelinsky said. "Give us some space."

Two forensic technicians stepped back from the wall where they had been working. There above a meth drying pan on a folding table was the victim's severed hand, pinned to the wall by the long-bladed knife most likely used to hack it off the body. The fingers had been manipulated. The thumb and first two fingers were up and tightly together, the second two were folded down over the palm. On the wall surrounding the hand was a circle drawn in the victim's blood.

"Seen anything like that before, Agent Dixon?" Zelinsky asked.

Dixon didn't answer. He leaned down and in close to the wall and studied the hand. Blood had dripped down the wall into the drying pan below.

"Kind of like the Cub Scout salute, if you ask me," Zelinsky added. "You know, two fingers up?"

"No," Dixon said. "It's not that."

Zelinsky was silent. He waited. Dixon straightened up and turned to him. He held his hand up, making the same gesture as the hand pinned to the wall.

"It's the gesture of divinity often seen in the paintings and sculptures of the Renaissance period," Dixon said.

"Really?" Zelinsky said.

"Have you ever heard of Hieronymus Bosch, Detective Zelinsky?"

"Uh, no. What or who is that?"

"I've seen enough here. Let's go outside and talk."

Under the canopy they cleared space on a table and Dixon took the end cap off the cardboard tube. He slipped out a rolled print of a painting and stretched it out on the table, using the boxes of latex gloves and paper booties to weight the ends.

"This is a to-scale print of the third panel of a painting that hangs in the Prado in Madrid, Spain," Dixon said. "The original is five centuries old, and the artist who painted it was named Hieronymus Bosch."

"Okay," Zelinsky said, his tone betraying in the one word that he knew that an already weird case was about to go weirder.

"It's part of a triptych—three panels—considered to be Bosch's masterwork. *The Garden of Earthly Delights.* You may never have heard of this guy, but he was sort of the dark genius of the Renaissance. While Michelangelo and Leonardo da Vinci were painting angels and cherubs down in Italy, Bosch was up in northern Europe creating this nightmare vision."

Dixon gestured to the print. It was a tableau of vicious creatures torturing and maiming humans in all kinds of religious and sexually suggestive ways. Sharp-toothed animals moved naked men and women through a dark labyrinth leading toward the fires of hell.

"Have you seen this before?" Dixon asked.

"Fuck no," Zelinsky said.

"Fuck no," added Captain Henry, who had stepped over to the table.

"The first two panels, which I don't have here, are bright and blue because they are about earthly matters. The first is a depiction of Adam and Eve and the garden and the apple and so forth, the Creation story from the Bible. The second—the centerpiece—is about what came after. The debauchery and life without moral responsibility and respect for the word of God. This, the third panel, is about Judgment Day and where the wages of sin lead."

"All I can say is, this guy had one hell of a warped mind," Henry said.

Dixon nodded and pointed to a face at the center point of the panel.

"That's supposedly the artist there," he said.

"Pious son of a bitch," Henry said.

"Okay," Zelinsky said. "So he was a dark fucking guy and all of that, but he's been dead five hundred years and is not our suspect. What are you telling us? What do we have here?"

"You have the third panel uprising," Dixon said.

"What the fuck is that?" Henry asked.

"Dixon tapped his finger on several images on the print.

"Let's start with the arrows," he said. "As you can see, the weapon of choice here is the arrow. Supposedly the arrow in Bosch's work symbolized a message. This is what the scholars tell us. The arrow shooting from one individual to another meant the sending of a message. So there is that, and there is this."

Now Dixon tapped heavily on a specific point on the print. Both Zelinsky and Henry leaned down over the table to see the tiny detail. Depicted in the lower left quadrant of the panel was a man being pressed against what looked like the slab of a tomb by a demon animal with a round blue shield on its back. A knife piercing a severed hand was stabbed into the shield. The fingers of the hand were configured like those of the hand attached to the wall inside the cook house behind them.

"So what are we talking about?" Zelinsky asked. "Religious zealots, end-of-the-world nut jobs, what? Who exactly are we looking for?"

"We don't know," Dixon said after a pause. "This is our third scene like this in fifteen months. The commonality is the targets are purveyors of human misery."

He gestured toward the house.

"They make meth here," he said. "This starts the trail to addiction and human misery. In March we found a similar scene in a warehouse in Orange County used by human traffickers. Three dead there. Graphite arrows. Purveyors of human misery."

"Sending a message," Zelinsky said.

Dixon nodded.

"Four months before Orange County we were in San Bernadino, where four members of a Chinese triad were slaughtered in the kitchen of a noodle restaurant. They were involved in extortion and smuggling in workers from mainland China to work in kitchens as slave labor while the triad held family members hostage back home. Three scenes, eleven dead, all of it tied together by this painting and this panel specifically. A piece of it re-created at all three scenes."

"By who?" Zelinsky asked. "You have any suspects?"

"No identified suspects," Dixon said. "But it's a group that calls itself T3P. Short for 'the third panel.' Within a day, maybe two, they will reach out to you in some way to take responsibility for this and to vow to continue the work they believe law enforcement is failing to do."

"Jesus Christ," Henry said.

"We believe they are an offshoot of something that started in Europe two years ago. It was the five hundredth anniversary of Bosch's death and his work was displayed in a Holland exhibition that drew tens of thousands and probably sparked the uprising. Since then there have been similar multideath attacks in France, Belgium, and the U.K.—all of them targeting the purveyors of human misery."

"It's sort of like they're terrorists against the bad guys," Henry said.

Dixon nodded.

"An international meeting with Interpol and Scotland Yard is scheduled for early next month," Dixon said. "I'll make sure you get the details."

"What I don't understand is why you haven't gone public with this," Henry said. "There's gotta be people out there who have to know who these people are."

"We most likely will after the international meeting," Dixon said. "We'll be forced to. But up until now we hoped the two cases were it and we'd have the chance to quietly identify and move in on them."

"Well, this one is going to go public," Henry vowed. "We are not going to wait around for fucking Interpol."

"That's a decision above my pay grade," Dixon said. "Right now I just came out to confirm the connection and I need to get the helicopter back. The special agent in charge of the Los Angeles Field Office will be reaching out to the sheriff's department to discuss task-force operations locally."

Dixon turned toward the helicopter. The reflection off the cockpit windows made it impossible to see the pilot. Dixon raised his arm and twirled a finger in the air. Almost immediately the turbine engine turned over and the rotor blade began to slowly turn. Dixon started peeling off the protection suit.

"Do you want to keep the print?" he asked. "We have others."

"I would, yes," Zelinsky said. "I want to study the fucking thing."

"Then it's yours," Dixon said. "I just need the tube—my last one."

The helicopter blade started kicking dust up again. Zelinsky reached up and grabbed one of the canopy's cross struts when the tent threatened to go airborne. Dixon put his suit jacket back on but kept the mask on to guard against breathing the dust. He picked up the empty tube and recapped it, then tucked it under his arm.

"If you need anything else, you know where to reach me," he said. "We'll talk soon, gentlemen."

Dixon shook their hands, then trotted back toward the helicopter as the turbine began to obliterate all other sound. Soon he was inside the cockpit and the chopper lifted off. As it rose Zelinsky saw that the *F* in the FBI decal was starting to peel off in the downdraft from the rotor.

The craft banked left and headed south, back toward L.A.

Zelinsky and Henry watched it go, keeping a steady altitude of no more than 200 feet above the hardscape. As it headed toward the horizon the sheriff's men then noticed the kickup of dust from an approaching vehicle. It had lights in its grille that were flashing, and it was moving fast.

"Now who the hell is this?" Henry asked.

"They're in a hurry, that's for sure," Zelinsky added.

The vehicle took another minute to get to them, and when it arrived it was clear it was a government vehicle. It pulled to a halt behind the other vehicles scattered on the road in front of the cook house. Two men in suits and sunglasses got out and made their way to the canopy tent.

They pulled badges as they approached, and Zelinsky recognized the FBI insignia.

"Captain Henry?" one of them said. "Special Agent Ross Dixon with the Bureau. I believe we spoke earlier? This is my partner, Agent Cosgrove."

"You're Dixon?" Henry said.

"That's right," Dixon said.

"Then who the hell was that?" Henry said.

He pointed toward the horizon, where the black helicopter was now about the size of a fly and still getting smaller.

"What are you talking about, Captain Henry?" Cosgrove asked.

Henry kept his arm up and pointing at the horizon as he began to explain about the helicopter and the man who had gotten off it.

Zelinsky turned to the equipment table and looked at the print of the third panel. He realized that the only thing the man from the helicopter had touched before gloving up was the cardboard tube and he had taken it with him. He moved the boxes that weighted the print and flipped it over. On the back there was a printed message.

T3P
WE SHALL NOT STOP
PURVEYORS OF MISERY
BE WARNED
T3P

Zelinsky stepped out from the cover of the canopy and looked off toward the horizon. He scanned and then sighted the black helicopter. It was flying too low to be picked up on FAA radar. It was no more than a distant black dot against the gray desert sky.

In another moment it was gone.

JOHN M. FLOYD

Gun Work

FROM *Coast to Coast*

WILL PARKER SAT ALONE on the wooden platform beside the pulpit in the empty church. He was watching, through one of the side windows, the bay horse he'd tied to the hitching rail half an hour ago and the rippling rust-colored leaves of the trees in the distance. It was a sunny October morning, bright enough to light up every corner of the little sanctuary, and the breeze through the open windows was cool but not cold.

Parker crossed his legs, took off his hat, and balanced it on one knee. The pews facing him were as empty as the church, but he had chosen this seat—which wasn't really a seat—because it offered a clear view of the front door. Whenever possible he sat this way, facing a room with his back to a wall. He remembered what had happened to Bill Hickok.

For the tenth time, Parker checked his pocket watch. He'd been intentionally early, but it was now twenty minutes past the time his client had set for this meeting.

His client. That still sounded strange to him, even after several years as a private investigator. But Parker liked the job, and the agency he and his brother had founded in San Francisco had been surprisingly successful. Granted, most of his recent work was dull—checking backgrounds, locating beneficiaries of a will, uncovering shady deals and/or relationships, etc. (unlike the tough assignments he'd had during his short time with the Pinkerton Agency years ago)—but occasionally he was given something interesting and challenging. He had a feeling this case might be both. After all, he wasn't often instructed to meet a client at a church in the middle of the week, in the middle of nowhere.

"Mr. Parker?" a voice said.

He looked up to see a tall man in a brown hat and vest standing in the front doorway. Parker had heard no hoofbeats, no footsteps. A quick glance confirmed that his own horse, rented from the livery stable in Dodge early this morning, was still alone at the hitch rail. So much for being watchful.

"Who else would I be?" he said. "We're probably the only two people within miles."

"Sorry I'm late," the tall man said.

Parker stayed seated, watching him. "How'd you get here?"

"Quietly. My horse is tied some distance away." A smile touched the man's lips, but only for a moment, there and gone. "The cautious, I have found, live longer."

"Cautious of what?"

"Of everything."

With that, the man strode casually down the aisle and extended his hand. "Cole Bennett."

They shook hands and Bennett took a seat in the front pew, facing Parker from a distance of eight feet or so. Cole Bennett appeared to be in his late fifties, maybe ten years older than Parker. But he looked strong and fit, and had what Parker's wife, Bitsy, would call a world-weary face. Bennett took off his hat and set it down beside him. "Thanks for coming," he said.

"You paid for my transportation," Parker reminded him. "I arrived on last night's stage."

"But not from San Francisco. Your brother wired me that you were already fairly close to here at the moment. Redemption, he said?"

"Yes—my wife lived there when I met her. We're visiting her parents."

"That was convenient for me."

"Convenient for *me*, actually. Less expensive for you." Parker hooked his thumbs in his gunbelt. "How can I help you, Mr. Bennett?"

Bennett blew out a long sigh. "First I need to tell you a story."

"I'm listening."

"Do you remember the Ford brothers? Jesse and Dalton?"

"Barely."

Again Bennett hesitated, obviously choosing his words. "Some time ago," he began, "a U.S. marshal, Sam Ewing, shot Dalton Ford during what was said to be the robbery of a bank up in Hays City. The marshal lived here in Dodge but was in Hays the day this happened. Anyhow, Marshal Ewing shot Ford and killed him. Afterward one of the witnesses said Ford was in the bank, sure enough, but wasn't robbing it—he said Ford was chatting with one of the tellers. Whichever way it happened, the marshal got word he was there, entered the bank, and Dalton Ford—a man wanted for multiple crimes—wound up dead as a pine knot. Dalton's brother Jesse, who was in prison at the time, heard about the killing, and when he was released a year later he showed up at Ewing's house just outside Dodge with two of his buddies."

"Looking for revenge."

"Yes," Bennett said. He paused and studied his folded hands.

Will Parker waited, saying nothing.

"According to the official report," Bennett continued, "Jesse Ford—I'll just call him Jesse from now on—and his friends arrived one day in July to find Ewing and his twelve-year-old son, Andrew, home in their farmhouse north of town. Not far from here, actually. Mrs. Ewing had died three months earlier, some kind of fever, and Ewing had retired as marshal and took to raising crops and some cattle. Apparently Jesse and his men surprised them. They struck Ewing in the head in the kitchen, held him and the boy at gunpoint, and Jesse ordered his two men to go outside and wait. Five minutes later Ewing got the jump on Jesse and shot him dead, then went out and killed one of Jesse's friends as well. The other one got away."

Parker thought that over. "The official report, you said?"

"Yes. It's what Ewing told the sheriff afterward."

"Go on."

"No more to tell. That's the background," Bennett said. "The current situation is, I received word recently that things didn't happen the way everyone thought they did that day at Ewing's house. I've been told that Jesse Ford was shot in the back. One of his two companions was killed with an entry wound in the chest, just like Ewing reported, but—again—Jesse's wound showed that he was shot from behind."

"And how did you find all this out?"

"From an old friend of mine. He'd been a sheriff's deputy in

Dodge, back when the incident took place, and saw the two bodies the sheriff brought in. He told me this a few weeks ago, on his deathbed. A week or so after that, I noticed an ad in the newspaper about your agency and sent the wire requesting your services."

Parker waited for more. When it didn't come, he asked, "So what is it that you need?"

Bennett turned to look out the window at the small stand of oaks Parker had been watching earlier. The wind had died; the leaves were still. Like Bennett's expression.

"I need to know what happened that day," Bennett said. "What really happened."

"Why don't you just ask the sheriff?"

"Because the sheriff is dead. So is former marshal Sam Ewing, and even his son, Andrew. The son died young, from an accident on a cattle drive, south of here. They're all gone now."

Parker studied Cole Bennett for a moment. "What haven't you told me, Mr. Bennett?"

"I haven't told you *when* all this happened."

"When did it happen?"

Bennett let out a lungful of air. "Sam Ewing shot Jesse Ford twenty-two years ago."

"What?"

"My friend—the deputy—said he kept the secret all those years because the sheriff asked him to. Said everybody in town loved Sam Ewing, all the Ewings. Said the sheriff figured what good would it do to tell the whole story? Jesse Ford was dead, along with one of his cutthroat friends, and the world was better off for it. Why complicate things? The deputy said he and the sheriff, and of course Ewing and his son, were the only people who knew Jesse was back-shot. And that only the two Ewings knew *how* it happened."

Bennett went quiet then, staring down at his boots as if in deep thought.

Parker let the silence drag out, then said, "I think we have a problem here, Mr. Bennett. If this took place more than twenty years ago and everyone involved is deceased, why do you think I could find out any more than what you just told me?"

Bennett raised his head. "Because I don't think they're all deceased."

"You just said—"

"I said the deputy told me Sam Ewing and his son were the only people who saw exactly what happened. But I think there's some-one else." He leaned forward in his seat, his eyes locked on Park-er's. "I heard Sam Ewing's son, Andrew, had a childhood friend his own age, and I heard that in the summers they were inseparable, those two boys, especially in the months after Sam's wife passed. Way I heard it, this kid was at little Andrew Ewing's house most every day." Bennett paused, drew a breath, and said, "I'd be willing to bet—in fact, I guess I am betting, by hiring you—that whoever this boy was, he was probably there with Andrew the day Jesse Ford and his men came to call. I'm betting he never got mentioned because everyone involved was trying to protect him. Again, why make a simple matter complicated?"

Parker gave this some thought. "Do you have a name?"

"No. But I have confidence you'll come up with one. And when you do . . ." Bennett paused again, his face solemn. "When you find him, maybe he has what I need to know."

Another question was nagging at Parker. An important question.

"Why *do* you need to know?"

Cole Bennett settled back into the pew. "My wife," he said, "was a Ford. Jesse and Dalton, as worthless as they were, were her neph-ews. Her brother's sons. I told her what my deputy friend, before he died, told me about Jesse's death, and it's driving her crazy. She says she has to know what really happened in that kitchen that day."

Parker mulled that over. "All due respect," he said, "why do you need *me*? Why couldn't *you* ask the same kinds of questions you want me to ask?"

"Because you're the expert. I checked out the references your brother gave me." Bennett picked up his hat and stood. "I'm trusting you to solve this for me, Mr. Parker."

Parker, who had spent a lot of time doing this kind of work, knew a lie when he heard it. He knew Cole Bennett didn't want to ask around about this matter for the same reason Bennett had picked a remote spot for their meeting today: he couldn't afford to be connected to all this. *What are you hiding, Mr. Bennett?*

Parker rose to his feet also, and the two men stood facing each other.

"Your brother told me your name's Will," Bennett said.

"That's right."

"It occurred to me that you bear some resemblance to another

Parker, well known in this part of the country years ago. By reputation, at least."

"What kind of reputation?"

"He was a gunman. A killer, I'm told."

"Is that so."

Bennett tilted his head, narrowed his eyes. "This man's name was Charlie Parker."

Parker felt himself shrug. "Sorry. No relation."

Bennett studied him a moment more, nodded, and left. Parker remained standing where he was. This time he did hear hoofbeats, moments later, receding into the distance.

Parker sighed. *All God's chillun got secrets,* he thought.

After another minute or so, Charles William Parker walked outside to the hitching rail, mounted the bay, and headed back to town.

It took Parker less than six hours to narrow things down a bit. Unlike the procedures he'd followed to gather information the last time he'd visited these parts—a missing-person case in the small town of Redemption—he didn't bother with the saloons and the stables and the blacksmith and the stockyards. This time he concentrated on places where he could find and talk with the womenfolk. After several hours of visiting the general store, a dress shop, the schoolhouse, and a church—this one with more pews and more windows than the one this morning—he'd discovered that young Andrew Ewing was well remembered by some of the older teachers and ladies. One, a widow with the unfortunate name of Ophelia Reardon, recalled that Andrew had indeed made one especially close friend during his long-ago school years.

"Truitt," Mrs. Reardon said, smiling at the memory. "Can't recall his first name, but little Andrew Ewing played a lot with Daisy Truitt's boy. Never saw one of them without the other."

"When exactly was that?" Parker asked. "When they were teenagers?"

"Earlier. When they were eleven or twelve, probably." A thought seemed to come to her, and Mrs. Reardon's smile faded a bit. "Around the time Andrew's mama died, and that outlaw Ford came and tried to kill Marshal Ewing," she said.

Which was exactly what Parker wanted to hear.

"Is Mrs. Truitt still here in Dodge?" he asked, holding his breath.

"Sure is. Husband died five years ago. She and her son live on the other end of town." Ophelia Reardon pointed toward the reddening sunset. "You turn left there at the stage office, their place is about a mile south, on the right side of the road. White house with a tall barn."

Parker thanked her and set out in that direction. Five minutes later he climbed the front steps of a white-painted home and rapped on the front door. The small woman who answered the knock looked about as old as Cole Bennett was, which made sense. Twenty-two years ago she would've been about the right age to have a twelve-year-old child. She was holding what looked like a damp washcloth.

Mentally crossing his fingers, Parker identified himself and, without giving a reason, asked if he might meet her son and ask him a few questions.

She stared at Parker a long time before answering. "You can certainly meet him," she said at last. "But I'm afraid questions won't do any good."

"Excuse me?"

She heaved a sigh and motioned him inside. The house was old but neatly kept. Parker followed her down a dark hallway and through a door to a room containing nothing but a bed and two small tables on each side. Propped up on pillows in the bed was a pale, thin-faced man in his thirties, with sandy hair. His eyes were closed, his breathing slow and peaceful. His forehead and cheeks looked wet. Parker now understood the washcloth.

When Parker turned to look at her, Daisy Truitt gave him a sad smile. "My poor boy Wilson. He's been that way six months now," she said. "Got kicked by a mare while he was trying to shoe her. Doc says it caught him square in the left temple, at just the wrong place. When his brother got here he went out and shot the horse dead, not that that did anybody any good." She studied her visitor again and added, "He can't speak, Mr. Parker—he can't even hear us. Could I be of some help instead, with your questions?"

Parker, stunned, shook his head. "I doubt it, ma'am. Unless he might possibly have told you something—anything—about the day Jesse Ford was killed, up at the Ewing place."

She looked shocked. "Wilson? No, I'm afraid not. I doubt he knew anything about that."

"Well, then, I'm sorry to have bothered you."

"No bother at all."

They retraced their steps to the front door, but Parker was barely aware of it. His legs felt heavy, like chunks of firewood. What a disappointing way to end his search. And his assignment.

Parker thanked Mrs. Truitt again at the door and was turning to leave when it hit him. He stopped and looked at her in the gathering twilight. "You said his *brother* shot the horse?"

"That's right. My second son."

"You have another son?"

"Two years younger," she said. "His name's Tommy."

Parker swallowed. "Could he have known Andrew Ewing? The marshal's boy?"

"Oh my, yes. Those two were best friends."

Tommy Truitt, it turned out, lived in the town of Hopeful, about half a day's ride from Dodge. Will Parker, hopeful now also, sent a wire that night to his wife and another to his brother, Robert, at the agency's home office. He assured Bitsy he'd try to be back by the end of the week and informed his brother that he had met with Cole Bennett and was making progress. He rewarded himself with a thick steak at a café called Delmonico's and a beer at the Long Branch, and after that retired to his hotel to sleep the sleep of the weary and guiltless.

Or at least the weary.

It was hard, Parker had decided, to escape the past. Years ago, young and reckless, he had chosen all the wrong friends and all the wrong endeavors, and his steely nerves and uncanny skill with firearms soon found him steady employment and built him a reputation from Fort Smith to Deadwood. Inevitably, many who heard about Charlie Parker wanted to challenge him, and those who did died. When maturity and self-preservation finally convinced him to give up gun work, he went East, started using his middle name instead, and landed a job with the Pinkertons in Washington, one that required brains over bravado. Since then he'd done some security work, even a stint as a deputy, before joining his brother at Parker Investigations in San Francisco.

Even now, though, after all this time, a lot of people remembered the name Charlie Parker. When that happened he usually pled ignorance, which occasionally worked. He doubted that it had worked with Cole Bennett.

What a career change, Parker thought. He'd gone from being a hired gun to being a liar.

He fell asleep wondering which was worse.

Will Parker got up early, had a leisurely breakfast, and rode into Hopeful just past noon. The town was appropriately named, he decided; there seemed to be nowhere for it to go but up. He counted a dozen dreary houses and half-a-dozen dreary stores, all clustered around the intersection of a sluggish creek and a muddy road. He hoped Tommy Truitt lived on this side of the creek. The wooden bridge looked too rickety to support a man, much less a man on a horse.

At one of the buildings — a sort of combination saloon and dry-goods store — he was told that Truitt owned a small ranch west of town. There was no real road out that way, but the directions Parker received seemed simple enough. An hour later he found the spread.

He also found Tommy Truitt, on his knees in the doorway of a barn, shoeing a gray horse. Given the family history, Parker figured it to be a scary task. The horseshoer looked up as Parker rode in and eased the gray's foreleg to the ground. Something about the man's eyes verified that he was the son of the woman Parker had spoken to the night before.

Parker stopped ten feet away and propped both arms on his saddle horn. "I've come a ways to find you, Mr. Truitt. Can I interrupt your work for a while?"

Truitt put down his tools, stood, and sleeved sweat from his brow. "Don't know. I'm having an awful good time here."

Both of them smiled.

"Help yourself to water for you and your horse," Truitt said, pointing to a well and bucket. "I'll be right with you."

Fifteen minutes later introductions were made and Parker's task was explained. The two of them sat in rockers on the front porch of the house. Truitt's wife and daughter, he said, were visiting his wife's mother, in town. Chickens pecked and strutted in the dusty yard, and small white clouds cast moving pools of shade across the flatlands. The wind was chilly.

Tommy Truitt exhaled a deep sigh. "Yes, I was there that day," he answered. "And no, I've never spoken of it to anybody, not even my ma and pa."

"You didn't tell your brother?"

"So you know about Wilson? A sad thing, that horse kicking him. I go over as often as I can, help Ma with chores . . ." Truitt paused, adrift in his thoughts. Then he blinked and said, "No, I never told him. Wilson was a bit older, and for some reason we never got along. Guess that's why I played so much with Andrew."

Parker, wondering how to proceed, decided to be direct. "Do you remember what happened that day?"

"I'll never forget it," Tommy Truitt murmured.

A silence fell, during which Parker had the good sense to keep quiet. After a full minute or more, Truitt took a long breath and said, "We'd been playing in a patch of woods behind his house, with a bow and arrow we'd made out of sticks and a springy branch. We were trying to shoot a rabbit, and Andrew kept saying we needed that old eight-gauge shotgun his pa had, not a homemade bow and a little stick with an arrowhead tied to the end. He said his pa had put away all his weapons when he retired, but Andrew knew where the shotgun was stored. He said we ought to sneak it out and shoot that rabbit. Said there wouldn't be nothing left but a cotton tail."

He stopped for a beat, and Parker saw him smiling a little at the memory. The smile didn't last long.

"That was when we heard hoofbeats, coming down the road from town," Truitt said. "By the time we got back to the house—"

—three horses were tied to the porch rail. Tommy Truitt didn't recognize any of them.

He and Andrew climbed the steps, crept inside, and found three men in the kitchen with guns drawn and Andrew's father sprawled on the floor with blood on his forehead. Greenish white peas were scattered on the floor, some still in their hulls, along with a broken bowl and an overturned chair. Tommy figured the intruders must've caught the marshal shelling peas and hit him with a gun barrel. "Pa?" Andrew cried.

When Marshal Ewing saw them—Andrew's pa would always be Marshal Ewing to Tommy—he propped himself up on one elbow and groaned, "Run, boys. Get outta here."

One of the three men told him, in a bored voice, to shut up. This was the ringleader, Tommy could see that. He was the oldest and the meanest-looking too. He had dragged one of the kitchen chairs over to the wall beside the spot where Andrew's father was lying and was sitting in it, leaning back against the wall. The glare he gave the two boys sent chills up Tommy's spine. The man said to one of his friends, 'Get rid of 'em, Dixon."

For just a second Tommy wondered what he meant, and then understood. The man the leader had spoken to seemed to understand too. "No," he said.

The leader turned to face Dixon. "What did you say?"

"I said no. I'm not shootin' any kids, Jesse."

It was then that Tommy knew who the leader was. Jesse Ford. He'd heard the name mentioned in town. Tommy had thought Ford was in jail.

But he wasn't. He was here, in Andrew's house, sitting in a chair against the wall and pointing a gun at Andrew's pa, lying at his feet. It felt like a dream, a scary one. But it was real.

"Then I guess *I'll* have to," Jesse Ford said.

"No." Dixon shook his head. "Nobody's shootin' a kid."

The two men stared at each other for what seemed a long time. Sam Ewing was still propped on one elbow, opening and closing his eyes and breathing hard. Finally Ford said, "What do you suggest, then? We can't let 'em go—they done seen us, and can tell the Law."

"So can that woman we saw in the field a few miles back. She got a good look at us."

"We shoulda killed her too," Ford muttered.

"Jesse's right, Dixon," the other man said, a short guy with a face like a weasel's. "I'll do it if you won't."

Ignoring him, Dixon said, "We don't have to kill 'em. We could tie 'em up. Or lock 'em up someplace. All we need is time to get this done and get far enough away."

"You could lock us in the pantry," young Andrew said, speaking for the first time. Tommy turned in surprise to look at him, and so did everyone else. Even Marshal Ewing's eyes were open now, and watching.

"It's right there," Andrew added, his voice shaky, and pointed to the wall against which Jesse Ford's chair was leaning. "The only door's just around the corner, and it locks."

"Who in the hell would put a lock on a pantry?" Ford growled.

"My ma, years ago. She kept stuff in there, kerosene and poison and such, that I wasn't supposed to get into."

Dixon walked to the corner, then came back. "It has a latch, with an open padlock on it."

Jesse Ford sighed and nodded. "Get 'em in there, then."

Within seconds the two boys found themselves inside the long, dim pantry. Dixon had steered them through the door, and afterward Tommy heard the lock snap shut. Narrow bars of light seeped in under the door and through the spaces between the wall boards.

The first thing Tommy heard, from the other side of the shared wall, was Jesse Ford's voice: "You men go outside, you and Dixon both. Bring the horses round to the back door here and wait for me. I won't be long."

"You gonna kill him?" Weasel Face said.

"That's what I came here for. Now get out, both of you."

Tommy, who had been listening and peering into the kitchen through the tiny slits between the boards, heard Andrew moving around in the back of the pantry. "What are you doing?" he whispered. Andrew didn't answer.

On the other side of the wall—Tommy could see the dark outline of Jesse Ford's back as he sat in the chair only inches away—Ford said, "Well, well, Marshal. Here we are, just you and me. You beginning to be sorry you killed my brother?"

Weakly, Sam Ewing said, "Wish I'd had a chance to kill you too."

Ford cackled a laugh. "I got news for you, Marshal. Them two boys of yours are gonna die too, soon as I finish with you. I'll just shoot the lock off the door and take care of 'em both. Might have to shoot Dixon too, afterwards. Looks like he ain't got the grit I thought he had."

All of a sudden Tommy felt Andrew pushing him aside. Andrew had something in his hands, but Tommy couldn't make it out. He was about to whisper a question when Andrew placed one end of whatever he was holding—a long stick?—against the wall Ford was leaning back on and squatted down behind it.

"Ain't no use wastin' time," Ford's voice said. Tommy heard the click of a pistol being cocked. "This is for Dalt—"

Jesse Ford never finished the sentence. Tommy heard an explosion—it sounded like a blast of dynamite only inches from his right ear—and suddenly there was a fist-sized hole in the pantry wall. Light poured in from the kitchen, smoky gray light, and then he saw Andrew standing beside him. Andrew was saying something to him, shouting it, his lips moving, but Tommy could hear nothing. Finally he saw Andrew motion to him to get down. Tommy ducked and heard yet another explosion, above his head. He looked up to see that the pantry door was open, the wood splintered in a huge circle around the spot where the lock had been. Andrew stormed past him and out the door, holding his pa's double-barreled eight-gauge, and Tommy stumbled after him, ears ringing. Andrew was reloading as he ran, stuffing in fresh shells.

There was no need. They rounded the corner to find the kitchen empty. Jesse Ford's body was lying in the middle of the floor, lying where Andrew had blown him out of the chair and forward six or seven feet. Marshal Ewing was nowhere to be seen. Blood was everywhere.

Before Tommy could get his mind around all this, he heard—through his left ear—a pistol shot, and followed Andrew out the back door. Standing there in the yard were two men: Dixon and Marshal Ewing. Dixon had his hands raised, and Ewing was leaning against a tree, his smoking revolver pointed and rock-steady. At first Tommy wondered where Ewing had found a pistol, then realized it must've been Jesse Ford's, picked up off the kitchen floor after Andrew had shot him. A short distance away, lying at the feet of one of the three horses, was the motionless body of Weasel Face. His shirt was bloody and a gun lay in the dust beside him.

For a long moment no one said a word. The boys gawked at the two men and the two men stared at each other. Somewhere nearby a crow cawed.

With the back of his hand Andrew's father wiped blood from his eyes. He was covered with it, from head to toe, and Tommy realized most of it was Jesse Ford's.

"Give me a reason I shouldn't kill you," Marshal Ewing said.

Dixon shook his head. He looked sad, and strangely unafraid. "I can't."

Ewing cast a quick glance at his son and Tommy, then said to Dixon, "You don't seem the same kind of man as those other two were. What are you doing in this bunch?"

"I'm more like them than not," Dixon said. "But there's some things I won't do."

"Like murder a child."

"Yes."

Another long silence passed.

"Get out of here, Mr. Dixon. And don't come back."

Without a word, Dixon lowered his hands, walked to his horse, mounted up, and rode away. Tommy and the two Ewings watched until he disappeared around the curve of the trail.

Then Andrew put the shotgun down and ran to his father. Tommy did too. Marshal Ewing scooped both of them into his arms, then stopped when his son cried out in pain. As it turned out, Andrew's right shoulder was badly sprained from the kick of the eight-gauge. And he had even fired it a second time, Tommy remembered, to blow away the door lock.

All three of them, as if at a signal, turned to look at the shotgun lying in the dirt.

"Guess I won't bother hiding it anymore," Ewing said.

"And that's what happened." Tommy Truitt looked at Parker and shrugged. "They're all gone now. Marshal Ewing, Andrew, everybody. Except me."

Parker nodded. He had started out taking notes but had soon quit and just listened. "You all agreed, I guess, never to talk about it."

"That's right. To anybody. And the marshal insisted on hiding the fact that Andrew was the one who killed Jesse Ford and that I was even there at all. If anyone else ever showed up looking for revenge, he said, simpler was better. Three men came, two died, one got away."

Parker wondered what it would feel like to live through that and never tell anyone about it. Maybe telling it, at long last, had helped a little.

"Andrew was a tough kid," Truitt said. "And smart. He talked a bunch of killers into locking us in a room that had a gun hidden in it."

Parker nodded. "Smart *and* lucky. Lucky two of the three men were outside, lucky that Jesse Ford sat where he did, lucky that Sam Ewing was on the floor, underneath the line of fire."

Truitt didn't reply. He just sat, slowly rocking, looking out at the flat plains and his memories. After a while he blinked and studied Parker's face. "You said you came a long way for this. Did you get what you needed?"

"I got what my client needed. You cleared up a lot of things."

"Now I plan to forget about it," Truitt said.

He rose to his feet, and Parker followed.

"You're welcome to stay for supper," Truitt said. "My family'll be home soon."

"Much obliged, but I need to go." Parker turned to leave, then paused. "One question. You said you'd heard the name Jesse Ford before all this happened."

"That's right."

"Well, he wasn't the only one did gun work back then. Ever hear of Pete Lawson, or Merrill Smith, or Charlie Parker?"

Truitt thought a moment, then shook his head. "Don't think so."

"Good," Parker said.

The temperature dropped like a stone that night, and the following afternoon was windy and cold and overcast. The orange, yellow, and red leaves of the trees outside the small country church seemed to be struggling to stay on the branches, and many of them failed. Parker arrived just before three o'clock. This time Bennett was early; Parker found him standing at the head of the center aisle. They shook hands and settled again into the same seats they'd taken earlier.

"Let's hear it," Bennett said.

Twenty minutes later the story had been told. Parker left nothing out. Using many of Tommy Truitt's own words, he told Bennett about the intrusion, the spoken threat to the two boys, Dixon's challenge to Jesse Ford's order, the locking of the boys in the pantry, the shotgun blast through the wall, the shootout in the back yard, the departure of the third attacker.

"I believe every word he said," Parker concluded. "That's the way it happened."

For a long time Bennett sat there in silence, fingering the buttons of his overcoat. At last he said, "It makes sense. I couldn't see Sam Ewing as a back-shooter. But I had to know." He stood up. "You've done good work, Mr. Parker. I'll be sending full payment to your office tomorrow morning." He turned and moved away toward the front of the church.

"Give my best wishes to Mrs. Dixon," Parker said.

Bennett stopped in his tracks. For several seconds he stood motionless, then turned again and locked eyes with Parker. Parker hadn't moved. He was still sitting there, on the platform beside the pulpit.

Very slowly Bennett walked back to the first pew. It was so quiet in the church Parker could hear the wood creak as Bennett sagged into the seat. His face was blank.

"Are you even married?" Parker asked him. "Or was that a lie too?"

"I'm married. But my wife wasn't a Ford. And she has no nephews." Bennett paused for a beat, then said, "How did you know?"

"That you were the third man?" Parker sighed. "I'm not sure. Maybe it takes somebody with a guilty conscience to recognize it in someone else. Besides, you were so certain that Andrew had a playmate who would've been there at the time. Why were you so sure? And something else that bothered me from the start was that you felt you couldn't pursue this on your own. I finally realized that if you had, if you'd discovered the identity of Andrew's friend and approached him yourself to ask him questions—"

"He might've recognized me. From that day."

"Right," Parker said. "And I assumed you had a reason why you'd rather not call attention to your past."

"My reason is I'm an elected official now. A mayor. Back East a ways."

"I know. And I know where. My brother checked, and contacted me this morning."

Bennett stayed quiet a minute, gazing out the window.

"You think anyone'll find out?" he asked.

"About your former life? That you rode with Jesse Ford? No. Even if they do, so what? You're a changed man."

"What about Tommy Truitt?"

"The two of you live far apart. I doubt you'll ever meet."

Bennett rubbed his face wearily. "Maybe we should." He looked Parker in the eye and said, "I went there that day to help murder an innocent man. What I did got two people killed."

"What you did saved three people too."

Bennett gave that some thought, and nodded. This time both of them stood. "Thank you, Mr. Parker."

"What should I call you?"

"My name's Morris Dixon."

They shook hands. "Have a safe journey home, Mr. Mayor."

"You too."

Parker watched through the window as Dixon rode away, then he pulled up the collar of his coat and stomped outside to his own horse. He had already swung into the saddle when he saw a grizzled old man in a fur hat and a bearskin trudging up the road toward him. Parker loped over to the man and reined in.

The old-timer looked up and patted the shotgun he held in the crook of his arm. "Good day for squirrel huntin'," he said.

Parker burrowed deeper into his coat. "If you say so."

The old man chuckled, then frowned. He leaned forward and squinted. Parker knew what was coming.

"I know you from someplace," the hunter said. "Ain't you Charlie Parker?"

Parker raised his head a moment, gazed up at the trees and the falling leaves and then at the woods and the straight, flat road that led to his wife and his brother and the rest of his life. He thought about past deeds and past decisions, and about Cole Bennett, also known as Morris Dixon. Then he looked back down at the old-timer.

"I used to be," Parker said.

DAVID EDGERLEY GATES

Cabin Fever

FROM *Alfred Hitchcock Mystery Magazine*

HECTOR'S TRUCK BROKE DOWN on a fire road in the Gallatin, on the west side of Custer National Forest. He was just south of the Needles, and GPS put him close to the Yellowstone, so he wasn't lost, but it was probably a good fifteen miles to the nearest campground, and he'd have to hike it, shank's mare. From up on the hogback where the truck had died, he could see out across the Absarokas, a couple of thousand feet higher in elevation. Down by Granite Peak, some thirty miles to the southeast, there was a late-afternoon storm system building, thunderheads, the flicker of lightning, a curtain of rain. It looked to be coming on fast, but with luck he could still beat the weather.

It was one of Katie's days at the Limestone clinic. Mondays, Wednesdays, and Fridays she was up in Billings. Local patients came to the clinic the other three days, and there was always a backlog. Katie took everybody who showed up, of course, which meant she didn't get off work before seven or eight most nights, but the practice of medicine was what she'd signed on for.

A charge nurse came back to the examination room.

"Dr. Faraday? There's somebody out front asking for Deputy Moody."

Hector had been Katie's boyfriend for the past year and a half. They hadn't moved in together yet, but that was probably the next step. A big step for Hector, who took things slow, she knew. Katie wasn't going to press it. She went out to the reception desk.

Frank Child, the new FBI guy assigned over at Crow Agency. He'd taken over from Andy Lame Deer, who was retired now, living down in Wind River.

They shook hands.

"Hector's over in the Gallatin," she told him. "Ranch hands at the Two Forks called in suspected rustling activity."

The ranchers ran cattle on federal land, under permit. The cows ranged fairly wide, and sometimes you lost track.

"Well, we've got a thing," Frank Child said.

Katie knew what cops meant by a "thing." It didn't usually presage good news.

"Prisoner transport was in an accident on the interstate, about halfway between Billings and Bozeman," he said. "Clipped by a semi. Went over the shoulder and rolled, cracked open like an egg. Econoline van."

"Anybody hurt?" she asked.

"Driver and the guard were wearing seat belts. Prisoners in the back got bounced around pretty good, but no broken bones."

She waited for the other shoe to drop.

"Two of the cons escaped. Both lifers. Violent felons, stone bad. One of them went down on aggravated assault, armed robbery, three strikes, the other guy's doing thirty to life for multiple homicide, domestic, killed his wife and both kids."

"You haven't been able to raise Hector on his cell?"

"He might not have a decent signal up in the Gallatin."

"Other agencies involved?"

"Full-court press," Child told her. "State police, tribal cops, Billings and Bozeman PD, county sheriff's departments in Stillwater and Sweet Grass. FBI is flying in Special Weapons and Tactical from Denver. Forest Service has been alerted. And we've asked for a National Guard unit to be deployed. There's an awful lot of rough ground out there to cover. We're going to need all the manpower we can get."

"What haven't you told me?" she asked him.

"They hijacked an SUV, family of four on a road trip. We found the vehicle abandoned at a highway rest stop east of Livingston. Four bodies in the camper shell, all of them shot in the head with the victim's own gun. These guys are armed and dangerous, and they've got nothing to lose."

"Why would they leave the highway?"

"Roadblocks, cops everywhere. Rules of engagement are shoot to kill, although you didn't hear that from me."

"Any idea which way they went?"

Child nodded. "They're not city boys. They can survive in the wild. They're in the backcountry."

"Where?"

"Last report, on their way south, into the Absarokas."

Which was probably where Hector was headed next.

He'd thought about staying with the truck but decided he was better off hoofing it out of there. The truck was exposed on the ridgeline, which meant you could see it from the air if anybody flew over, the park service, a private plane, but Hector didn't figure that was likely to happen in the next twenty-four hours, or even in the next week. And out in the open, the truck was a magnet in an electrical storm, no protection. His dad always claimed you were safe in a car because the rubber tires would ground a lightning strike. Hector knew that for an old wives' tale.

On the horizon the dark, boiling clouds were making up thicker, and already closer than Granite Peak, traveling at some fifteen miles an hour, north-northwest. He had a tarp and a waterproof poncho, but in less than two hours, if he didn't find shelter, he was going to get pretty damn wet. He had the other basic gear, canteen, compass, a folded USCGS map for this quadrant, laminated in plastic. And he knew the country, he'd been up here before, but he was experienced enough to know that anybody could get disoriented, even in daylight. He had his cell phone too, but out here cell reception was spotty at best.

He was surprised the dashboard GPS had read out accurately, if in fact it had. He'd gotten some beef jerky and a couple of energy bars out of the glove box. He was carrying the .40 Smith on his belt holster and the Ruger carbine off the rifle rack, the .44 mag, a brush gun. He felt about as prepared as he could be, given the circumstances. It wasn't the zombie apocalypse, it was just a little heavy weather. Hector thought about Katie, back in Limestone. *You're twice lucky,* he told himself.

The forest service maintained a summer campground over by

Tumble Mountain, fourteen, fifteen miles as the crow flies, but the way he remembered, there was a one-time dude ranch on the Boulder, abandoned and fallen into disrepair but only half the distance. He shot an azimuth with the compass, oriented himself on the map, and figured his heading at seventy-four degrees.

Four-thirty in the afternoon, three hours of hard climbing.

The manhunt had spread across three counties and there was a statewide APB, but they were beginning to tighten it up as possible sightings came in, although nothing positive as yet.

The state police had set up their command post at a forest ranger station in Pine Creek, as close as they could get by road to the western edge of the Beartooth. The search had narrowed to an area bounded north to south by the highway and the Wyoming state line, west to east from Pine Creek to the Stillwater. At a rough guess, some thirteen hundred square miles. They had two choppers in the air and a spotter plane, but there was weather moving in, a storm front from the south, and a big one that would ground the aircraft.

Frank Child was at the command post. He was in contact with the SWAT team. They were still an hour out from Bozeman, which was the nearest airstrip with runways long enough to accommodate the C-130. By the time they were on the ground and the unit fully deployed to Pine Creek, it would be after dark.

"Anything?" he asked the watch commander.

"One of the helicopters called in an abandoned vehicle on the Gallatin Trace," the state cop told him. "Went in to take a closer look. Light bar on the roof, Stillwater County Sheriff's Department markings. No sign of the driver, though."

Hector Moody. "If he left his truck, which direction would he travel?" Child asked.

"Six of one. He probably lost radio contact, and his cell wouldn't work out there. He could backtrack, go out the way he came in, but it's twenty miles to the nearest pay phone."

"What if he decided to go east instead?"

"Into the Absaroka watershed? Probably the better choice." The cop looked at the map. "Seasonal campsites scattered around inside a fifteen-mile radius, some old cabins, line shacks or Civilian Conservation Corps, if they haven't caved in by now. Up here on the Boulder there used to be a place called Beaver Lodge. Guest ranch, for dudes from back East."

Child knew himself for a dude from back East, and he didn't have the skills Hector had. "How bad's the weather?"

"Bad. He wouldn't want to get caught in the open."

Neither would their two fugitives, Child thought. "We have any chance of getting in there?" he asked.

"With the storm? We're going to have to suspend operations until daylight. Another hour, our visibility's down to zero."

"Not very promising."

"How soon do your people get here?"

"Too late to do Hector any good tonight," Child said.

"Well," the state cop said, smiling, "he's part Indian, he knows the terrain, and he doesn't expect anybody to come looking for him. He can take care of himself."

"He doesn't know about those cons in the woods."

"No way to get him word, either."

The storm broke overhead. It was a little past seven o'clock that night. The sun didn't set until after eight, but the sky was already black, the thunderclouds a heavy mass, lit from beneath by the occasional crack of lightning. Wind thrashed the trees, and then the rain came, in a sudden burst, like bullets.

Hector was on the final leg, moving downslope toward the confluence of the Boulder and Beaver Creek, where the old dude ranch was. The thick conifers gave him some cover from the force of the downpour, but water was already trickling downhill, and the pine needles slithered underfoot.

About a hundred yards out the trees thinned, and beyond that was space once cleared for pasture, now overgrown with weeds and wildflowers. The fences and corrals had collapsed, but through the sheets of rain Hector could see that a couple of the ranch buildings themselves were still standing.

As soon as he left the trees and started into the open, he was immediately soaked all the way through. Fighting a path across the pasture, his feet getting caught in the tall, tangled grass, his wet boots felt as heavy as sandbags, and even under the poncho his uniform was wicking water like a downspout. His skin felt raw, and he shivered with chill. The rainfall was so heavy he had trouble getting his bearings, but he managed at last to flounder up onto the porch of what had once been the bunkhouse. The roof was leaking, and Hector crowded up against the cabin wall, breathing hard. The windows were dirty and broken, but there was a glimmer of light from inside. Hector thought his eyes were playing tricks on him or the flashes of lightning had burned his retinas. He tugged the door latch open and stepped into the cabin.

There was a fire in the fireplace and somebody standing in front of it, rubbing his hands.

"Evening," the guy said, grinning at him. "You look like a drowned rat. Come over here and warm up."

Hector shook some of the water off his poncho and shucked it off. He took a step forward, into the firelight, and the guy who'd been in back of the door put the barrel of a gun against the base of his skull, just behind his right ear. "We shoot him now, Roy?" the guy with the gun asked.

Wet as it was, lightning strikes sparked a wildfire at the south end of the Beartooth, just above Yellowstone Park. It started small at first, right around midnight, but in the course of the early hours, before daylight, it grew to some thirty-five square miles. Winds out of the south were pushing it north, into the Absarokas. The problem was that nobody knew it was there until four o'clock the next morning, because there were no spotter planes aloft, and the watchers manning the fire towers didn't see anything until the storm blew over. But once the weather cleared and they had visibility, horizon to horizon, you could see the flames reflected against the night sky, and it meant all hands on deck.

The first firefighters to respond were the Bighorn Initial Attack crew, from the Crow reservation, since they were that close. They came through Limestone at 6 a.m. It was the nearest point of access. Katie already had her medical unit assembled, ready to go in with them. She wasn't about to take no for an answer. The crew chief, Joey Raven, knew they'd need her help. He also knew she was dating Hector Moody. He didn't turn her down.

"How bad?" she asked him.

"If it crowns, we're in deep shit, Doc," he said.

There were brush fires that burned through the slash and undergrowth, close to the ground, and then there were so-called crown fires, where it lit up the tops of the trees. Crown fires could move fast enough to outrun an animal, or a man.

"We're as ready as we're going to be, Joe," she told him.

He nodded. "Mount up," he said.

They'd taken his weapons and gear.

"You have a radio?" the guy named Roy asked.

"Two-way, back in the truck," Hector said.

"Which is where?"

"Maybe eight miles west of here, on the Gallatin Trace. No good to me, no good to you. Dead metal."

"And your cell phone doesn't work worth squat."

"Part of the problem that brought me here," Hector said.

"Which makes you part of my problem," Roy said.

"Aw, for Pete's sake," the other guy said. "Who needs this joker? He's bait for the law. Kill him and leave him."

"You never know, Little Eddie. Cop might come in handy, we have to work our way out of a tight spot."

"We're in a tight spot already."

"Well, bear with me," Roy said. He looked at Hector. "You got any bright ideas?"

"Give yourselves up. At least you'd be walking out of here in-stead of carried off in a meat wagon."

"Good advice. But we're both lifers, and neither one of us is go-ing back, not for another thirty years in the joint."

"All right," Hector said. "What's *your* bright idea?"

"You get us out of here," Roy said.

"How? There must be roadblocks, police presence, the whole nine yards. They've set up the end zone, you're inside it."

"Escape and evade."

"Never happen," Hector said.

"It better," he said. "Your life is going to depend on it, Deputy, not just ours."

Eddie came in from out back and thumped a big Bakelite box on the table between them. "Found this with the freeze-dried stuff in the storage shed, and the canned goods. Like they were getting ready for the end times."

Roy looked at the radio. "You know what this is?" he asked Hector.

Hector did. It was a basic survival tool, something useful in the third world, or post-apocalypse. No batteries, but a couple of paddles on each side, like bicycle pedals. You cranked it by hand, and it built up enough DC charge to give you half an hour of reception.

"Wind that sucker up," Roy said. "Buy yourself some time."

"This isn't helping," Frank Child said to the watch commander.

"Might flush 'em out, though," the state cop said.

"Along with every bunny rabbit and bear in the mountains."

They had the National Weather Service feed up, tracking the path of the fire on radar.

"Sitrep?" Child asked the FBI agent in charge of the SWAT team. They'd made it in from Bozeman a little before ten-thirty the night before.

"We can't mount an operation in these conditions," the SWAT guy told him.

"We can get the choppers back in the air first light," the state cop said. Oh six hundred, an hour away.

"Fire crews?" Child asked him.

"First responders are on the Stillwater, east of the fire, with a second squad establishing a perimeter on the near side of the Yellowstone, to the west. Smoke-jumpers are on their way. Any luck, we'll have a company of National Guard on duty by late morning. But they'll be assigned to the fire lines."

Child nodded. Everybody had a full plate. Nobody had time to look for two escaped cons and a missing deputy sheriff.

He signaled the SWAT team leader to one side. "Looks like we're the fifth wheel," Child said.

"My people aren't trained for this," the guy said, "but you issue us shovels, we'll volunteer."

"No," Child said. "Get your gear on the helicopters. Lock and load."

The team leader ducked his head. "We on the same page?" he asked, meaning they were violating chain of command.

"Anybody spots those guys, we'll need boots on the ground," Child said. "State police can't spare the personnel."

"Roger that. Anything else?"

"Save me a seat."

*

"What's wrong with this freakin' thing?" Little Eddie demanded. He gave the radio a shake, but it still wasn't pulling in a live signal.

"There's nothing wrong with it," Hector said. "It's thirty years old is all."

"It doesn't work."

"Sure it works. They're presets."

"What are you talking about?" Roy asked him.

"It's got crystals inside, for preset frequencies, that's why it doesn't have a dial. Back when these were made, there was an emergency broadcast system, 640 and 1240 AM, what used to be called the Civil Defense Network. Nuclear attack."

"So how do we hear anything?"

"There should be ten or a dozen dedicated channels."

"I think you're a lyin' sack of shit," Little Eddie said to him. "And about as useful as tits on a bull."

"Eddie," Roy said wearily, "why don't you go outside in the rain and hump the chickens? Leave the heavy lifting to me."

"I don't trust him," Little Eddie said.

"I don't trust him either," Roy said. "We have a choice?"

Little Eddie stalked off, radiating hostility.

"Looks like I'm not your only problem," Hector said.

"Well, when God passed out the brains, Eddie was at the end the line," Roy said. "He got seconds."

"Stupid people do dangerous things."

Roy shook his head and smiled. "Nice try, Deputy," he told him, "but if I leave anybody behind, it'll be you."

Hector, switching frequencies, picked something up.

"What have you got?" Roy asked.

Hector tipped his head closer to the tinny speakers. "NOAA weather radio," he said.

"We need local news, or police band."

Hector didn't change frequencies. "You'd better listen to this," he said. "They *are* reporting local conditions."

Roy leaned forward.

Hector turned up the volume, but it distorted the sound, so he turned it down a little.

Roy frowned, concentrating. He sat back. "You catch it?" he asked. "They're talking about something called the Sugarloaf fire, north of Yellowstone. Mean anything to you?"

"Where's that USCGS map you took off me?"

Roy went and got it out of Hector's backpack.

"Give me those coordinates again," Hector said.

Roy waited until they were repeated and wrote them down.

Hector squared up the map. 45 north, 110 degrees west. He checked it again and looked across the table at Roy.

Roy could read Hector's expression, and he didn't think the cop was good enough to fake it. "Let's have it," he said.

"Fifteen, maybe eighteen miles from here, winds blowing north-northwest. It's coming straight at us. We're in a funnel between the Beaver Creek watershed and the Boulder."

"How fast are the winds pushing it?"

Hector shrugged. "No way of knowing. We might have half a day, we might have half an hour."

Roy sucked on his teeth. "Cuts it thin," he said.

"We can't stay here," Hector said.

Katie had set up the aid station by the creek, where there was glacial runoff, but the water was flecked with ash and the air heavy with smoke.

The firefighters were deployed in a ragged line on the other side of the stream, working their way upslope, turning the soil and clearing away brush. It was hard, sweaty work, and a couple of them had already been sent back, smoke inhalation or heat exhaustion. Joey Raven came back to check on them. It was seven o'clock in the morning.

"I want you and the medical staff prepared to evacuate your position, Dr. Faraday," he told Katie.

"Formal request, Joey?" she asked him, smiling. He usually just called her Doc.

"On the record, ma'am," he said. "I'll put it in writing."

Katie shook her head. "No need," she said. "You're the guy in charge. I'm here in support. You tell me to pack it up, we'll be ready to pack it up."

"I appreciate the fact that you're here at all."

"I know," she said. "It wasn't an empty compliment."

"But if it goes bad, I won't have time to think about you."

"You don't have to, then," she said.

"We're going to start a back-burn, up on the ridge, top of the hill there. If we can keep the fire from jumping the creek and going into the trees on this side, we'll be ahead of it."

"Your other units calling in?"

He nodded.

"What's your reported containment?"

"Reported containment is zero. The fire's blown up, over a hundred square miles, last known, and rough country to get to."

"You have the men?"

"Good men, probably not enough of them. The hotshots jump at oh eight hundred, into the Absaroka, east of the Needles."

Into the Absaroka. Katie looked stricken.

Joey Raven was suddenly embarrassed. He swallowed the lump stuck to his Adam's apple. "He'll be okay," he told her.

"We can't go north, that's where the cops are," Eddie said.

"You can't go south," Hector told them, "or you want to get burned alive. That forest is alight. You think hell is hot?"

"I'm tired of listening to your mouth," Eddie said.

"Jesus, get over it," Roy said. "You want to take your chances on your own, then take your chances. I'm going out with Deputy Moody. He's my free ticket."

Little Eddie looked at his feet, sullen and intransigent.

"Oh, Christ, it's like pulling teeth," Roy said. "When were you going to get past being a moron?"

"I'm with you," Eddie said, but his feelings were obviously hurt. He cut a savage look at Hector.

"Let's take a walk," Roy said.

"Eddie's right," Hector said. "You can't go north, and you can't go south. Six of one."

"Then we go out through the fire lines," Roy said.

They had two choppers, twin Hueys. Fixed-wing wasn't of much use here, although there was an observer aircraft up, watching the fire. You could see smoke on the horizon, and when they got closer, they actually saw treetops bursting into flame, like Roman candles lit off on the Fourth of July. The fire was a greedy hunger, something that had to be fed, a living thing, and almost as if it had a will of its own.

"Swing around," Child said to the state police pilot.

"I don't know what you're looking for, sir."

"Circle over to the Gallatin Trace and find that truck."

Ten minutes later they spotted it, up on the hogback.

"Okay," Child said. "Make a pass, backtrack, see if we cut any sign."

They quartered across the ridgeline, flying into the smoke again. The fire was eating up ground. From their altitude, a couple of hundred feet, it was like looking straight down into a blast furnace.

"There," Child told the pilot. "The meadow, those cabins."

"Beaver Creek Ranch," the pilot said.

"Can you set her down?"

"I can't give you much of a window," the pilot said.

"Ten minutes?"

"If that."

"Do it," Child said.

They dropped into one of the corrals. The second chopper orbited overhead. On the ground you could feel the superheated air, and the acrid haze was thick. The team moved fast but stayed loose, checking the buildings. Time was tight. They had no margin for error.

"Somebody spent the night here," one of the SWAT guys said, coming out of the bunkhouse. "Fireplace is still warm."

"Ambient heat?" Child asked him.

"Nope. Freshly opened canned goods scattered around too."

"All right. Come on."

They dog-trotted back to the chopper and scrambled aboard.

"Wind it up," Child said to the pilot, buckling in.

They lifted off. "What's our heading?" the pilot asked.

"Which way would you go to outrun the fire?"

"Fire's traveling almost due north. I'd be moving east."

"Let's hope Hector made the same call," Child said.

They were walking into the sun, but the sun was only a smear of patchy light through the smoke. Behind them and back on the right, the woods were smoldering, heating up toward flashpoint. All it would take was a sudden gust of wind, or a backdraft, and the trees would ignite, quick as a matchhead. They were in a sort of a vortex, or vacuum, a self-sustained system. The fire had created its own momentum, its own pressure gradient, its own weather, sucking air in like the eye of a hurricane.

Hector was out in front, where the other two could keep him in their sights, Roy a few paces back, Little Eddie behind them both. It meant Hector was breaking trail, which was tiring, but it meant he was setting the course. Even without a compass, he could plot their general direction, using dead reckoning and the position of the sun. A little past 8 a.m., some six or seven miles until they reached the Stillwater and an uphill climb, but once across, they'd be on level ground, the fire downwind, and some protection with the creek at their back. Somewhere this side of the Stillwater, he knew, the early initial attack crews would be maintaining a firebreak. The way Hector saw it, he had to make sure none of them got in the way of an itchy trigger finger.

More to it than that, he knew. Roy had enough sense to button his lip and let Hector do the talking, even if Little Eddie was the wild card, but after Hector led them out, they'd have no real reason to keep him alive.

Hector wasn't out of the woods yet.

The slurry tankers came in at 500 feet and dropped chemical retardant on the leading edge of the fire. They were PBY Catalinas, with a load capacity of 1500 gallons apiece. The hotshots jumped at 2000 feet, from a Twin Otter flying above the Catalinas. Their drop zone was a burned-over area between the Boulder River and Iron Mountain, and their immediate objective was to suppress spot fires and contain any back-burn.

"Smoke-jumpers," the state police helicopter pilot told his passengers, pointing out the red chute canopies opening.

"They must have asbestos balls," one of the SWAT guys said. "That LZ's hotter than a cast-iron griddle."

They'd overflown the worst of it. Below them there was a lot of smoke, blanketing the trees like low-lying fog, but there were no flames they could see.

"Where are we on the map?" Child asked.

"That's the Stillwater down there," the pilot said. He put the chopper into a shallow bank, turning back west again.

"Fire line on the ridge?"

The pilot nodded. "If it breaks out and moves east, that's where they hope to stop it."

"Which way is the wind blowing?"

"Still steady, north-northwest, not as strong. Ten knots."

"Jesus, we could use some more rain."

"Ask," the pilot said. "He might be listening."

"God answers prayers," Child said, "it's his day job."

They saw the planes go over, two fairly low to the ground, one at higher altitude. Roy and Little Eddie crouched under the trees. Hector didn't bother. The aircraft were flying too fast and too far up to notice them.

"Get your ass down here," Roy snarled.

"We don't have time to waste," Hector said. "Get your own ass up and get it in gear. We have to be over the Stillwater in an hour or we're going to fry like bacon fat. Come on."

Hector didn't care one way or the other, of course. He would have been perfectly happy to leave them there, but he knew full well one of them would shoot him in the back.

He struck out again, and they followed.

"How far?" Roy asked him.

"Couple of miles, as the crow flies."

"Home free," Roy said, grinning.

And then they heard the choppers overhead.

Joey Raven, the fire boss, hadn't given Katie the word to pull out, so she'd stayed on station. They were treating a number of Joey's crew, some minor burns, abrasions, blisters, but mostly smoke in their lungs. The fire itself hadn't approached; they'd been lucky so far. She hoped their luck held.

"Fifteen percent," he told her. He meant containment, and it was better than expected, given the dry conditions.

"Chance of rain?" she asked.

"Sudden storm would be good," he said. "We'd need a real frog-strangler, flood out the canyons and drown the bastard, but there's nothing on the radar."

"You good?"

"I'm good, Doc," he said. His face was streaked with soot, and he looked exhausted.

"Come inside a minute," she said.

He stepped into her trailer.

Katie handed him a pint of Johnnie Walker Black.

"Shouldn't," he told her.

"Medicinal purposes," she said.

"Where were you when my first wife left me?" he asked.

"Probably in third grade," she said.

Joey uncapped the scotch and had a healthy jolt. "You're a good man, Doc," he said, screwing the top back on.

"You too, Joey," she said.

"Proof is in the pudding." He gave her the bottle and went outside again.

Katie turned the pint of Johnnie Walker in her hand. Hector didn't drink hard liquor, just beer. Katie usually only drank wine. She took the cap off again and tipped the bottle up. The whiskey burned her throat and brought tears to her eyes.

This time Roy grabbed Hector and pulled him to cover. The big Hueys came in down on the deck, close enough that the rotor wash whipped the trees and the engine noise hammered the earth.

"Don't even think about it," Roy hissed in Hector's ear, hugging him close, his whisker stubble scratching Hector's skin.

The heavy thump of the twin turbos faded as the choppers crossed the next ridgeline. They dropped into the valley on the other side, but the reverberations still echoed behind them.

"You see their insignia?" Roy asked.

Hector nodded. "State police," he said.

"Looking for me and Eddie."

"Not necessarily," Hector said. "I think the fire's their biggest priority right now. They're probably pulling emergency personnel from every available resource."

"Where does that leave us?"

"I'd say you two were under the radar. Just be cool, don't do anything stupid. And that goes double for him."

Little Eddie gave him a poisonous stare.

"I can walk you out of here, but only if nobody gets hurt," Hector said. "Any crazy shit goes down, we're all dead meat."

"You first, asshole," Little Eddie said.

Hector was watching Roy.

Roy nodded. "Okay," he said.

"You answer for Eddie?" Hector asked.

"I'll answer for him and me both," Roy said.

"Shit, you listening to this bush-league tin badge?" Little Eddie asked him. "He's going to sell us out."

"That's as may be," Roy said. "Just remember," he said to Hector. "You cross me, you put the law wise and they try to take me down, you'll have your guts in your lap before I hit the ground."

"I knew I could count on you," Hector said.

They set the helicopters down on a patch of open dirt behind the creek, near the field hospital unit. Child climbed out.

"You have enough fuel?" he asked the pilot.

"Two hours reserve."

"Better get some coffee," Child told the SWAT guys. "Mount up again in five."

He went into the medical tent.

"Hi," Katie said.

"Dr. Faraday."

"You look ridden hard and put away wet."

"No joy," he told her, without ceremony. "We saw his truck but we didn't find Hector."

"Your bedside manner needs a little work," she said.

He smiled. "Least said, soonest mended."

"What about your bad guys?"

"Apples and oranges," Child said.

"You sure?"

"Somebody spent the night at a dude ranch on the Boulder, maybe ten miles west of here. Might have been Hector, might be our fugitives. Either way, they'd head in this direction. It's their only safe way out of the fire."

"How much time do they have?"

"Depends. If the wind shifts—" He stopped.

"What?"

"He's alive, Katie. I'd bet money on it. Hector could walk away from a plane wreck and give you frequent-flier miles. Thing is, he's not the only guy with a ticket."

"You think they might be with him, and he's a hostage."

"It's one possibility," Child told her. "I'm just covering my ass."

"That makes two of us," she said.

Crossing the fire line turned out to be easy. Joey Raven even detailed one of his men to take them back to the aid station, the three guys stumbling out of the burning woods, smudged with soot and bruised by what was a very close call. They were lucky to be alive, the crew chief figured.

As they made their way down the hillside toward the creek, the choppers were lifting off again from the beaten earth behind the field hospital.

Roy glanced at Hector.

Hector shrugged. Who knew?

When they got to the banks of the creek, Joey's guy left them there and trudged back upslope to the smouldering firebreak on the ridge.

The three of them waded across the shallow streambed.

"Home free," Roy said, grinning.

Don't count your chickens, Hector thought.

"Not firefighters," the SWAT commander said, checking them out through his field glasses, the recon second nature. "Guy in the middle's a uniformed LEO."

Child raised his own binoculars, turning back to look just as the helicopter overflew the top of the ridge. "Son of a bitch," he said. "Put this bird down and do it now," he said to the pilot.

"Aid station's the nearest LZ," the pilot said.

"No," Child said. "It's got to be up here. They're a hundred yards from the field hospital. They see us coming back, we'll have civilian collateral damage, big-time."

"I can't land in the trees."

Child glanced at the SWAT guy. "How close to the ground do we have to be?" he asked him.

"Thirty feet or less."

"Can you hover that low?" Child asked the pilot.

"We've got a lot of updraft. The rising air's hot. Tricky trim problem. You're looking at an unstable jump platform."

"Time to cowboy," the SWAT commander said.

"I'm good with it," Child said.

The state cop took them down to treetop level. The SWAT team opened the cargo bay doors, hooked up, and began the rappel to the ground. Frank Child had never done this before in his life. The chopper was bucking like a rodeo horse, veering and yawing, sliding in the currents of hot air. Child was nauseous, and frozen with vertigo.

"I don't care if you puke," the SWAT commander said. "Just go out the damn door or get out of my way."

Child's feet were stuck to the lurching cargo deck.

The guy behind him put both hands in the small of Child's back and put all his weight into it. Child's feet slithered on the deck plates, and he found himself treading empty air.

"I'm thinking this is where we part company, Deputy," Roy said to Hector. "Time to trade up to a newer model year, no offense. Something modest, low-profile."

Parked in back of the field hospital were a couple of vehicles, two pickups and a silver Isuzu Trooper, a little the worse for wear, rust spots covered with primer. Hector knew the Trooper belonged to Katie Faraday.

"So far we've been lucky," he said. "You think your luck's going to hold?"

"Maybe that's up to you."

"Okay," Hector said. "We take one of the trucks. I'll go in, I'll get the keys. No secret handshake, no Captain Midnight decoder ring, straight and simple. Police business."

"You talk good game," Roy said.

"Let's do it easy. No reason to do it hard."

"They've got roadblocks as far east as Billings."

"I can evade the checkpoints, or alibi my way past them. I'm wearing the star, right? Once you get past Billings, it's a straight shot into the Dakotas. You'd have a head start."

"And you think I'd let you go?"

"No," Hector said. "But it's a fair trade. Keep it clean. Don't complicate things. Nobody's dead yet."

"Well, you're wrong about that," Roy said. "Sorry to say."

"Something happened."

"Yeah. Call it an unhappy accident. Little Eddie got kind of a hair across his ass."

"I only shot the first one," Eddie said. "The guy went for his gun. You did the others."

"You left me no play, kid," Roy said. "Fortunes of war."

"Capital murder," Hector said.

"Something you might keep in mind," Roy said.

"I'll remember," Hector told him.

"Let's go talk to these people inside the tent," Roy said.

The choice Hector had been trying to steer him away from.

"You know what your problem is?" Roy asked. "You wear your heart on your sleeve. It shows on your face."

"All right," Hector said. "Let's go talk to them."

"Short and sweet," Roy said.

They'd bellied up to the ridge, where they were overlooking the creek. The estimated range was about five hundred yards, the declination some ten degrees. You had to compensate for the shot. Uphill you aimed high, downhill you aimed low, which was counterintuitive. The team carried M4s, in 5.56, the barrels chopped down for work in close quarters, with muzzle suppressors and high-cap mags, two of them duct-taped end to end, but the designated shooter was posting a Winchester model 70 with a Leupold infrared scope, a .308 bolt gun, still the Marine sniper rifle of choice, even in this day and age. The guy behind the sights had been a force recon Marine for twelve years before the FBI recruited him. Now his name and rank were classified.

"I don't like the way this is shaping up," Child said.

"We've got good position," the SWAT commander said. "We're on top of it. It's not Waco."

Your lips to God's ears, Child thought.

Katie was enormously relieved to see him, but something about his body English warned her off. Hector was avoiding direct eye contact. She didn't step forward right away. The two men with him. They spelled trouble, or even danger. She remembered what Frank Child had told her, killers with nothing to lose.

"We need to commandeer a vehicle," Hector said, addressing the group at large. His eyes grazed past Katie, but he didn't focus on her. "Get us as far as Limestone, I'll leave it at the sheriff's substation, take a car from the motor pool."

Katie looked at the three nurses who'd come with her from the clinic. They all knew Hector was bluffing. There was no motor pool in Limestone. He drove his own truck, and the county reimbursed him for mileage and maintenance.

"Who owns the Trooper?" Hector asked them.

Now they knew for a fact that something was very wrong, but nobody gave him away.

"I do," Katie said. She fished the keys out of her jacket pocket and handed them to him. "Gas tank's half full. Just pay me back for what you use."

Hector nodded and thanked her.

There was a loaded Beretta M9 under the front seat too. She carried it for emergencies, and Hector knew that. Which was why he'd asked to borrow her truck.

"Wait a minute, little lady," the bigger of the two men with Hector said. "Whyn't you come along for the ride, keep the deputy company."

"I'm sorry?" Katie asked him, frowning and pretending to be puzzled, although she knew why. "I'm the only doctor here."

"All to the good," the guy told her. "We might need one."

"This isn't a smart move at all," Hector said to him.

"You let me be the judge of that," Roy said.

Little Eddie grinned. He was liking this better now.

It was shaping up worse, Child saw, watching them through the binoculars. They had two hostages instead of one, and the four of them were bunched too close to take the shot.

"Your guy think on his feet?" the SWAT commander asked.

"Hector can think on his hands and knees," Child said. Not that Child wanted it to come to that.

"Let 'em get clear of the background," the team leader said to the rifleman. He meant away from anybody in the tent.

The shooter nodded. He dialed in the range.

"On my mark," the team leader told him. "Condition Zero."

The shooter put his targets in the crosshairs.

"Keep it tight," Roy said. He had Katie's arm pinned painfully behind her back. Hector was a step in front and Little Eddie a step behind.

Hector caught something in his peripheral vision, a flicker of reflected sunlight up on the ridge, and then it was gone.

They got to the Trooper. Hector shook out Katie's keys to find the right one. He unlocked the driver's door and tugged it open, but he dropped the keys in the dirt.

"Quit dicking around," Roy said.

Hector crouched down to pick up the keys and slid his hand under the driver's seat.

Roy looked at Eddie. "There's always some wetbrain has to douche the cat," Roy said, tired of coddling morons.

Straightening up, Hector uncoiled like a spring, pivoting off the balls of his feet, and hit Katie so hard in a body block it knocked the wind right out of her lungs.

"You stinking *prick,*" Roy shouted at him, the three of them going down in a tangle of armpits and elbows.

The sniper round was a jacketed hollowpoint, a 180-grain rebated Silvertip boattail moving at a velocity approaching twenty-one hundred feet per second, without buffeting or deflection. It hit Eddie at the base of the skull, on a downward trajectory, and blew his spine through his throat like a wet rope.

Hector rolled clear of Katie and ground the muzzle of the Beretta into the socket of Roy's left eye. "Your call," he said to him. "Doesn't matter to me one way or the other."

Roy's shoulders sagged.

Katie sat up and coughed. It hurt to catch her breath.

"Damn," Child said, putting the glasses down. He glanced over at the shooter. The ex-Marine ejected his spent round and policed up the brass, force of habit. "I never saw anybody take a shot like that, cold-bore," Child said.

The shooter looked at him. "No, you never did," he said.

The SWAT commander got on the radio and called the choppers back in, requesting emergency evac.

Hector helped Katie get to her feet. She flinched with the pain. "You okay?" he asked.

"I'm okay, but don't hug me quite so hard," she said. "You broke one of my ribs."

Hector let go and gave her room to breathe.

"I was afraid you weren't coming out," she said.

"So was I," he told her.

"Aw, you're like a bad penny. You always turn up."

"Heads or tails?" Hector asked, smiling.

"You know what's the matter with you?"

"No, what?" he asked her.

"I wish I knew," Katie said.

Small Signs

FROM *Ellery Queen Mystery Magazine*

DAVID ANGOLA WAS leaning against Anne DeWitt's car in the Travis High School parking lot. The bright early-fall sun shone on his newly shaved dark head. It was four-thirty on a Friday afternoon, and the lot was almost empty.

Anne did not get the surprise David had (perhaps) intended. She always looked out the window of her office after she'd collected her take-home paperwork.

Anne hadn't stayed alive as long as she had by being careless.

After a few moments of inner debate, she decided to go home as usual. She might as well find out what David wanted. Anne was utterly alert as she walked toward him, her hand on the knife in her jacket pocket. She was very good with sharp instruments.

"I come in peace," he called, smiling, holding out his hands to show they were empty. His white teeth flashed in a broad smile.

The last time Anne had seen David they'd been friends, or at least as close to friends as they could be. But that had been years ago. She stopped ten feet away. "Who's minding Camp West while you're gone?" she said.

"Chloe," he said.

"Don't remember her."

"Chloe Montgomery," he said. "Short blond hair? Six feet tall?"

"The one who went to Japan to study martial arts?"

David nodded.

"I didn't like her, but you obviously have a different opinion." Anne was only marking time with the conversation until she got a feel for the situation. She had no idea why David was here. Ignorance did not sit well with her.

"Not up to me," David said.

Anne absorbed that. "How could she not be your choice? Last I knew, you were still calling the shots."

For the past eight years David Angola had been the head of Camp West, a very clandestine California training facility specializing in survival under harsh conditions . . . and harsh interrogation.

Anne had been his opposite number at Camp East, located in the Allegheny Mountains. Since the training was so rigorous, at least every other year a student didn't survive. This was the cost of doing business. However, a senator's daughter had died at Camp East. Anne had been fired.

"I was calling the shots until there were some discrepancies in the accounts." David looked away as he said that.

"You got fired over a decimal point?" Anne could scarcely believe it.

"Let's call it a leave of absence while the situation's being investigated," he said easily. But his whole posture read "tense" to Anne, and that contrasted with his camouflage as an average citizen. David always blended in. Though Anne remembered his taste as leaning toward silk T-shirts and designer jeans, today he wore a golf shirt and khakis under a tan windbreaker. Half the men in North Carolina were wearing some version of the same costume.

Anne considered her next question. "So, you came here to do what?"

"I couldn't be in town and not lay eyes on you, darlin'. I like the new nose, but the dark hair suited you better."

Anne shrugged. Her hair was an unremarkable chestnut. Her nose was shorter and thinner. Her eyebrows had been reshaped. She looked attractive enough. The point was that she did not look like Twyla Burnside. "You've seen me. Now what?"

"I mainly want to see my man," David said easily. "I thought it was only good sense to check in with you first."

Anne was not surprised that David had come to see his former second-in-command, Holt Halsey. David had sent Holt to keep an eye on Anne when she'd gotten some death threats . . . at least, that was the explanation Holt had given Anne. She'd taken it with a pinch of salt.

"So go see him." Anne glanced down at her watch. "Holt should have locked up the gym by now. He's probably on his way home. I'm sure you have his address." Aside from that one quick glance, she'd kept her eyes on David. His hands were empty, but that meant nothing to someone as skilled as he was. They'd both been instructors before they'd gotten promoted.

David straightened up and took a step toward his car, a rental. "I hated to see you get the ax. Cassie's not a patch on you."

"Water under the bridge," Anne said stiffly.

"Holt had a similar issue," David said casually. Apparently he was fishing to find out if Anne knew why Holt had left Camp West.

Anne didn't, and she'd never asked. "What is this really about, David?"

"I'm at loose ends. I haven't taken a vacation in two years. I'm always at the camp. But until they find out who actually took the money, they don't want me around. I didn't have anything to do. So I came to see Greg. Holt."

That wasn't totally ridiculous. "I think he'll be glad to see you," Anne said. "When will you know the verdict?"

"Soon, I hope. There's an independent audit going on. It'll prove I'm innocent. You know me. I always had a lot of trouble with the budgeting part of my job. Holt did most of the work. Makes it more of a joke, that Oversight thinks I'm sophisticated enough to embezzle."

"That's Oversight's job, to be suspicious." Embezzling. No wonder David had taken a trip across country. You didn't want to be in Oversight's crosshairs if the news was bad.

"Okay, I'm on my way," he said, slapping the hood of his white Nissan.

"Have a good visit," Anne said.

"Sure thing." David straightened and sauntered to his rental car. "Holt's place is close?"

"About six miles south. It's a small complex on the left, all town-homes. Crow Creek Village. He's number eight."

"Has he taken to North Carolina?"

"You can ask him," she said, smiling pleasantly. Would this conversation never end?

He nodded. "Good to see you . . . Anne."

Anne watched until David's car was out of sight. Then she allowed herself to relax. She pulled her cell phone from her purse and tapped a number on speed dial.

"Anne," Holt said. "I was—"

"David Angola is here," she said. "He was waiting for me when I came out of the school."

Holt was silent for a moment. "Why?"

"He says they asked him to leave the camp while the books are being audited. Money's missing. He's on his way to see you."

"Okay." Holt didn't sound especially alarmed or excited.

They hung up simultaneously.

Anne wondered if Holt was worried about this unexpected visit. Or maybe he was simply happy his former boss was in town.

Maybe he'd even known David was coming, but Anne thought not. *I've fallen into bad habits. I felt secure. I quit questioning things I should have questioned.* Anne was more shaken than she wanted to admit to herself when she entertained the thought that Holt might have been playing a long game.

The short drive home was anything but pleasant.

Anne's home was on an attractive cul-de-sac surrounded by a thin circle of woodland. She'd never had a house before, and she'd looked at many places before she'd picked this two-story red brick with white trim. It was somewhat beyond her salary, but Anne let it be understood that the insurance payout from her husband's death had formed the down payment.

Anne noted with satisfaction that the yard crew had come in her absence. The flower beds had been readied for winter. She'd tried working outside—it seemed so domestic, so in character for her new persona—but it had bored her profoundly.

Sooner or later the surrounding area would all be developed. But for now the woods baffled the sound from the nearby state road. The little neighborhood was both peaceful and cordial. None of the homeowners were out in their front yards, though at the end of the cul-de-sac a couple of teenage boys were shooting hoops on their driveway.

The grinding noise of the garage door opening seemed very loud. Anne eased in, parking neatly in half of the space. She'd begun leaving the other side open for Holt's truck.

There was a movement in the corner of her eye. Anne's head whipped around. Someone had slipped in with the car and run to the front of the garage, quick as a cat. The intruder was a small, hard woman in her forties with harshly dyed black hair.

Anne thought of pinning the woman to the garage wall. But the intruder was smart enough to stand off to the side, out of the path of the car, and also out of the reach of a flung-open door.

This was Anne's day for encountering dangerous people.

The woman pantomimed rolling down a window, and Anne pressed the button.

"Hello, Cassie," Anne said. "What a surprise."

"Lower the garage door. Turn the engine off. Get out slowly. We're going inside to talk."

There was a gun in Anne's center console, but by the time she'd extracted it, Cassie would have shot her. At least the knife was still in Anne's pocket.

"Hurry up!" Cassie was impatient.

Anne pressed the button to lower the garage door. Following Cassie's repeated instructions, she put the car in park and turned it off. She could not throw her knife at the best angle to wound Cassie. There was no point delaying; she opened the car door and stood.

"It's been a long time." Cassie looked rough. Anne's former subordinate had never worn makeup, and she certainly hadn't gotten that dye job in any salon.

"Not long enough," Cassie said. She pushed her hood completely off her head. Dark hoodie, dark sweatpants. Completely forgettable.

"If you don't want to talk to me, why are you here? Why the ambush?"

"We need to have a conversation. I figured you'd shoot first and ask questions later," Cassie said. "All things considered."

"Considering you threw me under the bus?"

When Senator Miriam Epperson's daughter had died in the mountain-survival test, Cassie had laid the blame directly on Anne's shoulders. At the time Anne had thought that strategy was understandable, even reasonable. It didn't matter that Cassie had been the one who'd kept telling Dorcas Epperson to suck it up when the girl claimed she was ill. Anne clearly understood that the buck would stop with her, because she was in charge of Camp East. There was no need for both of them to go down.

Understanding Cassie's motivation did not mean Anne had forgotten.

"It was my chance to take charge," Cassie said. "Let's go in the house. Get out your keys, then zip your purse."

"So why aren't you at the farm on this fine day? Snow training will begin in a few weeks," Anne said. She unlocked the back door and punched in the alarm code. She walked into the kitchen slowly, her hands held out from her side.

From behind her Cassie said, "Have you seen David Angola lately?"

Anne had expected that question. She kept walking across the kitchen and into the living room. She bypassed the couch and went to the armchair, her normal seat. She turned to face Cassie. "I'd be more surprised to see David than I am to see you, but I'd be happier. He's still running Farm West?"

"He was," Cassie said. She was savagely angry. "We're both on probation until . . . never mind. I figured he'd head here, since you're such a *favorite* of his. I just found out Greg is here too. He was always David's man, to the bone."

"Surely that's a melodramatic way to look at it?" And inaccurate. Holt was his own man. At least Anne had believed so.

Now she was leaving margin for error.

"I don't know why both of you are living new lives here," Cassie said. "In the same town. In North Carolina, for God's sake. No two people have ever been placed together."

"Most people get dead," Anne said. "The point of being here is that my location is secret."

"It took some doing to find out," Cassie said. "But by the usual means, I discovered it." She smiled, very unpleasantly.

"Coercion? Torture? Sex?" Anne added the last option deliberately. Cassie didn't answer, but she smiled in a smug way. Sex it was.

That's a leak that needs to be plugged, Anne noted. She should have taken care of it the first time someone from her past had shown up in her house and tried to kill her. At the time Anne had dismissed it as a one-off, a past enemy with super tracking ability and a lot of funds. Now she knew there was someone who was talking. A weak person, but one who had access to records . . .

"Gary Pomeroy in tech support," Anne said, making an informed guess. Cassie's eyes flickered. *Bingo.*

"Doesn't make any difference, does it?" Cassie now stood in front of the couch, still on guard, a careful distance away. She gestured with the gun. "Strip. Throw each garment over to me."

Anne was angry, though it didn't show on her face. *No one can tell me to strip in my own house,* she thought. But what she said was, "What are we going to talk about?" She stepped out of her pumps and unzipped her pants.

"Where Angola hid the money," Cassie said.

"You'll have to tell me what you're talking about," Anne said. "I'm totally out of the loop." Anne's jacket came off (her knife in its pocket), then her blouse. When she was down to her bra and underpants, she turned in a circle to prove there was nothing concealed under them. "So, what money?"

Her eyes fixed on Anne, Cassie ran the fingers of her left hand over every garment, tossing the jacket behind the couch when she felt the knife. "Someone in accounting sent up a flare," she said. "After that, the accountants settled in. Like flies on a carcass." Cassie waved her gun toward an easy chair. After Anne sat, she tossed Anne's pants and blouse back within her reach. While Anne got dressed, keeping her movements slow and steady, Cassie sat on the couch, still too wary and too far away for a successful attack.

"Both camps got audited?" Anne said, buttoning up her blouse.

"Yes, the whole program. Our accounts got frozen. Everyone was buzzing. Bottom line, in the past few years over half a million dollars vanished."

Anne was surprised at the modesty of the amount. It wasn't cheap to run clandestine training facilities staffed with expert instructors, much less to keep a fully staffed and equipped infirmary. "The money was missing from the budget? Or from the enemy fund?"

"The fund." Both farms contributed to a common pool of money confiscated—or stolen outright—from criminals of all sorts, or from people simply deemed enemies. The existence of this fund was known only to the upper managers and to Oversight . . . and because it couldn't be helped, a high-clearance branch of the tech team responsible for data handling also had access to the figures.

Cassie continued, "It would have been too obvious if it had only disappeared from David's allocation. It came from the undivided fund. Oversight's pretending they suspect David. I know they really think I did it. *I'm* suffering for it. Even when I'm cleared, and I will be, and get reinstated . . . they've halved the number of trainees for next year because of the deficit. I'll have to let two instructors go."

This was not a novel situation. A money crunch had happened

at least two times during Anne's tenure. "Consolidating the camps would save a lot of money," Anne said, because that had been the rumor every time a pinch had been felt. She'd scored a direct hit, from the way Cassie's face changed. Cassie was the younger administrator; she'd be the one to go if the camps combined.

"Not going to happen," Cassie said.

Anne knew denial when she saw it. "What do you think I can do about this?"

"David and I are both on suspension until the money is tracked down. I'm sure David will come to see Greg. They're thick as thieves. Maybe literally."

"I've been here for three years, Holt for two," Anne said. "It's hard to see how either of us could be responsible." *But it's not impossible,* she thought. "What do you plan to do if you find David?"

Cassie didn't answer. "I'll find him. Are you telling me the truth? You haven't seen him?"

"That's what I said." Why would Cassie expect Anne to tell the truth?

"What's Greg's new name?"

"Holt Halsey. Baseball coach." Anne could see no need to keep the secret. She planned to make sure Cassie never told anyone.

"As soon as it's dark we're going to pay Coach Halsey a little visit," Cassie said. She sat back on the couch and fell silent. But she stayed vigilant.

Anne had plenty to think about. She'd grown into her new identity. She'd become proficient in making her school the best it could be . . . though sometimes through very unconventional methods. She found it intolerable to believe she was on the brink of losing it all.

Anne was mapping out possible scenarios, imagining various contingencies, and (most important) planning an unannounced visit to Gary Pomeroy as soon as she could spare the time.

Assuming she had any left. Cassie was an emotional wreck, but she was also dangerous and capable.

It would be dark in less than an hour. Anne figured Cassie planned her move—whatever it was—for after dark. But that left an hour she'd have to spend in Cassie's company. "Want to play cards?" Anne asked. "More to the point, do you want me to touch up your roots? Jesus, girl, go to a salon."

"Shut up, Twyla."

"Did you fly into Raleigh-Durham? Surely you didn't drive all the way?" It was remotely possible Cassie had driven her personal vehicle all the way from Pennsylvania.

Cassie looked at her in stony silence.

It had been worth a try. Anne did not speak again, but she wasn't idle. She had a lot to plan. A lot to lose. There were weapons here in her living room if she could reach them. She counted steps to each one. Each time she came up just a little short.

"That your family?" Cassie said, and Anne's mind snapped to the present. Cassie waved her gun at the set of pictures on a narrow table against the wall. The table looked like a family heirloom, maybe passed down from the fifties.

"Yes," Anne said.

"Your mom and dad?"

"Someone's mom and dad."

"Where'd they find the guy posing as your husband? He looks familiar." Cassie was looking at a picture of Anne and her husband, standing in the fall woods, a golden retriever on a leash. His arm was around Anne's shoulders. Both were smiling; maybe the dog was too.

"He's in the acting pool." Actors came in very handy in training exercises.

"Was the dog from the acting pool too?" Cassie tilted her head toward the framed picture.

"Waffle," Anne said. "The cook's dog."

"How'd your husband die?"

"Skiing accident." That had been Anne's choice.

"Who's the girl?"

Anne had a studio portrait of a young woman on the credenza in her office, so she'd picked an informal shot of the same woman to place in her home. The woman looked not unlike Anne, and she was wearing nurse's scrubs and holding a plaque. (She'd been named nurse of the year.) "That's my sister, Teresa," Anne said. "She lives in San Diego."

Cassie looked at Anne with a mixture of incredulity and distaste. She said, "At my job I can be who I am. I don't have to fake a family. And no one underestimates me. How can you stand being here with civilians? Being *less*?"

"But I'm not less," Anne said. Anne had never thought of herself as a civilian, the instructors' term for noncombatants. Anne was still a fighter and strategist. Her regime at the school was sure, focused, and covertly ruthless; very much Anne, no matter what name she was using. She could have told Cassie about the gradual improvement in the school grade-point average, the better win-to-loss ratio of the school teams. (Except girls' volleyball, Anne remembered; she had to do something about Melissa Horvath, the volleyball coach.)

Anne locked away her concerns with Melissa Horvath. She might not be around to correct the volleyball coach. She couldn't discount the danger of her situation.

Cassie was obviously pleased to have her former boss at her mercy. That came as no surprise to Anne; Cassie had always wanted to be top dog (or top bitch). She'd never been good at hiding that. She'd waited for the death of Dorcas Epperson, one cold night in a marsh. Then she'd seized her opportunity.

"Did you take care of Epperson?" Anne asked. It was a new possibility, one she hadn't considered before.

"No," Cassie said, outraged.

Anne thought, *She means it. She wanted to get rid of me, but she didn't plan the death that brought me down. Idiot.*

Anne's cell phone rang.

"You can get it," Cassie said after a moment. "No cry for help, or you're dead."

Anne nodded. Moving slowly, she rose to go to the kitchen counter. She pulled her phone from her purse. There was a gun hidden not two feet away, and this might be as close as Anne would get to a weapon. But Cassie had stood and was facing Anne, on the watch.

"Hello," Anne said. She'd seen the caller ID; she knew who it was.

"Are we still on for tonight?" Holt's voice was cautious.

Anne had been expecting this call since the clock had read five-thirty.

Anne was never late.

"I'm so sorry, I have to cancel," she said evenly. "I've had an unexpected visitor. I don't get to see her often, so we plan to spend the evening catching up."

After a moment's silence, Holt said, "Okay. I'm sorry to miss our dinner."

"Is it Holt?" Cassie mouthed.

Anne nodded.

"Tell him to come," Cassie hissed.

"Why don't you come over here?" Anne said obediently. "I've got plenty of salad and some rolls. I'd love you to meet my friend." Anne really enjoyed Cassie's face when she said that.

"You sure you have enough lamb?" Holt asked. Anne never ate lamb.

"I've got enough lamb for all of us."

"I'll be right over," he said. "I'm really looking forward to it."

"Me too," Anne said sincerely. She ended the conversation. "He's coming over," she told Cassie.

"You two are on dinner terms?"

"Every now and then." *At least three nights a week, sometimes more.*

"Are you bed buddies?"

"My business."

Cassie could not control her face as well as Anne could. She reddened. Anne had a very faint memory of an instructor telling her that Cassie'd made a play for Holt when they were both at some planning session. That play had been spectacularly unsuccessful.

Even if Anne had not heard the rumor (she was surprised she remembered it, she hadn't known Holt well at all), Cassie had clearly signaled that she had a history with him, at least in her own mind.

Since Anne had worked closely with Cassie, she'd quickly become aware that her subordinate was very touchy about her looks, doubtful of her own sex appeal. It was a point of vulnerability. Anne began to wonder if this search for David Angola had more than one layer. Interesting, but not important.

After ten minutes there was a knock at the door. When Cassie nodded, Anne answered it.

Holt was clutching a bag of groceries to his chest with his left hand. His right hand was concealed. He'd come armed.

"You'll never guess who's here," Anne said, standing to one side to give him a clear shot if he wanted to take it. "You remember Cassie Boynton?"

Holt smiled and stepped inside. "I did not expect to see you, Cassie," he said. "It's been a long time. What are you doing in this neck of the woods?" Anne quietly shut the door behind Holt.

Cassie held up her gun. "I'm looking for some answers," she said. "Are you going to try to stop me?"

"I am," said David, behind her. He'd used Holt's key to come in the back door.

Cassie whirled, but David wasn't where she thought he'd be. He'd moved as soon as he'd spoken. Holt, who'd begun moving with *me*, leaped behind Cassie and took her in a chokehold. Cassie clawed at Holt's arm with her free hand and tried to bring the gun to bear with her other.

Holt made Cassie release her gun by slamming her hand with the butt of his own. Anne heard a bone crack.

And just that quickly it was over, without a shot fired.

Anne had broken a finger once (or twice), so she knew how painful it was. Cassie did not scream. Fairly impressive.

"You're unarmed," David said. "You're under our control. If this was a training situation, what would you tell yourself?"

Cassie did not speak. Her rage filled the room like a red cloud.

"You'd say, 'Bang, you're dead,'" David told her. "Did you follow me all this way to try to kill me? Are you trying to prove I stole the money?"

"You *did*," Cassie said. Though they were all liars by trade, Cassie believed what she said.

David's dark face was impassive as he said, "I never took a cent."

"I didn't either." Suddenly Cassie launched herself backward, drawing up her knees to explode forward in a kick that hit David's chest. He staggered back. Since Cassie's whole weight was suddenly hanging from Holt's arm, his hold broke.

With a beautiful precision, Anne pivoted on her left foot and kicked Cassie in the temple with her right. Cassie's head rocked back, her eyes went strange, and she crumpled.

David had regained his feet by then and he was striving to catch his breath. He held his gun on Cassie, but after a few seconds he was sure she was out. His arm fell to his side, and he sat heavily.

Holt had stepped away from Cassie in case David shot her.

"She sounded like she was telling the truth," Holt said, after a moment of silence.

"She did, didn't she?" David looked troubled. "I was so sure it was her."

"She was sure it was you," Anne said.

David appeared both confused and angry. "Do you believe I'm an embezzler? Twyla, Greg?"

Twyla said, "Anne," at the same moment Greg said, "Holt."

"Does it matter what we think?" Holt continued. "One of you will take the blame. I hope it's her."

Anne began to pick up the items that had scattered from the grocery sack. Among them was a knife. Anne smiled. She retrieved her own from her jacket. Then, just in case, she got her gun out of the drawer and put it in a handy spot. After all, everyone else in the room was armed.

She was waiting for the inevitable question. Holt obliged by saying, "What do you want to do with her, David?"

"The options are limited," David said slowly. "We call Camp East and tell—who, Jay Pargeter, I guess?—to come get her. Or we wait until she wakes up, and we ask her some questions. Or we let her go. Or we kill her now."

"We're not part of the system anymore," Anne told David, pointing from Holt to herself. "We shouldn't take part in an interrogation."

"You can't let her go," Holt said.

David looked down at Cassie unhappily. "If she was anyone else, I'd put her down. But she's earned some respect. She's done a good job since you left, Anne. Until now."

Holt glanced at Anne and then said, "There's another choice. You could take Cassie up to Camp East yourself."

David looked at Holt with narrow eyes. "Why?"

"Enough people know where Anne is already," Holt said. "Someone had to tell Cassie. If you call from here, at least ten more people will know. Anne, did Cassie say how she found you?"

"Gary Pomeroy in tech support. She also knew you were here, so she figured David might visit."

"Son of a bitch," David said, disgusted. "I'll pay Gary back. Maybe officially. Maybe on my own time."

"If you don't, I will," Anne said. "I don't want to have to start all over again. It seems to be too easy to pry the information out of Gary. At least we'll assume it was him."

"What's that supposed to mean?" David tensed.

"You knew all along where I was. You sent Holt here."

"You were getting death threats!"

"Like that's new. I never believed that's the only reason he came."

David looked at Holt. "So you've never told her why you left?"

"We never talked about it," Holt said calmly.

"We don't talk about the past a lot," Anne said, which was absolutely true.

"Well, *Anne*, you might be interested to know that *Holt* here, back when he was Greg Baer, was suspected in the disappearance — and probable murder — of a doctor in Grand Rapids, Michigan," David said.

"And?" Anne was unconcerned.

"I got tipped off Greg was going to be arrested," David said. "We couldn't let the police come to the facility, obviously. They believe it's a wilderness camp for adults, but if they had a closer look, that wouldn't fly. I had to drive Greg into town to meet with them. They'd flown in from Michigan."

"They took me to the local police station and put me through the wringer," Holt said, smiling. "But considering where I work, it was nothing."

David stared at him. "Man, they were going to arrest you!"

"Maybe." Holt didn't sound worried.

"Oversight voted to hide him, on my strong recommendation," David told Anne, though he sounded as if he considered that was a mistake just at the moment. "Otherwise his background might raise a red flag, though I swore to them that Greg wouldn't talk about the program. His background fit the opening here. He had his ears modified and his tattoos removed. A nose job. I figured you wouldn't recognize him right away. You two hadn't actually met, as far as Greg could remember. You could get to know him as Holt."

"You're right, I didn't recognize him." He'd made her vaguely uneasy, though, and it had explained a lot when he let her know who he'd been.

David nodded, pleased. "Oversight charged me with arranging your identities. No one else knew."

"Except Gary in tech support," Holt said in disgust.

"Except him."

"Thanks, then," Anne said. She smiled brightly. Holt was going to have some talking to do after this. From his face, he knew that.

David looked from Holt to Anne. "All right, I'll take Cassie with me. I'll call Pennsylvania once I've gotten a couple of hours under my belt so no one can find out where I started. I disabled the GPS on the rental. It's a seven-hour drive?"

"Yes," Anne said. "Thereabouts. One of us could go with you, fly back. You might need help."

"No, thanks," David said. "I need to think. Someone took that money. It wasn't me, and I believe it wasn't Cassie. But we both might lose our jobs."

Holt and Anne glanced at each other, quickly looked away. Yes, they needed to talk.

"Where's your car?" Anne asked David.

"We drove over here in it," Holt said. He was staring at Cassie, sizing up her shape and weight. He was a practical man.

"Good. We need to find her car."

"Search," Holt said briefly. Since it was possible Cassie was playing possum—though Anne didn't think so—Anne stood a safe distance away, with Holt's gun aimed at the prone figure. Holt knelt to search her. In a practiced way he rolled Cassie to one side, then the other. He pulled two sets of keys from her pockets and stood. "Rental," he said, "and personal."

"She's got a cabin five miles from camp," Anne said. "If she hasn't moved."

"She won't stay out for much longer," David said. "If I get stopped . . . I'm a black man. Just saying." He was saying that not only might he get stopped no matter how carefully he kept to the speed limit, but also that he didn't want to have to kill policemen. But it would be very, very awkward if he was arrested with a tied-up white woman who was screaming bloody murder.

"I have something to keep her out until you get there," Anne said. "You sure you don't want me to come? I could manage her. But I'd have to be back by Monday morning for school."

"You have no idea how weird it is to hear you say that," David said, smiling reluctantly. "I'll take her solo, if she's drugged. What do you have to keep her quiet?"

Anne ran up the stairs to her attic to open her carefully concealed stash of things she'd figured might prove handy. She was a "waste not, want not" kind of person.

"This should be two doses of thiopental," Anne said when she returned. She handed the vials of freeze-dried powder to David, along with sterile water and two hypodermics.

"You keep that around? Geez, Anne. What else you got?" David withdrew 20cc of sterile water and injected it into the first vial of thiopental. He shook the solution vigorously and withdrew it into the syringe.

"Oh, this is a holdover from Camp East," she said. "I picked it up in the infirmary after a trainee broke his leg. I thought it might come in handy someday. I stuck it in my go-kit and I didn't clean it out . . . in the haste of my departure." (In the middle of the night. With two armed and wary "escorts." Not her favorite memory.)

"Thanks," David said. He gave Cassie the first injection and prepared the next one, capping the syringe and pocketing it. "Is the other side of your garage free?"

"Yes, there's a control button by the kitchen door. You can drive right in. Might as well leave the kitchen door open."

In a few seconds — not long enough to have a conversation — Anne heard the garage door rumble up. She nodded to Holt, who squatted to take Cassie's feet. Anne took her shoulders. Cassie's body drooped between them like a hammock.

David had lowered the garage door and opened the trunk. "I've disabled the safety latch," he said. "I'll keep an eye on the clock and stop to give her the second shot. Four hours?"

Anne and Holt laboriously dumped Cassie into the trunk. It was lucky she wasn't tall.

"Four hours should be right," Holt said. "Sure you can stay awake?"

"Or I make you a to-go cup of coffee," Anne said helpfully. She predicted David's reaction.

Sure enough, he stared at her with ill-concealed suspicion. He said, "No, thanks."

"Let us know when you get there." Holt clapped David on the shoulder.

"I hope they find out who took the money," Anne said.

That was as much goodbye as any of them wanted.

As soon as David backed out, Anne closed the garage door. She and Holt stood in the chilly space.

He was waiting for her to say something first.

"When you were Greg, you had a real family," Anne said. It was not a guess.

He nodded. "Mom, Dad, brother. My father had stomach cancer. He was having a lot of pain. The roads were icy, and my brother was out of state. So Mom took him to the emergency-care clinic at three in the morning, because it was lots closer than the hospital. I drove from my hotel to meet them there. The doctor on duty was either incompetent or sleepy or both. He gave Dad the wrong drug. Dad died. He would have died soon anyway, I know. And he was suffering. But it wasn't his time just yet. Mom was sure she'd get to take him home."

"So you took care of the doctor."

"Waited three weeks and then went into his house at night." He smiled. "Snatched him right out of bed and vanished him."

"Did the police really have evidence against you?"

"I'd said a few things to him that night. So they had a lot of suspicion. When they checked into my background, they had even more. And a neighbor saw a car like my rental backing out of his driveway that night."

"Nothing decisive."

"Enough to haul me in for questioning. David didn't let that happen."

Anne said, "You did the right thing. So did David. Not that you need me to tell you that."

He nodded. "Was that really thiopental you gave Cassie?" he said.

"If I'd had something stronger I would have brought it down," she admitted. "All I'd kept was the thiopental. Cassie might not survive the trip anyway. She was out a lot longer than I'd thought she'd be, and I know she's had more than one concussion over the years."

Holt looked hopeful. "That would make things simpler."

They went into the house. Anne opened a cabinet and brought out a whiskey bottle, raising it in silent query. Holt nodded. She poured and handed him a shot glass, filled one for herself. She leaned against the kitchen island on one side while Holt sat on a stool on the other. They regarded each other.

"Cancer treatment is very expensive," Anne said at last.

Holt regarded her steadily. "Dad had a long illness. That trip to the clinic was only one of many. The bills . . . you could hardly believe how much, and the insurance only covered a fraction of the cost. My mother and my brother were scared shitless. The debt would loom over them the rest of their lives. They think I have some hush-hush military job, and they know the military doesn't pay well. They didn't expect I could help much. They were really understanding about that. It burned me up inside."

"So you siphoned off the money from the enemy fund."

"Yeah. I did."

So there it was.

"You did a good job covering your tracks. How'd you plan it?"

"It helped that David's never been confident with numbers. He always sweated budget time, needed a lot of help from me. I remembered a genius accountant, a guy I'd roomed with in college," Holt said. "Tom was doing the books for a lot of the wrong people. That was how I knew where he was. Tom was glad to help; he's one of those people who loves to beat the system, any system."

"Is Tom still around? Can they interrogate him?"

"He began doing bookkeeping for the wrong people. He disappeared a year ago."

Anne eyed Holt narrowly. "Really?"

"Yes, really." Holt managed a small smile. "Nothing to do with me. But convenient."

"So what now?"

Holt's smile vanished. He looked very grim. "When David showed up today, I felt like the bottom had fallen out. I hated that he was suspected of something I'd done when he'd done nothing but back me up. As people like us go, he's a good man."

Anne had thought of suggesting they follow David and run his car off the road. She was glad she hadn't said that out loud.

Anne had the feeling they were stepping on thin ice, new and fragile territory in their relationship. The two regarded each other in silence.

Finally Anne said, "Do you think David suspects you?"

"No," Holt said immediately. "He would have tried to take me out. An honor thing."

"Your family does not know where the money came from. They couldn't reveal anything accidentally?"

"I told them I'd invested money in an online shopping program and it had taken off. They were too relieved to ask for any details."

"You think Oversight will come back with questions about your dad's bills being paid off?"

"If the bills had been paid in one lump sum, it would be suspicious. But I paid in irregular amounts spread out over two and a half years, some of it channeled through my family's accounts. Less conspicuous." His mouth twitched in a smile. "And I haven't worked at Camp West in more than two years. I live on my coach's salary."

"And the money's stopped disappearing. No one's stealing from the enemy fund now."

"They'll still be looking. No one makes a fool out of Oversight."

"But they might be glad to find a scapegoat."

"What are you thinking, Anne?"

"I'm thinking we can find Cassie's rental. We can drive it to Pennsylvania and get there ahead of David. Two drivers instead of one."

Hoyt looked interested. "Then what?"

"Then we plant money in Cassie's house, gold or bearer bonds. Untraceable stuff."

"Anne, I don't have anything like that. I don't even have much cash stashed away. Not enough to make them believe she stole everything."

"I have some backup funds," Anne said. She looked away.

Holt leaned forward and took her hand. She couldn't avoid his eyes. "You'd do that?"

"Yes," she said stiffly. "I would."

"No regret?"

"No regret."

Holt struggled to find words of gratitude, but Anne held up her hand to keep him silent. "If they find unexplained money in Cassie's house, David's in the clear, Cassie will vanish, and they'll consider the theft explained. It's all good. I know where her house is, and we've got the keys."

"Let's get on the road," Holt said.

Anne retrieved half of her escape fund from its secret hiding place — the same place the thiopental had been stored — and she was back down the stairs in less than two minutes.

"If we find the rental quickly," she said, "it'll be a sign that we're doing the right thing."

Anne and Holt knew where to start looking. Using the key fob to make the lights blink, they found it in four minutes, parked behind a house for sale on the other side of the street.

During the long drive north they made some plans for spring break.

Those plans involved Gary Pomeroy.

ROB HART

Takeout

FROM *Mystery Tribune*

HAROLD WAS DOZING, his head rested against the tiled wall behind his chair, when Mr. Mo placed the brown paper bag in front of him. The bag was nested inside a milky-white plastic shopping bag, through which Harold could make out plastic utensils, packets of soy sauce, napkins, and a folded-up menu. Stapled to the top was a slip with an address on Mott Street.

"Crispy-skin fish rolls," Mr. Mo said, his high voice cracking like a whip.

Harold looked up at Mr. Mo. The man's face was flat and unreadable. His blue polo shirt stained with splotches of cooking grease, his slight potbelly and narrow limbs not really fitting into the shirt right. He could have been thirty or fifty. He only ever spoke English when he gave Harold a delivery.

He spoke English one other time, on Harold's first night. Harold had sat down and pulled an electronic poker game up on his phone. Mr. Mo took the phone out of his hand, turned it off, and smacked it on the table. He placed a Chinese-language newspaper over the phone.

"No play," he said. "Read."

"But I can't read Chinese," Harold protested.

"Read," Mr. Mo said, tapping his finger against the newsprint.

It had been three weeks, and Harold's Chinese hadn't gotten any better, so he looked at the pictures or dozed off until it was time to work.

Harold picked up the latest delivery and exited Happy Dumpling. The evening air was the kind of humid that made it hard to breathe. It was late, probably getting close to midnight, which meant this would, with any luck, be his last trip for the evening.

He hefted the bag, trying to guess at the contents. Then he pulled out his phone and punched in the address. It was close — just below Grand. He walked north, cut down Hester, and made a right. Found an apartment building with a nail salon on the first floor. The number 4 was circled on the receipt, so Harold hit 4 on the ancient buzzer.

After a few moments the door screamed at him and he pushed it open, climbed the narrow staircase to the fourth floor, where he found himself in front of a door painted glossy black, chipped in spots, gunmetal gray underneath. There was a peephole set at eye level.

The door was ajar, and it opened as soon as Harold stepped in front of it. A frail Chinese man in a wrinkled dress shirt and slacks, his white hair thinning, peered out from inside of the darkened apartment.

Harold opened the bag, first undoing the staple that held it closed, then reaching in for the white takeout container.

He hated this part. The anticipation.

Sometimes he had to bring something back to Mr. Mo. Sometimes he didn't. He wasn't always sure which. Mr. Mo wasn't big on instructions. This was the first time he'd gotten an order for crispy-skin fish rolls and he wasn't sure what that meant.

Harold placed the bag on the ground and opened up the take-out container, his hands shaking a little. Inside was a single pear. He looked at it for a moment, then took it out and offered it to the man, who breathed in sharply and put his hand to his mouth. Tears cut down his cheeks and he began to shake.

Harold pushed the pear forward into the space between them, but the man refused to take it. Instead he took a step back. Harold got the sense he wouldn't be bringing anything back to Mr. Mo tonight, so he put the pear on the floor in front of the door and left.

As he climbed down the stairs, he thought he heard the man weeping.

"Pears are taboo in Chinese culture," said Wen, putting his pint glass on the bar top, missing the coaster by a wide margin. He wiped the sleeve of his MTA-issue baby-blue dress shirt across his mouth. "The Chinese word for *pear* sounds like the Chinese word for *parting*. If I had to guess, it was a warning or threat. Mr. Mo is going to take something from him."

"Not like . . . his life or something?" Harold asked, his voice low, glancing around the mostly empty bar to make sure no one else was listening. The only person even close to earshot was the bartender, a pretty college girl in a halter top and a cowboy hat. She was down at the other end of the bar and seemed more interested in the Yankees game playing on the television mounted in the corner.

"Probably not," Wen said, undoing his ponytail, then doing it back up. After a moment he repeated himself. "Probably not."

"Weird," Harold said, taking a small pull of his beer. "Something is unlucky just because it sounds like something else that's not good."

"We're a superstitious people," Wen said. "In China the number four is *sì*. It sounds like *sǐ*, the word for death. So four is a very unlucky number. In buildings in China there's no fourth floor, or fourteenth, or twenty-fourth."

"Why so superstitious?" Harold asked. "I thought Chinese people were supposed to be like . . . smart?"

"First, that's offensive," Wen said. "There are plenty of superstitious people in the world. Race has nothing to do with it. Second, it's just a cultural thing. But I'm second generation. I don't actually understand any of this stuff. Mostly just what I remember from my grandparents."

Harold exhaled. Contemplated his half-empty beer. It was already warm, but he couldn't afford another. So he'd have to make this last a little while longer, because it felt good to be out. To pretend like Wen was a real friend and not just another sad sack he shared bar space with.

"At least I didn't have to deliver anything more than fruit," Harold said. "Just, you know, I was a little worried when I started this. The kind of stuff he might want me to do."

"Mr. Mo doesn't make his delivery boys do any real dirty work," said Wen. "He has triad goons for the real hardcore stuff."

"I can't wait until this is over," Harold said. "It's hell on my nerves."

The Yankees batter knocked in a home run, putting the team up by two. Wen pumped his fist. Probably had money on the game. "You made your bed," he said. "Now it's time to curl up and get some sleep."

"You're the one who got me wrapped up in this."

Wen shook his head, threw Harold a side-eye glance. "I got you in the door. You lost big and ran a tab on the house. I told you that was a bad idea. That's on you."

As much as Harold wanted to protest, Wen was right.

He had no one to blame but himself.

As per usual.

Harold pushed through the door of Happy Dumpling. It was just before the dinner rush, but the restaurant still had more full tables than empty tables.

He walked to the back, and the man at the register didn't acknowledge him as he ducked past the curtain separating the kitchen from the seating area. Harold's glasses fogged up from steam coming off the dishwashing station. He took them off to rub dry on his shirt and waved to Bai, who was hunched over a wok, swirling something around with a large metal spatula.

Bai looked up, smiled, and nodded, sweat dripping down his bald head.

Harold was glad Bai was working. The line cook would occasionally come out and offer him plates of food. Dishes he recognized — beef chow fun or pork fried rice — but sometimes things he wasn't used to, like crispy chicken feet, or a meat he couldn't identify in a chili bean sauce. All of it absurdly delicious.

That, at least, was something to look forward to.

Harold cut a hard left, into a narrow stairwell. At the top of the stairs was a red door. He knocked and waited until an older woman wearing a green accountant's visor opened it. She looked at him like he was a stray dog.

"*Gweilo,*" she said under her breath.

Which meant "white devil."

They sure knew how to make him feel welcome.

Harold stepped into the main room, crowded with elderly Chinese immigrants, mostly from the Fuijan province. They were huddled around flimsy poker tables, playing pai gow and mahjong, the tiles clacking like insects. Nearly everyone was smoking, and with the windows boarded up, the smoke didn't have much to do but collect into a heavy cloud that hung in the air.

Harold crossed the room, turning sideways to slide through the thin pathways between chairs, and stepped into the back room, where the blackjack and poker tables were empty. They wouldn't fill up for another few hours at least.

Mr. Mo was sitting at the small desk in the corner, a cigarette dangling from his lip, counting out a thick stack of money. Harold looked at the stack and his breath caught in his chest. They were high-denomination bills. A lot of them. He ran the math in his head. Just a quick guess, based on the thickness and the speed at which Mr. Mo was counting. There had to be at least ten grand there, maybe more.

That was two months' rent, his phone bill, and a few child-support payments.

It was enough to make the next few months of his life very comfortable.

He thought about how easy it would be to pick up something heavy, lay it hard over Mr. Mo's head. The man was often surrounded by young guys with ornate tattoos and cement faces. The triad goons. None of them were here today. There was no one to defend him, just senior citizens who couldn't be budged from their pai gow for anything short of a nuclear strike.

Mr. Mo stopped counting and looked up.

Did he know what Harold was considering? Harold felt dread bubbling in his stomach, threatening to escape his mouth and heave onto the floor.

After what seemed like a full minute Mr. Mo shrugged, as if to ask, *What?*

"I'm on tonight?" Harold asked.

Harold came in every day to ask, and Mr. Mo would tell him to work or not. Presumably one day he would tell him he was done, but Harold had no idea how long the terms of the assignment were for. With a debt to the house of $25,000, he didn't expect it would be anytime soon.

Still, he held his breath. Prayed Mr. Mo would shoo him away, tell him never to return. Harold would give anything for that.

But Mr. Mo nodded. That meant Harold was on duty.

He crossed back through the smoke-filled room. Down the stairs and through the kitchen to the front of the restaurant, the smell of cigarettes clinging to his clothes. He sat at the small table in the corner by the register that no one else ever sat at, next to the fish tank filled with silver and orange fish floating through murky water. He opened the Chinese newspaper that was waiting and flipped through slowly, looking at the pictures.

*

"Clams in chicken soup," Mr. Mo said, placing a bag down in front of Harold.

Clams in chicken soup. This one he remembered. It was a collection. The Chinese food container would be empty, and he would have to wait for something to be placed inside, then bring it back.

Usually the addresses he delivered to were within a ten-block radius of the restaurant, but this one was different. On Eighth Avenue, up in the twenties. It would take about forty minutes to walk there. That was too much. Though Harold was generally in favor of wasting time, he didn't feel comfortable taking that long, so he headed for the F train, which would get him most of the way there.

He was happy to see there weren't any cops down in the station. No one in the token booth either. He stood by the gate for five minutes before a mother pushing a stroller came through. He reached over to hold it for her as she maneuvered the stroller out, and he ducked in before it closed.

Seeing the stroller made his chest ache. Cindy was older now, six or seven by his best guess. He only ever remembered her as small enough to push around in a carriage. Back before Marguerite changed the locks and left a packed suitcase outside the apartment door for him to find one morning, when he finally mustered the courage to stumble home.

As he waited for the train, the ache in Harold's chest grew bigger. He promised himself that when this gig with Mr. Mo was done, he would make the changes he needed to make.

Get treatment for his addiction.

Find a steady job.

Take those tiny little baby steps that, once accumulated, would maybe allow him to see his daughter again.

He knew things would never be the same, knew he could never make up for it entirely. But he was sure he could at least make things better than this.

Another narrow stairway, another red door. This one had a small security camera mounted to the ceiling above it. Harold looked into the bulbous eye before knocking on the sign that said RED SPA 22 on a white sign in red lettering.

Red was a color of good luck. This is also why Chinese takeout containers had red script on them, even though they were an American invention. More trivia, courtesy of Wen.

The door opened and a petite woman peeked out. She was barefoot, wearing a slinky black dress, her hair pulled back into a tight bun. Older, odd strands of hair gone gray, but she had the energy and smile of a young woman. She reached for Harold's hand, pulled him inside.

There was a main room with a desk, and to Harold's left a long hallway with six doors. The lighting was dim, and soft music played from hidden speakers. He was pretty sure it was Debussy's "Clair de Lune," the delicate piano notes falling around them like raindrops. The woman smiled and snapped her fingers. Another door opened, this time to the right, and three girls came out. All of them much younger. All smiling and done up for a night on the town, also barefoot.

"You choose favorite," the woman said.

Harold shook his head. "No, no. Delivery."

He held up the bag, tried to hide how nervous he was, because the women were pretty and it had been a long time since he'd been around a pretty woman, let alone several.

"Mr. Mo," he said.

The woman's smile disappeared. She snapped her fingers again and the women disappeared too. She took the bag from Harold and walked to the desk. Took out the Chinese food container and filled it with rolled-up wads of cash.

When she was done she could barely close it, but she managed to get the flaps down and placed it back in the bag and handed it to Harold. She was robotic now, all business. She quickly moved around him and opened the door. Harold stepped into the hallway and she closed it. The deadbolt scratched as it slid into place.

Harold made it down to the sidewalk and stood under the awning of the fried chicken restaurant on the first floor of the building. It was starting to rain, fat drops smacking the pavement. He clutched the bag to his chest.

Thought about the money.

Not as much as Mr. Mo had earlier in the day, but still, it looked like a lot.

Maybe enough?

Harold took out his cell and dialed Wen. He'd never called Wen before, only texted, so when Wen answered, his "What's up?" was weighted with surprise and concern.

"Just had a question I needed to run by you," Harold said. "Some advice."

"Okay. Shoot."

"Mr. Mo. How dangerous is he, exactly?"

"Ah." Wen laughed. "Let me guess. You're running some money for him right now? And you're thinking of taking off?"

"Can you blame me?"

Pause. "Listen, just do the job like you're supposed to."

"How would he even find me?"

"Jeez, Harold. You don't want to mess with this guy. I know it's tempting, but look, I know you're trying to make good right now. This isn't the way to do it. Besides, I wouldn't be surprised if he has someone keeping an eye on you right now. So get the hell off the phone and get back to the restaurant."

Harold's heart skipped around in his chest. He surveyed the street. It was late, and most passersby were young people, stumbling home or headed to the next bar. But across the street was a man leaning against a parking meter, smoking a cigarette, wearing a gray hoodie, the hood pulled up over his head so his face was cast in shadow.

He wasn't looking at Harold, but he was looking in Harold's direction.

"Okay," Harold said. "Thanks, Wen."

"You'll be fine. Remember, I had to do this once too. It'll all be over soon. Maybe I can talk to him. See if we can speed things along."

Relief washed over Harold. "Thank you. I would really appreciate it."

"Hey, what are friends for?" Wen asked.

Harold hung up. Looked across the street and saw the man was still there, still looking in his direction. Harold stepped to the curb and hailed a cab. He didn't want to spend the money, but thought it would be better for his overall health to hurry back.

As soon as Harold walked in the door, Mr. Mo handed him another bag.

"Crispy-skin fish rolls," he said.

Another pear then. A little depressing, but easy enough.

This address was close. The rain had picked up on the cab ride over. Harold walked closer to the buildings, ducking under awnings to stay out of it, not doing a great job. By the time he got to the address he was nearly soaked.

There was a Chinese grocery on the first floor. It reeked of fish. An older couple sprayed down the empty display cases out front, foamy water running into the street.

Harold found the door propped open and climbed to the second floor, his shoes squeaking and squishing on the steps. He knocked on the green-painted metal door. It flung open and a young Chinese man with spiked hair and black plastic glasses looked at him with confusion and, upon seeing the bag, rolled his eyes.

The man tore the bag from Harold's hands, opened it, and took out the container, letting the bag fall to the floor. He opened the container and took out the pear, took a deep breath, and threw it at Harold's chest as he yelled something in Chinese.

The pear thumped hard enough to make Harold wince. He took a step back and put up his hands. "I'm sorry, I don't understand . . ."

The man threw out his fist. Harold moved to the side and it glanced off his head, knocking his glasses to the floor. He stumbled over his own feet and fell to the ground as the man drove his foot into Harold's head. Harold put his arms up, tried to protect himself as the man threw his foot into him again and again.

After a dozen or so kicks, the man spat and went inside the apartment, slamming the door. Harold searched for his glasses, and was happy to find they were still intact. Waves of pain pummeled his body and he was content to lie on the linoleum tile for a few minutes until the worst of it subsided, but he changed his mind when he saw a fat, shiny roach scuttling toward him.

Mr. Mo sat at his desk, cigarette dangling from his lip, as Harold told him what happened. After Harold finished, Mr. Mo continued to stare at him, like there was more story to tell. Harold shrugged and let his arms flop down to his sides.

Mr. Mo took the cigarette out of his mouth, tapped the end of it into the overflowing ashtray on the desk, and nodded. Harold wondered if Mr. Mo even understood half of what he said. It never seemed like he did.

Harold went back downstairs. Stopped in the dingy bathroom to survey the wreckage of his face, found there was a cut on his hairline, a thin stream of blood trickling down to his eyebrow. A fat bruise blooming under his left eye.

He wet some paper towels, cleaned himself up the best he could, and went back out to his table and chair. It wasn't long before Bai came out and put down a plate of steamed dumplings with a dark brown dipping sauce.

Bai looked at Harold's face and placed his hand on Harold's shoulder.

"I'm sorry," he said.

Harold was a little surprised to find the man spoke English. They'd never exchanged words before, outside of a passing introduction on Harold's first day.

"Not your fault," Harold said. "Thank you for the food. I appreciate it."

"It's not usually like this," Bai said. "It shouldn't be for too much longer."

"My friend Wen said he's going to help me," Harold said.

Bai made a face, and Harold got very nervous. Like maybe he shouldn't have said that. The man worked for Mr. Mo. Maybe it would have been better to just keep his mouth shut.

But Bai looked around. The man at the register was on the phone and the restaurant was mostly empty. After confirming there was no one close to them, Bai said, "Your friend Wen is the reason you're here."

Harold felt his stomach twist. "What does that mean?"

The curtain behind them parted and Mr. Mo peeked out. Bai smiled, said something in Chinese, and ducked back into the kitchen.

After Mr. Mo dismissed him for the night, Harold wasn't sure what to do. He wanted to go home, to sleep, because his body ached and his head hurt and he thought one of his teeth might be loose.

But he couldn't shake what Bai had said.

So he walked toward Dizzy's, where he and Wen would often wind up. He wondered if Wen would be there, or if tonight he was working, driving the M23 bus back and forth across midtown Manhattan.

Harold thought back to the night they met. They had both been tossed out of a late-night poker spot in the basement of a West Village bar on the corner of Sullivan. Harold for running a debt, Wen for arguing with the owner over the jacked-up price of the beer.

Before that night they'd been familiar to each other. Two addicts orbiting each other in the darkness of the city's less-than-legal gambling dens. As they stood on the curb, Harold smoking a cigarette he bummed off a friendly bartender, he wondered if Wen might be a kindred sprit. Someone to grab a drink and commiserate with. Harold asked Wen if he wanted to hit a nearby bar he knew served cheap beers and didn't get too busy on the weeknights.

Wen responded with an offer to bring him to a gambling den on Mulberry Street.

Harold was nervous from the get. He'd heard about the spots in Chinatown, and he was curious about them. Without someone to show him the way, he had no idea how to find them. But he didn't know the customs. He figured language would be an issue. It was a very different, intimidating universe.

At that moment all he wanted was a beer. To quit while he was ahead, or at least not any further down, and for a gambler that was a major personal victory.

But Wen had the kind of easy smile and warm personality that made you want to say yes when he asked you for something. He insisted the place on Mulberry Street had good food and friendly dealers. The language barrier wouldn't be an issue. Anyway, the regular spots in the West Village were getting too expensive, too full of young kids who watched the World Series of Poker on ESPN and suddenly decided they were experts.

Plus, they had beer on Mulberry Street.

Why not, Harold thought.

Maybe this was the moment his luck would finally turn.

Wen was sitting at the bar, nursing an amber beer, watching the Yankees game on the television mounted in the corner. Harold sat down next to him.

The pretty bartender in the cowboy hat didn't wait for him to order, just filled a pint glass with the cheapest beer they had and placed it onto a coaster in front of him. Harold dug a couple of singles out of his pocket and placed them on the bar.

Wen looked at Harold's face and said, "Jeez, man, what happened to you?"

"You did."

"What do you mean?"

"Why did you bring me to Happy Dumpling?" Harold asked. "That night we first hung out. Why did you bring me there?"

Wen exhaled. Undid and redid his ponytail. It didn't take a gambler to see it was a tell. After a few moments Wen said, "C'mon, man. I was just looking to help a fellow player out. You looked like you were still up for some action."

Harold took a sip of his beer. "You said you worked for Mr. Mo."

"I did."

"When?"

"Before."

"How long did you have to do it for?"

Wen pursed his lips, his words taking on a tone of aggravation. "One day he told me I was done. He sent me home."

Harold twisted the stool around until he was looking at Wen. "Why did you bring me there?"

"Look, man, what happened happened," Wen said. "You should have kept yourself in check. You didn't. I told you to be careful. But I've been thinking about what you said. About . . ."

Wen arched his back, looked around the bar. The bartender was down at the other end. No one was sitting close. He leaned in to Harold's ear. "I've been thinking of what you said. You're getting pretty used to the routine now. Mr. Mo is comfortable with you. Maybe we can work together. Give something a try."

"Something what?"

Wen smiled. "You know how much money goes through that place?"

"You mean knock him off?" Harold asked. "You told me he was dangerous."

"Where did you say your wife and daughter moved to?" Wen asked.

"Iowa."

"One big score. You up and leave to Iowa. Get closer to them. Never come back to this nightmare town again. I'm not saying we have to do it right now, but keep your eyes open. If you see there's something we can exploit, let's sit down and have a conversation about it, you know?"

Harold thought about his daughter and the ache in his chest.

Wen held up his pint glass and smiled. Harold picked up his own glass and clinked it against Wen's.

"Partners," Wen said.

"Sure," Harold said.

Finally he saw his way out.

*

Harold wasn't sure if it was Wen's plan all along to get him into position and plant the seeds of a heist. Maybe he came up with the plan on the spot, to derail Harold's train of thought.

It didn't matter. Either way, Harold was pretty sure he'd been a sacrificial lamb. That Wen was stuck doing deliveries for Mr. Mo and realized the only way out was to push some *gweilo* into the job. He almost didn't blame Wen. Harold briefly wondered if he could pull off the same. Find some desperate gambler looking for a fix, willing to run up a stupid debt.

Then he just got angry.

That anger festered in his gut, making him feel sick. He'd thought they were friends. And after years of reneging on loans and breaking promises, Wen seemed to be the only friend he had left.

A long time ago, so long he couldn't even remember when, Harold decided the life of wearing a suit and tie and sitting in a gray box to make some rich person richer was not the life he wanted for himself.

Gambling was a natural fit. He was good with numbers. Gutsy enough to make bold moves but cautious enough to sit on a mediocre hand. For a while he made some nice money. And it was fun. But as the bills stacked up, he got desperate.

Made bolder moves. Sat on hands less.

When Marguerite left and the alimony payments piled up, it got worse.

Maybe he could exploit some weakness in Mr. Mo's operation. Maybe he and Wen could come up with a plan that would score them some quick cash, and Harold could get on a plane. Mr. Mo seemed to have juice, but probably not out in Iowa. Even if he couldn't get back in with his family, at least he'd be well away from here.

But how long would it last?

What if they came out of the job with a couple of grand each? It would float him for a little bit, but he'd end up in the same spot. The spot that got him into this situation in the first place.

So he chose not to end up there.

And as he explained Wen's idea to Mr. Mo, he felt something approaching serenity. That he was finally making a decision to better himself. Because it was the smart decision. Smarter than a heist. Smarter than maybe getting himself shot or beaten to death by vengeful triads.

He got himself into this mess. He would ride it out, finish it, and move on.

No more gambling.

He was making his own luck.

Mr. Mo listened silently, that cigarette dangling from his lip. Harold thought at the end maybe he should barter for early release, but thought it best to just let the truth percolate. Mr. Mo was harsh, but didn't seem unreasonable.

After finishing the story, Harold thought he saw a hint of a smile on Mr. Mo's face. Like something flitting on the edge of his vision, but when he looked, found there was nothing there.

Mr. Mo raised his hand and waved him off. Harold went downstairs and smiled at Bai and sat at his chair. It wasn't long before Mr. Mo placed a bag down in front of Harold.

"Last delivery," he said. "Braised frog. After, you go home."

That was a new one. He hadn't delivered braised frog before. Harold picked up the bag and Mr. Mo grabbed his wrist.

"After, you go home," he said, drawing out the words. "You don't come back. Ever."

Harold nodded. He thought about thanking Mr. Mo, but decided against it. It felt perverse to thank him. The only thing he was thankful for was the fact that he'd never see this man again.

The address was for a street Harold didn't recognize. He stepped out of the restaurant and typed it into his phone. It came up in Coney Island. That meant more than an hour, round-trip. But Harold didn't mind. It would be worth it, just to be done.

He walked to the N stop at Canal, sat on the train with the bag nestled in his lap, thinking about what he would do with the rest of his day. No beers with Wen, that was for sure. Another person he hoped to never see again.

As the train made its way down the aboveground tracks of Brooklyn, Harold pulled out his cell phone and tapped Marguerite's name on his contact list. Maybe he'd catch her in a good mood and she'd put him on the phone with Cindy.

A gruff voice answered. "Hello?"

"Hi, I'm looking for Marguerite?"

"She changed her number," the voice said. "Number got reassigned."

"I'm sorry. Listen, did she leave a forwarding number?"

The man clicked off.

Harold closed the phone and looked at it. Put it back in his pocket. Felt the ache in his chest grow bigger. Marguerite probably forgot to tell him. Maybe she emailed it to him. He hadn't checked his email in days.

He brushed it off. It was nothing. A mistake. He'd get word to her somehow. Chances are she wouldn't believe him, because he'd given her this song and dance before. But this time he would follow it up with action.

That, he promised himself.

When the doors opened at Stillwell he could smell the salt heavy in the air that came off the ocean. He followed the exit signs down to the sidewalk and checked his phone, found the address was a couple of blocks away.

On the walk back, he would hit Nathan's. Get a hot dog. Maybe some cheese fries, if he could afford it. He was all the way down here, maybe not ever coming back to New York. One last hot dog at Nathan's seemed like a proper sendoff.

He walked the long stretches of suburban sidewalks to the little pulsing blue dot on his phone, finally finding it, but the number on the front didn't match the number on the ticket. He looked at it again and realized there was a second mailbox with the correct number. Must be a side apartment.

Harold walked down the empty driveway to the door with an awning and a single step. He stood in the shadow cast by the house next door and rang the bell before placing the bag on the step, opening it up, and pulling out the Chinese takeout container inside. His heart racing, head spinning, so pleased to almost be done.

The takeout container felt heavier than normal. He pried open the cardboard flaps as the door opened. Harold looked up from the container to see Wen in a tank top and boxers, bleary-eyed and hair unkempt, peering out from inside the darkened apartment.

They stared at each other in confusion.

Then Wen saw the container and his lips parted a little.

Harold looked down into the white folds and found a small, compact handgun.

"Please tell me that's just a pear," Wen said as Harold contemplated the ache in his chest.

DAVID H. HENDRICKSON

Death in the Serengeti

FROM *Fiction River*

THE SMELL OF newly rotting flesh hit Jakaya Makinda. He stopped his Land Rover, grabbed his binoculars off the seat beside him, and trained them in the direction of the odor's source.

Eighty meters away, mostly hidden by a rocky outcropping of man-sized boulders, lay the carcasses of a dozen or more slaughtered elephants.

Poachers.

Anger coursed through Makinda. He grabbed his Remington pump-action shotgun and, with his broad-brimmed hat shielding his eyes from the early-morning sun, used the binoculars to scan the Serengeti's tall grass for predators. The poachers were long since gone, but he wasn't some damn fool white tourist, stepping out of the security of his vehicle, thinking how cute the animals were, all set to launch into "Hakuna Matata."

Out here, humans were food. Short and wiry, he'd be less of a meal than the overweight Americans whose entry fees paid his salary as senior park ranger, but he had no interest in being any creature's gristly lunch.

He approached the rocky outcropping cautiously, binoculars dangling from his neck, his shotgun ready and his .38 holstered but loaded.

His stomach gave way when he stepped past the two largest boulders and saw the full extent of the carnage. Beside what had to be close to twenty dead elephants, their missing tusks sawn off at the roots, lay the carcasses of five hyenas, three jackals, and a couple dozen vultures.

The poachers, as they'd come to do, had poisoned the elephants with cyanide, killing them and everything that came to feast on their corpses, most importantly the vultures, who wouldn't be left circling overhead for rangers such as himself to notice. The poison killed everything in its path but made for an easier getaway.

Makinda gripped his shotgun tightly. He'd get these devils, these parasites who'd invaded even the Serengeti, Tanzania's greatest treasure. He'd get them if it was the last thing—

Behind him, his Land Rover exploded.

The force of the concussion knocked Makinda face-forward onto the ground. He tasted the tall grass in his mouth. Felt grains of the hard soil between his fingers. His ears rang.

He looked back over his shoulder and saw flames shooting up from the wrecked carcass of his vehicle. Makinda stared in disbelief and horror.

Makinda shot to his feet, grasping the shotgun, and ran toward the flaming wreckage of the Land Rover. He didn't know why. It was useless to him now. The two-way radio, referred to by safari companies as the "bush telegraph," would be destroyed, as was its backup.

He hadn't called in the slaughter because he knew the safari companies listened in on the rangers' frequency and would flock to this less popular section of the park to gawk at the butchery. Makinda had wanted to report this in person back at HQ and shield tourists from the ugliness. Let them think Tanzania was perfect.

So now he was stranded.

Alone.

And with no cell phone coverage in this sector of the Serengeti, there was now no way to reach the other rangers. No way to alert them that a group of poachers bold enough to blow up his vehicle weren't settling for elephant tusks. They'd be going for the staggering rewards of rhinoceros horns, which made those from elephant tusks pale by comparison.

Ever since that damned Vietnamese politician claimed rhino-horn powder had cured his cancer, demand had shot through the roof faster than Makinda's head would have if he'd remained in the Land Rover. The street value now of an average-sized rhino horn was a quarter of a million dollars, and not surprisingly, rhino poaching deaths had skyrocketed every bit as furiously, though mostly outside of the protected national parks. Even so, in this sector of the Serengeti there were only seven rhinos left.

Makinda had always declined the thinly veiled bribe offers, no matter how they escalated. He could be a wealthy man right now, retired in dirty luxury at the age of thirty-nine instead of struggling to care for both his own family of six and that of his late brother, Jephter, whose wife and seven children Makinda had of course taken in.

The only time the temptation had come close to overwhelming him was when Jephter had lain dying of cancer in a Bunda clinic and a poacher, a fat white American with a southern drawl named Luther Ricker, had whispered in his ear, "Save your brother. We'll give you enough of the rhino powder to make him well. You need not dirty your hands with our money, but save your brother."

Makinda knew the claims of the rhino powder's powers were nonsense; all the scientists here said it was so. But he had almost given in that one time.

And perhaps he should have, he sometimes thought. The experts weren't always right.

Makinda spat, trying to rid the bitter taste of that memory from his mouth. As the smell of burning metal and electronics filled the air, he struggled to gather his thoughts. His vehicle's explosion had only been the opening gambit. The rhinos would be next, if not his fellow rangers, and he couldn't just stand by and allow either group to be wiped out.

He had to move. Predators be damned, he had to get to some group that would help him contact his fellow rangers. He'd warn them and get them to the watering holes where the rhinos would be visiting, easy targets for the poachers if not protected.

Makinda had taken no more than five steps up the road when far to the north a soft explosion sounded. Distant and muted, little more than a *poof.*

But unmistakable.

The hairs on the back of Makinda's neck stood up.

The north. Rashidi. That was where Makinda's top assistant was supposed to be this morning. Near the big hippo watering hole.

"No . . ." Makinda groaned.

But maybe, he thought, it hadn't really been an explosion. It had just been his overactive imagination, overwrought at barely escaping his own death. It couldn't—

A second explosion echoed off to the west.

The west. Another soft *poof.*

That would be Samson.

If Makinda was right, and in his suddenly nauseous gut he knew he was right, that left only Brayson, Salim, and Philipo. Brayson in the northwest, Salim in the east, and Philipo in the south.

In rapid fire, soft explosions echoed off to the east and south. *Poof! Poof!*

The taste of bile filled the back of Makinda's throat. Salim and Philipo. Makinda closed his eyes and waited for the fifth and final explosion.

Brayson's. The one that would complete the elimination of Makinda's entire staff. Wipe out their entire sector. Sure, there were many other rangers in the Serengeti, but that covered almost 15,000 square kilometers. Their sector was isolated.

They were on their own. Just him and Brayson.

Makinda waited, but the fifth explosion didn't sound. Had he missed it? If it had detonated simultaneously with his own, as had perhaps been the plan for them all, he'd never have heard it.

But Makinda's instincts told him otherwise. When the fifth explosion never sounded, he knew it had not come simultaneously with his own.

Brayson was a traitor.

He had sold them out, the son of a bitch.

Makinda began to run down the road, shotgun slung over his shoulder and binoculars jangling about his neck. His boots clopped noisily, kicking up dirt in his wake. He didn't care if he had to run a hundred miles. When he got to Brayson, he'd throttle the traitor's sweaty, grime-covered throat and squeeze until Brayson's greedy eyes popped out.

If he was guilty.

One look and Makinda would know for sure. But with a sinking, angry heart, he knew already. Brayson liked the night life too much. Handsome. Too handsome for his own good. A ladies' man. A gambler. A drinker and maybe more. Trekking off to Mwanza whenever he had two straight days off.

The appetites that gave birth to greed. And the murders of Rashidi, Samson, Salim, and Philipo.

And the attempt on Makinda himself, which would have been

successful if not for Makinda's lucky discovery of the butchered elephants, almost totally hidden from the road with the usually telltale circling vultures instead lying dead in the field.

A greed with no conscience.

In retrospect, it was obvious. Brayson had betrayed them all. He'd betrayed himself.

Makinda picked up the pace, and in no time his effort was rewarded.

A cloud of dust appeared on the horizon. Makinda stopped and broke into a smile. A lucky break! Not a long shot, but still a much quicker arrival of a safari group than he could have expected.

He jumped up and down, ignored the jostling of the shotgun on his shoulder, and began to wave wildly with both hands. It wasn't exactly dignified behavior befitting a senior park ranger, but he didn't give a damn. He'd get them to stop even if he had to shoot out the tires, though that shouldn't be necessary. Any safari company's driver would know to stop for a clearly identified park ranger.

But when he peered through the binoculars, Makinda's smile faltered. His hands fell to his sides.

Something was wrong. He couldn't pinpoint exactly what from this distance, but something about the vehicle looked wrong.

Makinda dropped into a crouch and sprinted for the brush. He spotted a meter-high boulder diagonally ahead to his right. He made a beeline for it, bent over double all the way, then continued away from the oncoming Land Rover and back to where the wreckage of his own vehicle still smoldered.

He dove behind another large boulder, tasted the tall grass once again and a bit of dry soil as well, and scrambled around to face the dirt road. His belly lay flat on the ground, the binoculars uncomfortably pinned against his lower ribcage. He readied the shotgun, touched his finger to the trigger, and tried to calm his hammering heart.

The Land Rover that approached looked different from those of all the safari companies he'd ever seen in the Serengeti. It still had the elevated roof that allowed tourists to stand on their seats, poke their heads out, and shoot photographs. Three African men stared out from just such a perch.

But they didn't hold cameras or binoculars. They held AK-47s.

The side windows were darkened. Makinda couldn't see if more compatriots of the men brandishing the AK-47s sat below or if the space was instead filled with cargo. Elephant tusks. Rhino horns.

A bitter taste again filled Makinda's mouth. He wanted to shoot now and ask questions later, but one pump-action shotgun against at least three AK-47s didn't sound like good odds to him, even if he got off the first two shots.

Makinda released the pressure of his finger on the trigger. Realized he was holding his breath. Exhaled slowly and as quietly as he could manage.

They stopped twenty meters short of what was left of his ruined vehicle: tortured, blackened steel with wisps of black smoke curling up from it.

Four men climbed out, three slender Africans, though none of them looked Tanzanian, and Luther Ricker, the fat American who'd tried to corrupt Makinda with the words *Save your brother.* All of them wore nondescript long-sleeved khaki shirts and matching trousers and boots. One of the Africans wore a dark blue baseball cap. They all carried AK-47s as they walked to the wreckage of Makinda's vehicle.

"Nice work," Ricker said in his southern drawl, the *nice* long and drawn out. *Niiice.* It sent a chill up and down Makinda's spine. "You blew this one to kingdom come. He's having a little talk with Jesus right now. With Jesus and his brother." Ricker laughed, setting off waves of stomach fat rolling.

Makinda's finger tightened on the trigger.

"I don't see him," the African with the baseball cap said in Swahili.

"English!" Ricker yelled.

The man repeated what he'd said, this time in English.

"You vaporized the sucker!" Ricker said. "Blew him into *tiiiny* bits of dust. That's all that's left of him."

"No blood?" the African said.

"You think he survived this blast?" Ricker said in a tone Makinda associated with talking to children and stupid people. "You want to look for his severed head, be my guest. But get your scrawny ass back here in three minutes. I ain't got no time for trophy hunting. We got some money to make."

Ricker lumbered back to their Land Rover and slid in the driver's seat, on the right, the near side facing Makinda. The three Africans looked at each other, gave slight shrugs, and loaded back into their vehicle.

"That better be all of them," Makinda whispered to himself long after they were gone. "If there's a separate group for each ranger they took out . . ."

He didn't want to think about that. Four against one was bad enough odds.

Although he knew it was worse than that. Much worse.

Four plus Brayson against him. Four AK-47s plus whatever Brayson was carrying now against one pump-action shotgun and a .38.

A Land Rover, actually two counting Brayson's, against a man walking on foot.

He didn't stand a chance.

Makinda started walking. After ten steps, he began to run.

After three kilometers, Makinda finally got lucky. Sweat ran in his eyes. His feet felt like he was walking on eggshells; his boots were not meant for running. His shirt was dripping wet.

But he'd only encountered a half-dozen giraffes, a herd of about twenty elephants, and a hundred or so impalas of one variety or another. None of them had shown him any interest.

He'd pushed to get to a particular intersection of the dirt roads, knowing it was likely some safari group would pass it soon.

And he was right.

He was there at the crossing for less than two minutes when he spotted clouds of dust in the east billowing up from the road. Makinda considered wading into the tall grass far enough to hide himself until he was sure it was Nikons and Canons that were pointing out of the tops of the vehicles and not AK-47s, but he figured he'd take his chances with the Land Rover over whatever hidden surprise waited for him in the tall grass.

As it turned out, it was an Ace African Safaris Land Rover, driven by Chibuzo Akunyili, a man Makinda had dealt with for years and called Chi. Makinda waved him down.

"What's up, chief?" Chi said. "What are you doing out here all alone?"

"Hello, Chi. May I step inside? I've got a private message I need to give you."

Makinda liked Chi and thought he could trust him, but knew that what he was about to say would not be popular. He couldn't imagine any driver taking off and leaving him standing there—

there'd be hell to pay if anyone did — but the morning's events had shaken him. Makinda was taking no chances.

"Sure, hop in."

Makinda stepped aboard and quickly introduced himself to the five tourists arrayed on three rows of blue seats, the first two rows consisting only of a single seat on each side, the last row the only one that stretched from side to side.

Sweat dripping off his face, he ducked down to speak to Chi, seated on the right side, the driver's side, of course. On the left was a large flyswatter to nail the occasional tsetse fly and a brown cardboard box filled with a dozen or so white boxed lunches.

"I've got a very dangerous situation here," Makinda whispered to Chi. "I need your complete discretion."

Chi's brow furrowed. "Of course." He was a broad-shouldered man of about fifty-five with short gray hair. A white nameplate with black printing identified him at the front of the vehicle; a smaller one hung above the left pocket of his dark green shirt.

"You can't tell anyone about this," Makinda said. "My life depends on it. Possibly others." He pointed to the two-way radio and the square black microphone that hung from a chrome metal clip. "Nothing on the bush telegraph. It's going to be difficult, but I'm counting on you."

Chi nodded vigorously. "What's wrong?"

"I've got to commandeer this vehicle."

"Jakaya, these tourists paid top dollar! I can't—"

"Mine got blown up by poachers. I was supposed to be in it."

Chi fell silent.

"How many vehicles in this group you're hosting?" Makinda asked.

"Three. Four including this one."

"I need you to find them right away. We need to offload these people into those other three vehicles. Do you know where they are?"

"Sure. The other three are less than a kilometer away from here. They're viewing a pride of lions another group found. All of us heard on the bush telegraph and went rushing to join them. We were the farthest away. We're the last group getting there."

Makinda swore. He closed his eyes tightly. "Get going while I think."

The Land Rover lurched forward along the uneven dirt road.

"I can't have this going out over bush telegraph," Makinda said.

"Not from you or any of the other drivers in your group. Or for that matter any of the drivers in the other groups with other safari companies that will wonder why we're offloading people from this vehicle to the other three. Nothing can look unusual. Nothing can look suspicious."

"We can't offload people with lions out there," Chi said.

"I know. I know. How many other safari companies are already at the site?"

Chi got back on the two-way radio and asked.

"Close to a dozen," came the static-filled answer in Swahili.

Makinda shook his head. "We can't make the offload there. It's too dangerous. Besides, we can't let that many other drivers see us. The bush telegraph will talk about nothing else. The wrong ears will hear it." He squeezed Chi's shoulder tight. "Surprise is the only thing I have on my side."

Chi got Ace African Safari's other three drivers on the radio. "Problems with my vehicle. Bad differential. Rendezvous with me a half kilometer down the road, due east."

He hung up. "They're not happy. Two were in prime viewing position. They're going to get an earful over this for days. But they're coming. And they'll be quiet. I said the magic words."

"Bad differential?"

Chi nodded. "Bad differential is our code for silence."

Makinda nodded. "Thank you."

"After we ditch the cargo"—Chi nodded toward the back—"do you need a driver?"

"I couldn't ask. This is too dangerous."

"Do you need a driver?"

"I believe these poachers killed four other rangers and would have killed me if I wasn't lucky. I probably won't get out of this alive. If you join me, you'll be every bit as much at risk."

"These poachers. They're going after the black rhinos?"

Makinda hated the name "black rhino." There was almost no color difference between the "white" and "black" variants, but the names had been given to the two species by the colonialists—based on the white version being more docile and the black more savage —and the racist titles had stuck. But now wasn't the time to quibble.

"I'd bet my life on it," Makinda said.

"Double that wager. Count me in."

*

They headed northwest, toward the last noted location of the nearest rhino. Makinda filled him in on all the details. If the man was going to die, he had a right to know. Chi drove with a sense of unspeakable fury over the pitted dirt roads, bouncing the two of them wildly in the air, straining at their seat belts every time he hit a pothole or partially submerged rock at top speed.

But they arrived too late for the first rhino.

Vultures circled overhead. Others filled a nearby tree. Flies swarmed through the air. The smell of blood and death was palpable.

The fallen rhino lay on its side, the armor of its lower torso blown apart by what must have been a shotgun blast at point-blank range, its horns hacked from its mighty head. Makinda stared at the magnificent creature. Almost four meters long and well over a thousand kilos.

Its only natural enemy: humans.

Humans and their greed and stupidity.

Makinda thought that if the Vietnamese politician were here right now—the one responsible for stoking the fires of this poaching greed—Makinda would shoot the man with no remorse at all.

They came upon a second felled rhino, its midsection blown apart and its horns hacked off just like its brother's.

And then a third.

Each time Makinda and Chi found the carcass further northwest than the one before. The guiding hand, of course, was Brayson's. No one else, not even the best of the safari tour guides, could have told the poachers where to find the rhinos so quickly.

Makinda spat on the ground, then they headed further northwest.

Soon they saw vultures flying overhead and followed them to where fifteen more slaughtered elephants lay, huge holes ripped in their heads by shotgun blasts. Their tusks had, of course, been sawn off.

"I thought you said they used cyanide on the other elephants," Chi said. "Why shotguns now?"

"It's faster," Makinda said. "They think I'm dead along with all the other rangers, other than their buddy Brayson, of course. There's no need to cover your tracks if there's no one left to catch you."

As if to underscore his point, a chorus of gunshots boomed in the distance. Makinda stared in that direction, then connected the dots of each slaughter in the map inside his mind.

Suddenly Makinda knew the poachers' destination.

The tiny airstrip.

He hadn't expected that. He'd assumed that the poachers would exit the country using the same vehicle, taking no chances, sticking to back roads, staying as invisible as possible, and finding some unguarded path out of the country. Or use a standard exit point where there was a corrupt guard.

But via the airstrip? To get out of the country? The more he thought about it, the more sense it made, flying low beneath radar detection, especially if their destination was somewhere beyond one of the neighboring countries.

It was a tiny airstrip with a short dirt runway suitable only for prop planes, so remote that it had once had a plane crash because a hippo had wandered onto the strip. It serviced only a handful of planes each day, if that.

"While they harvest those tusks," Makinda said, "we'll race to the airstrip. That's where they're going. I'm sure of it. If we're lucky, we'll get there first."

"Chief," Chi said hesitantly. "They've still got all the AK-47s. We've got one shotgun and a revolver."

Makinda explained his plan.

Chi stared at him. "Really?"

Makinda and Chi waited, hiding in the thick trees that lined the short, six-hundred-meter dirt runway and its grass curtain. They crouched on one knee at the opposite end from where a small, nondescript white bush plane rested beside the tiny white wooden shack that serviced the airstrip. Other than the buzzing of insects and the chirping of birds in the trees around them, the place appeared lifeless. Not a soul was visible, although presumably someone was working in the shack, the same person whose battered old jeep was parked outside, the lone vehicle visible in the open grassy area that passed for a parking lot.

Makinda and Chi had hidden their Land Rover a short distance past the airstrip, then raced back, crouching low and working around to their current position, not quite at the end of the strip on the opposite side from the jeep and the shack, always staying under the cover of the trees.

In an ideal world, Makinda thought, he would arrest these men and bring them to justice along with Brayson. He would look directly into the eyes of Ricker, whose sadistic words, *Save your brother,* haunted him still.

But a host of AK-47s against a single shotgun and a .38 didn't amount to an ideal world. He'd be lucky if he got any kind of justice at all.

Makinda was starting to wonder if he'd been wrong and the airstrip wasn't the poachers' destination after all when they drove up in their Land Rover and parked haphazardly next to the jeep. The four men emerged, Ricker and the three Africans, AK-47s at their sides, shielded from view of the shack.

Makinda trained his binoculars on them as they walked single file into the shack. A solitary cry of outrage rang out briefly, then was silenced a split second later as the AK-47s roared to life.

Moments later, while Ricker strolled casually to the plane, unlocked it, and pulled down the stairs, the three Africans returned to the Land Rover. They unloaded stacks of curved white elephant tusks, then carried them to the plane and stuffed them inside, angling the longer ones around the corner of the door. It took several trips for the three men until finally the one in the blue baseball cap carried a green, blood-stained duffel into the plane and, with the four poachers all aboard, closed the door.

"The duffel has the rhino horns," Makinda said. "I'm sure of it."

As the propeller blades whirled, he peered into the binoculars, needing to see inside the cabin, and muttered, "Good!" when he saw Ricker in the pilot's seat.

His assumption had been correct. There were no innocents aboard. Only the four poachers. It was time to make them pay for the deaths of the four rangers and whomever they'd just shot in the shack. For the butchered rhinos and the elephants. It was time to make sure they never returned to kill again.

"This revolver isn't going to do squat," Chi said.

"Aim for the propeller blades. Give it a chance."

The plane accelerated down the runway, at first moving at barely more than a standstill, then faster, speeding closer and closer to the two men waiting in ambush.

The plane roared, drowning out all sound, its propellers a blur. Makinda tasted bile at the back of his throat. His heart hammered, but he felt strangely at peace.

"Come get it," he said, his voice steady.

The plane drew closer. Almost on top of them.

It began to take off, angling upward.

"Three . . . two . . . one," he said.

It lifted off the ground.

"Now!" Makinda yelled.

They burst out of their cover, firing. Makinda's shotgun boomed its deafening blast and the pilot-side window blew out. He pumped in another round, thinking he heard the ping of Chi's shot hitting the thin metal of a propeller, then Makinda fired again, this time ripping a hole in the bush plane's white underbelly as it drew beside them.

Makinda pumped and fired, pumped and fired, aiming at the fuel tank as the plane shot past.

It wobbled at eye level, wings dipping wildly, groaned, then righted itself, inching higher off the ground.

He pumped and fired. Pumped and fired.

But the plane continued to climb.

Fifteen feet off the ground.

Twenty, then thirty.

And just when it appeared that they had failed, the plane fell silent. At first Makinda, his ears ringing from the shotgun blasts, didn't realize it except on some subconscious level.

He pumped and fired, having long since lost count of the shots but sure the Remington's external magazine was almost spent. He pumped and fired even as the plane stalled and then plummeted, nose down.

It crashed, and just as Makinda and Chi both fired one last shot, the plane exploded violently, the concussion knocking the two men backward through the air.

A fiery ball shot high into the sky from the mangled wreckage of the plane. The smell of burning fuel and human flesh filled the air.

After a time, Makinda turned to Chi and hollered, "You up for a visit to Brayson's house?"

Chi nodded. "Wouldn't miss it for the world."

ANDREW KLAVAN

All Our Yesterdays

FROM *Ellery Queen Mystery Magazine*

A SCREAMING BRIGHT madness of noise and fire—then nothing.

Brooks wasn't afraid after he went over the top. Before, yes. In the moments just before the assault began, the fear was almost unbearable. As he stood there with his boots sunk in the sucking puddle, rifle lifted, bayonet fixed, the rat-infested dung hole of a trench seemed to him transformed: it had become hearth and home and mother all rolled into one. He would have sold his soul to stay there, never mind the filth of it, never mind the endless crump and boom of the shells falling all around him, that noise that he'd thought, just hours before, was going to drive him mad. Now he hungered to curl up and hide here in the dirt and the din and even the madness. He just wanted to go on living, that's all.

He stared up white-faced at the trench rim. He sensed all the blanched faces of his men around him, staring too. All these weeks, that's how he'd thought of them: his men, his charges, though he was younger than most of the platoon. Now they were suddenly strangers, each one alone in his feral terror. He couldn't do a thing for them, nor they for him—not a single thing that would keep a man from becoming a bloated corpse like Moore had or Wilson or a shrieking legless torso like Miller was when they dragged him to the wagon half a week ago. Brooks knew now what they all knew: they would each of them go through this—this assault, this war, this life, this death—in utter solitude.

It occurred to him he ought to pray. Then the sergeant blew the whistle and Brooks led the way up the ladder, screaming.

They were all screaming, all around him. You didn't think about screaming, you just did. You screamed and you ran. And what he felt then wasn't fear anymore. Fear was no longer the right word for it. It was just a kind of blank, blind fever of being. He screamed and he ran through acid-black smoke, over a mud-drenched moonscape lit by shellfire, studded with corpses.

Six months before it had been the rolling green countryside of France.

That was all Brooks remembered—running like that, screaming like that; the intensity of feeling. He was told that the concussion from a Jack Johnson shell had sent him flying through the air "like a rag doll." He was told he'd been found buried in the mud when the assault was over, just his lifted right hand and the center of his face visible. He didn't remember any of it.

The trip back home to England—that was gone too, except for one cloudy flash of a jostling train ride, which he may only have imagined. He was told they took some shrapnel out of his brain. They laid him on a long cook's table—so he was told—out under the grand staircase in the main hall because there was a little bathroom there with running water. After that, he spent the next few days going in and out of consciousness, asking the same questions over and over of anyone who happened to be passing by. This too he simply did not remember.

His first clear memory was when he awoke out of an absolute darkness that almost seemed like peace. He opened his eyes and saw Jesus Christ ascending into heaven.

He was in Gloucestershire somewhere, as it turned out. In a stately home called Gladwell Grange. Its owner, Lord Farrington, had given it over for use as a hospital, his family's contribution to the war effort.

Brooks's bed was one of twelve in a hall decorated with enormous Baroque paintings in the Dutch and Spanish styles. A lion hunt. The rape of the Sabine women. David slaying Goliath. And the Christ ascending, which hung directly across from him. Brooks found the picture soothing somehow. It showed the Savior swirling up into heaven like a bright wisp of white smoke, the base world half swallowed in gloom all around him. When Brooks became agitated or fearful, he would focus on it, and it sometimes calmed him down.

"Is it a Velázquez?" he asked the doctor.

The doctor's name was William Haven. He was about sixty. On the short side, but very sturdy, broad-shouldered, with a cool but kind manner and steady hands. He had smooth, handsome features and tidy silver hair, and his face seemed wreathed in a sort of sorrowful wisdom, as if he had seen all and forgiven all. Brooks had liked him on sight.

Sitting beside him, holding his wrist, taking his pulse, the doctor glanced up at the painting as if he hadn't noticed it before. "I wouldn't know. You like it?"

"Yes," said Brooks. "Reminds me of my childhood somehow. I find it steadies me to look at it. It keeps my mind off . . . the other things. The things I saw."

"Probably for the best," the doctor said. "No point thinking about all that now."

While Haven listened to his chest with a stethoscope, Brooks let his eyes range over the hall. The inlaid panels. The flocked wallpaper. The portraits of the Farrington family flanking the Baroque works. Everything about the place made him feel an enormous emptiness inside himself, a painful nostalgia for his boyhood, a yearning for the world as it had been before the war.

"It will never be the same, will it?" he said.

The doctor pulled the stethoscope from his ears. "The house?"

Brooks nodded. "The house. England. The world. It won't be what it was after this. It can't be."

For the first time since they'd met, the doctor seemed to look at him, really look at him, as a person rather than a patient. One corner of Haven's mouth lifted in what Brooks thought might have been a smile of appreciation. He thought the doctor might have been realizing what he himself had known right away: despite the difference in their ages, the two of them were kindred spirits.

"No," the doctor said. "I don't suppose any of it can be the same. A war will do that. Change things. Some people look forward to it. Clears the air. Like in 'Maud,' you know."

"'I embrace the purpose of God and the doom assigned,'" said Brooks, and the doctor gave that small smile again. Because Brooks had understood his reference, had quoted the Tennyson from memory; they were kindred spirits.

But then Brooks remembered some of the things he had seen: what the young men looked like lying in the mud between the trenches, the fresh bodies bloated with gas, the older ones sunk into themselves as if they'd been mummified.

"I don't think it can be," he said. And when the doctor raised his chin in a question, Brooks looked at the Christ on the wall again and said, "I don't think it can be 'the purpose of God.'"

He didn't tell the doctor about the blackouts, not that visit and not later either. As his health returned and he was able to move about a little, he would sometimes find himself in various rooms of the house or out in the garden in back, and he would not be able to remember how he'd come to be there. It made him sick with fright when it happened the first time. And the second time was even worse, because he'd convinced himself the first time had been a fluke.

He knew he ought to tell the doctor, but he couldn't work up the nerve. He wasn't sure what he was afraid of exactly. Maybe that Haven would operate on him again or put him in an institution of some sort. He just kept hoping the blackouts would go away and there'd be no need to bring the subject up.

He didn't tell the doctor about the rages either. Brooks's father ran a school in Yorkshire. He had trained his son — as he had trained all his pupils — in a grimly cheerful faux-heroic stoicism. The Victorian ethos and all that: keep your head when all about you are losing theirs, etc. When Brooks had enlisted, his father clasped him briefly by the shoulders and said, "Good lad." Brooks answered with a curt nod. That was all. The point was, Brooks was well able to control his emotions, to hide his passions, even at their height. No one could tell when the rages came over him. But they were there all right.

It would happen without warning, a blaze rising out of the pit of his stomach. The anger would be general and amorphous at first — and then, very quickly, something would draw his attention, some small thing, and he would focus on that with terrible fury. A nurse once dropped a tray, for instance, making a clatter. And Brooks's heart flared at her. He called her things — only in his mind, silently — but still, they were awful things, words that he had never spoken aloud, not even in the trenches, where they were all lads, cursing together. He wanted to teach the nurse a lesson. Teach her to be a bit more careful. Making all that noise in a sickroom. He wanted to punch her in the face, or rip her blouse open and molest her . . .

These fantasies horrified him. He had never experienced anything like them before. He knew it must be an effect of the shrap-nel or the concussion, same as the blackouts were. And again, as with the blackouts, he told himself the rages would go away on their own.

Then one day—one cool September evening—he found himself out in the hills above Moreham, the nearby village. It must've been half an hour's walk at least from the Grange, yet he couldn't re-member a single second of it.

His first reaction was that sickening fear, almost a panic. How had he got here? Why couldn't he remember? He wanted to turn around and run back to his hospital bed—as if he could erase the fact that he had come to this place at all. But then he looked down the slope at the village, a road lined with cottages of Cotswold stone and shingled roofs, the yellow gaslights burning in their windows. It was a sweet homely scene in the blue dusk. It made the nostalgia flare in him, and he ached painfully for the old days and another England, England as it was. He didn't want to leave the scene just yet, so he walked down into the village.

He strolled along the road, stealing glances through cottage windows as he went past. The sight of a family at dinner, or gath-ered in their sitting room, gave him a warm, peaceful feeling. It was women and old men at home mostly, some children. All the young men, of course, were gone.

At the end of the village was a pub, The Chimes, set on a ledge of land above the banks of the river. Brooks went in and ordered a pint. The barmaid—the publican's daughter—was a surprisingly delicate-looking girl of about eighteen. Brooks found her attrac-tive but very modern-looking, with her raven hair bobbed above her pert birdlike features. Brooks found the gaze of her blue eyes almost mannishly direct.

"You up at the Grange, then?" she asked him. He still had a ban-dage on one side of his head so it was obvious he was, but Brooks knew she wanted to talk to him because there weren't any other young men around.

He wanted to talk to her too. "I am. I'm done, they tell me. I won't be going back."

She said her name was Nancy—said it in such a way that he knew she wanted him to romance her. Her bold manner made him feel edgy, almost hostile toward her. He thought to himself that girls had been gentler, more reticent and more modest, before the war, and that people in general had been more aware of their social standing. Still, he hid his misgivings and they had a friendly chat while he drank his ale. Then he went out into the night again.

He continued on a little ways past the pub, listening to the burble of the river water and the breeze whispering in the willows that clustered on the banks. He was just about to turn back when he saw a final cottage at a small remove from the others. He glanced through the window and saw Haven there, the doctor, writing at a small roll-top desk.

On impulse, Brooks knocked on the doctor's door.

"Brooks, is it?" said Haven, startled. "What are you doing out here? And in your shirtsleeves. It won't do my reputation any good if you come down with pneumonia."

"It was warmer when I started out," Brooks said. But the fact was he couldn't remember when he started. He felt guilty about the lie, but he still couldn't bring himself to tell the doctor about the blackouts. It would make them real somehow.

The doctor seemed glad to see him and had him in. They sat together in the sitting room, each with a whiskey. The look of the room puzzled Brooks at first. Very prim and Victorian. Plush furniture crowded together, lots of throw pillows on it. Lots of pastoral paintings and pottery hanging on the wall. There was even a framed portrait of the queen in her later years set on the mantel. Brooks would've sworn a woman had decorated the place. An older housewife, even a grandmother. But he knew the doctor lived alone.

Haven must have read his thoughts. "I've just taken the place for the year," he said. "I only came down from London to help out at the Grange. The owners are in Yorkshire with their daughter. A sweet old couple."

"That explains it," said Brooks with a smile. "I like the feel of it, actually. I do. The old days. I envy you to have lived back then. It was a better time."

The doctor raised one shoulder, made a face. "One time's pretty much like any other."

Brooks gave a little noise of disbelief. "You can't believe that. The way people are nowadays." He thought of Nancy at the pub. "Just the way girls are, for instance. You don't think standards have fallen?"

"You don't like the ladies in trousers, eh?"

Brooks laughed, but he said, "I don't. I like the old styles. Some modesty. I like a girl who's a girl. A lady. Like in Victoria's time."

The doctor only shrugged again. "There were ladies then, but there were the other kinds of women too, and plenty of them. Good men and bad men, just like now. That's what I meant about times being the same, taken altogether."

"I suppose. You don't look back with . . . I don't know: longing? I do, and I wasn't even there. I was a child when she died," Brooks said, with a gesture of his glass toward the queen's portrait.

Haven glanced at her, and then let his eyes linger. "Look back with longing?" he said. "No. No, I don't. I don't look back at all, really. Let bygones be bygones, I say. I try never to think about the past."

But Brooks, more and more these days, found himself thinking of little else. The past. How things used to be. How they were changing and would never be the same. He daydreamed for hours about living in an age of fine manners and high morals, with the women in bustle dresses. And when the rages came over him, he would go into a dark fugue and brood about it. How corrupt the times were now. Radicals and perverts like that Strachey character everywhere. Respect between the classes breaking down, men speaking to their betters as if they were equals. And the way men and women congregated, easy as friends, but not friends because there was always that other-sex element involved. When the rages came over him, Brooks would wonder grimly if he'd even be able to find himself a good girl, a pure girl, when he was ready to settle down.

He visited the doctor's house often. He tried to get Haven to reminisce about the past. The doctor was always reluctant at first and would plead with him to change the subject, but he would come around if Brooks pressed him hard enough. Sometimes even then he would try to dampen Brooks's nostalgia with harsh stories about his days as a doctor in a hospital in London's East End.

"Terrible poverty," he said one evening. "Disease." He shook his head. "Ever see a man die of syphilis? I have. It isn't pretty. That was part of those days too, remember. You can't just look at the magazine drawings."

But Brooks continued to press him. He wanted to hear about other things, good things. He hungered to hear about them. It was as if he wanted peaceful images of the Victorian old days that he could use to cover over and replace the images of what he'd seen in the trenches, at the front.

"Were you ever married?" he asked the doctor once.

"I was, yes. She died young, I'm afraid. In childbed."

"I'm sorry."

"Thank you. So was I. She was a fine girl." The doctor hesitated, as if uncertain of what he wanted to say next. But then, in an apparent enthusiasm of affection for his remembered wife, he rose from his chair and said, "Here, I'll show her to you."

He got up and went through a door at the far end of the room. The door had always been closed when Brooks was there. As the doctor went through, Brooks caught a glimpse of a four-poster bed in the room beyond. Then Haven shut the door behind him. A minute or two later he emerged with a small photograph in an old silver frame. He handed the photograph to Brooks and stood over him while he examined it.

"That was her," Haven said. "That was my Emma."

The effect of the picture on Brooks was so powerful he instinctively hid his reaction to it. If he had conjured from his own imagination some perfect icon of old-fashioned beauty and modesty and goodness to soothe away the front's images of mutilation and savagery and death, this would have been the figure and the face. Emma was lovely, tall and shapely in a light-colored, floor-length dress, sashed at the waist. Smooth-featured, fair-haired, with the kindest and most sympathetic expression that Brooks thought he had ever seen.

"That was June 1886," the doctor said. "About a month before our wedding. Almost two years to the day before she . . ."

Brooks did not want to let the picture go or give it back, but he felt if he held on to it another moment he would give himself away, expose the power of his feelings. "I truly am sorry," he said again as he returned the photograph to Haven.

Haven glanced down at the picture himself, and Brooks saw all the longing and desire and affection in the doctor's eyes that he felt in his own heart.

"I suppose that's why you don't like to talk about the past," Brooks said.

"Mm," Haven murmured. "I suppose so."

*

That night, as Brooks walked home through the village, his thoughts were far away—in the past, as he imagined it—and his mind was still full of Haven's Emma. As he neared The Chimes, he heard a noise coming from the shadows of the willows by the river. A young woman gave a low, sensual, two-note giggle. Jarred out of his distraction, Brooks stopped short and looked toward the sound. All at once the woman broke out of the dark up ahead of him and stepped out onto the moonlit road. She didn't notice Brooks standing there but immediately hurried away. Brooks got a good look at her as she passed beneath the lantern above the pub's front door: dark-haired, husky, blunt-faced, young.

A moment or two later a man stepped out from under the same trees. He was a rough-looking tradesman, older than the girl, about forty or so. He paused to light a cigarette, his hands cupped around the match. Brooks saw his face in the glow of the flame. He looked very pleased with himself.

The man ambled back to the pub, and Brooks continued on his way up the road toward the Grange.

Later, it was determined that that was the night of the murder.

Brooks found out about it three days later. The doctor came to the Grange to make his rounds, and Brooks noticed at once that he was wearing a solemn, "official" expression.

"Walk with me," Haven said.

They went out into the garden in back of the house. They walked together side by side over the square spiral path that wound among the purple belladonna. Haven had his hands clasped behind his back, his face bent down to watch his shoes moving through the brown dust. Brooks waited for him to speak. He didn't know why, but he felt a flutter of nervousness. What was the doctor about to say?

"The constable came to visit me this morning," Haven said. "A girl's body was found under the willows down by the river. Police say she was murdered."

"Murdered?" Brooks's heart beat faster, so fast he began to feel lightheaded.

"It was a Land Girl, apparently," Haven said. "Working at one of the farms nearby. I had to do the postmortem. Someone had taken a knife to her. Butchered her."

The horrible image of it flashed into Brooks's mind, as clear as a memory. A girl lying on her back in the grass under a willow tree, her mouth open, her eyes open, staring, lifeless. Her throat was slashed, her chest mutilated, her blouse soaked in gore. It was the girl he had seen by the river: the girl who had giggled and then run out from under the trees. He wondered, why should he assume it was she who had been killed? But he knew it was.

"That's awful," he managed to answer finally. "Do they know who did it?"

Still watching his feet, Haven murmured, "Not yet. It's not the sort of thing that happens around here much."

"No, I shouldn't think it was."

"The constable was very keen to hear about the patients up here. Anyone I might have qualms about."

"Here . . . ?" was all Brooks could say.

"Because you're all strangers. And soldiers. You know." They walked a little longer in silence, side by side. Brooks felt so weak and unsteady now he wondered if Haven noticed.

Then, all at once, the doctor turned his head and pinned him with a sharp glance. "How often are you having blackouts?" he asked. Brooks could not hide his stunned surprise: his mouth fell open. Haven went on, "The nurses noticed it. So did I, come to that. I visited you a week back. I could tell you didn't remember sitting with me the night before. You'd forgot our entire conversation."

"I . . ." Brooks began, but nothing more would come.

"Any other symptoms? Uncontrollable emotions? Sudden bouts of fear or anger?"

Before he could even think, he had shaken his head no. He had lied.

"You're certain?"

"Of course I'm certain. Why are you asking me?"

"Don't go thick on me, Brooks. It's me asking or it's the police. I had the devil of a time keeping them away. Practically had to wave the flag and sing 'By Jingo.' All the same, they'll be up here asking questions sooner rather than later, so it's best you tell me straight out. The murder happened three nights ago. That was the last night you came to see me. Do you remember that?"

"Yes, yes," Brooks said irritably. He was feeling persecuted now.

"Did you happen to see a girl on your way home? Dark-haired girl, broad-shouldered, a bit heavy in the hips. Down by the river near the pub."

"Yes. Yes, I saw her. There was a man with her too," Brooks added eagerly. "Rough-looking chap . . ."

"Yes, that was Ned Morton. Tradesman from over in Gilesbury. He and the girl had been carrying on a romance."

"Well, then . . ."

"The police are still questioning him. That's the only reason they're not here. But last I heard, it seems he couldn't have done it. Local busybody saw them together. It seems his movements are accounted for."

Now Brooks's temper flared. He stopped and the doctor stopped and they faced each other squarely.

"Why don't you come out with it? Are you accusing me?" Brooks said, trying to keep his voice even.

Haven didn't waver. "Do you remember what happened that night?" he asked again.

"Of course I remember. I'm not insane. I left your house and walked back here. That's all. I remember every moment."

Haven considered. Then he smiled that sad, wise smile of his, just the corner of his mouth lifting. He gave Brooks a doctorly pat on the shoulder.

"Good man," he said. "I had to ask. You understand, don't you?"

Brooks drew a deep breath, fighting to compose himself. "Yes. Yes, of course. It's nothing. It's fine."

But it was not nothing. It was not fine at all. Because while Brooks thought he remembered walking home that night, how could he be certain? If a whole conversation with Haven had vanished from his memory, if even the nurses had noticed what he thought he had hidden so well, how could he be certain of anything?

He lay awake in his bed that night with fear gnawing at him so relentlessly it was as if he were back in the trenches waiting for an assault. His stomach was unsettled. His skin was clammy. His breath was short, his heartbeat rapid. He stared through the shadows at the Christ ascending. It seemed to him a ghostly and accusatory figure now in the wavering glow of the nightlight just outside the door. Brooks yearned to be able to cry out to the Savior for help, but he felt no connection to him. Ever since his return from the front, he barely felt connected to other people, let alone to God. The world he had known was slipping away from him—he himself, the man he had been, was slipping away—and there was nothing to fill his empty places but darkness and rage.

The next morning he felt ill and exhausted. All through the day he was worried and sick. He imagined the nurses were casting sidelong glances at him. He expected to hear the police pounding on the Grange door any minute. A sense of dread gathered in him like clouds. And it darkened, like clouds just before a storm . . .

Then, suddenly—just like that—he was walking through the village with Nancy beside him. It was night, but he could not remember nightfall. He could feel he had had a pint, maybe two, but he could not remember that either. He could not remember anything after the slow approach of sunset beyond the windows of the Grange. He was just suddenly there, just suddenly with her.

Fear burst in him like a shell, one of those coal-box shells the Huns used that filled the air with black smoke after it exploded. The fear filled him like that. He wanted to turn and run away from Nancy as fast as he could, without even a word of explanation. But he didn't.

"This is me," she said. They had stopped outside a cottage only a few yards from The Chimes. "Thanks for walking me. It's so close, I know, but after what happened to that poor girl . . ."

She stood on tiptoe and kissed his lips, her mouth warm and soft on his. Brooks was taken aback by it. *Don't,* he thought. In fact, he almost panicked and said it out loud. Not that he didn't like the touch of her. He liked it very much. But he was afraid. He had the vague but powerful sense that she was in danger here. She touched his cheek with her fingertips—lightly, fondly. It made him angry somehow. Why did she keep on like this? he thought. Why wouldn't she stop? What was she trying to do to him?

She turned away quickly then and opened the door. The cottage was dark inside, quiet, empty. He wanted to ask her where her father was, but he felt certain that she'd already told him back in the pub; he just couldn't remember. He didn't want to give himself away, so he stood there, silent, and watched her go inside.

The moment she shut the door, he hurried up the road as fast as he could, toward the doctor's house. Enough was enough. He had to tell Haven everything, the whole truth. About the blackouts. About the rages. He thought of the Land Girl, murdered under the willows. Good God, if he was the one who had hurt her . . . Well, he didn't know what. He would just have to take what was coming to him, that's all. Maybe the authorities would consider his injuries and show mercy. Maybe they would consider his service and decide not to hang him.

Maybe they would understand. It was the war. The war had changed everything.

The doctor's house was lighted inside, but when Brooks knocked no one answered. He tried the door. It was unlocked. He slipped inside quickly, as if escaping a pursuer. He called out from the foyer: "Doctor. It's Brooks." No answer. He was already so agitated, so fearful, that he immediately grew concerned. He stepped into the sitting room and called again, "Doctor?"

When there was still no answer, he looked around. He saw the door on the far wall, the door to the bedroom that was always closed.

"Doctor?" he said again, more softly now. He was already moving toward the door. Another moment and the knob was in his hand. He was turning it. The door was coming open. The lights were on in the bedroom too, as if someone had just stepped out and would be back any moment. Standing on the threshold, Brooks saw the four-poster bed, and the dresser with the mirror on it, and the door into the bathroom.

And he saw the box and the picture of Emma.

The box was a slatted milk crate, wholly out of place in that setting. It was sticking out from under the bed, as if someone had tried to hide it there in a hurry but hadn't quite managed to shove it under all the way. The box was stacked full of papers. Brooks could see the photograph of Emma lying on top, and through the slats he could see the yellowed pages underneath it.

The sense of urgency that had driven him here was immediately replaced by the impulse—the *desire*—to have another look at that photograph. It was as if he thought he had stumbled on the magic cure for his anxiety and his fear and his anger: her image. Her image to replace the images in his mind, her world to replace this world. Before he even considered what he was doing, he was moving across the small room toward the bed, toward the crate. *Just a glance*, he was thinking. And then he was lifting the picture of Emma in both hands and gazing down at it, his soul hungry for her.

But he was distracted by what he saw on the pages beneath,

the headlines he saw on the old yellowed newspapers in the crate. The moment he read the words there, they set off a series of associations in him, memories linked to memories. The doctor's reluctance to discuss the past. The hospital where he'd worked in London's East End, where men were dying of syphilis. Emma, his beloved wife, who had died in childbirth in the late spring of 1888. And then these newspapers—these headlines—these *souvenirs* of the spate of bloody, rage-filled murders that had begun only a few weeks later—murders of prostitutes in the East End near the hospital—in Whitechapel.

Even before the series of thoughts was finished, Brooks was running. Out of the house. Through the night. Back up the road toward Nancy's cottage. He saw them before he reached the door. Saw their silhouettes in the moonlight moving over the sloping grass toward the river. The woman, rigid with fear; the man, with one hand gripping her arm, the other held out of sight close to her midsection, as he led her away from the road and down toward the trees and the deep shadows.

Brooks charged them, screaming wildly, as he had charged screaming out of his trench and raced across the dead fields of France. Haven heard the sound and turned and saw him coming. The doctor pushed Nancy aside and brought his arm sweeping up in a vicious arc toward Brooks's throat, the dagger flashing in his hand.

Brooks halted fast and dodged back and the blade went by him. Then he stepped in close and blocked the doctor's knife arm and punched him in the chin. Haven staggered back as Brooks stalked after him, crouched low, fists raised. The doctor's eyes flashed just as the knife had flashed.

"You had to bring it all back," Haven said in a broken whine. "I begged you not to."

With that, he turned and ran for it.

On instinct Brooks took a step after him, but then he remembered Nancy and stopped. He turned back to her, went to her, took her arm, his eyes traveling over her, looking for blood.

"Are you all right?"

She managed to nod, but she was crying hard and had no voice. In his relief, Brooks held her to himself and stroked her hair. Only after several minutes did she manage to sob out some words. "He came . . . right after you left . . . I thought it was you . . ."

Brooks didn't answer. But he understood: The doctor had been watching him. Using him. Using his rages, his blackouts, his confusion. Because Haven knew he could set Brooks up for his own crimes. Gently he held Nancy away at arm's length. "Don't be afraid. We'll go get help, we'll . . ."

But something caught her eye over his shoulder, and she cried out, "Behind you!"

Behind him, up away from the river, down the road, there was a dancing flicker of fire, painfully bright and alive in the darkness. Brooks knew what it was immediately. He sent Nancy to raise the alarm and ran toward the flames alone.

By the time he reached the doctor's cottage, it was fully ablaze. He could see the fire inside through the window, like some sort of multi-tentacled creature dismantling and devouring the walls, already starting to reach up through the rafters into the night.

And there was the doctor, Haven, calmly standing at the window. The sitting room behind him—the room where he and Brooks had talked together—was just beginning to burn. Brooks pulled up on the road outside and stood still, looking through the pane at the older man. Haven was holding the photograph of Emma in his two hands, just as Brooks had held it. He was looking down at her image in a dazed confusion of sorrow and terrible longing.

Then, perhaps sensing Brooks's presence outside, Haven lowered the photograph and raised his eyes. The two men looked at one another through the glass. Brooks saw black smoke curling up over the plush furniture and the flocked wallpaper. He saw red flames gleefully licking at the plates and pastoral paintings on the wall and the knickknacks on the mantel and the portrait of the queen. Everything that surrounded Haven was burning as Brooks watched.

They gazed at each other for another long moment. One corner of the doctor's mouth lifted a little: that sad, wise smile. He lowered his chin in a nod, and Brooks felt a sense of release and surrender. Then the black smoke closed over the room like a curtain closing, and there was nothing left of the old house but flames.

Brooks turned away and began walking up the road toward The Chimes.

MARTIN LIMÓN

PX Christmas

FROM *The Usual Santas*

STAFF SERGEANT RILEY slapped his pointer against the flip chart and barked out the title of today's training session. "Suicide Prevention," he shouted. Then he lowered the pointer and paced in a small circle as if contemplating all the burdens of the universe. He looked up suddenly and aimed the pointer at me.

"Sueño. How many Eighth Army personnel committed suicide during last year's holiday season?"

I shook my head. "*Molla* the hell out of me."

He growled, glancing around the room. There were about thirty GIs in various stages of somnolence slouched listlessly in hard wooden seats. About half were 8th Army criminal investigation agents and the other half MPI, Military Police investigators.

Riley slammed his pointer on the table in front of him. "On your *feet!*" he shouted.

Slowly, every student rose to a mostly upright position. The last person up, as usual, was my investigative partner, Ernie Bascom.

"Okay, Bascom. Do you know who General Nettles is?"

"He's the *freaking* chief of staff," Ernie replied.

"Out*standing*," Riley said. "And do you know how many ways he can screw up your life if he takes a mind to?"

"About thirty?" Ernie ventured.

"At least," Riley said. "He can mess up your life and the life of every swinging dick in this room in about as many ways as you can imagine." Riley paused to let the dramatic tension grow. "And there's no doubt in my military mind that that's exactly what he'll do if the 8th Army Christmas suicide rate doesn't come down and come down *fast*. Is that understood?"

A few bored voices said, "Understood." Then someone asked, "Can we sit back down now?" Riley barked, "Take your *seats!*" Which everyone did.

My name is George Sueño. I'm an agent for the 8th United States Army Criminal Investigation Division in Seoul, Republic of Korea. Riley wasn't telling us anything we didn't know. When you're stationed overseas, pretty much constantly harassed by the pressures of military life, and Christmas rolls around and you're pulling patrol along the demilitarized zone between North and South Korea, life can become pretty depressing. Some guys fire a 7.62mm round into their cranium. Others eat a hand grenade. This, of course, causes quite a bit of consternation back home. Not only do the moms and dads and wives and brothers and sisters complain about the suicide rate, but, more importantly—as far as the honchos of 8th Army are concerned—Congress complains about it. And Congress controls military funding. So the Department of the Army rolls the shitball downhill from the Pentagon to the Pacific Command to 8th Army headquarters to the provost marshal's office until it splats into those of us working law enforcement on the front lines.

Now that Riley had our attention, he said, "You're probably wondering what law enforcement personnel have to do with suicide prevention." Then he grinned, taking on the visage of a death's head. "The chief of staff is initiating a new program. We're going to be proactive. All personnel who seem to be displaying evidence of depression or suicidal thoughts will be placed in the new twenty-four-hour, seven-day-a-week Suicide Prevention Program. They'll be provided counseling and psychiatric treatment if necessary and they'll be kept under observation at all times."

"They'll be locked up," Ernie said.

Riley glared at him. "Not locked up. They'll be provided extra care. And extra training. We want to make sure they make it through the season without harming themselves."

Another of the investigators raised his hand. "Once they're stuck in this Suicide Prevention Program, will they be allowed to leave?"

Riley looked embarrassed and turned to his flip chart. After tossing back a few sheets, he found his answer. "They'll be allowed to leave upon release by medical personnel and the OIC." The officer in charge.

"So they'll be locked up," Ernie repeated.

"Can it, Bascom," Riley told him.

"What about us?" another guy asked. "What are we supposed to do?"

"You'll be picking them up."

"You mean, taking them into custody."

Riley shrugged. "It's thought that since CID agents and MP investigators work in civilian clothes, it will be less obtrusive if you take them in rather than having armed and uniformed MPs make the pickup."

"You want to make it look as if we're not treating them as criminals."

"Which we are," Ernie added.

"I told you to *can* it, Bascom."

Riley flipped through the sheets until he found a map of the Korean Peninsula. Assignments were made based on geography, starting in Seoul, then working south and north. We'd be receiving a list daily as to who to pick up, the name of the unit they were assigned to, and where they worked. Then we were to transport them over to the new Suicide Prevention facility behind the 121st Evacuation Hospital here on Yongsan Compound South Post.

"Any questions?" Riley shouted.

Ernie raised his hand. "What about me and Sueño? You didn't give us an assignment."

"You two are staying on the black market detail."

A guffaw went up from the crowd. Some wise guy said, "Somebody has to protect the PX from the *yobos*." The derogatory term for the Korean wives of enlisted soldiers.

Ernie flipped him the bird.

As everyone filed out of the training room, somebody murmured, "Lock 'em up. That'll help lift their spirits."

We sat in Ernie's jeep outside of the Yongsan Main PX, the largest U.S. Army Post Exchange in Korea. With only ten shopping days until Christmas, the place was packed.

"I don't get it," Ernie said. "What the hell are they *buying*?"

"Presents," I said.

"Like *what*?"

Ernie stared at me, honestly wanting an answer.

"Like toys for kids," I told him, "or clothes for the family or decorations for the house. How the hell would I know?"

We were both single, in our twenties, and we both lived in the barracks. About the only things we ever purchased were laundry soap and shoe polish for the Korean houseboys to make our beds and keep our uniforms looking sharp. And consumables, like beer, liquor, and the occasional meal of *kalbi,* marinated short ribs, or *yakimandu,* fried dumplings dipped in soy sauce. That was about all we ever went shopping for.

Here in the mid-1970s, in the middle of the Cold War, one would've thought that the honchos of 8th Army would've been primarily concerned about the 700,000 Communist North Korean soldiers just thirty miles north of here along the Korean DMZ and the fact that war could break out at any moment. One would've been wrong. What seemed to obsess the 8th Army bosses most was stopping the black marketing out of the PX and the commissary.

Twenty years ago, at the end of the Korean War, the economy of the ROK was flat on its back. In Seoul and almost every other city in the country, hardly a building remained standing. Even the rice paddies, which had been plowed out of the fertile earth millennia ago, were fallow and overgrown with weeds. During the fighting that raged up and down the peninsula, virtually everyone had become a refugee. And those were the lucky ones. Estimates varied, but it was believed that between 2 and 3 million Koreans had been killed during the war, this out of a population of about 25 million. Things were getting better. People for the most part had roofs over their heads and were employed. However, wages were desperately low, and if you cleared a hundred bucks a month you were doing just fine.

Still, the demand for imported products was growing. Such things as American cigarettes, blended scotch, maraschino cherries, freeze-dried coffee, instant orange juice, and powdered milk. The Korean economy wasn't producing those things. Not yet. And it was a crime for GIs to buy such items on base and sell them off base. The official reason was supposedly so fledgling Korean industries wouldn't have to compete with cheap foreign products, thereby giving them a chance to grow.

The real reason was more visceral. On a crowded shopping day like today, American officers and their wives hated to stand in long lines behind the *yobos,* the Korean wives of GIs. Once legally married, the Korean wife was issued a military dependent ID card so she could come on base, and a ration control plate, which allowed her to buy a specified dollar amount each month in the PX and the commissary. Some of the wives resold what they purchased to black marketeers for twice or even three times what they paid for it. The extra money, for the most part, wasn't wasted. Often they had elderly parents to take care of or younger brothers and sisters to support. The money garnered from black marketing could often be the difference between continued misery for a family versus having a sporting chance to rise out of poverty. However, the 8th Army honchos didn't look at that side of it. They only knew that *their* PX and *their* commissary were being invaded by foreigners.

It was my job, and Ernie's, to arrest these women for black marketing and thus keep the world safe for colonels and their wives to be able to buy all the Tang and Spam and Pop-Tarts their little hearts desired.

"So who should we bust?" Ernie asked.

We were watching the women parade out of the front door of the PX, pushing their carts toward the taxi line.

"Those illuminated nativity scenes seem to be popular this year," I said.

"What?"

"Those." I pointed. "In the large cardboard box. Cheap plastic replicas of a manger and three wise men bowing before Baby Jesus. Just screw in a bulb and plug it into the wall."

"Koreans buy those?"

"Yeah. It makes sense. They can keep it indoors. Makes them seem modern."

"Modern? That happened two thousand years ago."

"Christianity came to Korea less than a century ago."

"They consider that modern?"

"Korea's four thousand years old, Ernie."

"Damn. People have been eating *kimchi* and rice all that time?"

I ignored him and studied the line. "Let's make one bust this morning and another this afternoon. That should keep the provost marshal off our butts."

"How about her?" Ernie said.

A statuesque young Korean woman wearing her black hair up in a bun and a blue dress that clung to her figure pushed a cart toward the taxi stand. The wait wasn't long. A black-jacketed Korean cabdriver helped her put her bags in the trunk of his big Ford Granada, including one of the illuminated nativity scenes. After she was seated in back, the driver drove off. Ernie and I followed.

The driver wound his way through the narrow lanes of the district known as Itaewon and finally came to a stop in front of a wooden double door in a ten-foot-high stone fence. Keeping well back, Ernie stopped the jeep and I climbed out and crept up to the alleyway and peered around the corner. The trunk remained open as the statuesque woman conferred with an elderly woman whom Ernie and I both recognized as a well-known black market mama-san. Money changed hands and then some product. I motioned to Ernie and he started the jeep's engine and rolled forward, blocking the taxi's escape. I hurried forward, showed the woman my badge, and told her she was under arrest for the illegal sale of PX-purchased goods. Even in the U.S. it's illegal to resell PX goods. The idea is that the shipment and the warehousing of the goods is subsidized by the U.S. taxpayer, to keep prices low for servicemen and their families. To resell under those conditions would be to rip off the taxpayer who is footing much of the bill.

We had no jurisdiction over the mama-san who purchased the goods. We could've reported her to the Korean National Police, but they already knew about her operation and were probably receiving a cut of her profits. We didn't bother. The younger woman was nervous and close to tears but willing to comply. Ernie pulled forward and allowed the cabdriver to leave. Then we sat the distraught woman in the back of the jeep and drove her to the 8th Army MP station.

While I filled out the arrest report, Ernie called her husband, one Roland R. Garfield, specialist four, assigned to the 19th Support Group, Electronic Repair Detachment (Mobile). When he arrived his face was grim. His wife, whose name I'd determined was Sooki, nervously fondled a pink handkerchief and dabbed tears from her eyes.

He was a slender man, with moist brown eyes and a narrow face that was filled out by surprisingly full cheeks. I didn't bother to shake his hand. He didn't seem to be in the mood. I showed him the arrest report, had him sign it, and turned over an onion-skin copy.

"You're responsible at all times for the actions of your dependent," I told him.

"I know that."

"You'll retain PX and commissary privileges, but the amount of the monthly ration will be reduced." By about ninety percent, but I saw no reason to rub it in. "Take this form over to Ration Control and they'll issue you and your wife new plates."

He nodded but said nothing. His wife continued to stare at the floor.

"Kuenchana," he said to her. It doesn't matter.

That made her cry more.

After coaxing her to stand, he held her elbow lightly, and they walked out the door.

The Suicide Prevention Program was going swimmingly. After only two days, according to Riley, the original facility was full and more Quonset huts had to be identified to provide housing for the "inmates," as he was now calling them. In fact, the program was going so well that Ernie and I were taken off the black market detail and handed a list of a half-dozen GIs to pick up.

I showed the list to Ernie. "Look at this," I said, pointing.

"Garfield, spec four," he read. "Yeah. What of it?"

"That's the guy whose wife we busted for black market a few days ago."

"Oh, yeah. The tall gal in the blue dress."

"Yeah. Her."

"Garfield didn't seem so depressed then. Pissed off, sure, but not depressed."

"Guess you never know."

"No, I guess you don't."

We picked up everyone on the list, saving Garfield for last.

When he emerged from the back of the electronics truck, his fleshy cheeks were covered with bruises.

"What the hell happened to you?" Ernie asked.

Garfield glanced around. No one seemed to be within earshot but he said, "Not here."

We'd already given the paperwork to his commanding officer, so we had him hop in back of the jeep and we drove him over to the

121st Evac. In the gravel lot in front of the new Suicide Prevention Center he said, "I need your help."

I turned in my seat and looked at him. "What is it?"

"My wife." He hung his head for a few seconds and looked back up at me. "She took the black market bust pretty hard. I told her to forget it, but it means a lot to her. The money she was making she was sending to her family. I knew about it, but I didn't put a stop to it. Her father's sick and her mother still has a son and a daughter of school age, and they can't even afford uniforms, much less the tuition."

Ernie and I sat silently, waiting.

"She went to Mukyo-dong," he said. "Do you know where that is?"

"Sure," Ernie replied. "The high-class nightclub district in downtown Seoul."

"Most GIs don't know about it," Garfield said.

"Most GIs can't afford their prices."

"Right. Sooki's resourceful, and good-looking. You saw that. She landed a job. Dancing, I think. Maybe as a hostess. Serving drinks and lighting cigarettes for those rich Japanese businessmen. I told her to stop, but she said she had no choice. If she stopped sending money home, her brother and sister would have to drop out of school, and worse, they'd probably go hungry."

"How about your paycheck?" Ernie asked.

"We're barely making the rent as it is. We can send some, but not enough."

"You're not command-sponsored?"

"No."

Officers and higher-ranking NCOs often are assigned to billets that are considered "command-sponsored." That is, although Korea is generally considered an "unaccompanied" tour, if you are command-sponsored you can bring your wife and children over here and you're given a housing allowance to help you make the outrageous downtown Seoul rents. Low-ranking enlisted men, like Garfield, are seldom offered command sponsorship—especially if they have Korean wives.

"Okay," I said. "Things are tough. I get that. What do you want us to do?"

"She didn't come home," he told me. "For two nights in a row.

Last night I went down there, to the nightclub where she works. The sons of bitches wouldn't let me see her. I tried to push my way in and the bastards did this to me."

He touched the bruises on his cheek and then unbuttoned his fatigue shirt. Red welts lined a row of ribs.

"When the CO saw me this morning, he asked me what had happened. I couldn't tell him. I didn't want the entire unit to know what she's doing."

"So he called Suicide Prevention," Ernie said.

"Seems like the popular thing to do these days." He shook his head and rebuttoned his shirt. "I'll break out of this place," he said, nodding toward the Suicide Prevention Center. "And this time I'll take something with me."

"You mean like a weapon?"

"That's exactly what I mean. For all I know, they're holding Sooki against her will."

"Unlikely," I said. "She's probably fine."

"Says you."

Ernie and I looked at each other. He grinned and said, "Hell, I haven't been to Mukyo-dong in ages."

Garfield's eyes lit up. "You'll check on her for me?"

I was of two minds. Getting between a husband and wife always spelled trouble. But we couldn't let Garfield go down there with blood in his eye. By getting beaten up, he'd already proven that he didn't know what he was doing. "All right," I said, "my partner and I will go down there for you. Tonight. We'll check on her and make sure she's all right. But that's it."

Garfield patted his pockets. "I don't have much money. It's expensive down there."

"Don't worry," Ernie replied. "My partner here is rolling in dough."

Inwardly, I groaned.

"I don't know how to thank you."

"Wait until tomorrow," I said. "Thank us then."

According to Specialist Four Garfield, the name of the nightclub Sooki was working in was the Golden Dragon. He didn't know the Korean name, which is sometimes different than the English translation, but I made a guess and asked our cabdriver to find a place called the Kulryong or something with a similar name. Mukyo-dong parallels a bustling main road lined with two huge department stores and smaller boutique shops catering to the upwardly mobile elite of South Korea. Down the side streets, barely wide enough for a Hyundai sedan, is where the action is. Especially at night. First open-air chophouses serving noodles and live fish in tanks and various delicacies such as octopus marinated in hot pepper sauce. Then, down even narrower lanes, stone pathways lead to bars and underground nightclubs. Some of them blare rock and roll for youngsters, others are designed for the packs of businessmen in suits wandering drunkenly from one flashing neon sign to another.

The driver stepped on his brakes and pointed down a flight of steps. "Kulryong Lou," he said. The Chamber of the Golden Dragon.

Ernie spotted a shimmering golden serpent. "This must be it," he said.

I paid the driver and we climbed out. Just as we did so, a black sedan pulled up below in a narrow road on the far side of the Golden Dragon. A liveried doorman in white gloves opened the back door and out popped three businessmen in what appeared to be expensive suits.

"Class joint," Ernie said. "They're going to be happy to see us."

Down here GIs are considered to be Cheap Charlies, and our presence only upsets the more free-spending Japanese and Korean clientele, who don't necessarily want crude barbarian GIs intruding on their space.

"Front door?" Ernie asked.

"No," I said. "Let's try the back."

The chain-link fence behind the nightclub was locked. Inside, in an area about the size of a two-car garage, trash cans were lined up and stacked wooden cases held empty beer and *soju* bottles.

"After you, maestro," Ernie said.

I grabbed a spread-fingered hold on the chain link and pulled myself up. The tricky part was at the top. I swung my leg over rusty razor wire and managed by stretching and then twisting like a ballerina to grab a toehold on the other side. Gingerly I swung my crotch and then my other leg after. Once I grabbed another handhold, I dropped to the ground. Ernie climbed over, performing the same procedure in about half the time.

I'm a land animal. Whenever possible, I keep two feet on the ground.

The back door to the Golden Dragon was locked.

"Apparently they've had unexpected visitors before," Ernie said.

So we crouched on either side of the door and waited.

"Kokchong hajimaseyo," I told the elderly cook as we pushed him down the hallway. Don't worry.

He'd popped the back door open carrying a bag of garbage, and Ernie'd been on him before he could pull it shut. I continued speaking to him in Korean. "Do you know who Sooki is?"

He shook his head.

"Tall woman," I said. "Only started work two or three days ago."

He claimed ignorance, which figured, because an old man like this doing the drudge work in the kitchen would have little or nothing to do with the elegant young female hostesses.

When we reached the kitchen, I let him go and thanked him for his patience. He stared at me, completely befuddled. Some Koreans have had little or no contact with foreigners, and when they hear one of us speak their language, to them it's like hearing a chimpanzee recite Shakespeare. Through a double door, the floor turned from tile to carpet and I knew we were close. Finally we entered a sizable hall with an elevated ceiling. On the right stretched a long bar; the wall on the left side of the room arced in a graceful curve lined with high-backed plush leather booths. In the center of the room were a half-dozen tables draped in white linen.

Ernie and I held back, peering over a paneled room divider. He scanned the left, I scanned the right.

"There she is," I said.

"Where?"

I pointed. "In that booth. You can barely see her. She's against the wall, behind those two businessmen."

"We could wait until she goes to the ladies' room."

"No way. We're lucky the bouncers haven't spotted us already."

"Then there's no time like the present."

Ernie stepped out from behind the divider and started walking across the room. A few people looked up from their drinks, and then more. The mouths of some of the elegantly dressed hostesses fell open. Apparently the elderly kitchen worker had dropped a dime on us, because hurried steps approached from the hallway behind me. Near the front entrance, two men peered in to see what was causing the commotion.

Ernie stood in front of the booth that contained Sooki, also known as Mrs. Roland R. Garfield, and started speaking to her in English. She didn't look up at him but instead peered straight down at the table. Ashamed.

One of the businessmen seated next to her said, *"Igon dodechei muoya?"* What the hell is this?

The bouncers approached Ernie, and one of them grabbed his elbow. He swung his fist back fiercely and shouted at them to keep their hands off him. I hurried across the room, holding my badge up and shouting *"Kyongchal!"* Police.

Apparently they weren't impressed. Another bouncer approached me from behind, and as I was explaining to him that we were here on police business, Ernie punched somebody. And then they were wrestling, two men on Ernie, and I tried to pull one of them off him and then somebody was on me and in a big sweating mass we knocked over first one table and then another. Women screamed and men cursed and soon I was on the floor.

Ernie managed to keep his feet and was winging big roundhouse rights when the front door burst open and a shrill whistle sounded. Cops. The next thing I knew I was in handcuffs and heading toward the rear door of a Korean National Police paddy wagon.

A crowd of upset customers gathered in front. Some of the hostesses were wide-eyed and clinging to one another. One of them was crying. But Sooki Garfield was nowhere to be seen.

Ernie was shoved into the back door of the wagon, and after cussing out his assailants he slid over on the bench next to me.

"Assholes," he said. When they shut the door, he reached in his pocket and pulled out a liter bottle of *soju*. I stared at him with a puzzled look. "Grabbed it on the way out," he said. Then he pried off the cap with his teeth, took a swig, wiped the lip clean, and offered the bottle of rice liquor to me. Grasping it with two hands, I tossed back a glug and then coughed, feeling it burn all the way down.

"At least we know Sooki's all right," Ernie said.

"Maybe," I replied.

"Why? What are you worried about?"

"They're pissed now. And they know she's a *yang kalbo*." A GI whore.

"She's not a *yang kalbo*," Ernie said. "She's a wife."

"Same difference to them."

Ernie raised the *soju* bottle and sipped thoughtfully. "Maybe you're right," he said.

Captain Gil Kwon-up of the Korean National Police allowed me to use the telephone on his desk. It took twenty minutes to get through to the Yongsan Compound exchange and two minutes after that I was talking to Staff Sergeant Riley.

"We're going to be late," I told him.

"*Late?* You're supposed to be in this office standing tall at zero eight hundred hours." I imagined him checking his watch. "You have fifteen minutes."

"Like I told you," I said. "We're going to be late. We're tracking down a lead."

He sputtered, and before he could form words, I hung up the phone.

"Everything all right?" Mr. Kill asked me.

"Just fine," I told him. "They're very understanding."

We called him Mr. Kill, a GI corruption of his real name, Gil. It made a certain kind of sense, since he was the chief homicide inspector for the Korean National Police. Ernie and I knew him well after working a number of cases with him.

After taking in a GI, normal procedure is for the KNPs to call the U.S. Army Military Police. Last night I headed that off by speaking to the desk sergeant in Korean and explaining to him that I knew Mr. Kill, and stretched the truth by claiming that we were currently working with him on a case. He was suspicious but didn't want to risk irritating a superior officer, so he said he'd wait until the next morning to confirm my statement with Kill. Ernie and I spent the night in our own cell, segregated from the raving lunatics in the drunk tank. Special treatment for foreigners. True to his word, the desk sergeant contacted Gil Kwon-up first thing in the morning, and he'd immediately ordered that we be brought up to his office.

"What's her name?" Mr. Kill asked me. I didn't know Sooki's full Korean name. Sooki was a nickname, probably short for Sook-ja or Sook-ai, or something close to that. Her legal name now was Mrs. Roland R. Garfield. He jotted the information down and I gave him her general description.

Then he looked up at me. He'd been educated in the States and his English was excellent. "Why didn't you contact me," he asked, "before almost starting a riot in the Golden Dragon?"

"Sorry," I said.

The truth was, I didn't like to bother him unless I had to. He was too valuable a resource.

He pressed the intercom button on his desk and spoke to another officer. I didn't understand everything that was said, but the gist of it was that he ordered two men to go over to the Golden Dragon and pick up the woman called Sooki and bring her in. It was going to take some time. While we waited, Ernie and I sat outside on two hard chairs in the hallway. Ernie was already snoring and I'd started to doze when Mr. Kill appeared in front of us. My eyes popped open.

"She's disappeared," he said.

Once he realized I was fully alert, he continued. "The thugs who own the Golden Dragon are well known to us. We took one of them in and we had Mr. Bam have a little talk with him."

Bam was the lead KNP interrogator.

"According to what he told us, orders came down to pull Mrs. Garfield out of the Golden Dragon and send her to one of their subsidiary operations."

Ernie was awake now. "Subsidiary operations?" he said.

"Yes. A brothel." He handed me a folded sheet of paper. "I won't be able to help you further."

"Why not?" Ernie asked.

Mr. Kill just stared at him, saying nothing. He looked at me, seeing if I understood. I did.

"How high does it go?" I asked.

"Within the police hierarchy," Mr. Kill answered. "Not higher. Which leaves you a certain latitude."

I nodded. "Thank you, sir, for this information."

Then he said, "One more thing. The man in charge of the operation is known as Huk. A Manchurian name. You are aware that Manchuria invaded us a few centuries ago?"

"Yes, sir. I know."

"Be very careful when dealing with him. You'll be on your own. My colleagues and I need to keep our hands off this operation for as long as we are able."

Mr. Kill held eye contact with me until he was sure I understood, then swiveled on the cement floor and strode briskly away.

Ernie glanced at me. Confused.

"What just happened?"

I took a deep breath. "Mr. Kill can't do anything officially," I said, keeping my voice down.

"Why not?"

"Think about it," I told him. "This guy Huk, whoever he is, not only runs the Golden Dragon but also has subsidiary brothels. He makes a lot of money and couldn't be doing that unless he had protection."

Ernie nodded, getting it now. "Somebody high up in the police hierarchy is protecting him."

"Yes," I said, standing up. "Mr. Kill doesn't like it, but that's the world he lives in."

"So Huk's protected," Ernie said.

"Yes. He's protected from the Korean National Police." I paused, thinking it over. "But he's not protected from us."

Relations with the U.S. military are considered to be so important that they are reserved for the very highest levels of government: for President Park Chung-hee and his most trusted advisors. Whoever was protecting Huk wouldn't have that much pull and therefore wouldn't have a chance in hell of calling off American law enforcement. Mr. Kill was making it clear to me that although his hands were tied, Ernie and I had an open field for action.

I stuck the sheet of paper in my breast pocket, and Ernie and I hurried out of the police station.

Back at the CID office, I found the address Mr. Kill had given me on our wall-sized map of Seoul.

"Here," I told Ernie.

"Why'd they send her there?"

"They're pissed. She caused a disruption. Embarrassed them."

"*We* caused the disruption," Ernie said.

"Because of her. And she has a ration control plate. They'll probably work her two ways. Not only in the brothel but probably by forcing her to buy beyond her ration at the PX and commissary."

"She'll be caught."

"But not for a month or two. It takes that long for the reports to be collated. Only then will the ration control violations make their way to Garfield's unit commander."

"And he might not act right away."

"That's what they're hoping for."

"How can they do this?" Ernie asked. "Okay, I get it. The KNPs won't touch this guy, Huk, but why doesn't she look for her own chance and then run away?"

"Because now they know her situation and they know the jam she's in. You can bet that they already have a bead on her mother and her brother and her sister and are using them to threaten her."

"What kind of country *is* this?" Ernie asked.

I shrugged. "It's like most countries. Big money talks. Women are expendable."

"So are GIs," Ernie replied.

Riley volunteered to be the first in.

"About time we kicked some ass," he said.

"Easy, Tiger," I told him. "We have a plan, remember? You need to follow it."

"Sure. A commando raid. I get it."

"No. We're faking an MP bust. That's it."

The midnight curfew would hit in a little more than an hour, and the entire city of Seoul would shut down. We sat in the shadows in a neighborhood near the Han River known as Ichon-dong. Ernie's jeep was parked about a half-block from a dilapidated three-story wooden building that looked as if it had been built on the cheap and would fall down during the next strong wind. So far we'd seen working-class Korean men go in, linger, and come out about a half-hour later, and we'd seen women's silhouettes in the upstairs windows. Light from a dirty yellow bulb flooded down a short flight of steps at the entranceway.

Ernie sat behind the steering wheel, I sat in the passenger seat, and Staff Sergeant Riley and the fourth member of our "commando team," Sergeant First Class Harvey, better known as Strange, sat in back. He had a reputation for being a pervert, but on this mission all I required was that he be dressed in fatigues and one of the MP helmets I'd borrowed—and that he be armed with an M16 rifle. Riley was similarly outfitted. Their job was not to shoot anyone but to back us up as we ran our bluff.

Ernie and I had come up with the plan this afternoon. We couldn't go to the provost marshal and ask for a detachment of real MPs to help us, because what we were planning to do wasn't only outside of our jurisdiction, it was illegal. Plenty illegal. So we had to enlist the only two guys we knew who were crazy enough to help: Riley and Strange.

"How about this guy Huk?" Strange asked. "He must be a pretty cool customer."

"Not cool," I replied. "According to Mr. Kill, he started as a petty thief after the war and worked his way up to becoming a pimp, and after he landed a few well-placed connections he graduated to becoming a nightclub owner."

"How are we going to recognize him?"

"He has a disfigured nose. 'Mangled' is the word Mr. Kill used."

"Lost it in a knife fight?"

"No. Nothing so glamorous. Not all of Huk's girls knuckle under to him. Apparently somewhere along the line one of them fought back. According to Mr. Kill, she not only bit into his nose but almost chewed his face off."

"Korean women are *bold*," Riley said, almost in awe.

"What happened to her?" Strange asked.

I glanced toward the Han River. It was only two blocks downhill and glistened in the wavering moonlight. "What do you think?"

After a moment of silence, Riley spoke up. "You sure his office is here?"

"Yes. He never goes to the Golden Dragon or his other properties. Frightens the customers. He stays here in the slums, pulling the strings."

"In the mud where he came from," Ernie said.

"All right," I said. "Everybody has a job to do. Let's go over it one more time."

We did. It was a simple plan, brutal but elegant. If we only had to grab Sooki and return her to her husband, life would've been easy. But it was more complicated than that. We had to assume that Huk and his boys knew about her family, knew where they lived, and they knew how to find them. That was their modus operandi and the secret of their control. Promise the women they trafficked that if they didn't do exactly as they were told, their families would pay with their lives. So we had to liberate not only Sooki but also her family from the threat of Huk and his gang of thugs.

After the verbal rehearsal, I said, "Okay, everybody got it?"

Three nods.

"According to Mr. Kill, Huk's office and his living quarters are on the third floor. That's where I'm going. So don't shoot me on the way down."

Strange waggled his cigarette holder.

"And you better take off those damn shades," I told him.

"What? And ruin my style?"

"To hell with your style," Ernie said. "Do what the man says."

Strange took off his sunglasses and stuck them in the breast pocket of his fatigue shirt. Now I understood why he wore them. His eyes were like desiccated green olives lost in a moist excretion of dough.

We climbed out of the jeep. Ernie took the lead, holding his .45 pointed at the sky. Riley and Strange ran after him across the street and the three of them burst into the entranceway to the Ichondong brothel. Once inside, Ernie blasted his whistle and started shouting. Riley and Strange fanned out upstairs to the second floor like we practiced. They were also shouting. It didn't matter much what they said, because English would be incomprehensible to these people anyway. It was their job to make sure that everyone understood that this was a raid by the Military Police and to intimidate the customers and move them out while at the same time herding the girls into a safe place. It was Ernie's job to find Sooki.

My job was to grab Huk.

The central staircase was made of cement. Korean men in various stages of undress flooded out, frantic to escape before we placed them under arrest. I pushed against the descending crowd, running upstairs two steps at a time. On the third floor, a long hallway greeted me. At first I didn't see any doors. Just flimsy curtains and thin blankets hanging from a network of overhead wire. Inside these makeshift partitions, cots and mats were arrayed at odd angles and female clothing hung from metal hooks. At the end of the hallway loomed a wooden door. A cement wall partitioned this end of the third floor, and this had to be Huk's office and living quarters.

I kicked the door in.

He was standing, arms akimbo, staring right at me. He was a small man, wearing blue jeans and sneakers and some sort of red-checked shirt with long sleeves and a collar. If he put on a Stetson, he would've looked like a short Asian cowboy. His face was square, almost wider than it was long, and the mangled scars on his face, from eyes to chin, seemed immobile. Dark eyes smoldered through squinting lids. His fists were clenched and he was slightly hunched over, as if prepared to take a blow.

And, to my relief, he was unarmed.

Behind him sat a rickety wooden desk and a diesel space heater and what appeared to be a pilfered army cot. The desk supported a large red phone atop a knitted pad. He reached for the phone. I fired a round into the wall.

Apparently that convinced him I meant business. He held perfectly still.

"*Iriwara!*" I told him, in very disrespectful Korean. *Come here!*

He hesitated but then stepped slowly toward me. I ordered him to turn around and I cuffed his hands behind his back. Grabbing a knot of his curly black hair, I pushed him outside his office and held the .45 against his back as we stepped downstairs. Ernie had located Sooki. She was crying and covering her face.

Strange and Riley joined us, both of them panting and sweating, their faces flushed red with victory. Mr. Kill had already warned the local KNPs to back off and not respond to any calls that might come from the Ichon-dong brothel. At least not too quickly. Still, I didn't want to press our luck.

"*Kapshida!*" I said. Let's go.

Everyone understood and we ran outside and down the stairs and across the dark street to the jeep.

Ernie drove. I sat up front with Huk kneeling on the metal floor in front of the passenger seat. Every time he squirmed, I kicked him. Riley had left his green army sedan parked near the Han-gang Railroad Bridge. When we pulled up next to the sedan, Riley and Strange hopped out. They took Sooki with them. I thanked them for their help. Ernie warned them not to shoot themselves with their M16s. As they drove off, Sooki sat in the back seat of the sedan, still crying.

Ernie and I sat alone in the quiet night with Huk, watching the string of lights that spanned the bridge. A slowly rising moon illuminated a few small fishing boats straggling back to their home ports.

"How soon until the next train?" Ernie asked.

"One last train comes in from Pusan just before the midnight curfew. Should be along soon."

We pulled Huk out of the jeep. The expression on his face, such as it was, didn't change. I spoke to him in Korean.

"Sooki doesn't belong to you anymore," I told him. When he didn't answer, I continued. "You will not bother her in the future and you will not bother her family. Do you understand?"

Again he just stared at me, eyes squinting, mangled face impassive. Ernie slugged him in the stomach. When he came up for air, the only change in his face was a bubbling gasp from his small round mouth.

We walked him toward the railroad tracks. There was no one out here, just a few abandoned warehouses and what appeared to be cats prowling for rats.

"You understand," I told him. "You can't get to us. We live on the U.S. military compound. You have no power there. Your thugs can't gain entry, and even if they could, it's a big compound and they have no idea where to find us. We're safe from you." I shoved his narrow shoulders and he knelt into gravel. Deftly Ernie pushed the tip of a short bicycle chain beneath a crosstie and, using the jeep's crowbar, dug a pathway for the chain under the thick plank. Once it was through, he locked the two ends together and then, as Huk stared at his work, he unlocked one of his cuffs and looped it through the bicycle chain and relocked it with a snap.

Huk now knelt in the center of the railroad tracks, like a worshiper waiting for the next train. Ernie switched on his flashlight to make sure Huk could fully appreciate his predicament. A trickle of sweat formed just above Huk's eyebrows. He had yet to speak a word.

I knelt next to him.

"You must promise us not to hurt Sooki, not to hurt her husband, and not to hurt Sooki's family. Once you do that, we will let you go."

Huk said nothing.

"If you break your promise," I continued, "then my friend and I will come after you. We know where your businesses are. We know how to find you. And the next time we won't be so nice. We will shoot you with one of these." I pressed the business end of my .45 up against the twisted mass of flesh that was his nose. "The Korean National Police won't care. Not about you. And they won't care about us. They don't like to bother the U.S. Army. And their bosses in the Korean government don't like to bother the U.S. Army. No one will investigate your murder. No one will come on our compound to bother me or my friend. You will be dead. Someone else will take your place at the Golden Dragon and at the Ichon-dong brothel. Do you understand?"

His oddly shaped face still remained impassive and he said nothing.

"Dumb shit," Ernie said and kicked him.

I stood up. I had to admit that he was one tough cookie, and I could see why he'd risen to the top of the rackets. I was through wasting breath on him. Ernie and I walked back to the jeep. From this distance, about twenty yards, we watched Huk kneeling on the tracks.

I had no idea what was going through his mind. He didn't yank on the handcuffs, trying to get away. He just knelt there without moving.

Ernie glanced behind us. "Maybe he figures somebody is going to come and save him," he said.

"No way. He doesn't have thugs at the brothel because he doesn't need them. He's protected by the money he pays at a high level."

"Maybe those high-level people will catch wind of this and send the KNPs."

"I don't think so. My guess is that the KNPs are just as pissed about this setup as we are. Mr. Kill warned them off and they'll stay away. Even if the word comes down from on high that they need to save Huk, they'll hesitate. They can always claim that they didn't know where he was; which is true, they don't know."

"So we just stand here and watch him die?" Ernie said.

"That's the plan."

He glanced at me. "Can you handle it?"

"You saw those girls in the brothel," I replied. "Some of them still had their schoolgirl haircuts, just barely out of middle school. Did they have cigarette burns on their forearms? Bruises on their shoulders? I didn't have time to look, but I bet they did."

"They did," Ernie said.

"So I can stand here and watch this creep be run over and smashed into pieces."

Ernie grinned, staring at me, but said nothing further.

In the distance the train whistle sounded.

The train from Pusan emerged along the banks of the Han River on the western side of the district known as Yongdungpo. The name Yongdungpo is composed of three Chinese characters that mean, literally, Eternally Rising Port. Or, more poetically, the Port of Eternal Ascension. Eighth Army had a supply depot over there for many years, and there was a place GIs called the Green Door that old-timers told me was one of the raunchiest brothels in Korea. But that was controlled by a different organization, not Huk's. Whether or not he was thinking about this while the train reached the bank of the Han River and turned east and then about two miles later made the left turn toward the railroad bridge, I didn't know. But when the train did make the turn, we saw the front light of the locomotive shine almost halfway across the bridge. It was heading toward us at about thirty miles per hour, all the massive tonnage of it, and I calculated it would arrive on this side of the Han River in less than a minute.

Ernie and I leaned against the jeep, arms crossed, waiting. I'm sure he was expecting me to crack first, but as it turned out, it wasn't me, it was him.

"Maybe we should unlock him," he said.

"Why?" I asked.

"This is going to be messy. Blood and flesh and bone splashed all over the place."

"Yeah," I said. "I suppose it is going to be messy."

Ernie studied me. "Are you serious? Do you really want to go through with this?" When I didn't answer, he glanced at the approaching train. A whistle sounded. "We don't have much time."

I kept my arms crossed, my face impassive, and then we heard a choked yell.

"*Okay!*"

It was Huk. Just the one word, but that was good enough for me. I ran forward, reaching in my right pocket for the keys. They weren't there. And then I remembered. I'd given them to Ernie.

I turned and shouted. "The *keys!*"

But Ernie was already on it. He ran past me and knelt next to Huk and started fumbling with the handcuffs. The train was only a hundred yards away now, its front light so bright that both Ernie and Huk were illuminated by its fierce glow. A screaming whistle sounded a warning, shattering the night.

Ernie continued to fumble with the keys. I was just about to run forward and snatch them from him and unlock the cuffs myself when I heard the snap. Ernie leapt off the tracks and rolled toward the stanchions on the edge of the bridge. Huk pulled away but for a moment the cuffs caught on something, and then frantically he jerked them up and down until something released and, like the rat that he was, he scurried toward the stanchions next to Ernie. Mesmerized, I realized that I had to back away too, and stepped quickly toward the end of the bridge until I was safely out of the path of the train.

With a great whining and clattering, the train reached us and, like a monster of metal and steam, ground its great iron wheels past, parading the full length of its dragonlike body until it finally pulled away, shrieking regally, into the dark night.

I ran along the tracks, grabbed Huk, and retrieved my handcuffs. He remained kneeling on the edge of the tracks, facing the water below, his face and the back of his neck slathered in sweat. As a memento of our visit, I kicked him in the thigh. Hard. Like the tough little shit he was, he took it without a whimper.

We left him there, clinging to the stanchion, staring into the river.

On shaking legs, Ernie and I marched back to the jeep, jumped in, and drove away from the Han-gang Railroad Bridge.

"You're kidding me," Ernie said.

The next morning we had just stepped through the entranceway to the Yongsan Main PX and stood gazing past rows of consumer goods and milling crowds of shoppers. Against the far wall a dais had been set up for children to be introduced to Father Christmas.

"Not *him*," Ernie said.

"Yes, him," I replied.

"Not Strange."

Sergeant First Class Harvey, also known as Strange, sat on a throne in the center of the dais dressed in a fake white beard and a bright red Santa Claus outfit, greeting the children one by one.

"I guess the Officers' Wives Club doesn't know he's a pervert," I said.

We pushed our way through the crowds of shoppers until we stood in front of the dais. After one of the children hopped off his red-trousered lap, Strange looked over at us and responded to the quizzical look in our eyes.

"I was *volunteered*," he said.

One of the ladies controlling the tittering line of children sent another youngster up. Strange let out a *"Ho ho ho!"* and lifted the child to his lap.

"Watch his hands," Ernie whispered.

We did. For about twenty minutes. Apparently he was on the up-and-up. So far.

"I guess children aren't his particular perversion," Ernie told me.

"Let's watch him anyway."

I went back into the PX administrative offices and found a couple of straight-backed chairs. Ernie and I set them out of the way but close enough to the dais so we could keep an eye on Strange.

"So Sooki's all right?" Ernie asked once we got settled.

"Yeah. She begged me not to tell her husband what had happened. I promised I wouldn't. Not all of it, anyway."

I had told Specialist Garfield that we'd broken Sooki out of the Golden Dragon, and that had been good enough for him. He didn't ask more questions. Maybe because he guessed he wouldn't like the answers.

"Huk is a complete shit," Ernie said. "What makes you think he'll keep his word?"

"He knows what I said is true. He can't get to us, not without a hell of a lot of expense and trouble. Even if he managed to take you and me out, he'd face the wrath of the KNPs and the Korean government, neither of which wants a big-time racketeer messing up their cozy relationship with the United States. Not worth it for a single girl in one of his brothels."

The United States government had not only provided South Korea with 50,000 troops to help in their defense against the Communist army up north, but we also gave them millions of dollars in economic and military aid annually. If there was one thing every faction in the South Korean government agreed on, it was keeping the relationship with the United States pristine, without the slightest blemish.

"So if we were bumped off," Ernie said, "the KNPs and the 8th Army honchos would go after Huk."

"Big-time."

"It's like in 'Nam," Ernie told me. "The army treats you like shit when you're alive. But once you're dead, you become a hero."

"Right. They'd probably dedicate a plaque to us."

"The only way we'll ever get one." Ernie thought about it for a minute and then continued. "Okay, so Huk knows he can't touch us. And after that performance on the Han-gang Railroad Bridge, he's also convinced that if he messes with Sooki's family, we'll take him out. So he'll leave her alone."

"It's the smart business decision," I said. "What's one girl, more or less? And besides, nobody in the Seoul underworld knows what happened. He doesn't lose face. As far as they're concerned, the MPs raided the Ichon-dong brothel and he shrugged them off and he's back in business the next day."

"He looks good."

"Right. And if he's smart, he'll leave it that way. Sooki told me that as soon as her husband's tour is up, they'll go back to the States and she'll put in the paperwork to have her parents and her brother and sister join them."

"The sooner, the better."

"Right. Because once we're gone, who knows what Huk will do?"

"Once we're gone? What are you talking about? I'm not going anywhere."

"You already have your request in for extension?"

"You better believe it. Riley hand-carried mine over to his pal Smitty at 8th Army Personnel. How about yours?"

"Already in."

Ernie surveyed the crowd of shoppers, and we watched Strange behave himself as we listened to the schmaltzy Christmas music wafting out of the PX sound system.

"Everybody talks about being homesick at Christmas," Ernie said. "They think that's why GIs off themselves."

"Isn't it?"

"For some," he said. "Maybe for most. For me, I'll only off myself if I end up back in some trailer park in the States and somebody reminds me of Korea."

"Or Vietnam?"

He nodded. "Or Vietnam." He motioned toward the long lines at the cashier stations. "They think buying shit is living. It ain't."

"What is?" I asked.

"This," he said.

I followed his gaze toward the entrance. Sooki walked in, paused, and glanced around the expanse of the busy PX. When she spotted us she smiled, waved, and headed straight toward us.

PAUL D. MARKS

Windward

FROM *Coast to Coast*

PETRICHOR. THAT FRESH SMELL of drying grass—or in
my case wet pavement after the rain. You didn't know there was
a word for it, did you? The rain had just cleared out. Everyone's
been cooped inside, pent-up energy building, seething. Bad guys
couldn't do their thing. The rain stops, they come out to play.
Shards of sun streak through a buttermilk sky. People in L.A. can't
deal with rain anyway.

Petrichor. There's a word for everything. The word for my life at
that moment was hell.

I was finishing up the job from hell, putting together the final bill
on the Rence case. Identity theft. If you ever want your life to turn
to shit, get your identity stolen. Not only did it turn Rence's life to
hell, but mine too. I'd spent three months on it, mostly barricaded
inside, chasing leads on the dark web from the *hole*, my office. Three
months of pure hell till I caught the bad actors—but Rence will
spend five years trying to get her name back. I like what I do for a
living, though lately, with computers and the Internet, it can get a little boring and tedious—they make it too easy to track people down.
Not that it wasn't boring before, sitting on stakeouts or gumshoeing
it, but at least then I was out in the world, among the living, even
if it meant sweltering inside a parked car or hiding behind bushes,
getting sunburned and having an excuse for all the crappy food.

A man opened the office door, the little bell on it rang. It's a
concession to the old days that makes people feel comfortable,
something they don't often feel when they have to hire a private investigator. It also makes a chime on my computer ring. I looked up,

saw him enter on the video monitor. There wasn't an inch of my office, inside or out, that wasn't covered in a crossfire of cameras. I even had a camera on the restaurant across the street, shooting the front of my building. I'd done a little work for Lou Hernandez, the owner, and instead of taking money from her I asked if I could put a camera on her place. She agreed. I liked watching my little storefront PI shop on Windward Avenue in Venice. I particularly liked watching it from the hole.

I opened the door to the small front office, covered in pix of Venice from the old days. The piers and amusement parks, people in old-fashioned bathing suits on the beach. The canals and oil wells. And a young surfer dude standing next to his stick, stabbed in the sand. Originally a color photo, I'd printed it in sepia so it would match the others. It reminded me of who I used to be—I didn't get much surfing in these days. Actually, I hadn't surfed in years. I thought about it a lot though.

I'm talking about Venice, California. Los Angeles. Hey, the other one in Italy has canals and grand thoroughfares with colonnaded arches. We have grand canals and streets with grand colonnaded arches. Okay, so we don't have such grand canals these days, most of them have been filled in, including the Grand Canal. And Venice didn't quite cut it as the cultural paradise-by-the-sea that Abbot Kinney, its founder, had envisioned. Today it was an ever-changing kaleidoscope of people, dudes dancing on skates, musicians, artists. Maybe a few pickpockets here or there. But it was home. And I liked it here.

"Jack Lassen?" the familiar-looking man said from behind expensive shades, entering my place. Tan, very tan. Maybe the kind you pay for, maybe the kind you get from sitting by the pool, sipping mojitos, or whatever the in drink was these days. Loafers without socks—that told me a lot about him. Pastel shirt, Rolex. Definitely not a walk-in off the beach looking for a handout.

I smiled. He didn't return it.

"You're a licensed private investigator in the state of California?"

"Want me to show you my photostat?" Of course we don't have photostats anymore, but he was playing with me, I played back.

"Funny."

"What can I do for you, Mr. . . ."

"Lambert, Patrick Lambert."

I knew the name. As in "A Patrick Lambert Production." Hey,

this is L.A. Everyone aspires to a credit like that or "A Film By." Few get there. Lambert had been there for twenty years with no signs of coming down. Back in the day he'd been a leading man of the George Clooney variety. Good-looking, athletic. Heart-throb. And richer than God's Uncle Larry. He'd drifted from act-ing to producing and become an even bigger player, if that was possible.

"Have a seat," I started to say. But he was already making himself comfortable, leaning back in one of the guest chairs like he owned the place.

My office was neat as a pin, clean as a whistle—what other cli-chés can I come up with to describe it? I wanted customers to feel confident in me. On the other hand, sometimes I worried they'd think I had no business if there weren't a lot of papers strewn here and there, piles of manila folders and the like.

"My wife, Emily, is missing. The cops aren't moving fast enough."

"You want me to find her?"

"You're good." He stretched.

"Am I boring you?"

"You sure you've done this before?"

"Just making small talk."

"I don't need small talk. I need someone to find my wife."

"Did you lose her?" I knew I'd better stop.

He got up, turned for the door. Most people have trouble get-ting to the point, so I do a little friendly jousting with them. Not him, he was all business, or should I say *biz*? Unlike all those down-and-out PIs in the movies, my business was doing okay and I didn't need the money. But I didn't like the guy—wasn't sure why, some-times you just don't. That didn't mean I wanted to let business just walk out the door—his money would buy me a meal or two at El Coyote as well as anybody's. Besides, I needed a break after the Rence case. You think it might have been that Hollywood swagger that put me off?

"Hey, Mr. Lambert, you come to a Venice PI, you get a Venice vibe. Did you come to me specifically or was I just the closest one to you?"

"You're not the closest. You have a good rep, though I'm begin-ning to wonder why."

"Tell me what's going on."

He seemed to collapse in on himself, lowered his voice. "My wife

Emily's been missing for about a week now. I think she's been kidnapped."

"You're rich."

His face startled. Hollywood folks, the successful ones, are very wealthy and like to pretend they're "of the people" while sitting in their modest 20,000-square-foot houses and their $150,000 Teslas.

"I'm just trying to figure out why someone would kidnap your wife. Motive and all that."

"We're comfortable. And to answer your next question, no, there's no ransom demand. Yet."

Comfortable, the old saw people said when they were way more than comfortable.

"I came home from work on Friday. Drawers dumped out. Whole house ransacked."

"Forcible entry?"

"The police said it looked like someone jimmied the sliding door open, but they think it was staged. They've lost interest. In fact, they think she ran off. That she faked the crime scene to make it look like she was kidnapped."

"Why would she do that?"

"She wouldn't." He sounded very sure of himself. Guys like that always sounded sure of themselves. They were, after all, God's gift to women and everyone else. Why would anyone ever want to ditch out on them?

"When I came home her car was gone. I think the kidnappers took her in it."

"Have the cops found the car?"

He shook his head. "Not yet."

"Alarm? Surveillance cameras?"

"Neither was on. We don't always have them on when we're home, especially during the day."

"Help? Servants?"

"Off that day."

Naturally.

He handed me a stiff piece of semiglossy paper with photos on it. Blond hair, full lips. Overly made up. Pretty in that typical SoCal *IWannaBeAnActress* way—and if you did want to be an actress, why not marry Patrick Lambert, one of the hottest producers around? Yeah, she was an actress. Hell, what he'd given me was a six-by-nine composite card, the kind that actors hand out to casting directors. It had the standard studio head shot, plus action shots, bikini at the beach, climbing a tree. I'm not kidding. The best for last, steely-eyed holding a Goncz GA-9 pistol—cool-looking high-tech gun, the kind Hollywood loves—dressed in a leather bustier and six-inch stilettos. I hoped that gun didn't have much recoil.

"Anything better? Normal, y'know, snapshots."

He slid a wallet-sized photo across the desk. Without makeup she really was pretty. "There's a ton of pictures of her on her Facebook page." He wrote down the password to her account. I wondered why he knew it.

I followed him to his *comfortable* Pacific Palisades house, er, mansion on an acre and a half overlooking the ocean. The house was small by Saudi prince standards but was definitely comfortable. He showed me where the break-in occurred. Sliding door off a pool patio, a slight dent in the doorframe.

"These are the official police photos." He showed me a dozen police pix from the crime scene. "I have some clout with the PD."

I bet you do.

The broken door. Ransacked dressers and closets. It was a little too perfect, everything just a little too perfectly out of place, strewn here, strewn there—like on a movie set maybe. But that didn't really mean anything. Bad guys don't always do everything according to Hoyle.

He said he'd wire me the money within the hour and gave me the names and numbers of Emily's besties and sister. He wanted her back, bad. I could see it in his eyes, or maybe he was just afraid what they would say in the tabloids?

I called Laurence Lautrec, a Detective II in the West L.A. station, from my cell. He was my department go-to. We'd worked together when I was on the force. Claimed he was related to Toulouse. The fact that Laurence was black and six feet tall and Toulouse white and barely five foot didn't seem to bother him. And who knows, down the ancestral line anything might happen.

Every once in a while we'd get together to go shooting or just shoot the breeze, sometimes with guns.

"It's not my case," he said. "But from what I hear, some-a the guys think she mighta pulled a Gone Girl and—"

"What, faked her own kidnapping? Why? She's an actress wannabe married to a player. Rich. Good-looking. Powerful. Nobody skips out on that."

He gave me a "who are you kidding" look, said he had to get back to work. He also said he'd send whatever he could regarding the case my way.

I hit Tito's Tacos on the way home. A little out of the way, but worth it, and I sure as hell didn't want any of those too-hip hipster joints. With my taco fix satisfied, I parked behind my building, went in, slid down the ladder back into the hole—a 1950s bomb shelter built by some previous owner of this little building during the Cold War, when trust was low and paranoia high. He was going to hide down here and be safe if the Big One came. Of course what he'd come up to when he opened the hatch might not have been much fun. The next owner had used this space for storage. The hatch door was solid steel, four inches thick. If I was down in the hole I could lock it so it couldn't be opened from the outside. I felt safe and snug down here, from bill collectors, home invaders and burglars, angry husbands and nukes. There was recirculating air and filters, electricity from batteries, generator, and solar, and enough food and water for one person for a month. Well, it might not have been the best food, but it would do—MREs. Plenty of books and DVDs. A link to the Internet. I could be happy here forever if I didn't have to earn a living. And it was bigger than you might think, taking up the entire square footage of the building . . . and then some. The biggest problem was getting things down the hatch, but I managed. I also added running water, a shower and toilet, and a great galley kitchen that HGTV would be proud of. Even had a chemical toilet in case the shit ever really did hit the fan topside and the regular one stopped working. All the comforts of home, including a million-dollar view of the Venice boardwalk from the Venice Beach live cam, spread out on a sixty-inch flatscreen. But it was quiet and that made up for a lot. And I didn't tell anyone except a handful of really good friends that it was here or where I lived.

By the time I got back to the hole, the material from Lautrec was already there. I downloaded it and perused the reports. Nothing jumped out at me.

I turned to Emily's Facebook page. A ton of pix. Nothing really out of the ordinary, no incriminating pictures. I printed a couple to show around along with the composite card should the need arise.

I made sure Lambert's payment cleared before I really dug into the job. Just because he's a big Hollywood muck doesn't mean he'll keep his word. I've been doing this gig for seven years on my own. Before that I had a partner for two. He preferred the safety of a steady paycheck—his wife's—and became a stay-at-home dad. Before that I was a cop for nine years, until I got shot in the hip, a nice euphemism for ass. I could have stayed on in the department, but I like my ass. It gives me something to sit on.

I scanned the monitors to make sure everything was good. Nothing unusual happening on the Venice Beach live cam either, where the unusual is usual. I then looked at the outer office. The pictures on the walls. A clean, well-lighted place. My board. Even though I was just yards off the beach, I never seemed to get around to surfing anymore. I don't know why. I guess sometimes you just have to grow up, do grown-up things. Little games are for little boys, as the song says. On top of that, I just didn't have the time I had when I was younger. Every day it seems to evaporate like the fog snuffed out by the sun. So I kept that board, leaning on the wall, to remind me of younger days, better days. Glory days—like the high school football star who made the game-winning touchdown, then didn't do much with his life after that.

Turning back to the computer, I checked all the usual resources on Emily Lambert, Spokeo and Intellius, DMV and military records. She'd led a pretty ordinary life except for marrying Lambert. And was wife number three for him.

Lambert called, wanting to know what I'd done. It'd been about three hours since I left his house, and already he's bugging me. Hollywood Power Player thinking he owns me or Guilty Guy protesting too much?

I pulled up to Emily's sister's place in the Spaulding Square neighborhood of Hollywood at 9 a.m. the next morning. Nice little Spanish-style houses built in the 1920s, around thirteen hundred square feet—on postage stamp lots of pure L.A. bliss going for a mil and a half—hell, my bomb shelter was bigger than that. Walking to the front door, I noticed she had torn out the front grass and put in an ugly xeriscape. Some xeriscapes are attractive. Not this one. It looked like the Iraqi desert after a brigade of American tanks had rolled over it two or three times. Erin Beckham, Emily's sister, answered the door. I intro'd myself, got the prelims out of the way.

She invited me in. The house was cozy. Offered me a cup of tea, which I declined. I took in everything about the room that I could, the decor, family photos, artwork. Several of the pix showed her with a man I assumed to be her husband. Buff and tough, like they're all trying to be today. Dirty-blond hair in a too-slick do. Another of him clowning, posing like the muscle men on Muscle Beach.

"Your brother-in-law, Patrick Lambert, is concerned that the police aren't doing enough to find your sister."

Her puckered lips, like she'd just tasted a sour lemon, gave away her feelings for her brother-in-law, even if she didn't say anything. "He's got a whole force of studio cops, but he hires you."

"I'm not chopped liver, you know. I have a pretty good rep, if I say so myself."

"I didn't mean to put you down. Just that the LAPD sort of shills for the studios. But either way, I don't know anything."

"She have any run-ins with anyone?"

"No."

"How does she get along with her husband?"

This time a raised eyebrow. "As far as I know they get along fine. I mean, they fight like everyone does. He might be a little controlling, but nothing out of the ordinary."

"Maybe I can talk to your husband?"

She glanced over at the photos on the mantel. "He's too busy and he doesn't know any more than I do, probably less."

"What about other siblings, friends?"

"No siblings, just us. And she didn't have a lot of friends lately."

I asked if I could use the head. I didn't really have to; I wanted to see more of the house. I satisfied myself that Emily wasn't there. I stayed another ten minutes or so thrusting and parrying with her, getting nowhere. Maybe she didn't really know anything, but it's my nature—and my job—to be suspicious of everyone and everything.

"I'm sorry I can't help you," she said, eyeing the door. A not-so-subtle hint.

"Are you?"

I wanted to slam the car door—but didn't want to show emotion. And she sure as hell wasn't showing any, hardly seemed concerned about her missing sister. People do worry in different ways, but I knew she was full of shit. Problem was, I didn't exactly know what she was full of shit about. Something didn't seem right.

"Strike one," I said, driving off, heading back toward the beach. Made some stops on the way to talk with some of Emily's coworkers, then hit Pink's on La Brea, hot dogs to the stars. Pink's is nothing more than a ramshackle shack. But an L.A. institution. I'd rather eat at places like that or Tito's any day of the week than those new cooler-than-cool places that last a year or three, then spontaneously combust.

I parked behind my building in the secure private lot. Made a pit stop at Lou Hernandez's restaurant for a beer and headed toward the boardwalk a few yards away instead of to the office. I popped the lid on a Lagunitas IPA and thought on it awhile.

Emily's coworkers, mostly actors and some below-the-line people, didn't have a lot to say. I figured they didn't want to get on Lambert's bad side and be blackballed. But they did turn me on to one of his exes—right in my own backyard. I looked her up on IMDb on my phone. She'd had a few small roles but was mostly an appendage to Lambert.

Since the pea soup of winter laid a cold, heavy hand on the waterfront, I didn't know if she'd be on the boardwalk at all. I walked down there, passing a man in a Speedo playing a grand piano, just a little the worse for wear from the weather. I still haven't figured out what they do with that piano at night. Some detective, huh? I passed the Sidewalk Café and Small World Books, and of course the ubiquitous tourists. Venice is the number one tourist destination in L.A., though for the life of me I can't figure out why. I guess they come to see the freaks. And since I lived here, I was one of them—my people.

After talking with several denizens—I like that word, don't you?—of the walk, Ja-ron, the fire eater, steered me to Haley Garrick Lambert. I'd seen her around but never paid any attention. She was younger than I'd expected, early thirties maybe. But still probably past her prime for Lambert. Short shorts and sandals—hey, it's an L.A. winter. Baubles and beads on bracelets and necklaces. A headscarf wrapped around long golden-brown hair that hung down below her shoulders. And two or three different-colored tank tops layered one over the other. Yeah, she belonged in

Venice. She worked selling handmade jewelry from a stand on the side of the walk.

I told her who I was, who I was working for. Asked the usual opening questions.

"I'd help you if I could," she said. That's more than Emily's sister had said. And why wasn't Erin worried? That worried me.

The sun cracked the clouds, glinting off Haley's dangly earrings, which sported a distinctive dolphin design.

"You're looking at my earrings."

"They're unusual."

"Yeah, and solid platinum. Patrick's very magnanimous. He gives all his exes earrings, 'cause he's sure stingy on the alimony." She squinted in the glaring sun. I could taste the sarcasm.

"How many does he have?"

"I'm the second. I guess Emily is the third now . . ."

"Can I ask you something?"

"That's what you're here for, isn't it?"

"What're you doing hawking this shit out here in Venice?"

"Oh, you think because I'm the great Patrick Lambert's ex that I should have my own alimony mansion in Bev Hills, right? I'll tell you, I signed a prenup. I get a little, and when I say a little—"

"You mean a little."

"Very little."

"So there's no love lost."

She hesitated. "I don't hate him, if that's what you mean. I started out wanting to be a star like every other halfway decent-looking girl in L.A. I thought Patrick was my ticket. We used each other. I didn't expect much on the back end. Just like in the movies, nobody gets their back-end money. Almost nobody."

"He do that to you?" I pointed to a pink scar on her leg.

"Oh hell, no. But it did happen on one of his locations in the Angeles National Forest. He finally gave me a bit in one his flicks, *The Atom Boys*."

"Don't know it."

"You're not missing anything, though it did make a lot of money. Anyway, I got hit by a falling light. You should have seen it right after. Searing red."

"I'll bet. So he didn't hit you, but maybe he was controlling?" I said, remembering Erin's comment and playing off my own hunch about Lambert.

"Everything from soup to nuts, as my grandmother would say. He's a control freakazoid." The venom gushed now. "I'd say that's why I left him, but he left me. Probably for Emily—probably had her waiting in the wings. But I don't care, I'm happy, I got the sun in the morning and the beach all day long. I'm not mad at him or her."

"You think he—"

"Well, yeah, sure. He could have taken Emily out. Well, not Patrick. He pays people to do his dirty work."

"Like me."

"Yeah, like you."

I went away knowing a little more than I had when the sun woke up this morning. Erin was closemouthed. Haley was friendlier. Maybe bitter about the breakup, about Emily taking her place. Motive to kill or kidnap her? Sure. She claimed not to hate Emily or her ex-husband. Nobody knew anything. Nothing they would cop to, anyway. And I was suspicious of them all.

My phone buzzed. Lautrec wanted a meet. We hooked up at the Sidewalk Café, not too far from Haley's stand. I knew something was up as soon as he walked in. Tense, unsmiling. Shoulders tight.

"Hey."

We took a table, shot the breeze—how's your wife, how's the bunker, that kind of thing. But something was wrong. The conversation stiff, avoiding the subject at hand until . . .

He leaned in. "We're definitely liking Lambert for it now."

That came out of the blue. "You think he's the doer?"

"New thinking is he killed her and staged the break-in to explain her disappearance." He downed a slug of Sam Adams. "This is under your hat."

I tipped an imaginary hat. "So why would he hire me if he killed her? You think he's trying to set me up?"

"Makes him look like he's doing something."

I toyed with my beer. "So what's wrong, that's not why you wanted a meet. I see it in your face."

"Every day it gets back-burnered a little more."

"That makes sense—much as anything, I guess. You think he's the doer and somebody's warning you off it."

"And now I'm warning you off," he said. "Fair warning."

"I get it, the studios are comin' down on you. L.A.'s a factory town and Hollywood's the factory. Wanna make sure one of theirs is protected."

"Get outta here."

I walked home, looking at the colonnades along Windward, echoes from another time, and feeling uneasy about my meal with Lautrec as I entered the office. As soon as I did I saw something on one of the monitors that pissed me off. A green minivan blocking the gate to my little parking lot in back. I have to police that area, because people will park there and go to the beach, even at night. Then I have to call a tow. It's a royal pain. I could see there were still people in the van; they didn't look like they were going anywhere. I went out back to tell them to move on. I walked by the van. Two men jumped out from behind a low wall, slapping something down over my head. Everything went black. They yanked the hood's drawstring tight, shoved me into the back of the van. I didn't think it was a random kidnapping. My first inclination was to laugh, crooks with a minivan. My second was, how the hell do I get out of here? Third, I left the damn door to my place unlocked. Shit.

Zip ties tore into my wrists as they lashed me to a cargo cleat in the back. I could smell the fear-sweat coming off them. The whole van was steamy and stunk up, like a gym on a humid night.

I tried to figure out where we were going, but it was hard to tell. My senses said we were heading north, up the coast somewhere. Nobody was talking. I tried to discern how many people there were from their movements. The two men who'd grabbed me were in back with me and a driver up front.

"You want to tell me what this is about?"

"Shut up."

The van bumped over rough gravel, probably a semipaved beach parking lot somewhere up the coast. It had to be around 6:30 p.m., probably not anyone out at this hour. They cut the zip ties, yanked me out, threw me on the ground. Rip—the skin on my forearm shredding. Fuck them. I owe you now. I could hear the waves crashing a few yards away.

Damn! A kick in the ribs.

"Stay the fuck away from Emily Lambert. Hear me?"

"I hear ya." I felt him too. The kick wasn't hard, but it hit the right spot to give me a blast of pain.

"Or we'll be back."

"Did anyone tell you boys that kidnapping is against the law?" I loosened the drawstring on the hood. A drift of fresh air blew in through the gap.

Light from the open van door sliced across one of the men's faces as he bent over me. Familiar face—one I'd seen in a photo. Dirty-blond hair and nicely cut gym rat muscles, the kind you'd find at Muscle Beach. Erin's husband, maybe, from what I could tell through the gap in the hood. Another kick. Wasn't very sharp. These weren't hard guys. They wanted to scare me off—why? They piled in the van. I threw a rock at the taillight, shattering it. They hit PCH heading south. I tried to figure out where I was. Maybe Will Rogers Beach. I had a good walk ahead of me.

I tucked the hood in my pocket, walked PCH back to Windward. Got home at seven bells on the dog watch. I didn't always think in those terms anymore, but I always liked *dog watch*. And I was dog-tired. I slid down into the hole, sealed the hatch, salved my scraped arm. Put a couple of tortillas on the open-flame burner, spread butter on them and then hot sauce. And that was dinner. I set the alarm clock, lay down on my bed, and drifted into some kind of dreamland where all the freaks on Venice Beach came out one at a time and kicked me in the shins, like in some demented Fellini movie. The alarm went off at midnight sharp. I jumped in the shower, dressed, and climbed up the ladder.

An eerie, cold, wet wind blew in off the ocean. I pointed the car east and drove, blasting Brigitte Handley and the Dark Shadows on fairly empty, fairly quiet weeknight streets. The part of Hollywood I was headed to wasn't quite as romantic as the one people imagine when they think of Hollywood. It was the part where people lived and played, changed diapers and had sex, though maybe not in that order.

I parked a block away from my destination and walked that block like I owned it. A Nora Jones song filtered down the street from an open window somewhere. At 0130 not even a TV flickered through a window in the quiet house. I let my eyes adjust to the darkness, padded down the driveway toward the back of the house, looking for the outcroppings of a security system. Found it, disabled it.

Breaking in was easy-peasy. I crept through the house on my steel-toed Doc Martins till I came to the master bedroom. I pushed the door open, quietly took a seat on the rocker by the foot of the bed, and rocked slowly.

"W-what's going on?" Erin jumped up in bed. Her husband

lurched up beside her. I shined the sun-bright LED flashlight at the end of my 9-million-volt stun gun in his eyes. He shielded them with a hand.

"Did you really think I couldn't figure out who you were?"

"What're you talking about?"

"Don't play fucking games." I hit the trigger on the stunner. *Zzzzzzzz*, it crackled. "You want this upside your neck?"

"What do you want?"

I enjoyed watching them squirm. "I think you know more than you're telling. You want to keep me out of the loop—fine. But stay the fuck away from me. You're in a league you're not equipped for." I held up a piece of taillight from the van. "Fuck with me again, I'll turn you in. This piece of taillight belongs to your van, the one in your driveway. The one with the broken taillight I just snapped a picture of."

"Not legal," Erin said.

"Neither is kidnapping. Let's call it even and forget about it. When you decide to stop playing games, you know where to find me."

The hole seemed particularly reassuring that night. Next morning I wrote up a report for Lambert. Jammed by his house.

"You're not making much progress."

"I've only been working the case a couple of days." I didn't tell him about my being kidnapped or my field trip to Erin's house in the middle of the night. "You sure you don't know what might have happened to Emily?"

"Are you accusing me—"

"No, just that you might know about someone who could have been angry with her—or you."

"I wish I did. I really want to find her." He sounded sincere, but what did that mean? Like Shakespeare said, "All the world's a stage, and all the men and women merely players." Maybe he was a player in more ways than one—and maybe he was playing me. Driving back to the office, I tried to figure out my next step.

I looked through the photos again. A woman approached on one of the monitors. She glanced up and down the street, as if she was embarrassed going into a PI's office. I was up and out of the hole by the time the little bell over the door rang.

"Mr. Lassen."

"Erin. I'm surprised to see you here." I guess my late-night visit with the stun baton had worked.

"I'm sorry about what happened. We were just trying to protect Emily."

"Protect her?"

"She's been kidnapped." She sank into one of the chairs.

"Have you heard from someone? Has there been a ransom demand?"

"No, but I think someone wants to get to her husband."

"How does your kidnapping me help Emily?"

"Well, if she was kidnapped and you're nosing around, they might hurt her." She squirmed. "I'm not sure how to say this, so I'm just going to tell you everything. I'd been getting texts from Emily every day saying she's okay. But I haven't heard anything now in three days."

"Texts?"

"Yes, but not from her phone, from a number I don't know. I guess whoever kidnapped her is making her do it so we know she's okay."

"Anyone can send a text. No phone calls?"

She shook her head.

"How do you know it's really her?"

"She always signs off 'Lee-Lee,' what we called her as a kid. No one else would know that, but these are signed that way."

She showed me the messages. Short, terse. *No cops or they kill me. Lee-Lee.*

"We can't go to the police. Don't you see? And that's why we did what we did last night. We wanted to scare you off."

"I get it." I thought I did, but my suspicious nature made me wonder if she was telling me the whole truth and nothing but. "Does Lambert know about these?"

"No."

I understood her reluctance to share the info with Lambert at this stage. She showed me the last text message. It said something about curtains.

"Curtains?"

"It's our code. For where we used to go camping with our family in the Angeles National Forest. There was a wall of trees like a huge curtain."

"What do you think it means?"

"I think they might be holding her there."

She told me how to get to the place.

I hit Highway 2 in La Cañada Flintridge, drove up into the forest, looking for the turnoff that Erin had described. She couldn't remember exactly how to get there. The Angeles National Forest is known as L.A.'s body dump, and I was looking for a body, hoping not to find one, at least not a dead one.

Driving in circles for an hour, waiting for the GPS to come back online, I wondered if Erin had sent me on a wild-goose chase. Then I saw it. Rabbit Run Road. Not much to the little dirt road. It ended in a small campground. I parked, walked into the site. Deserted. A sliver of red flashed through the patchwork of leaves, glinting in the sun. Red Mercedes SL Roadster, behind a curtain of trees. Covered with dust and leaves, it looked abandoned. Hadn't been broken into . . . yet, but unlocked. Both of which surprised me. I guess it was so far off the beaten path, and especially in the cold of winter, nobody had found it.

I slipped on latex gloves, pulled out my little point-and-shoot—I liked it better than my phone for things like this. Snapped pictures of every inch of the car and surrounding area. The car was empty. No purse. No personal items. No dead body. Nothing. Looked like it had already been cleaned out. Maybe whoever took Emily Lambert had sanitized it to get rid of any incriminating fingerprints or DNA evidence they might have left behind.

I did a three-sixty around the car, then walked in successively larger concentric circles, trying hard not to disturb the land, hoping I wouldn't find Emily's body in a shallow grave. No footprints or breadcrumbs or anything. Someone had tossed her purse in a pile of leaves a few yards from the car. Emily's wallet remained, but her cash and credit cards were missing. Driver's license was where it should be.

Heading back to the car, something caught my eye. Two-inch-wide dark tape wrapped around a tree branch, one end flapping in the breeze. Duct tape? Had they held her here? I walked over. No, gaffer's tape, similar to duct tape but used on movie sets, and I'd been on enough of them to know the difference. Walked back to my car, found a spot where my phone would work, called the cops. And waited, and thought. Gaffer's tape, movie sets. Lambert made movies. Was there a connection?

Something else caught my eye, shiny and sparkly, half covered by dirt. I picked up an earring. A familiar-looking earring.

I played Stratego on my phone till a black-and-white sheriff's SUV came trolling up the road.

"Jack Lassen?" Deputy Cantwell said. I knew his name from the badge on his shirt.

"Yes."

He made sure I wasn't armed. Luckily, I'd left my Beretta Nano in the car.

"Where's the car?"

I pointed.

"Stay here."

The deputy walked to Emily's car. Made sure there were no dead bodies in the passenger compartment. Popped the trunk. Clean. Scanned the immediate area around the car. Said something into his shoulder mic. Came back to me.

"You sure you didn't check out the car?"

"Me?" Mr. Innocent.

"How did you come to find the car?"

"The owner's husband hired me to find her. She'd been missing."

"And how did you end up here?"

"Look, I don't want to tell the story eighty-six times. I'll just wait till the detectives get here."

He shot me a pissed-off, don't-fuck-with-me look but basically left me alone. He looked around, mostly just waiting for the detectives and criminalists to show. They took their sweet time. And when they did they gave me the third degree. I gave them most of what I had and they let me go down the mountain.

Halfway down, I pulled into a turnout. Figured I was far enough away from the scene of the crime that they wouldn't notice. Pulled out the earring. Familiar. I'd seen it before. On Haley at the beach. She'd had two. I wondered if now she only had one. Ex-wife, jealous of new, arm candy wife. Thrown to the wolves with a prenup that gave her virtually nothing. Maybe she'd hatched a kidnapping plan with a new boyfriend to make up for being shorted on alimony? It'd been done before.

Haley was holding down the fort at the little stand on the boardwalk. A chill wind slashed in off the ocean, biting my cheeks.

She saw me coming, had nowhere to go.

"Remember me?"

The scorn in her eyes said she did. She was wearing a pair of pearl stud earrings.

"How 'bout this, remember this? I think you lost it." I dangled the earring in front of her face.

She glared at me. "I didn't kidnap her. I had nothing to do with it."

"Then what was this doing where I found her car?"

"How would I know?"

"And that part of the forest is an interesting place. Not only did I find the earring. I also found gaffer's tape. You know, like they use on movie sets. Like Patrick Lambert's movie *The Atom Boys,* which was shot in the Angeles National Forest and which you were in, according to IMDb and yourself."

"Get out of here. I don't have to talk to you."

"No, but you'll have to talk to the cops. You were there. Emily's car is there. I think there's a connection." I thought that was a good tagline, spun on my heel, walked off.

I could tell she was panicked. And she was definitely involved. She lost track of me in the crowd, crammed her phone to her ear. I ducked into an empty tattoo parlor, watching her from behind the window, like Bogart watched Geiger's bookstore from another shop across the street. Only I didn't have Dorothy Malone to keep me company. Haley closed up her little stand, double-timed up the boardwalk. I fell in behind her. She got into a Passat—I guess that was the ex-wife ride—and took off in a swirl of dust. I ran to my car. Beach traffic and red lights, the bane of L.A., slowed her down. I didn't have any trouble catching up to her. She drove PCH north, I drove PCH north, all the way to Santa Barbara. I could tell she was talking on the phone—I wished I knew to whom.

Santa Barbara. Nice place to be kidnapped, if there is such a thing.

She parked outside of a small real estate office—Josie Tremaine Realty—on State Street, the main drag. I went in the front door.

"Josie. Josie Tremaine." No sign of anyone. But I'd heard noises in the back when I first entered.

A woman came out. Pretty, not Hollywood-sexy, or should I say sexed-up? Dark hair, just a hint of makeup.

"I'm Josie."

I just looked at her, didn't have to say anything. She knew I wasn't here to buy a house. And I knew her name wasn't Josie. Her façade crumbled.

"You don't look any the worse for wear . . . Emily."

"Did my husband send you?" Emily said. "You're the PI, right?"

"I'm the PI. Your sister tell you about me?"

She sat, or maybe collapsed, in a chair. Game over. "I don't know why I thought I could get away with it."

"What're you trying to get away with? You wanna get some ransom money from your husband since you got screwed in the prenup like Haley?"

"Can't you just leave me alone? Pretend you never found me."

"I have a rep to protect." I was being flip. I don't think it worked. "Your husband's worried about you."

She stared past me. Through me. "I'm not going back. If you take me, it'll be kidnapping."

"Like your sister and her husband did to me. I think we're at a Mexican standoff here."

"Why do you care if I go back to my husband?"

I didn't have a good answer to that. "I don't. But he hired me to do a job."

"And you always get your man—or woman."

"Something like that."

"I'll pay you twice what he's paying you."

"Why are you so desperate to get away from him?"

She sat closed-mouthed. "What kind of man are you?"

"Huh?" Nobody'd ever asked me that before, not so directly. I hadn't given it much thought. But I guess like most people I thought I was a pretty good guy—wasn't I?

"What kind of man are you? Honest? Trustworthy? Or a bum?"

"I'm as honest as the next guy, maybe more so. I like to think I'm a pretty decent person, try to do the right thing."

"Then do the right thing now."

"What's that?"

"Let me be."

I ignored her comment. "So why'd your sister turn me on to your car up there in the forest?" I said it loud enough for the people in back to hear. I'd seen Erin's van next to Haley's Passat. "You can come out now."

"We thought you'd find it, tell the police, and they'd think that someone took her, murdered her. But that no one would ever find the body," Erin said as she and Haley warily emerged from the back room.

"And she'd just *disappear*," Haley said.

"But you didn't plan to lose an earring, a very distinctive earring." I looked at Haley. "There was no kidnapping."

"No," Emily said.

I sat down, burned out. I'd been running on fumes since the Rence case. I was tired of all the assjacks I had to deal with every day. Assjacks I made my living off, but still . . . "You're all in it together? The ex-wives club."

"And ex-sister-in-law," Erin said, cracking the slightest smile.

"Have you told the cops yet?" Emily asked.

"Not yet."

"And maybe you won't."

"Tell me about it."

She pulled a manila envelope out of a locked desk drawer. Handed it to me. Several photos of her, black and blue and purple. Bruised up and down her body. "He did that to me."

"How do I know it's real? Not a Hollywood makeup job."

"That's why I wanted to leave. He gets off on beating me and he was getting more violent every time. He would've killed me eventually. I know he would have. I've been planning this over a year. Squirreling money away, a little here, a lot there. He never missed it. I'd tell him I was doing spa days with the girls. But come up here, work in another real estate office, till I founded this place. I got my real estate license, set up this office. Changed my name."

"And that's why you left your driver's license behind. Just to make sure everyone knew it was you, would figure you'd been kidnapped or worse."

She nodded.

I couldn't figure yet if she was being straight with me. "There's no reports of your being abused. And you were married to Mr. Wonderful, the dream guy for every woman in America. Mr. Perfect."

"Mr. Perfect has good PR and makes lots of money for the studios . . ." She fidgeted with the buttons on her blouse. "It's not makeup." She lifted the blouse, exposing a purple-going-to-yellow bruise that spread like a Rorschach blot over her left kidney. "He thought he could buy me with money and promises of making me a star. I don't want the money—except what I took. And I don't want to be an actor anymore. He was never serious about that." She looked to Haley, who nodded. "It was just something to keep me hanging in. And I don't want him. He'll kill me if I go back. I'm sure it's only a matter of time. He's narcissistic. He doesn't know love."

I turned to Haley. "You too?"

"Yes. He beat me too." She showed me the scar that she'd earlier told me was from a falling light. "Then, if I wanted anything at all, I had to sign a confidentiality agreement as part of the divorce settlement so I couldn't go to the press or tell anyone what a bastard he was. So Emily and I hooked up. I also got my real estate license. I'm planning to move up here too."

"And you?"

"I'm just the enabler," Erin said.

"You won't tell him, will you?" Emily reached for my hand.

"I don't know." But I did know. "You know, it's pretty easy to be found these days with the Internet and all. Even changing your name. If I could find you, others will too. And Santa Barbara's pretty close to L.A., too close. One of his Hollywood friends'll see you around town or even come in here. If you really want to disappear, I'd move farther away, much farther, and someplace more off the beaten path."

I turned for the door.

"Thanks. I'll take your advice."

"Get a new Social Security number, if you haven't already. Both of you."

Emily nodded.

"If you don't know where to get one—"

"Down on Alameda."

"Yeah, but if you want a better one, give me a call."

She smiled. The door closed behind me.

On the way home I stopped at the Malibu pier. Walked to the end, listening to the waves crash, watching them roll in and out. The endless ocean. I reached in my pocket, pulled out Haley's dolphin earring, gave it one last look, and tossed it as far off the pier as I could. It barely made a splash in the roiling water.

Dark clouds blew in off the Pacific. Storm warning. *Red sky at night, sailor's delight. Red sky at morning, sailor's warning.* How often did that hold true? Funny what you think of at times. A sting of salty ocean spray slapped me in the face, snapping me back to the moment.

Everyone's running from something. Emily was running from Lambert. More than that, she was running from the Hollywood thing, the phoniness. What they used to call the rat race. She just wanted a normal life now.

What was I running from?

I hit Lambert's house. The housekeeper told me he was on location in Colorado. Really broken up about his missing wife. I drove home, clambered down into the hole, and gave him a call on his cell. Filled him in, made the case sound colder than it was.

"What do you mean you can't find her? You found her car, the sheriff's office told me."

"She's in the wind—or dead. Trail's cold. Yeah, I found the car, but after that it's dead ends everywhere I turn."

"You're one fucking lousy PI. Give me my money back."

I enjoyed hearing the rage in his voice. "It's not like the movies, Mr. Lambert. Everything can't be solved in two hours. The money is for my time. Results are incidental. Read your contract."

"I'll destroy you. You'll—"

"What, I'll never work in this town again?" I laughed.

"Fuck you!" He clicked off. I'm sure he missed the days when you could slam a phone down and really show the person on the other end how pissed you were. He didn't seem to miss his wife much—maybe he suspected what really happened. He probably already had a new starlet on the hook, and I didn't feel guilty about letting his wife get away or taking his money. He might be able to hurt my rep a little, but what would it be without integrity anyway? On the other hand, maybe it would help once I got the truth out. Besides, my purpose in life isn't to prop up the Patrick Lamberts of the world.

I scanned the monitors, nothing exciting. Then I saw it, leaning against the wall in the outer office. My stick. The one I hadn't used in what seemed like a lifetime. I climbed out of the hole, walked down Windward toward the beach, board under my arm, the wind pounding in from the ocean. I guess like all those people cooped up inside, with their nervous energy building, I didn't want to be cooped up anymore either.

Went surfing.

Phantomwise: 1972

FROM *Ellery Queen Mystery Magazine*

OUT OF THE STEEP snowy ravine. Clutching at rocks, her hands blood-
ied. And all the while snow falling, temperature dropping to zero degrees
Fahrenheit.

 How still, the soft-falling snow amid rocks! The yearning, the temptation
to lie down, sleep.

 He'd wanted her to die. He'd wanted to kill her with his hands. But she
has escaped him, he will not follow her. (She vows) he will not find her ever
again.

I.

By the time she allowed herself to think, *It has happened. To me,* it
was already too late.

 So unexpectedly it had begun. Almost, Alyce would think afterward, as if someone else had acted in her place. She'd stared in
astonishment from a little distance.

 She hadn't been *drunk*. Except so excited, so elated, so — *exhil-*
arated.

 That he'd even noticed her. Invited her to come with him after
the reception. After the lecture. He'd known the speaker, a visiting professor from the University of Edinburgh. Before the lecture
she'd seen him speaking with the distinguished white-haired professor, she'd seen them smiling, shaking hands.

 A theory of language. Theories of language. How does language
originate? — is consciousness a blank slate (as it had been once

thought by philosophers like John Locke), or is consciousness something like a field of shimmering possibilities, generated by the particularities of the human brain?

If consciousness can be disembodied, is there the possibility of consciousness persisting after physical death? Is there the possibility of *hauntedness?*

He'd asked what had she thought of the lecture and Alyce said she could give no opinion, she had not enough knowledge. And he'd said what sounded like, *Well, you will. You've only just begun.*

How flattering to Alyce Urquhart, at nineteen.

They were crossing the darkened campus. Afterward she would realize how subtly he was guiding her—a light touch to her arm, an indication *Yes, this way. Here.*

Afterward she would recall how at dusk the old gothic buildings of the campus took on a sepulchral air. And how a light mist seemed to radiate from streetlamps as if the very air had become blurred.

Tall straight fir trees rose out of sight. Entering the region of trees was like entering an enchanted forest marking the western edge of the campus.

Her heart swelled, she felt such happiness. If she were to die—if she had already died—it would be this moment she would remember most vividly: the fir trees that were so beautiful, and the young philosophy professor at her side who had singled her out for his attention that evening.

But she did not know him, her instructor, well enough to exclaim, *Oh, how beautiful! Look.*

Whatever Simon Meech said to Alyce Urquhart that evening, Alyce would not recall precisely. Even in the presence of persons whom she knew Alyce was inclined to shyness, and she did not know Simon Meech at all. Yet suddenly he meant much to her; she had not guessed how much. And only vaguely would she recall how without seeming to do so he led her away from her residence hall. Away from the bright-lit, overwarm, and buzzing dining hall, where at this hour of evening she'd have been pushing along a cafeteria tray in the company of other girls and listening or half listening to their chatter, in a pleasantly neutral state of mind—mindlessness —and not required to think, *But who am I, to be doing this? And what will come of it?*

*

What will come of it: the steep snowy ravine, bloodied hands grasping at rocks, the determination to haul herself up, not to surrender and not to die.

A misty and rain-lashed autumn. Her second year at the college she'd envisioned as a sort of floating island, an oasis-island, amid the rubble of her familial life.

And what will come of it. Of me.

Alyce's most cherished class was a creative-writing poetry seminar taught by an elderly visiting poet from Boston. Once, Roland B___ had known Edna St. Vincent Millay and Robert Frost, Ezra Pound and T. S. Eliot, Wallace Stevens, William Carlos Williams, and Marianne Moore. He counted himself a friendly acquaintance of Robert Lowell, Elizabeth Bishop, Anne Sexton. He'd known Sylvia Plath—"for a teasingly short while."

A smooth hairless dome of a head, which seemed too large for the narrow shoulders. Suety eyes deep-sunken like a turtle's eyes, yet luminous. Roland B___ seemed always cold, though dressed for the upstate New York winter: Harris tweed jackets with leather elbows, sweater vests, woolen scarves slung cavalierly around his neck. The backs of his delicate hands were unusually pale, the skin seemed soft, flaccid. Alyce had the idea that if she were to lean across the seminar table and press a forefinger into that skin, the indention would very slowly fill in.

Aloud in a hoarse reverent voice the elderly poet read, sometimes recited poetry as if he were alone and the students were privileged to overhear, straining to listen. Alyce complained that her neck ached after three hours in the seminar leaning forward not wanting to miss a syllable.

This was not an actual complaint, of course. Her heart beat with awe for the distinguished poet, so blissfully self-centered he seemed a very Buddha basking in his own divinity.

At the first class meeting Roland B___ asked each young poet to recite a favorite poem—"a poem of unqualified greatness." The request was a total surprise, no one was prepared.

Alyce recited a little-known poem by William Butler Yeats— "To a Friend Whose Work Has Come to Nothing." Technically the poem was fascinating to her: harsh, percussive, accusatory, with a formal rhyme scheme, rage tempered by art. As a first-year student she'd unconsciously memorized the poem out of her English literature anthology; one day she'd realized that she knew it by heart.

Liking the quiet rage of the final lines. *Amid a place of stone, /
Be secret and exult, / Because of all things known / That is most difficult.*

Whatever Roland B___ might have expected from an undergraduate at the university, it was clear that he hadn't expected
this impassioned poem by Yeats. "Well! A unique choice, Miss"—
squinting at the class list as Alyce provided her last name in an
embarrassed murmur—"'Urquhart.'"

"Ah, Urquhart." As if the name might mean something to him,
Roland B___ gazed at Alyce with an expression of wonder.

Clearly Roland B___ did not know what to make of her just yet.

2.

This season of reversals. A balmy autumn followed by an abrupt
snowstorm in early November. Leaves ripped from trees, the pale
sky mottled with clouds, a dank air in the "historic" eighteenth-century buildings modeled (it was said) after Cambridge University.

Not a season for romance. Not a season for sentiment. If others
in the residence hall could have guessed that Alyce Urquhart was
newly pregnant they would have been astonished, speechless. For
God's sake—*how?*

No one had seen Alyce Urquhart with any man or boy publicly.
Her lover was her Philosophy 101 quiz-section instructor, but each
was discreet in the presence of the other, and Alyce took care to
match Simon Meech's aloofness with her own.

Though Alyce would sometimes raise her hand in class to answer
a question Simon had put to several rows of students, that no one
else knew to answer or had answered inadequately. "Yes? Miss—"
Just perceptibly, Simon might smile. But Alyce did not mistake the
gesture as an invitation to smile back.

It was in this way that she'd attracted Simon Meech's attention,
of course. *Always* the bright young schoolgirl determined to be impressive to her teachers.

As a young instructor Simon inclined toward haughtiness, disdain. A kind of *Kinch*—James Joyce's notion of himself as Stephen
Dedalus, a brilliantly unhappy young man in his midtwenties, vain
and uncertain, insecure, eaten up with pride. Yet, in his way, *wanting to be good.*

Before coming to the university to earn a Ph.D. in philosophy,

Simon had been a seminary student for three years. He'd intended
to be a Catholic priest, a Jesuit, but, as he'd told Alyce, his plans
had not worked out.

Another girl would have asked, *But why not?* but Alyce understood that Simon did not want to be asked such a question.

Nothing personal, private! Nothing that pried into the young
man's soul. Alyce understood, for she did not want to be asked such
questions either.

Through lowered eyes Alyce observed him at the front of the
classroom, her lover. Though she did not consciously think *lover.*

For was *love* involved? She had not heard *love*—the word—uttered between them.

In class Alyce took careful notes. Or it appeared that Alyce took
careful notes. Leaning over her notebook in a trance of concentration, hair falling across the side of her face as she moved her pen
quickly across the page.

Now her feverish note-taking had a singular theme. What could
not be uttered aloud took shape beneath her pen. *I am afraid, Simon* . . .

But no. Why should she announce that she is *afraid.*

Instead she would say, *Simon, I think* . . .

But this too was weak, craven. Why should she say merely, *I think!*

Bravely she would say, *Simon, I am* . . .

But her resolve faded. Her courage melted away, a puddle at her
feet. How could she bring herself to tell her sardonic *Kinch*-lover,
I am pregnant.

The words would not come. She could not choke up such words,
which were both banal and terrible. Her tongue had gone numb, a
chill suffused her body.

Hurrying away from the classroom even as the bell clanged. If
Simon glanced after her with something like surprise, that Alyce
should be so eager to leave the classroom even as other students
lingered to speak with him, she didn't want to notice. *Away, away.
Must get away.*

Desperate to hide in the women's restroom, beneath the stairs.
To check another time. To determine *if.*

Though knowing—*No. Don't be ridiculous.*

In less than a week she'd become compulsive about checking
her underwear, to see if the bleeding had begun. Though knowing
that it had not.

In the morning after troubled sleep checking her nightgown, bedsheets. *But—is it? No.*

Haunting to her now, the dark menstrual blood that refused to appear. Like a shadow that, when you glance up, startled, has vanished—has not been there at all.

He'd tried to pull out of her at the crucial moment, Simon had. Tried, but had not, or had not exactly. Not *entirely.*

A groan of something like pain, anguish. The hawkish *Kinch*-face contorted for a long moment, the teeth bared.

She'd scarcely seen him. His lower body. His penis, which was (she would try to recall afterward, as one might try to recall a frightening dream, to master the dream) blunt and hard, hot with blood and angry-seeming.

Yet soft-skinned. Astonishingly soft, flaccid. When they'd lain together panting and sweating and whatever had passed through them like an electric current had vanished as if it had never been and she'd felt it—felt *him*—against her belly, sticky with mucus.

For this was love, was it? Naively she'd wanted to think, *It's a promise. Love will come.*

The truth was, she'd hardly known what was happening. What Simon was doing to her, or trying (awkwardly) to do to her, which yielded no pleasure for her, only just a sharp-piercing shocking hurt between her legs that had felt like an evisceration.

Clumsily they were lying together on a sofa in Simon's apartment, much too narrow for them. The sofa was not very clean, and now it would be less clean, a patina of grime on a nubby beige fabric. Without wishing to, Alyce had noted the frayed carpet, stains in the hardwood floor and in the faded wallpaper. A smell of cooking odors from the floor below. The apartment was furnished, Simon had said with a smiling shrug, as if to absolve himself of responsibility for it.

It was an interim life, Simon said. A between-life. Neither here nor there. Not yet.

She hadn't known what he meant. Much of his speech, airy, witty, self-conscious, Alyce didn't quite understand; but she understood that she was expected to react, with a smile, laughter, admiration.

In their lovemaking Simon had panted like a creature that has been hunted down, not like a hunter. Yet Alyce would recall he had hunted, pursued, chased down, all but coerced *her.*

Not rape. Nothing so physically coercive. Instead he'd made her feel shame, that she had caused him to misunderstand her.

"Why did you come back here with me, then? Why are you being disingenuous now?" He'd professed surprise, reproach when Alyce had seemed to resist him.

Disingenuous. She knew what this word meant though guessing he might assume that she did not know.

"I—I don't know . . . I'd thought—you wanted to . . ."

Spend time with me. Talk with me. About linguistics, philosophy of mind . . .

She'd been confused. Her brain wasn't functioning with its usual precision. Like a fine mechanism into which static has been introduced, to befuddle.

Simon had shocked her by addressing her with an air of disdain, sarcasm that was totally unlike the way he'd behaved at the reception or the way he behaved in the classroom. Oh, but didn't he *like* her? She'd thought he had *liked her.*

Like a child she was abashed, wounded. Naively wanting to say, *But I'd thought you liked me . . .*

But then, hearing the petulant edge in his own voice, Simon smiled, and was friendly again, and charming; holding her hand, stroking her arm, her shoulder. Telling her that she was very beautiful, he'd seen from the first day in their class that she was very beautiful, and quick to understand what others were slow to understand or never understood at all. He had seen that she was *special.* It was rare that any undergraduate had such an instinctive grasp of philosophy, especially a female undergraduate. (Had Simon been about to say *girl?* But he had not.) He'd had trouble looking away from her, he claimed, paying proper attention to the other students. He'd shown her first short paper, intriguingly titled "Zeno's Paradoxes and Our Own," to the professor who lectured in the course, who'd been impressed as well. Both had agreed on a grade of A.

He was leaning very close to Alyce and breathing audibly, hotly, like one who is not accustomed to such intimacy yet believes it to be his due.

Still, Alyce held herself stiff and unyielding. Her heart was beating rapidly as the heart of a creature that is trapped, that has not quite acknowledged it is trapped.

"Well. We can leave. We don't have to stay if you're not comfort-

able here, Alyce." Simon's voice was flat, dismissive. The enuncia-
tion of *Alyce* was not flattering.

"I—I think—yes, I would like to l-leave . . ."

Her voice trailed off. The misunderstanding had been hers, that
was clear. Yet, she had no idea what to say. Apologize? Simon saw how
she was hesitating, trying to smile, and put his hands on her, and his
mouth against her mouth, and so a kind of fury passed over them.

Not rape. Not—precisely.

Though her body tensed against him, unmistakably. Stiffening
in sheer physical panic, dread. Another man, a truer lover, would
have relented, drawn away. Would have soothed the frightened
young woman, comforted her, spoken to her. But not this man,
who'd lost awareness of Alyce except as a physical being, in oppo-
sition to him, but weaker than he, unable to withstand his greater
strength.

Oh Christ. Jesus! The cry was torn from him.

Not pleasure, such intensity of feeling. Convulsive, anguished.

Not guessing at the time, he would blame *her.*

Afterward she'd dressed quickly, in the bathroom of his apartment, a space so cramped she could barely move without colliding
with the sink, the toilet, a wall. Clumsily washing herself, not meeting her dazed and bloodshot eyes in the mirror, dragging wetted
fingers through her straggly hair.

He'd walked her back to the residence, mostly in silence. Long
*Kinch-*legs, eager to stride ahead of her. The air was colder, the mist
had thickened. The tall straight fir trees were near-invisible. She
would recall, her pride would insist, Simon had clasped her hand
for at least part of the walk, but in fact he'd only just gripped her
arm at the elbow from time to time, not so much to comfort as to
hurry her.

"I'll let you go, from here. It's not a great idea for us to be seen
together." He'd stopped at the sidewalk leading to her residence
and was already backing away.

No kiss. No final squeeze of Alyce's hand. She would tell herself,
of course, he was concerned for her, for her as well as himself.

She would not see him again. She would stay away from his class,
which met late on Thursday afternoons. He'd had so little awareness of her in that moment; he'd forgotten her entirely in the very
instant of penetrating her body.

Hating him. So very ashamed that she had not been able to withstand the man.

She *would not stay away* from class. Certainly not!

Why should she deprive herself of philosophy? She loved and
revered the texts she was reading for the first time—Plato, Aris-
totle, Marcus Aurelius, Spinoza, Locke, Hume. John Stuart Mill.
Ridiculous for her to stay away from class because of the man, and
risk a failing grade.

And she would see Simon Meech again. If he summoned Alyce,
she would come to him.

In all, five times. In the furnished apartment, arriving by stealth,
after dark. On that sofa. As winter deepened. As dark came earlier
each day, and snow muffled the stone walkways, and there were
more of Alyce's clothes to be tugged off by the man's impatient
hands. And afterward clumsily washing herself, her raw and chafed
and heated body, avoiding her reflection in the mirror. *Is this me?
Alyce? Doing such things?* The wonderment in it, dread and pride
commingled.

Touching her mouth, tenderly. Lips swollen from being kissed,
sucked.

Yes. It is you. No one else.

3.

And then Roland B___ interceded in her life.

No one could have anticipated. (Alyce could not have anticipated.) How crossing the snow-swept square in front of the university library a few days after she'd had no choice but to realize
that she must be pregnant she'd heard a familiar voice calling her
name—"Alyce?"

Blindly she'd been making her way. Head lowered, thoughts
abuzz with alarm, fear. *No. Can't. Not possible.*

The surprise of her name in this public place like a burst of
music.

She turned and saw—who was it? A gentlemanly older man—in
a brown winter overcoat with a sealskin collar, pumpkin-colored
knit cap pulled down over his head—crinkling his eyes at her in
delight. "Miss Urquhart? It *is* you."

Startling Alyce, the gentleman reached for her hands. She was too surprised to shrink back shyly.

"Alyce, I believe? Hel*lo*."

"H-Hello . . ."

It was an astonishment to be greeted this way by the visiting poet, who was so formal in his speech in the seminar. Rarely—indeed, never—had Professor B___ called any student by a first name that Alyce could remember. She wouldn't have dared to assume that the poet even knew her first name or that, outside the seminar room, he would recognize her.

"Have you seen the Poet's House, Alyce? No? Come, then. You will be my first visitor."

"I wish that I could, Professor, but . . ."

"It's close by. In this direction. My dear, come!"—linking his arm through Alyce's arm in a display of mock gallantry.

How playful Roland B___ was, in the bright, open air! Not a small tentative man as he'd appeared in the seminar room but as tall as Alyce, and quite forceful.

The Poet's House, as it was called, was a handsome old faded-red-brick Edwardian residence that looked as if it were held together by the thick-clustered ivy that covered its walls. Set back behind a wrought-iron fence and gate, it had the air of a quaint period piece; in its small front lawn was a statue in black marble of the Presbyterian minister who'd founded the college in 1847.

In the foyer a brass plaque noted that such distinguished poets as Robert Frost, Amy Lowell, Theodore Roethke, and Galway Kinnell had been residents in the house. The interior exuded an air of faded opulence: antique furniture, musty brick fireplace, French silk wallpaper, Steinway grand piano with several (muted) keys, which Roland B___ cheerfully struck as he led his visitor into the drawing room.

"Let me take your coat, dear. You will stay awhile, I hope."

"I—I can't stay long. I was on my way to the library . . ."

"And would you like tea, dear? I was going to prepare tea for myself."

No, no! I must leave.

"Y-Yes. Thank you."

Roland B___ was standing somewhat close to her, smiling.

She could see just his lower teeth, which were somewhat small, uneven, stained.

Roland B___ was observing her with a smile. The flush in his cheeks and glisten in his eyes made Alyce wonder if he'd been drinking in the afternoon.

No doubt it was lonely for him here, away from friends and companions in Boston. In the seminar he'd several times spoken of Boston with a wistful air.

"Your choice of tea, dear: green, Darjeeling, Earl Grey, Lapsang."

Whatever Roland B___ was having, Alyce said she would have.

"You are very agreeable, dear Alyce! In our seminar you are not so easily persuaded."

This seemed to Alyce a remark provocative as a nudge in the ribs. As if, through the weeks of the semester, the poet had been hoping to persuade her — of what?

How little he knew of her, or could guess! Alyce herself could not bear to think of her predicament, what grew in her belly like a tiny acorn, unstoppable.

Leading Alyce along a corridor into a rear bedroom with elaborate white molding at the ceiling. A four-poster bed with a brass headboard, threadbare Indian carpet, tables piled with books and magazines. A small chandelier hung from the ceiling, also brass, in need of polishing.

"Here you have a glimpse, my dear, of a bachelor's stoical life. When I was young I yearned to be alone, and got my wish. And now I am older, and the danger is past."

Seeing that the faded quilt on the bed was crooked, Roland B___ deftly smoothed out the wrinkles.

The four-poster bed was not large, an old-fashioned double bed, but you could see that the occupant used just one half of it, with large square pillows propped up against the headboard; on the bedside table, a notebook and a stack of books. There came to Alyce's nostrils a faint, musty smell of bedclothes not freshly laundered.

"D'you read in bed, Alyce?"

Alyce nodded *yes.*

"D'you write in bed? In a notebook?"

Alyce nodded *yes.*

"Reading poetry, scribbling poetry, dreaming poetry. Yes, I'm sure that you do."

Roland B___ was standing uncomfortably close to Alyce. She laughed nervously, and edged away.

In all of the rooms of the Poet's House that Alyce had seen, the poet kept books, papers, worksheets. You could see that wherever he went, Roland B___ had to have a book at his fingertips, and he had to have his work. In a bay window he'd positioned an antique writing desk so that he could sit and gaze out the window at the brick-walled courtyard filling up with snow.

"My dear Alyce, sit! Sit here."

Roland B___ urged Alyce to sit at the desk, hands on her shoulders. Then leaning over her, his chin grazing the top of her head.

Very peculiar, Alyce thought this. As if Roland B___ was imagining he might see through her eyes.

Alyce would have liked to throw off the poet's hands, leap to her feet, and escape. But a sensation of lethargy came over her, as if her limbs had lost their strength. She could barely move.

He sees that I am unhappy. An open wound.

"You are welcome, you know. At any time."

In the courtyard snow was falling steadily now. A swirl of white, mesmerizing. Soon the old, faded brick would be obscured by powdery snow. Footsteps would be muffled. Voices would be muffled. Within the movement of the snow flurrying to earth all was still. Alyce Urquhart and Roland B___ might have been alone together in a remote place, in a remote time. The elderly poet standing behind Alyce, hands on her shoulders, silent, staring out the window at the foreshortened view filling up with snow.

In that way it began.

All things begin in innocence.

That is to say, ignorance.

4.

God help me. Even if you don't love me.

5.

Feverishly her brain worked. Like a cornered rat, she thought herself. Scrawling lines of poetry until her fingers ached.

Yet she did nothing. Like one waiting for—what?

Each morning after a feverish night. Choking back waves of nausea she could not bear to think was *morning sickness.*

So banal! Shameful.

What had taken root inside her, without her awareness. What grew darkly, flourished. That tough rubbery little slug not to be named, still less confronted.

What she could not acknowledge, had revealed to no one. And could never, to her lover.

For he was *Kinch*, he would be repelled by her.

Futile pounding at her belly with her fists, as a child might pound, biting back tears of anger and self-derision. Each morning checking her nightgown, the bedsheets. So desperately did she wish to see coin-sized spangles of blood, streaks of blood, almost her eyes blurred with moisture saw these in the rumpled sheets.

God help me, just this once. I will never doubt you again.

It's your baby too, Simon. We are equally responsible. Therefore you must help me.

Could not bring herself to approach the man. Certainly not in the classroom, or in the university office that he shared with another young professor.

Nor could she envision herself walking (slowly? briskly?) across campus, making her way to the weathered Victorian house in which the man she loved (for she did love Simon Meech, that was the shameful fact) rented a furnished apartment. A lone figure in a film, dark-clad against snowy white. Climbing stairs, lifting her fist to knock on a door. Dear God, *no.*

Haunted by the thing inside her, in the pit of her belly, in her *uterus,* that was so tiny! Surely something might happen to it. How frequent were miscarriages, if Alyce continued not to eat, not to sleep, dazed and uncertain, descending staircases, crossing busy streets . . .

The fact was, Alyce had no idea how to procure an abortion, and she had no money to pay for an abortion, nor even any idea how much money would be required for an abortion. One hundred dollars? Five hundred? A thousand? In high school she'd heard rumors . . . Unexplained disappearances of girls, deaths.

What she did know: abortion was illegal. There was no region of the country in which abortion was legal. Simply to inquire about an abortion might be illegal—might be enough to get her expelled from the university. She dared not risk assuming that another girl would take pity on her and help her. And not report her to authority.

There was only Simon with whom she might plead. And yet there was not Simon.

He would stare at her in disbelief, dismay. Revulsion.

He'd seemed to praise, in certain of his remarks, the "celibate" life. The life that "transcends" the merely personal, trivial. The biological self that is a refutation of the spiritual self. The priestly life, far superior to the conjugal life. Several times he'd expressed impatience with Alyce when she tried to discuss such issues with him, as if there might be two sides to a question and not just his.

Like a candle flame extinguished by a single rude breath, the man's feeling for her. Erotic longing could not withstand such raw need. Alyce could not risk that.

How do you "abort" a fetus yourself? Not easily.

There were drugs, Alyce knew. Powerful abortifacients available only to physicians, for provoking miscarriages when something has gone wrong with a pregnancy. But these could be lethal if not administered by a doctor. And they were not available, in any case.

Wire coat hanger: the most common remedy. Possibly ice pick, long-bladed knife, chopstick . . . Alyce began to feel faint, dazed, at the mere thought.

6.

So lonely, could not say *no*.

Astonishing to Alyce to learn, in time, that Roland B___ wasn't old — not *old*. Just sixty-one.

Old enough to be Alyce's father (of course) but (possibly) not old enough to be her grandfather . . .

She was recalling: Sylvia Plath, patron saint of lost souls, had been only thirty at the time of her suicide.

Despite the bald dome of his head and the formality of his public manner, Roland B___ was a surprisingly youthful person. His face gave the impression of being unlined, though (as Alyce saw close up) his skin was a network of creases fine as cobwebs. His pebble-colored eyes were heavy-lidded at times, like a turtle's, though at other times alert and curious. What appeared to be a scattering of liver marks on the backs of his hands were freckles. Guarded and muted in the seminar, he was capable of quick spontaneous laughter in the privacy of the Poet's House, especially if he'd had a drink or two.

Red wine, occasionally whiskey. Alyce accepted a drink but (usually) left it untouched.

In the seminar, when Alyce spoke Roland B___ regarded her through half-shut eyes as if it wasn't Alyce's words but her voice that fascinated him. She reminded him of someone—did she? She'd wondered at first if he even knew who she was—which of the names on the student roster was hers.

And in the Poet's House Alyce wondered if he knew who she was among the many women and girls with whom he'd been intimately acquainted in his lifetime.

From his poetry Alyce knew that Roland B___ had had lovers. He spoke of a stoical bachelor's life as if with regret, but his had not been a bachelor's life, and probably not stoical. Only first names attached to the wraithlike presences that had drifted in and out of the poet's life when he'd been a younger man.

But he never forgot Alyce's name once he'd learned it. Very carefully he pronounced the name—"Alyce."

Telling her that he'd once met the original Alice: "Alice Liddell."

Alice Liddell? For a moment Alyce didn't recognize the name, then she recalled: of course, the child Alice, model for the Alice of *Alice's Adventures in Wonderland* and *Through the Looking-Glass and What Alice Found There.* The dark-eyed, dark-haired, dreamy little seven-year-old whom the Oxford mathematician Charles Dodgson ("Lewis Carroll") had photographed in poses of extraordinary tenderness and intimacy, of a kind that would be outlawed in the present time.

"Alice Liddell's family banished Lewis Carroll finally—no one knows exactly why, but we can imagine. His heart was broken."

Poor Alice Liddell, forever haunted by "Alice"—the child she'd never really been and could not escape; as an elderly woman brought to the United States by her ambitious son, who'd wished to peddle a book he'd written about her, obliged to meet with the press, pose for photographs, sign copies of the son's book. Roland B___ had been a young man at the time, newly arrived in New York City, and at a gathering at the National Arts Club he'd actually—for a fleeting moment—shaken the hand of the "original" Alice.

Still an attractive woman, he'd thought, despite being exploited by her son and his publishers. The following year, 1934, she'd died, at the age of eighty-two.

Nineteen thirty-four! Alyce was astonished, this was so long ago.

Roland B___ said thoughtfully, "All her life she'd had to endure seeing pictures of herself, growing ever older, set beside the Tenniel drawings of 'Alice'—perpetually a little girl, with beautiful eyes and thick ringlets of hair. Newspaper reporters fawning over her, to her face, then writing ironic profiles of her as an adult, aging woman."

Alyce agreed, that would be painful. A difficult life.

Haunted by your own child-self! A vision of you in another's eyes, and not in your own. Forever young, as you grew older.

Alyce told Roland B___ she'd thought the Alice books were frightening when she'd been a child. Even the illustrations by John Tenniel frightened her. So grotesque! And Alice so often looking pained, grown too big, or shrunken, made to carry freakish creatures in her arms, fleeing from a shrieking mad queen—*Off with her head! Off with her head!*

She recalled the Alice of the books as a child very different from herself. Rather, the British girl had seemed somewhat adult to Alyce. And an orphan.

An orphan? Roland B___ was curious.

Well, Alice has no parents in the Alice books. Down the rabbit-hole into Wonderland and through the mirror into the Looking-Glass World, Alice wanders entirely alone, lost, without even a last name.

"I suppose you are right, dear. I'd read the books so long ago, I scarcely remember details. It never occurred to me that, as you've said, Alice was *alone.*"

Roland B___ began to recite:

"A boat beneath a sunny sky,
Lingering onward dreamily
In an evening of July—
Children three that nestle near,
Eager eye and willing ear,
Pleased a simple tale to hear—
Long has paled that sunny sky:
Echoes fade and memories die:
Autumn frosts have slain July.
Still she haunts me, phantomwise,
Alice moving under skies
Never seen by waking eyes . . ."

The poet's voice trailed off with an air of melancholy, regret.

Alyce was feeling uneasy. In the poet's overheated drawing room, a sense of chill.

Fragments from the Alice books she was being made to recall, as one might recall fragments from disturbing dreams. Like bats with fluttering wings these beat about her head. "Curiouser and curiouser"—"'Twas brillig, and the slithy toves"—"beat him when he sneezes"—"six impossible things to believe before breakfast." The mad twins Tweedledee and Tweedledum screaming at each other. The elderly white king sleeping beneath a tree, dreaming of Alice, and if he wakes from dreaming of her, Alice will vanish. Oh, terrifying! The Walrus and the Carpenter, strolling along the beach and devouring baby oysters *one by one*. Alice is herself going to be eaten—it's only a matter of time. Alice is only protected by remaining entranced in Wonderland and in the Looking-Glass World by the game of chess in which the (unlikely) promise is she will become a queen. Recalling the elderly White Queen disappearing into a soup tureen, about to be eaten by a leg of mutton, and candles rising madly to the ceiling—*Something is about to happen!*

Alyce shuddered. She'd hated and feared the Alice books and had had bad dreams about finding herself captive inside their pages. She was only realizing now.

On his fingers Roland B___ calculated how old he'd have been when Alyce was seven: "Fifty, at least! More than the difference in years between Charles Dodgson and Alice Liddell."

But why was Roland B___ telling Alyce this? And why, with such a strange smile?

The poet dared to take her hands, to comfort her.

"'Still she haunts me, phantomwise.'"

Alyce tried to smile, embarrassed. The poet held her hands with surprising strength.

"You are an unusually beautiful girl, Alyce—I mean, your beauty is unusual. It is not at all conventional, and some might say—those lacking a discerning eye might say—that you are not 'conventionally attractive' at all. You remind me of the child Alice Liddell, actually—those dark, melancholy eyes."

Alyce drew a sharp breath. "Well. I am not Alice Liddell, Professor. And I think I will leave now."

And so the comforting hands released hers, startled. The eyelids hooded like turtles' eyelids fluttered in alarm. Alyce rose to her feet, smiling, to think, *Enough of goddamned dark, melancholy eyes. I have shocked you at last, haven't I.*

7.

Each morning the tiny slug held firm. Deep inside the dark-haired, dark-eyed girl who'd once been, no, had never been Alice Liddell.

No loosening of menstrual blood, fresh dark stains in the bedclothes. No.

God help me. Even if you don't love me.

And the blunt and unassailable answer came at once to her: *Die, then. The power is in your hands.*

The possibility of killing herself.

In the early hours of the morning suicide appeared to be more feasible than abortion, certainly more convenient, since it didn't involve others and would incur no expense.

Preposterous even to consider. A pregnancy would last only nine months, and nine months is not long in a normal lifetime. *Yes, but there would be no normal lifetime remaining after the pregnancy.*

Steeling her courage to ask one of the older girls in the residence if Alyce could speak with her in private about something serious, something private, rehearsing the faltering words she would say, but her weak courage failed, she could not bring herself to so expose herself, for she could not trust anyone. Could not.

Throwing oneself from a height, from a bridge, would be an effective means. Stepping in front of a speeding vehicle, preferably a truck or a bus. Alyce tried to imagine summoning such courage if she had not even the courage to approach someone to speak of her predicament.

Later in the pregnancy, when she became desperate. Maybe then. If desperate, fanatic, and obsessed, maybe you don't need courage.

For certainly Alyce would become desperate when others began to notice, to suspect. When her stomach swelled out and her clothes no longer fit.

How long did she have? Weeks? A death sentence—the pregnancy growing like a tumor that could not be stopped.

Slashing her wrists. All she would require was a razor or a sharp knife and the act could be executed in the night, without detection if she acted sensibly. In a bathtub with running water to dilute the flow of blood, carry it away to oblivion. In one of the bathrooms in the residence which were single occupancy, equipped with a bathtub and not a shower stall; a room that could be locked, where no one could interrupt and Alyce could sedate herself with aspirin and lower herself into hot steaming water, shut her eyes refusing to see, for she was a coward and could not bear to see streams of blood in water rushing down a drain, as her heart beat slower with the loss of blood a sweet comfort would come over her at last . . . But—would she have removed her clothes, as if for a bath? Or would she be dressed, or partly dressed, in her flannel nightgown perhaps? For she would not (oh, she *would not*) want to be discovered both naked and dead.

And how would *dead* be accomplished, exactly? Only one wrist could be slashed by the badly trembling right hand, not both wrists. The left wrist, or rather the inside of the left forearm, the tender flesh there would have to be cut (deeply, swiftly, unerringly) before pain overcame her and the razor or knife fell from her fingers into the splashing water . . .

Overdose of pills? Which pills? Alyce had no prescription pills, would have to buy pills at a drugstore, and what pills would these be? Sleeping pills? She had no idea. If she were at home she'd have access to the medications in her parents' medicine cabinet—pills for high blood pressure, angina, kidney trouble, arthritis. But if she swallowed enough pills to kill herself, that might be enough pills to cause her to vomit, for she was not accustomed to swallowing pills. Had no idea how her stomach would react. And if she didn't vomit enough she would sink into a sweaty stupor but not die, her heart continuing to beat like a stubborn metronome, waking hours or days later in her own vomit and excrement, taken by ambulance to an ER, where her stomach would be pumped—whatever *pumped* meant, it did not promise romance or dignity. Hospitalized for psychiatric evaluation, parents contacted, discovery of pregnancy, removed from the university, possibly brain-damaged, possibly "vegetative state" . . .

Alyce laughed. Three-twenty a.m. and she was standing flatfooted on a cold hardwood floor, having heaved herself up from the bed in which she'd failed to sleep since turning out the light several hours before.

Deciding, Goddamn, she *would not*. *Would not* kill herself, nor even make the attempt.

Returning from morning classes to discover a folded note in her mailbox, a phone message. Something like a sliver of glass piercing her heart at the thought that this was Simon summoning her to him at last, but in fact as her fluttering eyes barely made out through a scrim of tears the note was a phone message for her—*Dearest Alyce, Please call this number. R. B.*

8.

In this way her life was decided.

The gift of her life. So Alyce would think at the time.

Returning to the Poet's House. Her heart beating eagerly as Roland B___ opened the door with a playful bow.

"Dear Alyce! I have missed you. Come in."

It was decided, Alyce would act as Roland B___'s assistant and archivist. For that would be the formal title of her role in his life and (as she might have anticipated at the time) in his posthumous life—*assistant, archivist.*

"I will pay you, of course, Alyce. I don't expect you to give up your precious time for nothing."

And, "Please do call me Roland, dear. Will you at least try?"

It was touching to Alyce that the poet so readily forgave her for her rudeness to him. Brushing aside her embarrassed apology with a dismissive gesture—"Don't be absurd, dear. An old man is well advised to be put in his place when he oversteps boundaries. Good to remind me."

"Oh, but, Professor, you're not *old.*"

The words leapt from Alyce. She had no idea that she would speak at all in response to the poet's rueful remark.

She'd spoken laughingly, out of nervousness. Like Alice in the Looking-Glass World in which all things are reversed, comical.

But she saw how it was true. Roland B___, in his solitude, loneliness. At the university he was admired, often invited to receptions, luncheons, dinners, but he went everywhere alone and returned to the faded-brick Poet's House alone. In the antique-furnished bed-room, in the four-poster bed alone.

And Alyce in her solitude, loneliness. Surrounded by others her age, swarms of others on the university walkways, yet alone.

For Simon Meech had not contacted her, and in the classroom he seemed now scarcely to glance in her direction and to take no notice how she departed immediately when the class ended.

All of the colors of the drawing room in the Poet's House seemed brighter to her, richer and more beautiful than she recalled. Crimson velvet pillows on a dove-gray velvet sofa, a deep russet-brown Chinese vase on the fireplace mantel, portraits of stern-looking eighteenth-century gentlemen on the walls.

How comical, these portraits! As if, long dead, long forgotten, they were playing the roles now of ancestors.

"Come in, dear Alyce! Your hands are cold. Will you have tea?" Drawing her into the overheated interior, where, on the beautiful old grand piano, a crystal vase of red roses pulsed with vivid color—*For me? Those roses are for me.*

Here was someone who cherished her. Would not repudiate, hurt her.

Strange, since Alyce's previous visit there'd come to be a new mood between her and Roland B___ that was lighter, more playful and (just perceptibly) erotic.

She'd dared to speak sharply to the professor. She'd pushed away his hands and left him. Astonishing him, as she'd astonished herself, and now they were beginning anew.

He'd brought back from a local bakery delicious flaky-buttery scones. Serving these to his visitor, with Lapsang tea in Wedgwood teapot and cups. Though she'd been stricken with nausea only a few hours before, Alyce felt now a wave of hunger powerful enough to make her tremble.

"You do look pale, dear. I was noticing in our class the other day. You were very quiet while the others chattered so self-importantly. Is something troubling you? Or is it 'Time's wingèd chariot, hurry-ing near'?"

An obscure reference, surely to a poem. But not a poem that Alyce knew.

"But you're too young, I think, to be troubled by the rapid pass-ing of time as we others are . . ."

At this Alyce laughed again, spilling tea from the dainty Wedgwood teacup. As if *time passing* wasn't painful to her as an abscess. As if such rituals as tea mattered when a few hours ago she'd been crouched over a toilet, dry-heaving.

"If there is something in your life that troubles you, I hope that you can confide in me, dear. I realize that at your age, so much is undecided, undefined. Recall what Paul Bowles said — 'Things don't happen, it depends upon who comes along.'"

Alyce had no idea who Paul Bowles was, but from the tone of Roland B___'s voice, she gathered that he was a visionary of some sort.

How shaky Alyce was feeling, yet how elated, in the presence of this kindly man. The gleaming dome of a head, across which feathery strands of gray hair lay lightly. The pouched eyes, crinkling at their corners. The hopeful smile, exposing yellowed teeth. Alyce felt how brittle her composure, which could be broken by a tender word from this man, a caress.

But what had he asked her? Hungrily she'd devoured an entire scone, and emptied her cup of Lapsang tea. Her hands were still trembling.

"Well, dear. Perhaps in time you will confide in me, as your friend. From your poetry, I believe that I know you — inwardly. Please think of me as the 'friend of your soul.'"

On a mahogany table in the drawing room were manuscripts, drafts of poems, letters both handwritten and typed. On the floor, boxes of papers. Much of this was new since Alyce's most recent visit.

"I've had these boxes sent to me so that I can begin working on my archive here. D'you know what an archive is, dear?"

Alyce thought so, yes. Only the estimable merited *archives*.

"Virtually everything in a writer's life. But I've only saved papers, documents, publications, letters — hundreds of letters. Out-of-print books, limited editions. I've delayed for years — never answered inquiries from Harvard, Yale, Columbia — as I've delayed making out a will. It's damned difficult, you see, for those of us who fantasize that we will live forever, to think of ourselves as mortal, let alone posthumous . . . But if you could help me, dear, I think I could face the challenge."

"Of course, Professor. I can try."

Again she spoke without thinking. So yearning to please the elderly poet, so lonely, so desperate, she could barely contain herself in the presence of someone so seemingly kindly.

"Please, I've told you—Roland. *Professor* is for *les autres*."

"Roland." The name sounded unreal in Alyce's voice, unconvincing.

"Rol-*land*. Give it a French inflection, *s'il vous plais*."

"Rol-*land*." Like an overgrown child, Alyce was blushing with embarrassment.

"Well. That's an improvement, at least. *Merci!*"

Outside the drawing room windows, daylight was rapidly fading. In the chipped Wedgwood pot Lapsang tea cooled, forgotten. In a hearty mood Roland B___ poured whiskey into shot glasses for his visitor and himself and insisted that Alyce drink with him: "We have much to celebrate, my dear."

Soon a fever came into the poet's face; he was laughing happily; by the end of the evening, when Alyce prepared to return to her residence, Roland B___'s words had begun to slur and his fine-creased skin was deeply flushed. It was touching to Alyce, how in her presence the poet seemed to *warm*, even to *glow*.

Insisting, of course he would pay her. He would pay her very well. But she must tell no one else about their arrangement, none of Alyce's classmates in the seminar, not anyone, for fear that *les autres* would misunderstand.

Not wanting Alyce to leave. Please no! Not just yet.

She had a curfew, Alyce tried to explain, laughing. All undergraduate women who lived in university residences had midnight curfews.

Ridiculous! Alyce should move out of such a confining place to a place of her own. *He* would help her pay for it.

9.

How happy Alyce was, in the Poet's House! *It* did not have the power to paralyze her here.

That interlude of days nearing the winter solstice when Alyce arrived breathless and hopeful at the red-brick residence between 4:30 and 5 p.m. Bringing her schoolwork, anthologies and texts she had to read for courses, papers she had to write, her notebook in which she kept drafts of her poems, in the interstices of helping Roland B___ organize the archive.

"My dear, we are making progress! I'm proud of us."

By the time Alyce arrived Roland B___ would have had a whiskey or two, a glass of wine or two, or three. Grateful to see her. Trying to maintain dignity. Kissing her hand, hands.

Sometime between 8 and 9 p.m. they would eat a meal together, which Roland B___ ordered and paid for, delivered to the Poet's House from one of a half-dozen restaurants in town. By the time the food arrived Roland would have had another whiskey, or begun another glass of wine, and Alyce would have left the work table to set the dining-room table with beautiful if chipped and cracked china she'd discovered in a sideboard, tarnished silverware, white linen napkins, cut-glass water goblets. Candlestick holders, candles. Their food was delivered in Styrofoam packages, transferred by Alyce to platters set in an oven at 375 degrees Fahrenheit. The aroma of heating food made her mouth water, she'd never been so *ravenous*.

Interludes of nausea were behind her now, mostly. Her center of gravity was settling in the region of her pelvis, closer to the ground.

Five days a week Alyce came to the Poet's House. Soon then six days a week. Seven. For always there was much to do that was thrilling to do, and in addition Roland B___ paid her generously as he'd promised, often in twenty-dollar bills, hastily, scarcely troubling to count out the bills, as if *paying* were embarrassing to him, as *being paid* was embarrassing to Alyce. "You need not report this income, you know, dear," Roland B___ said quietly, "as I shall not. What passes between us, IRS *shall not know*."

On Roland B___'s sturdy old Remington typewriter Alyce typed ribbon copies of poems as well as numerous drafts of poems, personal letters of Roland B___ which she was entrusted with critiquing and even correcting.

Telling herself, *I am doing this for him, he is my friend. The more I do for him, the more he is my friend.*

Only when she left the overheated Poet's House to return across the snow-swept campus to her residence a quarter mile away did reality sweep in upon Alyce, jarring as a clanging bell.

What was happening to her! What must she *do*.

Out of compulsion checking her underwear, her nightgown. Bedclothes. Hardly recalling what it was she sought, smears of blood, barely recalling it was menstrual blood, which had begun to seem to her remote like an imperfectly recollected dream.

Yes, but: the swell of her belly. Definitely. She could feel.

No longer losing weight out of anxiety and nausea but gaining weight. Five pounds, six . . . Eight pounds.

Roland B___ remarked how beautiful Alyce was. How smooth her skin, how shining her eyes . . . She wasn't so thin as she'd been. Definitely she was looking healthier.

"You see, you are *my* Alice. Come into my life when Alice was required, like magic."

Alyce laughed, embarrassed. Did Roland B___ really mean such things, or was he being fanciful? Poetic?

She wondered if in his vanity the elderly poet might have thought that his undergraduate assistant was falling in love with *him*.

It was becoming ever more difficult for Alyce to politely decline Roland B___'s offers of drinks. Possibly she would take a few sips of wine. But whiskey — *no*.

Pointing out, primly, "You know, Professor — I'm underage."

Roland B___ protested, "My dear, this is a private residence. No one can intrude here. The state has no authority here. My domicile." Pausing, slyly considering: "*Our* domicile. *Our* Wonderland. Without a warrant no officer of the state can cross the threshold and certainly no officer of the state can arrest *me*."

Soon too wanting Alyce to stay the night.

And what were you thinking, Alyce? That it would just — go away?

As one might be fascinated by a lump in a breast, a thickening tumor. A kind of paralysis. Sleeping heavily, her limbs mired in something soft like mud. Warm mud.

Recalling overhearing her mother and an aunt speaking in lowered voices of a friend's daughter, who'd had a six-months miscarriage when no one, including (allegedly) the girl, had even known that she was pregnant. A stocky girl, wearing loose-fitting shirts, overalls, not a very attractive girl (so it was said, an important detail), utterly astonished the family had been, disbelieving, scandalized. It had seemed improbable at the time that the girl hadn't seemed to know she was pregnant, yet now Alyce understood. It was very easy not to think about *it*. Anxiety about the future was replaced by a sudden need for a nap.

A swoon of ignorance, the most refreshing of deep sleeps.

That somehow it would go away. Cease to exist.

And you would wake to discover that it was all a bad dream—like Alice
waking from her nightmare.

"My dear, unavoidably I must be away for the rest of the afternoon.
But I will hurry back, I promise!"

It was flattering to Alyce that Roland sometimes left the Poet's
House while she remained behind. The poet had come to trust
his assistant, deferring to her out of respect for her good judgment or out of a cavalier wish not to be bothered with details. Yes,
yes!—those were letters from T. S. Eliot, who was plain "Tom Eliot"
to anyone who knew him, indeed yes, as Robert Lowell was "Cal,"
Alyce was correct, such precious archival material needed to be
kept in plastic binders, but—where would you get such binders?
The university bookstore? Huge ghastly place with racks of insipid
bestsellers, dour textbooks, T-shirts and sweatshirts, couldn't bring
himself to step inside a second time . . .

Of course Alyce would acquire the binders. Far more capably
than Roland B___, Alyce did such mundane tasks.

Mesmerizing to Alyce, to lose herself in hours of close, exacting
reading, deciphering handwritten letters to Roland B___, faded
carbon copies of Roland B___'s letters, handwritten manuscripts
by the poet himself, annotated galleys. Hundreds of letters from
individuals whose names were known and from individuals whose
names were unknown. In the 1930s Roland B___ had begun publishing verse; by 1954 Roland B___ had become poetry editor of
the *Nation* and would correspond with dozens of poet-friends. You
could see—Alyce could see—how the young ambitious poet had
made his way, not unerringly but erratically, haphazardly, sending
poems to whoever would receive them and offer comment or publication, grateful for any attention, encouragement, acceptance
from any editor, like one who is climbing a wall of sheer rock,
grasping at slippery surfaces.

Often Alyce brought letters to the window, to read carefully.
Small crabbed handwriting, faded typewriter ink. A letter from
John Crowe Ransom, editor of *Kenyon Review,* praising and accept-
ing several poems. A short, scribbled letter from the poet Delmore
Schwartz thanking Roland B___ for some favor. A letter from Elizabeth Bishop on hotel stationery, a sequence of dashed-off sen-
tences, rueful complaints about "Cal"—had to be Robert Lowell.

In these letters there was an air of intimacy, intrigue, and gossip that fascinated Alyce, who had nothing like this in her life.

Very easily she could fold up such letters. Some of them were paper-thin — blue airmail stationery. Slip them into her bookbag. Roland B___ would never know, for Roland B___ was a very careless custodian of what was his.

Especially the poet's early limited-edition publications, what Roland B___ called chapbooks, carelessly crammed together in boxes.

One of these was *Phantomwise and Other Poems*, published in 1936, beautifully printed on stiff white paper, with a mother-of-pearl cover and, on the title page, Roland B___'s youthful grandiloquent signature.

According to the copyright page, there'd been just fifty copies of this *Phantomwise* printed. In the box were three copies, each water-stained and torn.

The epigraph was familiar to her:

Still she haunts me, phantomwise.

What was this: a line from *Alice in Wonderland?* Charles Dodgson looking back at the seven-year-old Alice, suffused with yearning.

Leafing through the water-stained little book, which was just twenty pages. A half-dozen poems of Roland B___'s which Alyce had never seen before, and did not fully understand. Probably forgotten now by the poet himself.

Quickly she returned the copy of *Phantomwise* to the box. Even if her eccentric employer never knew the book was missing, even if no one would ever care that it was missing, Alyce would not behave so dishonestly. She could not *steal.*

It would be a betrayal of Roland B___'s tender regard for her. Her regard for him. Their mutual respect, which was unlike anything else in Alyce's life.

"Which of these do you prefer, Alyce?" The poet was revising poems originally published years ago, in 1953, in preparation for a *Selected Poems;* with the tactlessness of the young, Alyce said, "The older version. It's much stronger."

"Really? The *older version?*"

"Yes."

The poem was a clever imitation of a Donne sonnet. Alyce,

who knew only a few poems of John Donne, knew this. The harsh rhythms, masculine accents. By adding lines Roland B___ had softened the poem.

Her remark had surprised him. As she'd surprised him, yes and pleased him enormously, entering the Poet's House with the little cracked opal ring on the smallest finger of her right hand.

The look on Roland B___'s face! Like a candle, lighted.

My dear. You have made me so happy.

But now he'd gone away, not so happy.

In the kitchen she heard him clattering about. Seeking a glass.

Often Alyce washed dishes after their meals. Liking the feel of hot soapy water. If she had not, the elderly poet would have left dirtied dishes in the sink, in a pool of scummy water, awaiting the cleaning woman on Wednesday mornings. He seemed incapable of washing even teacups and coffee mugs. Whiskey glasses, wineglasses accumulated, out of an impressive store in the Poet's House cupboards, until Alyce washed them, and left them sparkling on the shelves.

Of course, Roland B___ was getting a drink now. To soothe his jarred nerves.

Returning at last, whiskey in hand, to Alyce's relief no whiskey for her.

But he also had a gift for her—"In gratitude for your astute insight, and your honesty, dear Alyce. A 'collector's item'—supposedly."

It was a copy of *Phantomwise,* the slender chapbook with the mother-of-pearl cover. Alyce felt her face burn as if she'd been exposed as a thief.

But Roland B___'s face was crinkled in a wide smile, without irony.

Holding the water-stained little book out to her, opened to the title page—*For my dear Alyce, who brings the light of radiance into my life. With love, Roland.*

Alyce took the book from Roland B___'s fingers. Tears leaked from her eyes. It was not possible to keep from crying, Roland B___ was so kind.

"Oh Alyce, what's wrong? Why are you crying?"

Heard herself telling him, at last: she was pregnant.

That word, blunt and shaming: *pregnant.*

How long, how many weeks exactly, she didn't know.

Didn't want to know. Had not allowed herself to know.

Stammering, sobbing. Like a child. A broken girl. Her composure shattered as backbone might be shattered. Roland B___ tried to comfort her.

Later Alyce would realize that the elderly poet had not been so very surprised. Must have known, suspected—something . . .

Of course, he was very kind to Alyce. Sitting beside her on a sofa, gripping her hands to still them. Letting her speak in a rush of words, and letting her fall silent, choked with emotion. Such kindness was terrible to her, obliterating. She could not recall when anyone had been so kind to her. So sympathetically listened to her.

"My dear. My poor dear. This is not good news for you, is it?"

No. Not good news. Alyce laughed, wiping her eyes.

He was holding her. As an older relative might hold her.

Assuring her he would help her. If she would allow him.

In his arms Alyce wept. Heaving sobs, graceless. Her pride had vanished. She was exposed, helpless. The posture she'd so rigorously maintained in her classes, within the gaze of others, abandoned. Suddenly a pregnant creature, helpless.

"Marry me, dear. Make me your husband. I will take care of you and your baby. It will be our baby."

Roland B___ spoke urgently, his words slurred from the whiskey.

Alyce laughed, nervously. No, no! She could not.

"I know you don't love me—yet. I can love enough for both of us. You know, you are *my Alice*."

Alyce wanted to push away. Alyce wanted to snatch up her dignity, what remained of her dignity, and flee the Poet's House. Yet there was Alyce, weakly huddled in the poet's arms. As if shielded from a strong wind. Scarcely recalling the man's name. Yet her mind was working rapidly. *He will help me. He has saved me.*

In the four-poster bed, in the dim-lit bedroom. An antique bed with a hard mattress that creaked beneath their weight. It was too absurd, Alyce thought. This was not happening! The elderly man breathing loudly, panting as if he'd climbed a flight of stairs. Tenderly holding her, kissing her mouth, her throat. Feathery-light kisses that became by quick degrees harder, sucking kisses that took her breath away.

"No. Please. Don't." Alyce pushed at him, frightened.

"Sorry!"

The elderly lover would make a joke of it, if he could.

Still he was breathing hard. Harshly. Excused himself to go into the bathroom, swaying on his feet.

There came a sound of faucets, plumbing. Alyce sat up, swung her legs off the bed. What was she doing, why was she here? She would leave, before he returned. Or—she would wait for him in the drawing room, in her coat. For it would be rude, unconscionable, to rush away without speaking to him.

She would ask him for financial help. Please would he help her!

All she wanted was her old, lost body. The *not-pregnant* body. A girl's slender body with narrow hips, small hard breasts, flat belly and nothing inside the belly to make it swell like a balloon.

How happy she'd been, in that *not-pregnant* body. Wholly unaware, oblivious. And now.

She had no doubt Roland B___ could put her in contact with someone who could help her. Roland B___ could provide the money.

An abortion. A doctor who could perform an abortion.

These blunt words had to be uttered. She, Alyce, would have to utter them.

After some minutes Alyce returned hesitantly to the bedroom. But Roland B___ was still in the bathroom. Something fell to the tile floor, clattered. Alyce came closer to the door, not knowing what to do. She had not wanted to think that something might be wrong with the elderly poet, that his breathing had been harsh and laborious, almost as soon as he'd urged her into the bedroom and onto the bed.

Alyce had balked, like an overgrown girl. She had given in, but stiffly. She had not returned his kisses except weakly, out of a kind of politeness. For a man of his age he'd been surprisingly strong. He'd been surprisingly heavy. But then, he was not *old*. She knew that.

Her face was wet with tears. Hair in her face. At last daring to call, "R-Roland? Is something wrong?"

How the name *Roland* stuck in her mouth! She could hardly bear to speak it. Like playacting this felt, speaking a name in a script.

The panicked thought came to her, *Is he ill? Is he dying? Am I to be his witness?*

Alyce approached the bathroom door. Leaned her ear against it. "Hello? Excuse me? Is—something wrong?"

In poetry you chisel the most beautiful words out of language.

In life you stutter words. It is never possible to speak so beautifully as you wish to speak.

Inside, a response she could not quite hear. Maybe it was a reply, *No, yes, I am all right, go away.* Or maybe it was a groan. A cry. A muffled plea. *Help me, I am not all right. Do not go away.*

A terrifying thought, that the elderly poet was ill. At the very moment of his declaration of love for her, his wish to help her, to marry her . . . Alyce had long suspected that Roland B___ was not entirely well: hearing him breathing laboriously, moving with unnatural slowness at times. Wanting to think at the time, *Oh, he's been drinking. That's why.*

Like seeing a spark fly out of a chimney and fall into a carpet.

In the next instant the spark may become a flame. The flame may become fire.

Is he dying? He doesn't want to die alone . . .

Then, suddenly: the door was opened. Roland B___ emerged, trying to smile.

A ghastly smile. His skin pale as if drained of blood. And his eyelids fluttering. His hand pressed against his chest.

She would call 911, Alyce told him. They could not wait any longer.

Roland protested *no.* Not yet. His heart "played tricks" on him— sometimes . . .

No. No longer. Alyce would call 911, and save the poet's life.

10.

"He is expecting me. He needs me."

At the ER insisting that yes, she was Roland B___'s assistant, a student at the university enrolled in the professor's course. For she could not bring herself to say that she was the elderly poet's *friend.*

Still less that she was the poet's *Alice.* The girl he'd offered to marry.

"He needs me, he expects me. I would have ridden with him in the ambulance but there was no room . . ."

A nurse led Alyce into the interior of the ER. She could not stop from glancing into small rooms with doors ajar—dreading to see what, who was inside. Smells assailed her nostrils, her eyes filled with tears. She thought, *Oh God if he dies. If he has died.*

Barely could she recall her own condition. What was growing, flourishing in her belly. Her aching and oddly full breasts. How she'd confessed to the poet, and how he'd taken hold of her hands, his kindness. His wish to help her.

. . . love enough for both of us.

The nurse was handing Alyce—what? A half-mask of white gauze. Slipped a half-mask onto her own face. Explaining to Alyce that until bloodwork confirmed that the patient didn't have a contagious illness they must proceed as if he might have one, and that the contagion might be spread by airborne germs or viruses.

Contagious? Illness? Was this possible? Alyce fumbled affixing the mask to her face, and the nurse adjusted it for her.

Before the door to room 8. Preparing for what was inside, as the nurse opened the door.

And there was the elderly poet in bed, in a sitting-up position, bare-chested, partly conscious, staring and blinking at Alyce as if he couldn't see her clearly or was failing to recognize her in the mask. Without his glasses he looked much older than his age—disheveled, distraught. The pale dome of a head, shockingly bare.

"Oh, my dear . . . What have they done to *you.*"

Bravely Roland B___ was smiling at his visitor. Quickly she came to him, took his hand. Fingers cold as death.

Her first impression was one of shock, yet relief. Roland was alive, that was all that mattered.

Thanking Alyce for coming. Begging her not to leave him.

How misshapen, Roland B___'s body in the cranked-up hospital bed! He might have been a dwarf, with foreshortened legs. Alyce had never glimpsed the elderly poet unclothed, always he'd been quite formally clothed; in the Poet's House when he'd removed his tweed coat he wore long-sleeved shirts beneath, often sweaters, vests. Scarcely had Alyce thought of the poet as a physical being.

Until he'd urged her into his bedroom and onto his bed she had not once thought of him as a sexual being; such a thought was repugnant to her.

Now with dismayed eyes Alyce saw folds of flesh at the poet's chest and stomach, of the hue of lard. Sloping knobby-boned shoulders. The flabby chest was covered in a frizz of gray hairs and amid these a dozen electrodes, wires connected to a machine. Was this an EKG? Monitoring his heartbeat? An IV dripped fluids into his right arm: antibiotics? Medication to slow and stabilize the rapid heartbeat? Oxygen flowed into the patient's nostrils through plastic tubes. Like clockwork every several minutes a blood-pressure cuff tightened on the patient's left upper arm with an aggressive whirring sound, then relaxed like an exhaled breath. Alyce stared entranced at the monitor screen. The numerals meant nothing to her—84, 91, 18. Green, blue, white. During the course of this first visit Alyce would surmise that the numerals in the high 80s measured the patient's oxygen intake.

It was explained to her that Roland B___ would have a CAT scan and an echocardiogram in the morning. He would have further bloodwork after eight hours of antibiotics. The rapid heartbeat wasn't tachycardia but fibrillation, which was more serious. Possibly the elderly man had a viral infection, which had precipitated the attack. Possibly he had pneumonia. Alyce tugged at the mask, which fitted over her mouth and nose uncomfortably.

It alarmed her how Roland B___ was coughing. (Had he been coughing at the Poet's House? She didn't think so.)

"They don't know what is wrong with me, I'm afraid," Roland B___ said, with an attempt at his old gaiety, "but I'm sure it's nothing to worry about, dear. I hope it won't be a cause of worry to *you.*"

Alyce insisted she wasn't worried. Even as she felt sick, disoriented with worry.

Wondering if, in his physical distress, the elderly poet remembered what she had told him. If he remembered what he'd told her.

. . . *love enough for both of us.*

For hours that night sitting with Roland B___ in the small room, much of the time holding his hand.

Even when he drifted off to sleep, eyelids fluttering and lips twitching, holding his hand.

At 11:30 p.m., when the ER was closing to visitors, Alyce was told that she could remove the mask on her face. Blood tests had established that the patient didn't have a communicable disease.

Removing the damned mask, which the nurse directed her to discard in a bin labeled MEDICAL REFUSE.

Removing the mask so that Roland B___ could see her more clearly and unmistakably identify her: "My dear—Alyce."

"Yes—Alyce . . ."

"You are looking so—pale, dear. Please don't worry! I feel so much better already, just knowing that you've been here, and that

we—we have—we will settle matters between us, as soon as I am
back home. Won't we, dear? As we'd discussed?"

"Y-Yes."

"Kiss me goodnight, dear. I'm not contagious now. And will you
promise to see me in the morning?"

Alyce promised. How exhausted she was, and how badly she
wanted to escape the stricken man, to burrow into sleep in her
own bed.

But Roland was blinking at her, his eyes forlorn without his
glasses. The blood-pressure cuff jerked to life, squeezing his upper
arm as if in rebuke.

Lowering his voice, Roland B___ asked anxiously, "You are—I
mean, you *are not*—my wife yet? I think—not yet? No."

Was he joking? Alyce wanted to think so.

*The patient in room 8 did not survive the night. We had no number to call
and we regret to inform you . . .*

In fact when Alyce returned to the ER the next morning, trembling with fear, she was informed that Roland B___ had been
moved out of the ER to a room on the fifth floor. His heartbeat had
been stabilized: his condition was "much improved." Yet he would
probably remain in the hospital for several days, undergoing tests.

In relief Alyce bought Roland a small bouquet of fresh flowers in
the hospital gift shop. It was heartening to see how his face lighted
when he saw her, and the bright yellow flowers in her hand.

"My dear! You've come back. Thank you."

Leaning over the hospital bed to kiss his cheek. Resisting the
impulse to shut her eyes in a delirium of relief. *He is alive. Alive!
That is all that matters.*

She'd scarcely slept the previous night. Many times reliving the
shock of the poet's collapse, even as he'd vowed to protect her.

Marry her, and they would have a child together . . .

It was clear to her now, nothing mattered so much as Roland
B___. She had to be with him, at his bedside. For he had no one but
Alyce, whom he loved and had promised to protect.

She'd ceased thinking of the other. The man who'd impregnated her and now shunned her. She did not even hate him, who'd
so wounded her.

Roland had not asked Alyce who the father of the unborn baby
was. Alyce seemed to understand that he would not.

Saying to her only, in a discreet lowered voice so that no one might overhear, "And you, dear? *You* are all right also?"

"Yes! Oh, yes."

It was a relief to Alyce, Roland B___ did seem to have improved since the previous night. He was still inhaling oxygen through tubes in his nostrils, but the numbers on the monitor were higher, in the 90s. IV fluids were still dripping into his veins, but his color was warmer, his eyes more alert. With a droll gaiety he showed his visitor his poor bruised arms, from which "pints of blood" had been drawn.

As Roland B___'s assistant Alyce had much to do. She must notify his closest relatives, whose names he provided her; she must notify the English Department that he would be postponing his seminar for a week. Alyce did not want to say, *But are you sure, Roland? One week?*

Clearly he had a serious cardiac condition. Still there was a possibility that he had an infection, for he was running a slight temperature. Though he was eager to be discharged from the hospital, he tired easily and several times dropped off to sleep while speaking with Alyce; once, explaining to her what she should say to his relatives, to keep them informed but discourage them from visiting him.

As it turned out Roland B___'s relatives, who lived in the Boston area, were not very keen on visiting him. On the phone with Alyce they expressed surprise, alarm, concern, but said nothing about visiting him in the hospital. ("Is Roland out of the ER? Not in intensive care? That's a relief!") Alyce wanted to ask sarcastically why didn't they come to see him now, before he was in intensive care? Wouldn't that be more sensible?

Roland had said that he didn't want to speak with his relatives just yet. Nor did the relatives express much urgency in speaking with him.

Often when Roland slept he woke disoriented, frightened. A nurse suggested to Alyce that she remain close by him, to assure him. "Older patients need reassurance that they haven't been abandoned."

Abandoned! Alyce was determined that this should not happen.

If she missed more than a few classes she would fail her courses, Alyce was warned. She would have to apply for extensions through the dean's office, and even then such applications might be denied.

But Roland was dependent upon Alyce for tasks he could not do from his hospital bed. Letters he must write, or believed that he must write, which he dictated to Alyce, who dutifully typed them out on the Remington in the Poet's House, brought them back to him for proofreading, addressed, and mailed them. There were telephone calls Roland couldn't bring himself to make, that Alyce must make for him; he'd grown to hate the phone because no one spoke loudly or clearly enough any longer. Since the shock of his collapse and hospitalization Roland seemed determined to show how alert, energetic, and assertive he was, how *well*—though he was still a hospital patient attached to monitors beside his bed and dependent upon Alyce or a nurse to help him make his faltering way to the bathroom when he needed it.

He'd been insistent the damned catheter be removed from his penis. No more! A man's pride would not allow that insult.

Especially Roland wanted to display for Alyce his returning vitality, his good humor. He wanted the medical staff to see, his physician to see, how well he was becoming, in order that he might be discharged soon.

Wanting to suggest to Roland that she might spend fewer hours at the hospital so that she could return to her classes, catch up on her work. That she might write poetry of her own again, to read to him.

But she could not force herself to utter such words—*I need more time to myself, Roland. I am afraid that I will fail my courses . . .*

He would be hurt, she knew. Since his collapse he'd become extremely sensitive, thin-skinned and suspicious. If Alyce was late coming to the hospital by just a few minutes, he wondered where she'd been; if he dropped off to sleep and woke startled, not knowing at first where he was, he might stare at her almost with hostility, as if not recognizing her.

But then, when she spoke his name, it was wonderful how awareness and recognition flowed into his face again. "My dear! Dear Alyce. It is you, isn't it?"

"Yes. Of course."

"I love you, Alyce. You know that, I hope."

Alyce was deeply embarrassed. Could not bring herself to say, *Yes. I know.*

"When I am discharged—which will be next Monday, I've just been informed—we will make our plans, dear. We—have—many —plans—to make . . ."

It was the pregnancy to which he was alluding, Alyce supposed. Yet he could not quite name it. Nor had he asked who the father was, as if (Alyce was beginning to suspect) he preferred not to know.

Soon after their nighttime meal Roland fell asleep with a book in his hand, which Alyce extricated carefully from his fingers and set aside, with a bookmark to mark his place. She stooped and kissed the poet's high forehead with its faint creases which felt cool against her lips; she listened to his shallow but rhythmic breathing, which was comforting to her as a baby's breathing might be. Love for the man suffused her heart, but how vexing, just as she switched off the bright overhead light, preparing to leave the hospital for the night, a young nurse entered the room and switched it back on, rudely waking Roland, who fluttered his eyelids, confused.

Alyce watched as the nurse poked for a vein in his right arm, which was already discolored. "Be careful!" Alyce spoke sharply.

It was new to her, this sharpness. As if already she were the poet's young wife, destined to outlive him and to bring up their child by herself, the renowned poet's literary executrix whose life would be closely bound up with his.

Afterward she kissed the poet goodnight a second time and switched off the overhead light a second time, and in the corridor outside the nurse was waiting for her with a quizzical smile. "Is he your grandfather? Somebody said he's a famous professor?"

It had been Roland's third full day in the hospital, unless it had been the fourth.

I I.

In Alyce's mailbox when she returned late from the hospital a folded note with the terse message *Please call me. S.*

Clutching the note, her heart pounding. A rush of sensation came over her, of dread, apprehension, and yet such excitement, she felt for a moment that she might faint; had to lean against the wall, her head lowered, as a struck animal might lean, uncertain what has happened to it.

No. Go to hell. It's too late, I hate you.

And yet she could not say *no.*

Asking Alyce to meet him the next evening at a Greek restaurant some distance from the university, a place to which he'd never taken her, dim-lighted, near-deserted, where no one from the university was likely to see them together.

He'd heard, Simon said bluntly, with no preamble, two things about the visiting poet Roland B___: the man was in the hospital, and Alyce, one of his students, was visiting him daily.

Evasively Alyce said *yes.*

"And why would you do such a thing?"

"Why? I'm his assistant."

"'Assistant'? Since when?"

"And archivist."

"*Archivist?*" Simon stared at Alyce, incredulous. "You're an undergraduate, you know nothing about library archives. Why would anyone hire *you?*"

Alyce's face burned with resentment, and unease. This question had occurred to her too, more than once.

"Did you know this Roland B___ before?"

"Before—?"

"When you—when we—when we first met . . ."

"I told you, he's my professor."

"I mean, were you his assistant then? His 'archivist'? I hadn't been under that impression . . ."

Alyce had never seen Simon Meech so discomforted. He was not so eloquent now, his manner not poised, aloof as it was when he stood before a classroom. When she'd approached the booth in the restaurant in which Simon was sitting with a drink in front of him, she'd seen his eyes glide over her with something like surprise, as if he'd forgotten, or had wished to forget, what she looked like. He had not, it appeared, even shaved that day, or had shaved carelessly.

It had been five weeks since Simon had last brought Alyce back to his apartment. Five weeks since he'd spoken to her. In the interim she'd missed several philosophy classes, she'd neglected to hand in an assignment. He might have been concerned for Alyce, her health, her welfare, what was happening in her life, but in his frowning face Alyce saw that his concern wasn't for her but for himself.

A waiter approached. Simon jerked his head irritably, without glancing at the man, to signal, *Go away, this is a private conversation.*

"When did you start seeing this Roland B___, outside your class with him? That's what I'm asking."

"Why are you interrogating me, Simon? Why does it matter to you?"

Even her naming of him—*Simon*. This was startling to him, for she'd scarcely dared to call him any name at all previously.

"Let's leave here. We should talk, in a private place."

"In your apartment? No."

"Not—not there. I have a car . . ."

Almost Simon was pleading with Alyce. She wondered what he knew, or could guess.

How hard it was for him to speak. And amazing to Alyce, to hear the man uttering such words she might have fantasized hearing weeks before, when he had mattered to her.

Reaching for her hand. Squeezing her hand. As rarely he'd done when they were alone together. In a faltering voice telling her that he'd missed her. He had thought it was wisest—for her, for them both—not to continue to see her, but . . . "I've wanted to call. I haven't really known what to do, Alyce."

But—did Simon love her? Soon in her dazed state Alyce would imagine she was hearing the word *love*.

Staring at their hands. Badly wanting to extricate her hand from his. Yet he was gripping her hand hard. As Roland B___ had sometimes gripped her hand, as if in desperation of his life.

What a charade this was! Telling Alyce now that he missed her, when she no longer missed him.

"I didn't think you cared for me, Simon. I didn't think you even liked me." Almost spitefully she spoke, childishly. Those hours of hurt, shame, despair when she'd wished indeed that she could die, cease to exist, without the effort and pain of suicide, the man must pay for.

"That's ridiculous. Certainly you could tell—I felt strongly about you. I'm not accustomed to spilling my guts the way poets do."

Poets. The word was a sneer in Simon's mouth. Alyce was surprised that he remembered she'd been a poet, or had hoped to be. Fortunately she'd never dared to show him any of her (love) poems, nor had Simon asked to see any.

She had to leave, Alyce said. She had to return to the hospital. She'd been there for much of the day and had only returned to the campus briefly to get Roland B___'s mail and other items . . .

"Jesus, Alyce! What are you to that man? He's—what? Seventy years old? You're being used by him—exploited."

"He is not seventy. He is sixty—barely."

"Oh, ridiculous! You are doing this out of spite, to hurt *me*."

Simon spoke angrily, resentfully. His face flushed as if with fever. This was a new, rough familiarity between them that would have been astonishing to Alyce if she'd had time to contemplate it.

Stubbornly she said, "He's all alone. He doesn't have anyone else."

"Of course he has someone else! He probably has a wife somewhere, and grown children. He's just taking advantage of you."

Alyce didn't want to say, *Yes, but he loves me too. I am taking advantage of his love.*

It seemed that they would not be having a meal together at the Greek restaurant. A waiter hovered nearby, ignored by Simon, who was becoming increasingly distracted.

Not a meal, not even drinks. Unless Simon had had a drink before Alyce arrived.

He began to plead. He apologized. He was very sorry for his poor judgment. Would Alyce forgive him? Try to forgive him? See him again?

No. Not ever.

Goodbye!

Preparing to leave, extricating her hand from his (sweaty) hand, and taking pity on him, the look in his narrow pinched face, his broken *Kinch*-pride, almost Alyce might have gloated, *Now you know what it is like to be rejected, and humbled.*

Simon was asking if he could drive her to the hospital, at least? They could talk together during the drive. She owed him that much, he would have thought.

Owed him! No.

Seeing the look on Alyce's face, quickly amending: "I mean—since—since we've meant something to each other . . . At least, I'd thought that we did."

Alyce felt again that rush of pity, sympathy for the stricken man. He had not meant to hurt her, perhaps. He had not thought of her but of himself—not her weakness but his own.

Simon was a young man: not yet thirty. Several years in the seminary had kept him immature: he knew little of the fullness of life.

Before Alyce he had not had any lover. He seemed awkward at touching and being touched. Yet Simon was older than Alyce Urquhart by at least ten years. A (male) faculty member at the university, improperly involved with a (female) undergraduate.

Alyce had the power to sabotage his career, she supposed. If she reported him to the dean of students, if she described his sexual coercion of her, as she saw it now, her shyness and intimidation by him. *And the pregnancy. If she told anyone!*

Relenting, yes, all right. He could drive her to the hospital if he wished. And they could talk— "Though I don't really think we have anything to talk about, Simon."

This was bravely stated. Never in the raging despair of the previous weeks had Alyce imagined such a statement made to the man who had impregnated her and abandoned her.

They were standing beside the booth. Still the restaurant was near-deserted. Simon seemed about to embrace her but hesitated.

On the way to the car along a windy snow-swept street, Simon thanked her. His voice was elated, excited. She had forgotten his height—he was taller than she, by several inches. She had forgotten the intensity of which he was sometimes capable, so very different from his calm, cutting eloquence.

He was considering returning to the seminary, Simon said. His contract at the university was being negotiated for the following year. In fact, there was the possibility of a three-year contract, and tenure. But he was no longer certain that he wanted tenure, a career in the university.

"The lay world, the civilian world, is . . . thin. Everything seems flat. Bleached of color."

Simon spoke with bitterness that was a kind of wonder. Glancing about as if seeing in this very place, which to Alyce looked so solid, how flat and two-dimensional the world was, how empty. She tried to see the world as he might see it but could not.

"It's God that has drained away. The meaning of my life."

In the car, driving. Alyce was deeply moved that Simon Meech would speak to her in this way. As thinking out loud. Baring his soul.

The streets had been plowed recently. The air was very still and cold, and what Alyce could see of the night sky was beautifully illuminated by a partial moon, but Simon, behind the wheel of his vehicle, which rattled and shuddered, did not seem to notice. Belatedly she realized that he'd (probably) been drinking before she'd met him, he had hurriedly settled a bill on the way out of the restaurant.

"I think that I can regain it. Him. By returning to where I was before I left the seminary. The person I was."

Him. What a curious way in which to refer to God. As if this *him* were a fellow creature, with whom the seminarian would be on particularly good terms.

"Not everyone wants to live in the secular world. Some of us require a different air."

Alyce heard herself murmur *yes.* Perhaps she was disappointed, Simon didn't love her after all. There was no room for earthly love in his priestly heart.

"I think we need to talk, Alyce. I think there is much you have not told me."

Calmly he spoke. But Alyce could hear the rage quivering beneath.

Instead of driving Alyce directly to the hospital, Simon was taking a longer route that involved crossing a bridge over a wide, dark river edged with serrated jaws of ice.

Weakly Alyce protested, but Simon promised he wouldn't keep her long.

Driving away from the city. Into the countryside. Simon's foot on the gas pedal erratic, aggressive.

Very still Alyce sat, staring at the rushing road.

Understanding that possibly she'd made a mistake. Leaving the restaurant with Simon instead of walking quickly away. Accompanying him to his car parked on a side street. Stepping into the car, into which she'd never stepped before, out of a (vague, apologetic) wish to placate the man whom (she'd been encouraged by him to think) she had hurt.

In the darkness of the countryside asking her almost casually, glancing at her, a smirk of a smile, "You're pregnant, aren't you? That's why you've been avoiding me."

Alyce was stunned, speechless. That Simon had asked such a question. Never had she imagined that Simon Meech would be capable of uttering the word aloud—*pregnant.*

"N-No . . ."

"What do you mean, no? You are *not pregnant,* or you haven't been *avoiding me?*"

Still Alyce stared ahead, at the rushing road. Her thoughts beat frantically, she could not think how to reply.

"Well, are you? Look at me. Answer me."

"I—I am n-not . . ."

Realizing now she had not wanted the man to know. Not this man.

Not because he would cease to love her, he did not love her. But because he would wish to harm her, as his enemy.

"How long? How pregnant are you?"

Just short of jeering. Furious. In the restaurant he'd kept glancing at her, furtively. And now, with that look of reproach and disbelief.

Rapidly Alyce's brain worked. She must find a way to answer him, to placate him. A raging man beside her, a vehicle hurtling her into the snowy countryside.

Simon's foot on the gas pedal alternately pressing down, releasing, and pressing down again. Several times he asked her how long, how long *pregnant,* and Alyce managed to stammer that she was not, not *pregnant.* And still he asked her, *how long.*

She had not calculated. So long as the duration of the pregnancy was imprecise, not marked on any calendar, it did not seem altogether real to her, even as her belly was swelling, thickening. Even as her breasts were becoming the fatter, softer breasts of a stranger.

How many miles Simon drove, into the countryside, away from the lighted city, Alyce had not a clear idea. Seeing his hands on the steering wheel tight as fists.

She hadn't even known that he owned a car. But perhaps this wasn't Simon's car but one borrowed for the night.

At last turning into an area cleared partially of snow. Long swaths of snow left by a forked plow. A small parking lot, it appeared to be, a rest stop with shuttered restrooms, beside the state highway and overlooking the river.

Had he planned this place? Alyce wondered. It did not seem to her by chance, Simon's car turning into this remote place.

He has brought other girls here. It was his intention all along.

Telling Alyce that he knew what the situation was but wanted to hear from her. In her own words.

"No accident, is it? You knew. You wanted it."

She had no clear idea what he was talking about. But there was no mistaking his anger.

"Did you? Purposefully? Use me? To trap me? Or—for some reason of your own, you're too stupid even to know?"

Alyce licked her lips. To deny this, to cry *no,* would be a confirmation of his suspicion, a mistake.

She would not beg him to drive back to the city. She would not beg him. Desperately calculating how quickly she must act, to get out of the car before it was too late.

"I don't intend to let you ruin my life, Alyce. No one is going to do that. If—"

Alyce grasped the car door handle, managing to open it before Simon could stop her. Surprising the man, she was so quick, and so strong, pushing away his flailing hand.

Because she'd seemed mute, passive. Because she had not resisted. He had underestimated her, had no idea of her cunning.

Outside, cold wet air against her face. Running, slipping on icy pavement as the man pursues her, thudding footsteps, surprisingly fast, faster than Alyce would have thought the priestly *Kinch* capable of. Coming up behind her furious and cursing and suddenly near enough to strike her with his fist, a glancing blow that would knock her down if she were not in motion, ducking instinctively from him, silent, teeth gritted, knowing she must not infuriate him more by screaming, and she must not squander her breath.

And now she is down, falling heavily onto the freezing ground. And the man above her, face white and contorted. Kicking her. Grunting, cursing. As she tries to shield her face, her head. Kicking her back, her sides, her thighs. Trying to turn her over, to kick her belly. *Bitch. Whore. Did it on purpose. I will kill you.*

So quickly it has happened, the man's fury. As when he'd first touched her weeks ago. She'd felt the sudden flaring up of the man's desire like flames that ran over each of them, and each of them helpless to thwart it. Thinking, *But this can't be happening. He would not—no . . .*

In fury the man is sobbing. Oh, he had not meant to *kick her.*

Her fault, the woman's fault. Provoking his feet to kick. Not his fault but hers. Making a beast of him when it is she, the female, that is the beast, the bestial thing. How can he forgive her!

Seeing that Alyce lies very still in a paralysis of terror, he ceases kicking her. Very exhausted, panting—he relents. But blaming her nonetheless. *You! You did this. God damn your slut-soul to hell.*

Simon will think that she has died, possibly. Or, no—Simon

wipes tears from his eyes and can see that she is breathing, just perceptibly.

Backing off from the fallen girl, in disgust. Alyce can hear him muttering to himself. *Jesus, Mary, and Joseph!* It is a plea, the most succinct Catholic prayer for help, forgiveness.

Alyce groans, wracked with pain. The man has returned to his car. He will drive away now, he will abandon her in this freezing place.

Her head is throbbing, her eyesight blotched. Later she will discover that the cartilage of her nose is broken, blood flows freely. Close against her face, rivulets of ice like veins. The warm blood—not hot: lukewarm—will freeze against the ice, if she gives in, if she allows herself, as she so badly wants to do, to sleep.

Lying on the ground. Trying to breathe. Lying where he has flung her. Where he stood above her kicking her, her belly, her chest, she can scarcely draw breath, the pain is so strong. Ribs cracked, broken. Massive bruises on her chest, belly. The bleeding face, broken nose. Broken tooth crushed into the gum. Wanting to kill her, but he has not killed her. Whatever is growing inside her, the living thing, the *baby*, he has wanted to kill but did not.

Ruining his life. It is the *baby* that will ruin his life.

All this Alyce thinks. Calmly and almost coolly, as if (already) she were floating some distance overhead observing the abject fallen figure (her own), the figure crouched over her (Simon Meech) and then backing away.

Very still she lies, in the cunning of desperation. Willing the man to drive away and leave her. Willing the car engine to flare into life, the foot pumping the gas pedal.

But then she hears his footsteps—staggering and wayward in the hard-crusted snow like the footsteps of a drunken man. Is he returning to her, to murder her?

By this time Alyce has managed to rise from the ground. She is very dizzy. She is on her knees. Her stunned face is smeared with blood, she has no idea she has been cut. No idea her tooth has been smashed into her gum, for there is no sensation in her lower jaw. A fist in her face, the heel of the man's boot in her face. *Her face*, which has been so precious to her.

The man, infuriated, past all restraint, is returning to her. He is the priestly *Kinch*, he cannot help himself. Like one who must crush a beetle beneath his feet, cannot trust the badly wounded beetle to expire of its own volition, a filthy thing he must grind into oblivion. And Alyce fumbling to seize a rock too large for her hand, fist-sized, a rock covered in ice, as the man stoops over her, panting audibly, to strike her, to take hold of her, close his fingers around her neck.

Doesn't know what he is doing. Fingers around the girl's neck to squeeze, squeeze. Not planned. Not premeditated. There is innocence to it, almost. But Alyce slams the rock into his face, unbelievably. Somehow this has happened. Scarcely able to clutch the rock in her hand, yet Alyce summons the strength to slam the rock into the jeering face. Into the eyes and the bridge of his nose and she feels the *crack* of the bone and feels or imagines she feels the man's wet warm rushing blood against her fingers. Against her face. Hears him cry out in rage, disbelief.

Running from him, limping. In triumph.

In triumph carrying her life as one might carry a torch, shielded against the wind. Her life, and the precious life within her, a torch, a tremulous flame, shielded by her crouched and running body from the wind.

And behind her the man calling to her. Pleading, Al-yce! Al-yce! Where are you, come back, I wasn't serious. Al-yce!

Suffused with strength. Where moments before she'd been weak, paralyzed. Weak as if the tendons of her legs have been cut. As if the vertebrae of her upper back have been broken. As if her carotid artery has been slashed by an invisible knife wielded in the murderer's hand, but new strength flows into her. Running into a snowy field beyond the parking lot. Thick-crusted banks of snow. Pathways through the snow, trampled by myriad feet. But the surface of the snow is icy-hard, treacherous. There has been a thaw, and refreezing. Melting, and immediate refreezing. Alyce is slip-sliding down a hill, into a ravine of rocks, boulders. Trickling water she imagines she hears, amid columns of ice.

Fainter now, the man's uplifted voice. An attempt at laughter—Al-yce! I was only joking!

In the ravine she hides. A steep ravine, filled with snow. But beneath the snow, cast-off household things—broken chairs, sofa, stained carpet. The skeletal remains of a small creature—raccoon, dog. The man will drive into the interior of the park, along a winding road, calling to her—Al-yce! Darling! I love you, I was only joking! Come back! *Sees, or thinks she sees, the headlights of the vehicle on the road until finally the lights have vanished and the wind is still.*

Out of the steep snowy ravine. Clutching at rocks, her hands bloodied. And all the while snow falling, temperature dropping to zero degrees Fahrenheit.

How still, the soft-falling snow amid rocks! The yearning, the temptation to lie down, sleep.

Five miles back to the city. She will stagger to the highway, she will limp along the highway facing oncoming traffic. Blinded by headlights and her eyes aching where he'd kicked and punched and pummeled her until at last a motorist stops to pick her up.

Call ambulance? But no, Alyce insists *no*.

She is going to the hospital, no need of an ambulance.

Call police?—but no, Alyce insists *no*.

Trickle of blood between her legs. Not a sensation of heat but cold. Begins high in her belly, higher still in the region of her heart. Between her thighs clamped together tight, sticky clots she hopes won't leak out and through her clothing onto the vinyl seat of the stranger's car.

Thinking, *I am alive. That is all that matters.*

Elated to think so. Elated thanking the motorist for the ride.

Saying to the driver, *Thank you. We owe you everything!*

At the hospital, it is nearing midnight. At such an hour the front entrance of the building is locked, the foyer is darkened, and you must enter by the ER at the side of the building.

On foot, in light-falling snow. Lucky Alyce is wearing boots, these hours she has been walking, trudging, staggering in snow that has accumulated to a depth of four to five inches. On her hot skin, snowflakes melt at once. Laughing to see, as a child might see, how, behind her, there are no tracks in the fresh-fallen snow leading from the curb to the ER entrance.

"Hello? Hello? Hello? Hello? Let me in, please!"

A surprise to Alyce, the automated doors refuse to open. Locked from inside? She peers through the plate-glass window, baffled.

But yes, this is the ER. The reception area of the ER. Where they'd brought Roland B___ on a stretcher. An interior Alyce had not realized she'd memorized as one might memorize a poem unconsciously.

But at last someone comes to open the door. A medical worker in white nylon shirt, trousers. Alyce has no ID—Alyce has left her bookbag, her wallet, miles away. Fallen onto the floor of the man's

car, or out onto the frozen ground when she'd fled in terror of her
life, to be discovered by a snow-removal crew in the morning.

At first they will not admit her into the ER. But then the decision
comes to admit her.

Carefully it is explained to Alyce, she must take a back stairway
to the fifth floor to where Roland B___ awaits her.

"You are his—granddaughter?"

"Yes! I am his granddaughter," Alyce says, laughing. "He is expecting me. He won't have gone to sleep without me."

When she'd been alive she would have been deeply embarrassed. And the seeping-cold sensation between her legs, deeply
embarrassing if anyone sees.

Now, grateful to be here. For nothing else matters, Alyce sees
that now. The elderly poet awaits her. They will be together, he will
cherish and protect her.

On the fifth floor. She is breathless from the stairs, there are no
elevators at this hour. She is breathless from hurrying. The corridor
is deserted. Where is the nursing staff? The doors to several rooms
are ajar. And the door to room 526 is open, there is a blinding shaft
of sunshine inside.

"Alyce, my dear! My darling. Where have you been? My beautiful
ghost-girl, I have missed you."

*On the morning of December 11, 1972, the body of a young woman was
found by hikers in a snow-filled ravine in a wooded area of Tecumseh State
Park five miles north of Bridgewater. The young woman was initially believed to have been strangled to death, for there were multiple bruises on her
throat as well as elsewhere on her body, but the Tecumseh County coroner has
ruled the primary cause of death to be hypothermia. Subsequently identified
as nineteen-year-old Alyce Urquhart of Strykersville, New York, a sophomore
at the university, the victim is believed to have been left unconscious by her
assailant or assailants in a ravine, to freeze to death when the temperature
plummeted to a low of zero degrees Fahrenheit during the night.*

*If there were tire tracks on the roadway and in the parking lot near the
ravine, a five-inch snowfall had covered them.*

*The deceased young woman had been an undergraduate in the College
of Arts and Sciences at the university. Residents in her dormitory were reported to be shocked by the news of her death and spoke of her with respect
and admiration, saying,* You could see that Alyce was a very serious
student. The rest of us would goof around, but not Alyce. She was

always in the library. (At least, we thought Alyce was always in the library. We'd see her rushing off after class, she'd say she was going to study in the library where it was quiet, then she wouldn't return until midnight.)

No, Alyce didn't have a boyfriend, or a man friend. Never saw her at frat parties, or anywhere with a guy.

During her freshman year at the university Alyce Urquhart had earned high grades and was on the dean's list. Her current instructors have testified that the young woman was an outstanding student until mid-November, when with no explanation she ceased attending classes regularly and failed to complete assignments.

Her philosophy instructor, Dr. Simon Meech, testified to police that Alyce Urquhart had done "usually very good" work in his section of Introduction to Philosophy.

No, he had not had any personal contact with the victim. He'd only realized that she was one of his students when he'd seen the "shocking and tragic" article on the front page of the local newspaper and checked the name against his class list to discover Alyce Urquhart *on that list.*

Dr. Meech had begun to notice that Miss Urquhart was missing classes when she failed to turn in a written assignment in early December. She had not offered her instructor any explanation and there had been no contact between them. Our undergraduates are adults whom we treat accordingly, *Dr. Meech said.* They must be responsible for attending classes as for completing their coursework.

Yes. The deceased had turned in work of unusual quality for an undergraduate in philosophy, and especially for a young woman.

Bridgewater police officers are investigating the death, which has been classified as a homicide. At the present time there are no suspects. Anyone with information that might prove helpful to the case is asked to call the Bridgewater Police Department at 555-330-2293.

ALAN ORLOFF

Rule Number One

FROM *Snowbound*

"YOU LOOK LIKE CRAP, Pen."

Pendleton Rozier, my longtime mentor, opened the door wide, then coughed into the crook of his elbow. "If only I felt that good."

I stepped into the entryway of his shotgun shack in Revere, the dump he'd been living in since I met him, and handed over a brown takeout bag. "Here. This'll help."

He shuffled over to a beat-up recliner and plopped down, while I sat on a folding bridge chair across from him. He set the bag on a metal TV tray and fished inside. Removed a container of soup and a plastic spoon. "Chicken noodle?"

"They were out. I got lentil barley." I shrugged. "All they had."

Pen snapped off the flimsy lid and took a spoonful. Blew on it for fifteen seconds, hand shaking as he did.

I'd known Pen for almost thirty years and had pulled dozens of jobs with him, from the small holdups when I'd just been starting out to an all-out blitz at a UPS warehouse two years ago. He'd shown me the ropes, given me advice. Saved my life a couple of times too. Now my teacher—my friend—looked older than his sixty-four years. He'd been heading downhill for a while.

He slurped his soup, then made a gagging noise as he dropped the spoon onto the tray. "Blech. Who would ruin good soup with lentils, anyway?"

"Sorry."

He tried to fit the lid back on the container, but after a moment of fumbling around, he gave up and leaned back in his chair. "Kane, as much as it hurts me to say, I'm losing my edge. Afraid I'm going to make a mistake that'll cost me—or someone else. Feh. I'm gonna hang it up. Retire." His voice caught. "Right after this one last gig."

"Didn't you say you were going to do this until the day you died?" He'd been squawking about retiring for the past ten years, but this time his stone-cold eyes told me he was serious.

"Can't a guy change his mind? I'm going to relax for as long as I've got left. Move to a trailer park in Boca and enjoy some early-bird specials." Pen sputtered off into a coughing jag. When he finished, he wiped some spittle from his ashen face. "So, how's the job coming along? Ready for me yet? The ride is gassed up and rarin' to go."

I needed some clean wheels for when I dumped the van we were using, and Pen had always delivered. Despite his age—or maybe because of it, no one suspected a geezer waiting in an idling car—he was a damn good driver. At least he used to be. "You sure you're up to it?"

He waved his hand. "Don't let the coughing and wheezing deceive you. I've never failed on a job yet, and you know it. I got enough left in the tank for this. Wouldn't do it if I didn't."

"Sure, sure." The truth was, I didn't need Pen—what I had planned didn't require a fast getaway, and I didn't anticipate any problems. But I owed him for all he'd done for me, and it seemed fitting to throw a bone his way and send him off to sunny Florida with a few bucks in his pocket—50,000 of them. Call it a token of appreciation for showing me the ropes, watching out for me.

Pen squeezed my arm. "Thanks, Kane, for giving an old guy one last thrill."

The late-afternoon Allston Diner crowd had thinned, and the servers were stealing some downtime before the dinner rush began. *If* there was a dinner rush. I'd only eaten there once before, a few months ago, and that was at 8 a.m. after an especially profitable office burglary two exits down the Mass Pike.

Of course, compared to the latest haul, that job was chump change. Penny ante. A paltry piss in a deep lake.

Across from me, my unseasoned partners in crime—both in their thirties, younger than me by two decades—finished up their meals. Jimmy Fitzpatrick, the Irish thug wannabe from Southie with the nonstop mouth and the pasty skin, devoured anything as

long as it was fried and doused with ketchup. Nagelman, who always looked like he'd just been released from solitary, gaunt and
pallid, was vegan. Or some such crap. I couldn't keep up with all
the latest diet fads, and frankly, I didn't trust a guy who wouldn't
eat red meat. It didn't help that all the leftover slimy green gunk in
the bottom of Nagelman's bowl made me queasy.

I balled up my napkin, tossed it onto my empty plate, and
stretched an arm across the back of the vinyl booth.

"They got good pie here." Fitzpatrick wiped a ketchup smear off
his chin.

"Maybe we should discuss what we came here to discuss." Nagelman glanced around, then leaned forward and adjusted his thick-
lensed glasses.

"We can multitask," Fitzpatrick said. "We ain't idiots."

"I didn't say we were idiots. I just think we should get down to—"

"And who the eff put you in charge, anyway?"

I held up my hand. "Girls, girls. Relax. Why don't we talk business first, then those that want pie can get pie. Okay?"

"Yeah, yeah." Fitzpatrick glared at Nagelman. "Whatever."

"Fine," Nagelman said, glaring right back at Fitzpatrick.

I cleared my throat. Broke out a fresh smile. It was always much
more enjoyable to deliver good news than bad, although I sometimes *did* look forward to dumping bad news on those I despised.
"Our interested party is ready. Finally."

It had taken a few weeks before my fence had lined up customers for the unique—and highly identifiable—treasures we'd stolen from a truck bound for a chichi Back Bay museum. About a
dozen bejeweled pieces from some twelfth-century Russian dynasty.

"Wa-damn-hoo," Fitzpatrick said. "'Bout time. First stop, Vegas,
baby!" He tapped out a drum solo on the edge of the table with his
fat fingers.

Next to him, Nagelman issued an audible sigh, and the expression on his face screamed relief more than happiness. "Thank
God."

Did Nagelman ever smile? "He wants to meet tomorrow afternoon at three. That work in your schedule?"

Fitzpatrick nodded. "You bet."

"We'll all go to the meet, right? As planned?" Nagelman chewed
on the inside of his cheek while his pupils jittered.

"That's right, boys. Tomorrow at about this time we'll be one million bucks richer. Each of us." I'd planned the entire operation, but to keep peace—and because that honor-among-thieves notion was complete horse manure—we'd worked out an arrangement. Fitzpatrick and Nagelman would hold on to the goods in a secret location, and I wouldn't divulge the name of the fence until the deal was ready. As for Pen, I'd pay him fifty thou out of my share, but I hadn't mentioned his involvement at all, not wanting to get into any arguments about bringing in another guy.

After the exchange we'd split the proceeds and go on our merry ways, off to spend our loot.

At least that was the plan we'd all agreed upon.

Sometimes plans changed.

Nagelman wanted to run through the specifics again—what time to meet and where, who would take the lead during the meeting, contingencies if things went south—and we spent about thirty minutes hashing it all out. When we finished going through it all yet a third time, he seemed satisfied.

"So we're good?" I asked.

Two nods.

"Now can I order some pie?" Fitzpatrick said.

"Knock yourself out."

"I gotta take a leak first." Fitzpatrick got up. "If she comes while I'm gone, I want a big slice of Boston cream, got it? Maybe some extra whipped cream on top. And ask for a cherry too. I'm in the mood to celebrate, and nothing says celebration like a plump red cherry."

When Fitzpatrick was out of earshot, I leaned across the table. "You gonna be okay? We talked about this, right? Three mil divided in half is a lot more dough than it is split three ways."

Nagelman dabbed his sweaty forehead with his napkin. "I know. But . . . you don't think he's got a clue, do you?"

"Him? He wouldn't know a clue if it burst out of his chest like that monster in *Alien*. Trust me, he's a dolt." I glanced over my shoulder toward the restrooms. "But I don't trust *him*, so you need to keep an eye out. Make sure he doesn't get the idea that he can rip us off and sell the goods on his own."

"He couldn't."

"I know he couldn't; my guy's the only one around who will touch our stuff. But he might *think* he can. So watch him, okay?"

"I will, I will. Don't worry."

"I'm not worried in the least." I smiled. "You want some pie too?"

"No thanks. They probably use lard in the crust."

"Isn't that the best part?"

My phone rang. *Fitzpatrick.*

"What's up?" I said.

"Just checking in. We got the van," Fitzpatrick said. "Everything on track with the meet?"

"Yep. Where are you?"

"Gas station. Nagelman's in the can."

"How's he seem?" I asked.

"Like a mouse in a snake's cage. He could use a Xanax or three."

"Do you think he suspects anything?" I asked.

"Hard to tell, he's always so twitchy. I asked him a few questions to feel him out, and he got all sweaty, like he does when he's stressed. Best guess? I think he's afraid I know about him and you planning to double-cross me, although I suppose he might sense we're about to screw him. But so what? If he figures it out, I can snap him in half. His physique is certainly an argument for eating meat, huh?"

"Don't hurt him, Fitzpatrick. There's no need." I didn't have a problem stealing stuff from people—things can always be replaced. I drew the line at physical harm, unless absolutely necessary. I was an artful thief, not a two-bit goon. Not hurting people was one of Pen's top ten rules. Right below his numero uno directive: *never trust anyone.* "Just be cool."

"Whatever you say. You're the bossman."

My other line beeped. *Nagelman.* "Got another call. Listen, the last thing we need is you getting all macho and screwing this thing up. Remember, three mil divided by two is a lot more than if we have to divide it by three. See you in a little while."

I clicked over to the other line. "Yeah?"

"It's Nagelman. I think he might be onto us. Christ, he was—"

"Slow down, slow down. Take a deep breath. Now, where are you? Can you talk?"

I heard a slew of inhalations and exhalations, followed by Nagelman's only slightly less frantic answer. "Exxon restroom. Fitzpatrick's waiting for me in the van."

"Okay. Now tell me why you think he might be onto us."

"He was asking all kinds of questions. He suggested that me and him double-cross you, but the way he said it made me think he knew what we were up to. I'm pretty sure he was toying with me, Kane."

Goddamn Fitzpatrick, always looking for ways to mess with people. I hoped he hadn't somehow spooked Nagelman. Unpredictability made me nervous. "You're overthinking things here. I'm sure he honestly wants to screw me. He doesn't like me, and he sure doesn't respect me. What better way than to cut me out of my own job and steal my share of the take?"

"You didn't see his eyes, Kane. He's a psycho. And I'm afraid he knows about us crossing him. He'll probably kill us both and smile while he's doing it."

"Trust me, he doesn't know squat about our plan. This time tomorrow we'll be a hell of a lot richer, and we won't be worrying about Fitzpatrick. Or anybody else, for that matter."

"I'll feel so much better when this is over."

I wouldn't bet on that. "Sure you will. Now, just try to take it easy. And don't get into it with him. I know how much of an a-hole he can be, but do your best to play nice. Can you do that?"

"I'll try."

"Remember, kid, it's just you and me on this."

Nagelman drove the van; I rode shotgun and Fitzpatrick sat in the back. I hadn't known where they'd stored our haul until Nagelman brought the van to a stop right before the barricade arm leading into the Jiffy-Stor site. He rolled down the window, punched the code into the security pad, and the red-and-white arm rose with a jerk.

A few snowflakes from a developing storm blew in through the window.

Fitzpatrick leaned forward from the back, poking his head between the two front seats. "Some security. Hell, you could just drive right through that ridiculous arm and nobody would even notice for a week. This place is deserted."

Nagelman rolled through the entrance and wound his way up a slight hill to the storage facility. Like a thousand similar places, Jiffy-Stor comprised a series of sprawling warehouses, subdivided into hundreds of tiny units, each with a roll-up door and cheap-ass lock.

I didn't know why anyone would store anything truly valuable here; it was mostly surplus furniture and sentimental keepsakes

and junk that people thought they'd use again but never would
—like exercise equipment and sewing machines.

"Well, I got to hand it to you. You guys picked a safe place to
stash the stuff," I said. "No self-respecting crook would be caught
dead prowling around here."

"It was my idea," Fitzpatrick said.

"Actually, I think it was my idea," Nagelman said.

"Whoever's idea it was, good job," I said, cutting off further argument.

Nagelman drove to the back of the place, past five rows of units,
and hooked a right to follow the asphalt circuit.

"I can almost taste our dough," Fitzpatrick said, opening his
door before the van had even come to a stop in front of the unit
they'd rented.

He was out and fiddling with the lock as Nagelman and I came
up behind him.

"*Aaaand* here we are." Fitzpatrick snapped the lock open and
removed it from the hasp. Rolled the door up. Flicked the light
switch. Off to one side were six boxes. "Just to be safe, we marked
them OLD CLOTHES."

"Brilliant," I said. "Let's load them up and get going."

Fitzpatrick turned toward the boxes. Nagelman winked at me
and said, "So, Fitzpatrick, how are you going to spend your share?"

Fitzpatrick hoisted a box, smiled. "Hookers. Craps. Booze. The
usual." He walked past me toward the van, flashed me a conspirato-
rial look, and called out over his shoulder, "How about you, Nagelman? Big plans?"

"Gonna move to San Francisco. Buy into a buddy's smoothie
shop." Nagelman picked up a box and followed Fitzpatrick. I
grabbed a box too, and we loaded them into the van. Then we
each made another trip, and we were done. Three million dollars
in antique treasures weren't very bulky.

I thought about Pen lying on the beach in Florida in a few weeks.
Nice.

We climbed into the van, and Nagelman started it up.

"What about you, boss?" Fitzpatrick said. "What are you going to
do with your dough?"

I thought about Pen, living in squalor, too broke to go to the
doctor. "Mutual funds. I'm saving for retirement."

*

"We're almost there," I said.

"You sure this is the right way?" Nagelman asked, voice nasal, as he steered the van down a winding road three miles past the middle of nowhere. The snow swirled in the wind, mini white tornadoes. The forecasters were predicting somewhere between six and ten inches; so far, about an inch had accumulated on the roads. Maybe I'd copy Pen's idea and move to a warmer climate.

"Yep. GPS don't lie."

Nagelman jerked the wheel to avoid a pothole, then overcorrected, causing our precious cargo to shift abruptly.

"Hey, numbskull, try not to land us in a ditch, okay?" Fitzpatrick barked from the back of the van.

"You wanna drive?" Nagelman said. "Be my guest."

"I could drive better than you with my eyes closed, that's for sure."

"Will you two just cut it out?" After spending the last month immersed in this job with these two chuckleheads—planning it, executing it, waiting for a buyer to materialize—I now knew what it would have been like to have squabbling children. I pointed up ahead. "Hang a left here."

We bumped along for another three minutes down an ever-narrowing driveway until we came to a house. "This is the place."

"Here?" Nagelman looked around.

There wasn't another structure within sight.

"Right here."

"I don't like this," Nagelman said.

"You don't like anything," Fitzpatrick said. "Don't worry, it will all be over soon."

"Look, my guy likes privacy when he conducts business. He needs to control the scene. In fact," I said, pointing up into some nearby trees, "he's probably watching us right now, so don't do anything stupid." *Stupider than normal, anyway.*

Both Nagelman and Fitzpatrick craned their heads, trying to catch a glimpse of the security cameras through the van's windows.

"Let's go," I said.

We got out of the van and huddled near the driver's door as I issued the orders. "When we get inside, let me do the talking—all the talking. After I make sure he's got the money on hand, we'll bring the merchandise inside and wait for him to do an appraisal. Then we'll get our money and be off. No fuss, no muss. Okay?"

"Sure, boss," Fitzpatrick said.

Nagelman nodded. "I won't say a word."

"Good. Now, who wants to stay in the van with the stuff?" I asked.

Nagelman looked at Fitzpatrick.

Fitzpatrick looked at Nagelman.

Neither said a word. I knew each was trying to figure out if stay-ing with the goods or going inside with me was the best way not to get squeezed out of the deal.

"Well?" I asked. "Who's it going to be?"

"Why don't you stay," Fitzpatrick said to Nagelman, "and I'll go in? Just in case there's trouble, I can handle it better. No offense, of course."

"What if someone tries to hijack the van while you're inside?" Nagelman countered.

"I'm sensing some distrust here," I said. "Forget it. You can both come in with me. No one's going to hijack the van while we're in-side. I trust my guy completely. Come on."

I led the other two up a scuffed path toward the front door. Two shutters hung crookedly on ground-floor windows, and one upstairs window had been boarded up. A few optimistic wisps of grass poked through the snow on the front lawn.

When we got to the porch, I stopped, took a few steps backward, and pulled a gun from the waistband at the small of my back. "So here we are."

"I'll pat him down, boss." Fitzpatrick started toward Nagelman, sneer in place. "You idiot. You had no idea we were cutting you out, did you?"

"Hold it right there, Fitzpatrick," I said.

Fitzpatrick glanced at me, saw my gun pointed at him, and stopped, jaw clenched.

"Now who's the idiot?" Nagelman said, advancing on Fitzpatrick. "How does it feel to be the one getting—"

"You stop too, Nagelman," I said.

"What?" He examined my face, realized I wasn't joking around, and froze.

Fitzpatrick shook his head slowly. "Crap. I knew it. Triple-crossed."

Nagelman didn't say anything, but he looked as if he might puke.

"Very slowly, I want you to remove your guns and toss them on the ground, toward me. Flinch and I shoot. Fitzpatrick, you first."

"I'm not armed. You said we wouldn't need it," Fitzpatrick said.

"Me neither," Nagelman said.

"Sure you're not. Look, if it's easier for you, I can take them off your dead bodies. It doesn't matter much to me."

Fitzpatrick slowly removed a gun from the pocket of his coat and tossed it on the snowy ground a yard from my feet.

"Thanks. Your turn, Nagelman."

"It's on my ankle. Don't shoot me while I take it out." He bent down and removed his piece from the holster and tossed it near Fitzpatrick's gun.

"Now your phones," I said.

They tossed their phones next to their guns.

"I didn't trust you a bit," Fitzpatrick said. "Bastard."

"Well, someone very wise once told me you should never trust anybody. Good advice, don't you think?"

I picked up the phones and retrieved their weapons while keeping mine trained on my partners—my *ex*-partners. "Now, please get down on your knees."

They hesitated a moment, then Fitzpatrick dropped down at once, while Nagelman eased down one knee at a time.

"Please don't shoot us. Please," Nagelman whined.

"I'm not going to shoot you," I said. "Unless you get up before I drive off. Then I'll use you both for target practice."

"Bastard," Fitzpatrick said again.

"Nice doing business with you. And remember, don't trust anyone." I smiled. "Adios, amigos."

"Bastard," Fitzpatrick said a third time.

I trotted to the van, started it up, and roared off.

Three mil, not divided by anything, was best of all.

I pulled up next to a Volvo station wagon behind a grocery store about ten miles from where I'd left Fitzpatrick and Nagelman. Pen leaned against the Volvo's hood, smoking a cigarette. A white crown of snow topped his knit cap. When I hopped out and tracked around the back of the van, Pen had exchanged the butt in his hand for a Beretta, and it was aimed at my chest.

"What the hell?"

"Sorry, bud." Pen stood straighter and seemed to have more zest than yesterday. More color in his face too.

"Feeling better, I take it?" I asked.

"Amazing recovery, don't you think? I owe it all to clean living. Wanna toss me the keys to the van?"

I flipped them up in a graceful arc, and Pen snatched them cleanly out of the air. "No hard feelings, right?"

"No, Pen. I still love you."

"You remember all those times we talked about our dreams, how we couldn't wait to hit the big score so we could retire on some tropical island somewhere? Well, now I can, thanks to you. I really appreciate your effort."

"Don't mention it."

"I must say, though, I'm a little disappointed in you, Kane. Your failure to master rule number one — never trust anyone — reflects poorly on me as a teacher." He clicked his tongue against the roof of his mouth. "I guess that's how we learn, by making mistakes. Next time you'll remember."

I watched Pen drive off. He'd turned on me, and part of me stung from my old friend's betrayal. I'd been his prize pupil. I liked to think he'd really cared about me.

But another part of me was content, happy even, as I pictured the proud look on my teacher's face when he opened those boxes and found a jumble of old clothes. I *had* mastered the most basic lesson, and now I'd passed the final exam.

I'd stashed the merchandise in a safe place before I met up with Pen — an insurance policy against a cagey old pro. If he hadn't double-crossed me, we would have picked up the goods on the way to our buyer, and we'd have gone through with the deal, smooth sailing. Then I'd have given Pen his dough, and we would have parted ways with a smile and firm handshake — teacher and pupil, partners in crime, dear old friends.

Sad to see, Pen losing his edge. He hadn't even bothered to check the boxes before taking off.

Thankfully, he'd left the keys to the Volvo in the ignition. I hopped in and started it up, hoping the future would be kind to Pen.

Without the big score, I didn't think he would ever make it to his tropical island. Maybe one day I'd visit him in that rundown trailer park in Boca, and we could laugh about how things had transpired.

Or maybe not.

WILLIAM DYLAN POWELL

The Apex Predator

FROM *Switchblade*

> Texas Equusearch officials said they have evidence of more than
> 127 cars submerged in Houston's bayous and they think some
> could contain the bodies of missing people, perhaps murdered
> or lost . . . the cars could hold clues to the dozens of unsolved
> missing persons cases in the area.
> —The *Houston Chronicle*, May 13, 2014

THE LAYOFF. THE DIVORCE. The gradual erosion of my 401(k).
Getting that call from the Houston Police Department to help with
the Buffalo Bayou vehicle recovery felt like a birthday present. Especially now, when the economy seemed to be made exclusively of
bloodsucking lawyers, bakers of fru-fru cupcakes, and soulless tax
collectors.

But as I swam around that '87 Camaro, peering through the
muck, it was hard to get too excited.

The car was covered with silt, reminding me of the drilling mud
they use in oil-field drills. That's my normal gig. Offshore oil rigs.
Underwater. I ran my glove along the hood, leaving a bloody scar
across the algae, revealing the vehicle's original crimson.

Above me in an aluminum fishing boat an HPD officer named
McCleary and Stephanie, the cute paramedic, sat moored to an
oak tree. The police have their own dive team, but if they can go
cheaper contracting guys like me, they'll do it every time.

All week it had been the same: The computer nerds marked
the location and vehicle's general orientation. Trustees from Harris County Jail cleared brush from the bank, and the city brought
a winch truck. Then I made sure the vehicles weren't stuck on any-

thing, found a solid connecting point, and signaled the all-clear with my radio. Up and out they went.

The older ones rusted to skeletons; the newer ones retained their shape but lost their bones. Low-rider Chevys with fancy wheels long since tarnished. Minivans with toys floating around inside. Muscled-up Mustangs and staid company sedans still containing office files disintegrating upon touch. Frozen little time capsules of someone's everyday life on the move.

The job was scary and sad and strange when the underwater cars were occupied. More complicated too. HPD's crime lab got involved. More paperwork. The dive felt dirtier—the water connecting you with the dead, both of you just floating objects. Each night of the assignment when I lay down to sleep I smelled the sour, earthy small of the bayou, even fresh out of the shower.

The Camaro in question was wedged into the bank. Moving in slow motion like an astronaut, my rebreathing apparatus making me sound like Darth Vader, I worked my way around it.

No fallen trees near; that was a relief. Cottonmouths nested in them, their bodies tangling like ramen noodles in boiling water—hence the paramedic in the boat. I saw an unintelligible bumper sticker on the back of the car and ran my hand across it to clear off the algae. "Luv Ya Blue," with a Houston Oilers helmet. I should have known it held nothing but heartache.

I shined my flashlight into the driver's side window. The bayou's current, seeping in through various imperfections in the vehicle, tumbled everything inside like a clothes dryer—though with no open windows or doors everything seemed to stay contained. Along with the murky brown water something light blue brushed across the window, then more brown water, then an empty can of Big Tex beer, then something blue again, then a plastic grocery bag. It was like peering at a slot machine before it landed on a lemon or BAR or cherry. Only the next thing that came up wasn't a cherry or lemon. It was a badge.

The shield ticked against the window as it slid across on its tumble cycle, along with the light blue cloth of a uniform. I stared into the chocolate murk, waiting for it to come around in the current, but the next thing I saw wasn't a badge but a hundred-dollar bill. Then the Big Tex can again.

Opening the downstream door would cause everything to float straight down to the Lynchburg Ferry, then Trinity Bay and eventually the Gulf of Mexico itself. I told myself that it was the badge I was following up on, not the hundred-dollar bill.

Fighting the current, I opened the upstream door. A cotton-mouth slithered out of the back-seat area and snapped at me, its teeth striking my hard plastic diving mask.

A man likes to think he knows where he stands within the food chain of predators and prey; even among other men. But under-water everything gets all shuffled, your awkward limbs and limited breathing placing you much lower in the hierarchy. As I stood catching my breath and feeling the mask for holes from the snake, I saw the hundred-dollar bill float out of the car and shoot down-stream toward the Gulf. Damn.

Shining my light inside, a skull stared back at me. Its grin floated across the car's interior, rotating its head like a model at a photo shoot. A chill danced up my spine.

I'd closed the door and had my hand on my radio, as this was a crime scene now, when another hundred-dollar bill floated past the car's window. I took my thumb off the radio button. Watched a flathead catfish wiggle along the bottom.

In the days of $147/BBL oil, a hundred bucks wouldn't last an hour for me at the Pumpjack Pub on Eldridge. I used to find hun-dred-dollar bills in my truck or wadded up in the laundry hamper ev-ery time I was home from offshore. One month on, one month off.

Now, at $30/BBL oil and three years of divorce, I didn't think twice. I reopened the door, plucked the hundred from the water, and shined the light around inside the Camaro like I meant it.

Bones floated without gravity, like pens in those videos from the space station. Another skull bumped up against the steering wheel and two pale blue HPD uniforms drifted around the seats—angu-lar, irregular shapes. A school of perch flitted past me, one of them nibbling on bone that looked like a fingertip as it passed.

That's when I saw it. There, in the shotgun seat floorboard—a canvas bag. It took up the whole floor on that side of the car. I wedged a finger into the zipper and opened it, shining the light inside. Bricks of banded cash, seemingly luminescent on the pale green—loose edges floating in the current just begging to be set free.

I did it all so fast, without missing a beat. As if there were no actual decision to be made. No hesitation. No internal debate. I just . . . did it.

Untying some paracord from my wrist, I zipped the bag back up and floated it out of the car, walking it upstream. Then I wedged it in the mud between a cypress tree and the bank, tying it off. Looping an extra length around the bag and my ankle knife, I jammed the knife into the tree. Then I swam back and clicked three times on my radio.

A minute later I heard a pop and groan. The Camaro pulled free of the bank, swayed in the current, then disappeared into the sky above.

"What the hell took you so long, I've got 'stros tickets!" screamed Officer Cleary as I made my way into the boat. The cop and the paramedic made room for me as I fell inside awkwardly.

"I'm fine, guys, really, thanks," I said. I was trying to keep the conversation light, but my mind raced. If I hadn't been wet all over, they'd have seen me sweating.

"Seriously, that wasn't no five minutes," said the cop. "That was more like twenty! First pitch is at seven and it's the Rangers."

I unbuckled my air tank and leaned back against the side of the boat, catching my breath. "I've got bad news," I said in between panting. "I ran into a few of your colleagues." Just then Cleary's radio crackled.

"Eighty-two, dispatch."

Cleary craned his neck to speak into the radio clipped on his shoulder. "Eighty-two."

"Eighty-two, Sergeant Mills says pack up Aquaman and go wait by the tow truck for the lab guys. It's going to be a long night."

"Eighty-two, copy," he said into his radio. And then to us: "Well, shit, there goes the Astros game."

"They never beat the Rangers anyway," I said, squinting into the shadows at the cypress stumps, tangled oaks, and black mud on the banks to find landmarks of some kind, any kind, as the boat puttered away from the scene.

At 3 a.m. I gave up on sleep and threw back the covers. During the best of times, life at the Oaks of Davenport Apartment Homes held little peace. Each apartment was part of a single building split into fours. So it was flushing, thumping, fucking, cooking, bathing, and screaming all night every night. At least in the navy or out on the rigs everyone was equally tired and therefore equally quiet.

Tonight one neighbor was coughing like active tuberculosis was a real possibility and another was watching *Matlock* so loud I'd already figured out who'd done it. But I couldn't have slept no matter how quiet: I was planning on walking out that filthy door today and never coming back.

I shuffled over to my coffee maker and put in a new filter, added fresh grounds. Stood at my breakfast table looking out at the bleak apartment parking lot outside, at the beat-up pickups and Big Tex bottles and fast food wrappers and nervous cats as the coffeemaker gurgled and hissed.

Just past the parking lot, with a lack of zoning for which Houston is notorious, spread the wide verdant lawns and flickering gas lamps of the Oaks of Davenport neighborhood. Resembling my little stainfest apartment complex in name only, the comfortable and quiet, large-lot homes stood with darkened windows and peaceful lawns.

Flags fluttered in the night breeze. BMWs gleamed in driveways, azaleas bloomed twelve months per year; its residents seemed entirely composed of men in golf shirts and women in capri pants with their hands in their pockets laughing at jokes while standing in their driveways each evening. In the early '80s my apartments housed successful oil execs while their palatial homes were being built in the Oaks of Davenport neighborhood next door. Now the apartments' only upside was letting residents get away with saying they "lived in the Oaks of Davenport" and simply leaving it at that, letting others assume success without knowing that somehow, somewhere in their lives, something had gone horribly wrong. It wasn't the money I was so excited about, per se. It was the prospect of more laughing driveway moments like the guys in the neighborhood next door had, and fewer 3 a.m. episodes of *Matlock* heard through an asbestos-laden wall.

Ever since I had seen that bag of money, my mind was like a computer trying to process something big and getting stuck at every attempt at simple tasks. I kept calculating how much money would fit in a bag that size, plus or minus a few floaters. Ten thousand? One hundred thousand? More? I hadn't seen more than a couple hundred bucks at once in a decade. Everything was direct-deposit, auto-pay, and then just a handful of ashes at the end of the month. And that was when I worked steady.

Pouring my coffee into a thermos, I threw on a T-shirt and jeans, then stepped out into the Texas night. Driving my beat-up truck toward Buffalo Bayou, I rolled the window down and lit a cigarette. Glanced at my watch: 3:47 a.m. Johnny Cash was on the radio with "Sixteen Tons."

The air was hot and muggy even driving with open windows. The chirping of crickets and croaking of bullfrogs replaced the sounds of car horns, police helicopters, and rap music usually filling the streets of America's fourth-largest city. At the park, where we'd removed the car, a pop-up tent lab had been erected—lit up like the Astrodome and crawling with HPD officers, men in cheap suits, and workers in reflective vests. I slowed for a closer look.

The Camaro sat parked on the grass with its doors, hood, and trunk open. A canopy had been erected over the vehicle, with generators and floodlights blazing up the scene.

Crossing the bridge over the bayou, I turned into an unmarked, unlit wooded drive along the bayou. Shutting off the truck, I dug a waterproof flashlight out of the glove box and changed into my wetsuit. Not bothering with scuba gear, I settled for just a snorkel and mask. Then I picked my way down to the roiling blackness of the water.

Tangles of swamp chestnut oak, flame-leaf sumac, bald cypress, river birch, passionflower vines, and trumpet creeper meant nobody across the way processing the vehicle could see me wading in. Buffalo Bayou's gumbolike water swept me along like a slow train. I pushed hard for the far side, holding my breath and swimming hard until I saw purple and blue spots and thought my lungs might explode.

After catching my breath on the other side, I bobbed up and down the bank, running a hand through the slime along the way. After twenty minutes of feeling nothing but mud and algae and cypress stumps, something bit my finger. I shined my light onto the banks, expecting to see a cottonmouth or catfish with razor-sharp barbs. Instead I saw the gleam of my diving knife and the paracord snaking back to the huge duffel stuffed into the roots of the tree. *Houston, the Eagle has landed.*

I'd just hauled the bag out of the water and was drip-drying against a cypress, trying to catch my breath, when a white light blinded me.

"Who the hell are you?" someone said in a knife-hand voice. A deputy in a cowboy hat shined a flashlight point-blank in my face, resting his other hand on his sidearm. My stomach clenched as I held a hand out to shield my eyes.

"I'm Derrick Stevens, the diver," I said, pointing at my snorkeling mask. "I did the recovery this afternoon." The truth was all I could think of. I stepped toward the light as my brain raced, switching the bag to the opposite hand.

People think that fighting is the most valuable skill you learn in the military. Nope. My time in Uncle Sam's navy imparted the most useful tactical skill ever developed by humankind—and it's not swimming or fighting or tying knots. It's the art of bullshitting someone so you don't get in trouble.

I stepped to the officer and did my best official voice. "Sir, it's standard operating procedure for all Harris County contract divers to undergo a mandatory environmental reclamation of the recovery zone, making sure all of the ropes and hooks and flags and towels and things are picked up at the dive site," I said, raising the duffel bag for emphasis. Water still poured from the bag, and I prayed a hundred-dollar bill wouldn't slink out in the stream of dripping water.

"At four in the morning?" he said.

I shook my head. "No, I'm slated to do it at nine a.m. But I was hoping to take the wife to Pedernales Falls later today."

The officer turned off his light and stared at me, his square jaw chewing tobacco and his chest puffing like a gorilla's. He waited to see if I said anything else. I didn't.

"Stop creeping around in them damn bushes," he said finally. "You gonna get your ass shot." He turned without saying another word and walked up the hill toward the Camaro and surrounding makeshift crime lab. I followed.

I was now on the side of the bayou where we did the recovery; where the car was being processed, and not the side where I'd parked. But Officer Gorilla had already seen me; it would be weird to backtrack. So I walked straight through the worksite. In my mind the bright white work lights made the bag transparent, and the hammering of the power generator become incoming fire as the officers saw the money and sent warning shots over my head—or, worse, gave no warning shots at all. I imagined Officer Cleary, who did the dive with me, being there too, complaining about missing the Astros game and wanting to see what was in the bag. Or the cute paramedic wanting to know why my finger bled.

But nobody noticed the bag. Or me. Cleary wasn't there; neither was the paramedic. Just past the Camaro I gave a casual wave to the deputy. He ignored me, spitting into a Dr Pepper can and talking to his colleagues. With my head held high, I walked by them all as if my car were parked just ahead, turned onto the street just past the officers' field of view, and vomited on the sidewalk.

My haul for that morning's dive was $642,120.

The discovery of the policemen's remains never made it to the papers, not even the *Houston Press*. And I never did discover how two uniformed cops wound up with that much cash in a personal vehicle, dead in the bayou. But somebody knew. Somebody had to know; someone *always* knows when that much money goes missing.

Stealing makes most men edgy. Stealing from a gang? Worse. Stealing from a gang of cops up to no good? Mainline paranoia. Every time I saw an HPD cruiser I was sure that was my day. Whenever a cop pulled up behind me my knuckles went white and I saw those skulls in the underwater Camaro swirling like bull sharks; imagined a rapturous pit of cottonmouths slithering through my floating bones until they drifted into oblivion.

Figured I had no choice but to get ready for them when they came. Sure, those two were dead. But was there a third or fourth? And whose money was it originally? No way somebody wouldn't connect the dots, even if a few years had passed. Somebody ruthless. Somebody who'd want me to pay compound interest in blood.

The only question was, would I really be ready for them when they came? Would I be strong enough to keep what I'd found? Where would I be on the food chain then?

I always imagined what life would be like when I retired. Golf. Movies. Spending more time with my daughter, Jenna, who I'd hardly seen since the divorce.

But I didn't do any of those things. Not once. Instead I spent my time getting ready for the day when whatever sketchy group knew about that money finally caught up to me.

For the first year my preparations centered on the house I'd bought in the Oaks of Davenport—the real Oaks of Davenport —on the opposite site of the neighborhood from my old rundown apartments. I figure, who comes looking for a man right by where they were? But I didn't spend my time laughing at jokes in my driveway; I was a busy man.

Floor safe, over-the-top outside lighting, a security system straight out of *Mission Impossible*, and enough guns to overthrow a small African government. ARs, AKs, M1911s, Glock 9mm's, thousands of rounds of ammo—all strategically placed around the house so I could tactically funnel threats as needed. Crooked cops would be armed and I had to be *ready*, no bullshit. I dropped $50K on guns and security, easy.

After the house, it was all about me. Guns are worthless without training, so I invested in formal classes and long afternoons at the Artemis gun range. Then Krav Maga, the hand-to-hand system of the Israeli special forces. I spent evenings punching, kicking, grappling, and getting a reality check regarding what actual fighting is like as a middle-aged man. Where I stood on the predatory scale against other men. It was ugly, but I put in the work. I even made it a point to spar with different body types, from short fireplug fellows to huge knuckle-draggers. I'd work the heavy bag, putting my hip and full body weight behind combinations of hook punches, uppercuts, jabs, and elbows until the bag was slick with blood, all the while envisioning an army of skeletons in police uniforms waiting for me in the shadows. Never blinking. Never resting. Just waiting to attack.

On the day I finally found my place in the food chain, I'd walked to the Starbucks on Dairy Ashford and Ubered to Global Security Conversions to pick up my new truck. The Ford F350 had just 702 miles on it and had been taken apart and reassembled with armored plating, bulletproof glass, run-flat tires, and industrial brakes. The service technician, a thin man in blue overalls, whistled as he slid me the final invoice. "I don't know who you're scared of, but they've already fired the first shot," he said, chuckling as he lit up a cigarette and counted the stacks of bills I'd piled on the coffee-stained counter.

Sweat ran down my back as the hot blast from the truck's air conditioner hit my face when I cranked the engine. I cracked the windows so some of the summer heat could escape. I'd never ridden in a bulletproof vehicle before, and I've got to admit that it felt good. Felt safe. Felt like I could relax a little. Hell, I sort of felt like causing trouble. It's only natural. All the training. All these new resources. I felt ready for anything. Bring. It. On. Bitches. I was literally bulletproof. I turned on the radio and listened to Willie and Waylon's "Pancho and Lefty," whistling as I drove and taking the long way home.

Back at the house I locked the door behind me, checked the security system, and reset the video feed. Opening my safe room, I took off my shoes and plopped down into the leather desk chair. A former master bedroom, the safe room was now my armory and operational security center. At my desk a half-dozen police scanners were set to different frequencies—HPD, Harris County sheriff, constables—squawking out various goings-on around town. As I listened to the drone of the cop talk saying things like "10-32" and "welfare check" and "disregard," I sipped black coffee and cleaned a Glock .40 while glancing at the TV screens showing my home from dozens of different vantage points.

I was just about to put the gun back together when a face appeared in one of those screens. A woman's face.

Bespectacled and no more than five feet tall, she wore khaki slacks with clunky brown shoes and an ill-fitting blue blazer. She wore her hair in a tight bun, but strands had broken free and stuck to her chubby face in clumps. Her mouth came together in an expressionless dot as she checked her smartphone and adjusted her glasses before ringing the doorbell twice. She held only the phone and a business card.

In the frame of the camera, you could see her standing in front of my sign reading WE'RE TOO BROKE TO BUY ANYTHING. WE KNOW WHO WE'RE VOTING FOR. WE HAVE FOUND JESUS. GO AWAY. I'd thought the sign hilarious, but she merely glanced at it and returned her stare to the door, as if she'd seen it a thousand times before.

I set the Glock down and wiped my hands. Tapping the keys of the security system a few times, I got a 360-degree view of the house, street, and backyard. No cars around save a dented white Toyota Prius out front. Nothing but squirrels out back. I opened up the bedroom window and listened. No helicopters in evidence, just the *chik-chik-chik*ing of a neighbor's sprinkler. Hey, I know that sounds crazy, but you never know.

Picking up my coffee, I padded down the hall toward the door. My legs were killing me from an early-morning run, my biceps destroyed from a brutal sparring session at Krav Maga the previous night.

Scrunching my face into the most annoyed look I could muster,

I threw open the front door and said nothing, merely raising my eyebrows.

"Derrick Stevens?" asked the woman. She had a lisp, and my name came out like "Thtevenths."

"Yes?"

She handed me her card. In hindsight, I'd rather have faced a dozen crooked cops with AR-15s and armored Strykers. Or actual ninjas with poison throwing stars. Or rabid pit bulls. Hell, I'd rather she'd have just shot me in the face then and there.

"Mr. Thtevenths, I'm Agent Abigail Larson with the Internal Revenue Thervith," she said. "I need to talk to you about some glaring overthights in your most rethent Form 1040." She adjusted her glasses and awaited a reply. I stared down at the card, trying to process what the woman was saying.

All the 7.62mm rounds I'd put through my AK-47. All those nights at Krav Maga. All the cameras and protocols and lights. Five-foot-tall Abigail Larson, lisp and all, wielded the might of the federal government like the sword of a Viking berserker, starting with that very conversation. The lawyer's fees. The court dates. The asset forfeiture and garnishing of any future wages. Then, finally, the Texas State Penitentiary at Huntsville.

In hindsight, I should have run. Run far away to a place with great diving and no extradition, like Indonesia or São Tomé & Príncipe. If I thought the bayou was murky, taking on the IRS offered more snakes and snags than even the worst underwater nightmare. And I'd spent so much money on security, I couldn't have afforded a decent attorney even if they hadn't found what was left.

Huntsville is even louder than the Oaks of Davenport Apartment Homes, what with the clanging and coughing and dubious grunting of my fellow incarcerated citizens. Between the noise and the thin, scratchy blankets, I'm right back where I started not sleeping very well. And when I lie down at night, I still smell the stink of the bayou on my skin and see the visions of snakes and skeleton cops lurking in every shadow to demand their money at gunpoint. In the waking world, however, I no longer worry about the money's original owners catching up with me — not even stuck here in Huntsville, so easy to find. The money is gone, and gone for good. And anyone who ever comes asking about it could damn well take it up with Abigail Larson. But I wouldn't recommend it.

SCOTT LORING SANDERS

Waiting on Joe

FROM *Shooting Creek and Other Stories*

ERICK, MY LAB-CHOW MUTT, was down at the treeline chewing on something, content, gnawing and licking the marrow from whatever creature he'd rooted up. On the porch, I attempted to keep my wood shavings in a neat pile as I worked on a replica of Erick, made from a soft chunk of poplar. Wood, it seemed, consumed every aspect of my life. I lived in the woods, I worked on a Christmas tree farm, and during my free time I was either splitting firewood or whittling to avoid the wife.

It had been a tough winter for me and Deborah, cooped up together far longer than was tolerable. She'd been pretty removed lately, and I didn't possess the proper tools to cheer her, neither in my pants nor in my brain. She'd gotten laid off from her secretary job at the dentist's office (or possibly fired; she'd been a bit murky with the details), so we weren't exactly happy or flush.

I used the tip of my Buck knife to replicate Erick's muscular haunches while the real Erick sprawled in the not-yet-green grass, still chomping away. That dog was always scavenging, bringing stuff home—woodchucks, squirrels, a three-foot copperhead once. During the spring melt he'd often drag back field dressings the hunters had left behind, my lawn resembling a full-blown yard sale composed of deer parts.

Inside, Deborah rummaged around, finally awake. She seemed to be sleeping later and later these days, going to bed earlier and earlier. Always on the computer, Facebooking or whatever the hell. Some nights I wanted to climb on the roof and rip down that satellite dish, get rid of our Internet, television, the whole goddamned bundle, as it were, toss it in the fucking dumpster. Hard to justify such luxuries when we had bills to pay, groceries to buy. She'd often talked of getting her degree at Community, but I hadn't once seen her make a move in that direction. Come to think of it, the only move I'd seen her make lately was toward another beer. Which made me sick. Only added to the problems. I think it's a weak man (or woman) who uses alcohol to wash away their troubles. Me, well, I never had a taste for it.

My fingers had turned fat and thick from the cold, the unforgiving winter refusing to let go just yet, so my carving was over for the morning. I set my knife and miniature Erick on the table and opened and closed my frozen hands as if casting a spell, attempting to work some blood back in. I whistled for Erick and he popped to attention, his find still stuffed in his jaws.

As he trotted across the yard, wood smoke caught the breeze and trickled down from the chimney, lightly fogging him. Tinges of red shimmered in his black coat when the sun hit it right. He was a tough old bastard. Seventy pounds, solid muscle, total badass. Far as I was concerned, flawless. Deborah felt otherwise.

"He just puked up a baby rabbit on the new rug, Steven," she'd once said. "Jesus Christ, it stinks." And it had stunk, granted, but if a dead rabbit was rotting in *your* gut, you'd probably throw up too. He was just a dog being a dog, couldn't blame him for that.

He chewed a beer can all to shit one time, which Deborah consequently stepped on, slicing her big toe on the way to the toilet in the middle of the night. He'd puked up plastic Kroger bags on a few occasions. Ate a dirty diaper once. Also an entire junior-sized Wilson leather football. We didn't have kids and I sure as hell had never changed a diaper. Hadn't tossed a ball since grade school. Where he'd found such items was a mystery.

Deborah had issues with Erick, fair enough, but you can't hold a dog accountable for following its instincts. Like now, for instance.

As he got closer, I tried to determine what he held so happily. A naked baby doll? The coloring was right. Shoot, he'd found a football once, why not a Barbie? I went to the top stair to greet him, and that's when my heart stuttered. Clamped between his jowls was a human foot, sawed off three inches above the ankle, the skin ragged and jagged as if chewed by some toothy monster. Erick swooshed his tail proudly.

"Shit, Erick," I muttered, glancing behind me. I guess my body language suggested he'd done something wrong, because his tail stopped wagging, his head drooped to hangdog. "It's okay, boy," I half whispered. "Drop it."

He was having none of it. Sensing I was up to something, he tried to make a break for it, unwilling to surrender his trophy. I snatched his collar and grabbed his bottom jaw. "Drop it," I said again, more forcefully. Erick's ears pinned back, his front paws digging in. The foot's stiff toes brushed my wrist, which freaked me out. "Motherfucker," I grunted through clenched teeth, realizing my only choice was to grasp that slobber-coated foot like it was Erick's favorite tennis ball. He immediately took it for a game, like a goddamned tug-o-war, and we both pulled and held on with the stubbornness of snapping turtles. But when I said, "*Chase?* You wanna *chase?*" that did the trick and he let go.

He started barking when I didn't hold up my end of the bargain. "Be quiet," I whisper-pleaded, knowing Deborah would open that front door any second now, furious, only to discover me hugging a hairy human foot. I scurried up the steps, grabbed the sports section from a stack of old newspapers, and quickly wrapped that thing as if rolling the world's biggest joint. I twisted the ends, then rewrapped with the classifieds. Erick was going apeshit, pissed I'd stolen his treasure.

I held the package tight to my chest, then walked inside and beelined for the woodstove. Bacon sizzled in the kitchen, a spatula clinking against a skillet, no doubt Deborah making exactly five pieces for her own self and exactly zero for me, a perfect illustration of where our marriage stood.

"Shut that dog up," she yelled. I envisioned her bleached hair pulled up high on her head in a ponytail as she squinted, a nasty cigarette waggling in her squeezed lips, her face not nearly as pretty as it once was.

"I'll try, dear," I said, stuffing Erick's offering into the coals, using the poker to push it way back. The man's leg hairs ignited and I got a strong whiff before closing the door. Deborah didn't need to know about Erick's discovery. Not just yet. "Sorry. I think he's hungry is all."

"Well, feed him already. Christ, it's too early. I got a ripping headache."

I walked back outside, Erick still yammering about how I'd betrayed him. "Come on, boy," I said, then zipped my jacket snug, grabbed a shovel, headed for the woods. The snow, the ice, it could only keep evil doings hid for so long. "*Hike*, boy? Wanna go for a *hike?*"

It was a pretty sorry excuse for a grave. But when dug in haste, and with fatigue setting in after sawing and digging and lugging and burying, a bit of slack had to be extended when it came to the particulars.

Erick had really gone to town—dirt scattered every which way, dead leaves strewn about like feathers from a slaughtered goose. The only body part I saw was a leg wearing a scrap of blue jean, and that was enough for me; no reason to delve deeper. Wasn't like I needed to confirm his face; I knew good and well who he was. I hoped Erick hadn't already carried off the head or arms or whatever, leaving bits of the man scattered about like a trail of breadcrumbs.

Erick had led me right to the plot, using an established deer path that meandered through oaks and rhododendron thickets. It was also a path that, if followed for another half mile, would've taken me straight to Willie Koonz's back door. Willie, as it so happened, was the man currently half buried in the soil. He had two kids and a wife, them wondering where he'd run off to three months prior. He'd been my supervisor. The guy I'd worked with on the tree farm for five years. He was also the guy who'd been fucking my wife for the past eight months before he disappeared, sneaking through these very woods, on this very deer path, during lunch hour. Supposedly he went home to eat during our break while me and the Mexicans stayed in the fields, our boots dangling over pickup tailgates, me eating partially frozen peanut-butter-and-jelly sandwiches, them gorging on still-hot tamales wrapped tightly in corn husks that their pretty wives—with skin like warm honey—had, earlier that morning, cooked and sealed in foil, which in turn always made me envious, but I never had the gumption to ask if maybe (just once) they'd bring an extra for me, them probably thinking I was pleased as punch with the cold, stale *gringo* sandwiches I slapped together every morning because my wife sure as shit didn't make them for me, her still sleeping away, waiting for lunchtime so my boss could come over and give her the business in my own bed while my bony ass turned numb on the freezing metal ridges of that aforementioned tailgate.

So, yeah, there was that.

I'd figured out the affair a year back. The Mexicans were doing the season's first mowing while me and Willie planted seedlings on a hillside. Squatting, kneeling, digging little holes, dropping in trees no higher than a hand. Long, sunny days but not so damn hot like it would be in another month, when we'd be culling dead trees, the son-of-a-bitching yellow jackets in the ground, lying in wait for you to step on their nests, or the hornets in their paper globes tucked in the trees, praying you'd slice into their hive with your trimming machete so they could zoom out like a squadron of fighter jets, just for the fun of it. But in March and April things were still pleasant. The magenta of redbuds dotting the mountainsides, the white of dogwoods. Oaks dropping their tassels from the sky like heavenly pipe cleaners.

When it's just you and one other guy, and that guy's come back from lunch, and he smells strangely familiar, in fact smells not only like that perfume your wife insists on—which she can only find at select TJ Maxx stores—but also like the unmistakable sweaty sex of her puss, well, you start to wonder. Then, when the breeze shifts and Willie is upwind of you, and suddenly Deborah's fragrance filters down the slope and your nose starts twitching the same as Erick's when he whiffs an injured bunny rabbit, well, your brain starts connecting the dots, puts the pieces together. A man knows his wife's odor, that's all I'm saying.

That, in and of itself, wasn't enough proof. Hell, maybe Willie's wife smelled similar. I mean, maybe it's like snowflakes. Every one of them's different, but from a distance they all appear pretty damn equal. So it's not out of the realm of possibility that Deborah and Willie's wife could've had a nearly identical odor. They live within a mile of each other, probably our wells are tapped into the same aquifer—pardon the expression—so maybe it's in the water. Who's to say? All I know is when that pleasant breeze drifted down the hillside, there was no doubt Deborah's unique and particular aroma floated on that stream of lazy, warm air.

A few weeks later, me and Willie are fertilizing when he gets to ripping on me. He was always bullying, but that day it was with more oomph. "Don't you got goals, Steve? What're you doing with your life?"

I hated when people called me Steve. My name's Steven, I always introduced myself as such, and I'd corrected Willie many times.

"Doing about the same as you," I said. "We're both dipping our hands into dried-up horseshit, which, by some weird-ass miracle, makes trees grow."

"Yeah, but this is temporary for me," he said. "I got bigger plans."

"Five years on the job doesn't sound very temporary, Willie. Five years sounds pretty permanent."

He spit, wiping tobacco trickle into his beard. "I've got some stuff on the side," he said. "Me and my brother, we been investing in shit. You ever heard of semiconductors?"

"Like a part-time orchestra leader?" I said, messing with him. If there was one thing I knew, it was technology. I only had a high school diploma, but I was always playing with electronics, tinkering. Probably had the fastest Wi-Fi connection in the county, not that Deborah appreciated it. Something I'd learned over the years was that people generally thought I was stupid. No matter, because I'd found it to be an asset. When people assume you're dumb, they let down their guard.

"I don't know how they work," he said, "but Barth says it's related to cell phones. We've been dumping money into this company he knows of, got an inside tip, and it's about to hit big. That's what I mean, Steve. I got plans, man, more than baling and loading fucking Christmas trees the rest of my life."

"Semiconductors, huh? Like you talking about core cooling capacitors, that type of shit?" I was that kid you probably went to school with, the one always tearing apart radios, TVs, just to see how they worked, then putting them back together.

"Speak English, man. I swear you're worse than them goddamn wetbacks half the time. I don't know what the fuck you just said. Anyway, you need to think bigger." Willie reached into his fertilizer bag and tossed a handful around the base of a Fraser fir. "Stop acting like an idiot, wasting your time carving stupid shit out of wood. You need to plan for your future."

"Hmm, maybe so," I said. And I did start planning, right then, because I'd never discussed my whittling with him. In fact, I'd never mentioned it to anyone, other than Deb, obviously. It was private, just something I did. And me and Willie, we didn't mingle outside of work. When we'd first met, there'd been discussions of us and the wives getting together to grill burgers, the way new acquaintances will do, imagining they've found that perfect match where the wives have everything in common, scrapbooking and collecting

Longaberger baskets or Beanie Babies, and the guys love bow hunting and Earnhardt—but that never panned out. So there was no way he could've known about me carving "stupid shit out of wood" unless he'd been to my house. Not just *to* my house, but *inside,* and not just inside, but all the way back to my bedroom, where I kept my finished pieces on a dresser, mostly of Erick in various states of repose. So that, along with the stink of my wife on his clothes, well, that got me to planning for my future all right.

"You ever seen *Risky Business?*" continued Willie, chuckling. "God, what a great movie. 'Sometimes you just gotta say *What the fuck,* Steve.' Best line ever."

A stripe of spittle dripped from his beard like lace from a spider's ass, and I considered countering with a quote of my own, lifted from a fortune cookie I'd once cracked open. "Live life like a mighty river." I loved that. I was a mighty river, ready to unleash my power. But in my own way, on my own terms.

It was me who'd first discovered how bad off Joe actually was. I was late for work, zipping my old Charger tight around a corner, when I nearly hit him as he walked the road's edge, gimping along. I braked, rolled down the passenger window. "What do you know good, old man?" I said. He caught my eye, then kept on. I nudged the car forward. "Jump in, Joe, before you get killed. Where you heading?"

He glanced over but didn't stop. "Gotta see the doc. Alternator belt's shot on my truck."

"The doctor? In town? That's ten miles. Get your ass in here before I jump out and stuff you in."

"You wrassle with a rattlesnake, you bound to get bit," he said, taking a long, deep draw from his cigarette. Deborah had gotten her orneriness honestly, that's for sure, but he did concede, opened the door, started to enter.

"Whoa, hold up," I said, raising my free hand. "You can't smoke in here."

Joe stopped midstream, tightened his jaw, began walking again, not bothering to close my door. "Go piss your pants, you son of a bitch."

"Shit," I muttered, inching the car forward, careful not to slap his ass with the open door. I leaned across the huge front seat, yelled to him. "C'mon, I'm sorry. Finish up and get in."

He kept walking, ignoring me, but I wouldn't relent. Finally he flicked his cigarette into the broom sedge and entered, the whole process a struggle as he twisted that twisted body into the front seat. His chest heaved in small spurts.

"You really need to quit smoking, Joe."

"Just drive, peckerhead." He stared at me, his eyes as hard and dark as the coal he'd extracted from the ground for fifty years.

I liked Joe well enough. Grouchy old thing, tough as leather plow line, his body bent and mangled like a crashed car, but he always told it straight.

"What're you going in for?" I asked.

"Cain't breathe, Steve," he said, lighting a fresh cigarette. "Reckon doc's gonna tell me for certain what I already been knowing for years."

So it was me who'd been with Joe when he'd received the official news, only a month after I'd learned his daughter was screwing Willie. He had the black lung—which might sound horrible—but for a retired coal miner it meant a check he could live out his days on, something to leave for his family.

The doctor brought in X-rays, clamped them to the backlit screen. Joe hadn't wanted me in there, had said, "Get on to work before I slit your throat," but his rheumy eyes said something different. So I insisted, ignored his objections. Those X-rays looked like some foreign black universe with a splattering of white stars. Each star, explained the doc, was coal dust, scarring the lungs. Joe didn't ask questions, just gazed ahead, absorbing it as if he'd known since boyhood this day was inevitable. He'd left school in eighth grade to enter the mines, only exited a few years back. That was the shit of it all. Work fifty years underground just to be put back in it permanently, right when you'd finally come up for air. As if day by day, year by year, all you'd been doing was digging your own grave.

That was his life. Mines every day, a wife, two kids—Deborah, of course, and her older brother, Russ, who'd made it to eleventh grade before going underground, only to be blown up ten years back. After the explosion, with his son dead, with his wife gone many years before, Joe moved from the little mining town of Grundy—the only home he'd ever known—to a singlewide in the Blue Ridge to be closer to his daughter, for whatever that was worth. No love lost between those two. Saw each other maybe three times a year. It was me who often checked on him, made sure he was getting by all right, especially after the diagnosis.

It was also me who'd helped Joe get his tanks in order. At first those clear plastic tubes jammed up his nose drove him batshit. He'd hobble around, bitching, pulling his little cart behind him like a pissed-off caddy, the thin blue oxygen tank his golf clubs. Once a month I'd go over to Radford to the gas place for refills. As teenagers we used to hop their chain-link fence at night and steal tanks of nitrous oxide, then buy big punching balloons at the pharmacy, fill them, have insane parties, everybody so fucked up they'd stumble, fall, and sometimes convulse. The gas people eventually got wise—installed hurricane wire, locked the nitrous in a cage—but did we ever fry some brain cells for a while, our entire class whacked on dental-grade laughing gas most of senior year. Man, I'd changed a lot since then.

Several weeks after I determined Deborah was knocking boots with Willie, I drove to Crosshairs, the local hunting outfitter, to make a purchase. Not for a gun, but instead for a couple of trail cameras— the ones with motion sensors so hunters can discover what monster bucks roam their forests. Simple setup, really. I put one above the floodlight spotting the driveway and another in a tree along that trail leading to Willie's.

That following Monday, after Deborah was asleep, I checked the computer to confirm my suspicions. Sure enough, during lunch while I sat with the Mexicans, me fantasizing about their young, dark-skinned wives, guess who appeared on my trail cam software? That cocksucker Willie, that's who, sneaking through the woods. Then the house camera picked him up, strutting along my driveway, cool as a goddamn cucumber.

The same deal unfolded for the next several months. I stewed so bad I couldn't stand it. Not so much because I gave a hell about Deborah anymore or felt betrayed by my coworker, who had the balls to stick it to my wife nearly every day, then return to work an hour later and tell me my tree trimming was a bit sloppy, but more because I was scared Deb might file for divorce. Which wasn't an option. Not yet. That didn't jibe with my financial plans. But a man can only take so much. So I decided if they liked games, I'd play a few of my own. Mess with their tiny brains a bit.

*

Once, when I'd mentioned that Joe was a good man, Deborah had gone off. "Don't you dare. You don't know a goddamn thing about it." I'd assumed this meant Joe used to be rough on her as a child, maybe knocked her around a bit, but I was wrong. "He was a drunk. A real bastard. I don't think he remembered my name most days."

"Coal mining's a tough job. He probably—"

"Don't you dare defend him, Steven. You want an example of what a *good man* he was?"

I shrugged. "Sure, why not?"

"He used to go to the shelter and get cats, pretend he was adopting them, okay? Once home, he'd break their legs with a hammer, leave 'em mewing in the barn. Those cries still keep me up some nights. Then in the evenings he'd sit in the loft drinking beer, waiting to shoot the curious coyotes who wandered in. For the bounty."

"Well, it *was* just cats. And son of a bitching coyotes. Not like it was dogs or cattle or something."

"That's awful, Steven. Cats are God's creatures, same as dogs."

"I'll tell you right now, cats sure as shit *aren't* the same as dogs. Not even fucking close."

"Doesn't mean they should be abused."

"That's not what I meant. Shit, they were gonna die at that shelter anyway."

"You're disgusting. God loves all his miracles equally."

All I can say is, she never showed that sort of compassion toward Erick. Not once. And okay, fair enough, no animal should be abused—not even cats, I guess. But oh, Jesus, did it make me crazy when she preached her Bible bullshit. Full-on hypocrite. Prime example? When I'd gotten home from Joe's first doctor's visit and advised her of his prognosis, she'd said, "Hallelujah. About time."

What she meant, of course, was that the diagnosis equaled compensation. Money that would set us up good once Joe died. Her brother was dead from the mines, her mother a suicide—slit her wrists in a bathtub; Deborah found her when she'd gotten home from school, only a freshman—so Deborah was the sole heir. Wouldn't get rich, but between that and the settlement from Russ's death in the mine collapse, we'd be doing okay for a while.

So I had no interest in divorce. Last thing I wanted was for Willie to somehow get his hands on even one dime of that money. I needed to break them up.

*

Out in the fields, I put my sabotage plan in motion. Started dropping hints. "But it's weird, Willie. I mean, me and Deborah, well, we
haven't exactly been frisky in months. So if she really is pregnant . . .
shoot, I don't know what's going on." The way Willie shifted, the
way he nervously passed that trimming machete from one hand to
the other, man, it was priceless.

Toying with Deborah was even more fun, and one evening while
eating dinner, I laid it on thick. Vanna was on the tube pushing
letters as we sat in the living room, shoveling in peas and potatoes
from our potpies. I had a lemonade, she one of those Redd's Apple
Ale things that'd been on the commercials lately.

"So I was talking with Willie today," I said, "and you know what
he told me? He's a real jackass, that guy." I paused, all cool-like.
Wanted to watch her squirm. But she was staring at that screen,
only one blank left in the entire puzzle: THE P_INTED DESERT.
She shouted at the TV, "*The Pointed Desert,* you dumb shit," just as
the contestant on *Wheel* said the same exact thing (I swear to God)
minus the "dumb shit" part. Sajak said, "No, I'm sorry, but you still
have time." The guy sounded things out, repeated, "*The Pointed Desert,*" and Sajak, supercool as always, replied, "No matter how many
times you say it, the puzzle's not going to change." Deborah said,
"What the hell?" so I chimed in, "The *Painted* Desert," which of
course was the correct answer and what the next contestant said.
The woman got twenty-five hundred bucks for her winning efforts.
I got *nada.* "Did you hear me?" I said. "About Willie?"

"What? No," she snapped, staring down the television as if somehow betrayed. Like Sajak and company were running a conspiracy.
"What happened?"

"Willie said something today I couldn't believe. Said he was stepping out on his wife."

She lifted her bottle, paused midraise, wouldn't look at me.
"Huh, well, I guess there's trouble in paradise."

"Not according to him. Says he's just got another girl he likes
better. Wants to be with."

Did she half smile as she took a sip of Redd's? Possibly.

"Shit happens all the time, right?" she said, cutting some potpie
crust with her fork and stuffing it in, grinning like a wolf.

"I don't know, just seems lowdown. Blindsiding his wife like that.
Two kids and all. I mean, if it was you and me, I'd just tell you."

"Yeah."

"And you'd do the same, right? No behind-the-back stuff?"

"Yeah," she repeated, her eyes locked on the television, staring at that new creepy Colonel Sanders as he peddled chicken, her seeming to only half pay attention to me. But I assure you, I had her ear.

"He said he hooked up with that cute little thing down at the tavern. You know, that new blonde who waits tables?"

Her head whipped in my direction. "With *who*?"

"That woman—hell, *girl* really—at the tavern. Melody, I think her name is. Short skirts, legs to here," I said, raising my hand well above my head. This was fun.

Her lips pursed.

"Said they're going to take off on Saturday. His wife and kids are out of town, visiting her mother, and he's running away to Myrtle Beach. Leaving a note, and *poof*, just like that, he's gone. Crazy, huh?"

That bit about his wife going out of town was the only true part, by the way, Willie having mentioned it at work. You sprinkle in a few truths with your lies and people eat it up.

Deborah looked at Vanna, back from commercial. "Yeah, I reckon so."

"Good news for us is I'll get the foreman job. A few more bucks. Mr. Majors ain't gonna give it to no Mexican."

She grabbed her plate and walked toward the kitchen, her face blank. If I could've magically pried open the top of her head right then, I'd've seen those gears whirring at double-time, grinding like an unoiled machine, smoke pouring from the works.

The day after I'd messed with Deborah, something curious happened: Willie failed to return to work after lunch. That son of a bitch was a lot of things, but unreliable wasn't one of them. That evening I checked my trail cam software, and sure enough, he'd headed toward my house that afternoon, sneaking through the woods like a horny tomcat. But the footage never showed him leaving. What it did capture, however, precisely an hour and twenty-three minutes later, according to the timestamp, was Deborah passing by, pushing my wheelbarrow, which in all my days I'd never seen her do. Far as I knew, that woman didn't know which end of a hammer to hold. But as usual, I'd underestimated her. She was full of surprises.

Days and weeks later, small-town details funneled through the rumor mill. One in particular was that Willie had left a note stating he was leaving his family. Nobody seemed too surprised by this, least of all his wife. She never even bothered to call the cops when she got back from her weekend at her mother's, just assumed the no-good scoundrel had left her high and dry. Which turned out to be particularly good fortune for me and Deborah.

I didn't let on to Deborah that I knew anything about what she'd done. I had my reasons for keeping quiet. But it was weird, living in that house with her afterward, realizing what she was capable of. I'd find myself looking at her from across the table every once in a while, thinking, *Man, that's one wicked-assed woman.* But she was cool. You'd never guess, not in a million years, she'd sawed up her lover and buried him in the woods.

"I'm leaving you," said Deborah. This was three weeks after Erick had brought me the foot, several months since Willie had gone missing. I have no idea why it took her so long to make that decision, but I'm assuming she wanted to be sure the smoke had cleared.

"No," I said. "No, you're not."

"Bite me, Steven. I'll do whatever I damn well please."

"Mmm, no you won't." That's when I got off the couch and approached the front door—all smooth and cavalier, like I had all the power, all the answers—and ran my hand along the casing. "Let me show you something, Deb. I'm figuring you plugged these with chewing gum?" I said when my fingers located the first of the three patched bullet holes, almost like I was reading Braille. "Then smeared them with shoe polish?" I rubbed both my pointer and middle finger against my thumb, as if demonstrating the universal money sign, while showing her the inky residue. "Pretty good match, really. I'm impressed."

"Listen, baby, you got things a little mixed up," she said, playing it cool but unable to hide her panic. Plain as day I saw her envisioning where exactly my rifle was at that moment. Saw her calculating speed and time and distance to the closet, figuring whether she could race to it before I tackled her. Of course it didn't matter, since I'd already moved the gun. And unloaded it.

"I don't have a thing mixed up, Deborah. In fact, it's all clear as day."

"I don't know what you're talking about. I didn't do nothing."

That's when I popped in the flash drive, played the video. She stood over my shoulder and watched her own self, right there on the computer screen, all bloody and goopy, pushing body parts down the trail. Three separate trips. It was almost funny, in a sick, demented sort of way, I admit, but it was humorous watching Erick follow at her heels as she struggled with that wheelbarrow, strong-arming it down the trail. Even when she halted and clearly yelled at him, presumably ordering him back to the house, his tail just slapped back and forth like a windshield wiper. He ignored her completely.

One particular part of the video seemed to really unsettle her. Of Willie's head bouncing up and out of the barrow when the wheel clipped a rock, then rolling along the trail for a few feet like a kid's wayward ball. I glanced back to see her nose crinkle as she relived that scene: her scooting around the wheelbarrow, picking up his head, plopping it back in as if harvesting pumpkins. She could've closed her eyes as the video played, could've turned away or walked off, but she watched intently. Instead of being unsettled, as I'd first assumed, I realized she seemed almost fascinated. Suddenly it was me who felt uneasy.

"It's also saved to a second jump drive," I explained, "and stored in a safe place with instructions. Thought you should know, just in case you're considering cutting me up into bits like your boyfriend."

"Steven, you don't understand. There's—"

"I figured out most of it, Deb. Though, I confess, I still don't know how you forced him to write a note. You're good, I'll give you that. Damn smart."

And that, right there—along with the video—was the key to her spilling everything. Simple flattery. Who'd've thunk it? Offer her a little praise about a cold-blooded murder she'd committed, and boy, she ate it up. Actually chuckled. "He didn't write a note."

"He didn't?"

"I did."

"You?"

"He denied everything. Said there wasn't no other woman. Got all emotional, started boo-hooing, though I reckon a gun pointed straight at your chest has a way of doing that. Him crying got me all fired up and flustered. Then *bam bam bam,* and he's dead on the floor. I barely touched that trigger. Didn't even mean to do it.

"When I'm burying him, I find a receipt in his pocket. From the XPress Mart, right? Had his fingerprints on it, which got me to thinking. I walk to his house when I'm done, let myself in with his keys, scratch a note on the back of it. Simple block lettering. He wrote like a third grader, so it was easy."

I rubbed my whiskers, cupped my chin. "Pretty damn good, Deb. I gotta give credit where credit's due." Figured I'd keep buttering her up, see what other info I might squeeze.

She grinned wide and lit a smoke. I'd never seen her so proud. "Stashed his truck at Daddy's."

She was gushing now. Who was I to stop her? "So Joe knows?" I said.

"Knows enough not to ask questions. So like I said, I'm leaving."

I shook my head. "And like *I* said, no, you're not."

"What the hell, Steven? We're done. You know it, I know it. No reason to stick around, so don't play me."

"You and me, we're gonna sit tight, happy and hunky-dory. And wait."

"What do you mean, wait?"

"On Joe."

"On Daddy? Wait for goddamn what, goddamnit?" Her eyes darted, searching for her smokes even though one still smoldered between her fingers.

"Wait on him to croak. Doc says he's got a year left, max, probably only six months. Once I get my half, you're free to roll. But until then you're staying right by my side. For better or worse, remember?"

"You ain't getting half," she said, but the statement lacked conviction. She knew she was beat.

"I'm going out on the porch for the sunset," I said. "Give you a little time to ponder, maybe rewatch that video if you want. Think about what the cops might say if they got their hands on it somehow."

Thirty minutes later she joined me, a fresh smoke pinched in her fingers. Erick sat between my knees, getting his ears rubbed.

"I been thinking," she said.

"Uh-huh."

"I don't wanna wait."

"Well, Deb, in this particular instance, I'd say you don't got much choice."

It appeared she hadn't heard me. "You know, lately I've noticed Daddy's been down in the dumps. Suicidal, even. Maybe I should call his doctor, tell him I'm worried about his mental status or whatever."

"Stability?"

"Yeah, that." She paused as if waiting for me to fully comprehend her meaning. Her intentions. Like she was giving me a second to let it all sink in.

"Deb, it's only six months. Year at the most. Not long in the whole scheme of things."

"Or better yet," she continued, "what if them oxygen tubes accidentally got pinched under a table leg or something?"

"Jesus, Deb."

"Oh, Jesus yourself, Steven. Fuck Jesus."

I once again found myself fearful, and slightly in awe, of my wife. But if truth be told, it was exactly what I'd been expecting. And hoping for.

"You're a dark, dark woman, Deb."

She remained quiet, deep in thought. The only sound on the porch was the shuffle of her bare feet as she paced, and the faint crackle of cigarette paper, that cherry burning hot as it raced down the shaft on her inhale. She shot me a nasty look, but her expression softened when she saw my own. Maybe it was the way my mouth had turned up at the corners, not quite a smile, exactly, but something close. Or maybe it was my eyes, the way I imagined they glimmered as the evening sun lit them up just before vanishing behind the distant hills. Like we were communicating without saying a word.

"I've never been able to change your mind once it's set on something," I said, feeding her fire. "Like a bulldog, you are."

"Damn straight," she said, looking confident as she stared off at the shotgunned sky, a spattering of purples and oranges and blues.

I gave Erick a good rub on his head, realizing I might not have to wait on Joe nearly as long as I'd first thought. And that pleased me to no end. Pleased me real good.

BRIAN SILVERMAN

Breadfruit

FROM *Mystery Tribune*

I READ SOMEWHERE that breadfruit is one of the new super-
foods. They say it contains "high-quality protein." Not that I have a
clue what differentiates high-quality protein from low-quality protein. I do know that here on St. Pierre they have been eating breadfruit well before it was officially deemed a superfood. I've eaten
it enough here myself, and superfood or not, I prefer a potato,
which it resembles somewhat in taste, but a potato most likely has
low-quality protein. So when I saw the two large green globes of
breadfruit patterned with round bumps on its skin on the counter
of my bar, I was not excited. I was, however, very much puzzled.

I was outside in the back of the bar I ran on St. Pierre called the
Sporting Place. It was the middle of the day, a slow Tuesday, and I
didn't expect any customers for a couple of hours. I was working on
the foundation for a small addition to my bar, adding another five
hundred square feet. Since I had owned the piece of land and built
the sports-themed bar five years ago, business had grown. There
were times when I just couldn't handle the overflow crowds, like
when the Windward Islands All Star cricket team was playing Barba-
dos for the Caribbean title — and when I held an impromptu fete
for local calypso legend Lord Ram as he lay dying in St. Elizabeth
Hospital. There was space in the backyard of the bar for the addition. I was overdue to expand and had put it off long enough, but
I was in no rush. I was in no rush for anything, which was one of
the reasons I was living on the Caribbean island of St. Pierre. There
were other reasons, but the only one I cared about at the moment
was that there was no rush to finish the addition.

It was when I took a break from my work and went inside to grab a bottle of water that I noticed the breadfruit on the bar. I looked around but knew there was no one in the bar. I hadn't heard anything or anyone while I was working in the back. I took a step out of the front entrance and looked down the road to see if anyone was walking by or had just left. In the distance I saw a dark figure running down the slope of the road. The runner, whose face I could not recognize from the almost 150-yard distance, turned back toward where I stood and then continued to run, his pace quickening. I watched as he disappeared from my sight, turning right onto Victoria Highway, a fully paved, two-way flat of street that on St. Pierre constituted a highway and led into the island's capital and main port, Garrison.

I went back into the bar and examined the breadfruit. Picked one up in my hand. Its flesh was pliant, and it seemed a little lighter than I recalled a breadfruit being. I ran my thumb over the circular bumps on the green skin of the fruit. I picked up the other. They were almost identical in size and shape, and its weight was the same as the other's. Maybe they needed more time on the breadfruit tree to ripen. What did I know about breadfruit? I put them back where I found them.

Tubby Levett came in about an hour later. I was out in the back-yard again, now cleaning the hollowed-out oil canister we used as a smoker. "You see the two breadfruit on the bar?" he said to me, one foot in and one foot out of the doorway.

I looked up from my work. "I did," I replied.

He remained in his position straddling the back door. He was waiting for an explanation. When he realized he wasn't going to get one, he went back into the bar to help set up for the rush-hour crowd. When I say *crowd*, I mean never more than half a dozen to a dozen in the bar for a Tuesday.

"You want those breadfruits?" I asked Tubby when I came back into the bar, where he was assembling clean glasses on top of the bar.

"What I'm gonna do with more breadfruit?" He shook his head. "My ma has a tree behind the house. The breadfruit fall all year from that tree. We don't need no more breadfruit. But I wanna know who that is who bring you the breadfruit?"

"I'd like to know that too, Tubby."

He looked at me as if I wasn't telling him something or was playing a joke on him. I didn't know what I could say to him to make him believe that I really didn't know who brought the breadfruit into the Sporting Place. I didn't tell him about the runner I saw. What was there to tell, and what did the man running down West Road have to do with the breadfruit? Tubby, who was usually very gregarious, went about his work close-lipped. He thought I was putting something over on him and wasn't happy about it. He thought I was busting his balls, which, I admit, I did now and then.

"Seriously, Tubby, those breadfruits just appeared there this afternoon. I'm not making that up."

"Uh-huh," he mumbled, not looking at me.

The two breadfruit remained where I found them on the bar when Adolphus Grainey came in for his daily, excluding Sunday, afternoon beer. Grainey was a tall, very thin, very dark-skinned man who worked up at the base of the national park surrounding Mount Hadali, St. Pierre's centuries-dormant volcano, as one of the groundskeepers. He was in his late sixties, I think, and lived alone in a small house about a mile down the road toward Garrison. His wife died several years ago, before I arrived on the island, and he mentioned to me that he had a married daughter who lived in Toronto and a son working in Trinidad.

He took his usual seat on the bar and examined the breadfruit while I opened a cold Carib beer for him.

"You want them, they're yours," I said to him.

He nodded, holding one in his hand. "A light one," he muttered. "I roast them with a little butter and salt."

"Do whatever you like with them," I said.

"Thank you, Mr. Len," he said to me as he put them in the canvas satchel he carried along with the sharp cutlass he needed for his work clearing the brush that was constantly encroaching on the groomed grounds of the national park.

Though my first name is Len, I had assumed the name here on St. Pierre by many as "Mr. Len." No matter how many times I politely said just to call me Len, it always came out Mr. Len. I wasn't sure if it was a sign of respect, the inability to properly pronounce my last name, Buonfiglio, or maybe the people of St. Pierre just were not comfortable calling me by my last or first name without a proper title attached. It had a colonial, plantation, antebellum feel to it whenever anyone addressed me that way, and it bothered me each time I was called that, but I had long since given up correcting them when they addressed me. Even Tubby, who wasn't tubby at all—in fact there probably wasn't more than an ounce of fat on his lean, muscular frame—and who was my right-hand man at the Sporting Place, called me Mr. Len. And he called me that later in the evening, when I was out in the back of the bar organizing what I planned for the bar extension work the next day.

"Mr. Len," Tubby said, poking his head out of the back door. "A man here who say he want to have a talk with you."

Tubby kept looking at me. He was gesturing in some way, trying to tip me off about the man, but I wasn't picking up his meaning. I put down what was in my hands and went into the bar.

The man at the bar was our only customer seated at the bar; Thomas Griffin and Marvin Toon, two friends who worked at the Karime Rum distillery, the island's lone rum distillery, were seated at a table, bottles of Carib in front of them, and deep in discussion.

When I entered, the man turned to me and smiled. He wore tinted glasses even in the dimly lit bar; his dark hair was long and lank and he wore it wrapped in a bun with a scrunchy like a woman would on his head. A man bun. I'd seen other men do that to their long hair in New York—especially in Brooklyn, for some reason. In my opinion it looked silly, but who was I, with not much remaining hair on my own head, to judge what a man does with his hair. This man was very thin and wore a flowered, colorful short-sleeved shirt loose that hung over his beige khakis. As I got closer I could see that his yellowish brown skin was pockmarked. I also saw the tattoo near the back of his neck, just a bluish blur that looked more like a bad bruise than anything else. I couldn't tell how old he was; anywhere from thirty to fifty. "Joseph Arjoon here," he said, extending his hand. "And you are Mr. Buonfiglio, though from what I've learned also known as Mr. Len."

"That's what they call me here," I replied, trying again not to make claim to how I was addressed. I took his hand; it was a small, bony hand, but I didn't disrespect him by squeezing it too hard.

"Wonderful spot you have here," he said in a formal Caribbean lilt. Like others I met from some of the islands, he was a mix of many races. I could see East Indian in him, Chinese, some remnant was there of an indigenous race, and maybe even a trace of Spanish nobility. But he didn't look like he was from St. Pierre, where most of the locals were dark-skinned descendants of African slaves. And his very proper British Caribbean inflection belied his, to be frank, somewhat thuggish appearance.

"What can I do for you, Mr. Arjoon?" I said, moving behind the bar. He spun on his stool to face me, the smile still wide and revealing teeth that looked like they hadn't seen a dentist in decades.

"I'm a businessman from Guyana," Arjoon said. "Here on this tropical paradise of yours, or should I say, an island you've adopted, to do some business."

There was excess water on the polished mahogany bar in front of him. I wiped it down with a towel. I wondered what more he knew about me. "And what is your business?" I inquired.

He sipped from a bottle of Heineken and then put it down. Adjusting his tinted glasses and looking me in the eye, he said, "Breadfruit."

I froze for just a moment, and then realized Arjoon was studying my reaction to what he just said. I resumed wiping the bar, now trying not to look caught unawares, making sure my expression remained stoic as it was before he made his proclamation.

"I didn't know there was much of a business in breadfruit," I said, keeping my head down on the work I was doing.

"Oh, but there is, Mr. Buonfiglio. You would be surprised." He swiveled his beer bottle with his fingers as he talked. "Breadfruit, which we have in abundance on Guyana, has been classified by some as a new superfood. The world is just now beginning to realize its many health benefits."

"Yeah, I heard it has high protein," I said with a smile.

He returned my smile, keeping the eyes behind those tinted glasses on me. "So you do know something about breadfruit. But did you know that breadfruit has more potassium than a banana? Do you know what that means?"

"I don't, Mr. Arjoon."

"The more potassium, the better the blood flow. It helps those blood vessels relax. In other words, Mr. Buonfiglio, breadfruit does wonders for high blood pressure."

I tried to act amused and smiled back at him. "Well, if I have any problems in that area, I will make sure to load up on my breadfruit intake."

He laughed into his beer. "You do look fit and healthy. Island life, it seems, has been good for you."

I said nothing. This was getting a little too cute for me. He was talking but saying nothing.

Realizing my patience was beginning to wane, he went on with his pitch. "Now I'm sure you know that the climate here on St. Pierre is, as on Guyana and so many of these beautiful islands, also conducive to the cultivation of breadfruit."

"Yeah, the trees are everywhere," I said bluntly.

"And we can thank Captain Bligh for them," he said.

I looked at him. "What?"

"Captain Bligh. The mutiny on the *Bounty*. You know the story, don't you?"

"What's the mutiny on the *Bounty* got to do with breadfruit?" I asked, vaguely remembering the plot of the movie of the same name.

"Well, if Bligh's vessel wasn't mutinied, maybe the breadfruit plants he went to fetch in Tahiti would have gotten to these islands sooner," Arjoon said. "And maybe the fruit would have been accepted more readily in Western society. It's a marvelous story. So good they've made three movie versions of it."

"Yeah, didn't they make one with Marlon Brando? And he ended up with one of those Tahitian girls?" I asked.

He sipped his beer and laughed into it. "That he did, Mr. Buonfiglio. It's funny how the local girls seem attracted to the white westerner." He looked at me. How much more did he know about me? I wondered. "Anyway, that was one version. Before that it was Clark Gable playing Fletcher Christian and the great Charles Laughton as Captain Bligh. The most recent, called *The Bounty*, starred Mel Gibson and Anthony Hopkins as Bligh. Can you imagine three movies where breadfruit is a central plot device?"

"I thought it was the mutiny," I said, not knowing really what I was talking about but trying to make conversation about this nonsensical subject.

"That's a matter of opinion, Mr. Buonfiglio. I like to think that it was the breadfruit that propelled the action. There would be no voyage, no mutiny if it weren't for the task of returning to the West Indies with breadfruit plants. And to show his resilience, after being tossed from his vessel by his crew and then navigating himself to safety, Bligh was promoted to captain and sent back to Tahiti once more for breadfruit plants."

"He didn't get mutinied again, did he?" I asked, suddenly actually curious.

"No." Arjoon smiled. "He was successful in bringing back a few hundred plants to St. Vincent and then Jamaica. And now look. As you said. The trees are everywhere."

I nodded. "They are. And?"

"And a man who can harvest the fruit and export it to other countries to meet the growing demand overseas can make himself a lucrative business."

"Is that what you do, Mr. Arjoon?" I leaned back against the bar, my arms folded across my chest, now looking him in the eye. I wanted him now to know that we were communicating without the bullshit he was spewing. That I knew that he was playing with me.

"Something like that," he said. He went into the pocket of his flowery shirt and pulled out a business card. "We can discuss my business further if you like, at your convenience. That is my mobile number. I will be staying at LuJean's Guest House for the evening."

"LuJean's?"

"Yes, I hear she makes a delicious breakfast for her guests. I'm looking forward to it."

"Breadfruit pudding?" Even I knew about her famous breakfast.

He laughed loudly, his smile again showing off those sorry teeth. "Oh yes . . . it has quite the reputation, doesn't it?"

With that he slid his bony frame off the barstool and made his way to the front entrance. I thought he might turn around and smile again at me, but he didn't.

I waited a few moments behind the bar to make sure he wouldn't come back in and then I made my way to the door. Tubby was right behind me. Both of us saw the black Lexus SUV pull out of the small parking lot and head down West Road toward Garrison.

"Someone in that car waiting," Tubby told me as we stood at the doorway. "It was running all the time that man in here."

"I know," I said.

Tubby saw the concern on my face.

"What's going on? What that man say to you?"

"I'm really not sure." I paced a bit, moving from the front entrance again to the bar and back, peering into the dark quiet of West Road.

Toon and Griffin stopped their discussion to look at me. Neither said anything. They were waiting for my next move. I was waiting for my next move. I had suspicions, but that was all. And even if my suspicions were real, this was all new to me. I was a bar owner. I knew cops back in New York. They came to my bars. I talked to them. But I wasn't a cop. And those cops were not on this island. Something was pushing me forward here. I knew I had to act, but I didn't know how, or really what to do or why. In New York, even if I had suspicions of something not right, I wouldn't have done a thing. Here, though, it was different. Here I felt a responsibility I never felt before.

"Where does Grainey live?" I asked Tubby, a sick feeling rising up in my belly.

"Grainey? The man was here earlier," Tubby said, surprised by my question.

I grabbed the keys to my jeep. "Where does he live? Is he near the turnaround past the Blue Tyre Shop?"

Tubby sensed my urgency. He shook his head. "No, not that far down de road. Grainey, he live two house from the LeGrande Miracle Church. The house with the green door. Why you want to find Grainey?"

I didn't answer. I was out the door and into my jeep. I could see Tubby, along with Toon and Griffin, standing in the doorway, watching. Wondering.

I was wondering too. I had no idea what I was doing. But I had an idea what I would find. And I didn't think it would be good.

I saw the flashing lights in the darkness of a St. Pierre night from almost a mile away. All I had to do was follow them and I knew I would find Adolphus Grainey too. I had a feeling of dread that reminded me of what I anticipated that June morning back in New York. When I felt the ground shake under my feet.

They had just gotten him into the ambulance when I pulled up. A police car was next to the ambulance, and Superintendent Keith McWilliams was there talking to another policeman I recognized as Albert Haines. They stopped their conversation when they saw me arrive.

"What happened to Grainey? Did someone do something

to him?" McWilliams, who was very tall, thick in the chest, dark-skinned with bloodshot eyes, said nothing for a moment.

"Why would you say that, Mr. Len?" he said to me in his deep, sleepy voice.

"The ambulance. This is his house, isn't it?" I gestured.

"Yes, but why do you ask if someone did something to him?" I realized my error and was impressed that McWilliams, who, working as a policeman in St. Pierre for so long and not having to do much detective work, quickly picked up on my blunder.

I shrugged. "Why would the police be here if not," I muttered, hoping to cover up my carelessness.

He nodded slowly, still examining me. "It seems so, Mr. Len. He got beat up pretty bad. You don't know anything about this, do you?"

"Me? No . . . I was driving down to Garrison and saw the lights. Grainey is a friend. He stops into the Sporting Place almost every day."

McWilliams nodded. He was looking again for any hesitation or doubt. He was looking for the truth. And the truth was, I didn't know what was going on. All I had were hunches.

"Today?" McWilliams asked, keeping his unwavering eye on me.

"He was in today," I responded, with a nod.

"Did he say anything to you about someone after him? Was there anything different about today that you noticed?"

Yes, there were two breadfruits on my bar, which appeared out of nowhere. And I gave them to him. A few hours later a man appeared, inquiring about a breadfruit business. A man not from St. Pierre who had bad skin, bad teeth, a tattoo on his neck, and wore his hair in a male hair bun. That's what I probably should have told Superintendent McWilliams, but I didn't. What I muttered instead was a barely comprehensible "No . . . nothing."

"Poor Mr. Grainey . . . he de kindest man." All of us turned to see Netty Langford, covered in an old robe, thick glasses that were slightly crooked, and a net over her thin gray hair. She had been right behind us, listening to our conversation. "And de man stop by my house just a couple of hours ago."

"You say you were with him tonight?" McWilliams said to her in his deep, slow delivery.

"Before dark. I was in the yard tidying . . . he stopped to chat. We chat for just a little while and den he say he need to fix he supper. I offered to fix something for he, but de man, he never say yes to dat. Just a supper is all I offer he. Why de man think I want something else?" She looked at the three of us.

"Did you see or hear anything from his house after he left?" McWilliams asked her.

She thought for a moment. "I had the radio on . . . my hearing . . ." Her eyes, through those thick lenses, looked hurt, ashamed that her minor handicap prevented her, in some small way, from helping. "Why would someone hurt him? Please say de man recover?"

McWilliams looked down. "We certainly hope he will," he mumbled.

The ambulance sped off to St. Elizabeth Hospital, its siren blaring through the otherwise quiet night. I could see Netty Langford staring at it with worried eyes. "Jesus take care of the good," she muttered, and then she turned and shuffled back to her house.

I watched as she went back into her house. McWilliams turned to me. "I trust, Mr. Len, I will hear from you if you have any information for me." His red-rimmed, almost hound-dog eyes were boring into me.

"Of course," I said. "I'll do anything to help you find who did this to Grainey."

I waited in my jeep, pretending to talk on my cell phone, until McWilliams's police car left, and then I got out. I walked over to Netty Langford's house and knocked on her door. There was harmonic gospel playing from a radio. It was loud enough to be heard from outside. Through the screen door I could see her in her small living room, her Bible in her hand as she sat in her chair. I knocked again and she got up, turning toward the door. "It's me, Mrs. Langford," I said. "Len from the place up the hill."

"Yes," she said, slowly rising from her chair and turning to me. "Come in then."

I pushed the screen door open and entered. The kitchen was just to the right of the living room, the two rooms separated by a thin linoleum black-and-white-checkered walkway. There was a small round dining room table on the side of the room of the kitchen with three chairs around it. On top of the table were the two breadfruits I had given Adolphus Grainey.

"Grainey gave those to you?" I asked, looking at her as she made her way slowly to me.

"He did. De man such a kind one." She shook her head. "He say he get dem on the way back from his work. I tell him I don't need breadfruit, but he insist."

I thought about what had happened. What Grainey did. Or really, what he didn't do. What he must have endured by saying nothing. He knew what they were after, but he was protecting his neighbor. My eyes seemed to narrow as I realized more and more of what was going on. I had long ago learned to keep my mouth shut even when I wanted to roar. This was one of those moments. It took all I had to remain calm in front of Netty Langford. I picked one of the breadfruits up in my hand and then the other.

"Mrs. Langford, do you mind if I take these?" I asked, knowing my request would most likely puzzle her.

She laughed. "You can have dem. Dey no good anyway. I don't know where Mr. Grainey find breadfruit like dis."

"No good?" I looked from her to the breadfruit I held.

"You feel dem, sir. Dem breadfruit not real or something. A breadfruit heavier den dem you hold. Take dem. Dey good for nothing, not even for porridge." She shook her head.

I thanked her and, with the breadfruits in my hands, went back to my jeep. I sat in the jeep in the dark in front of Mrs. Langford's house for several minutes. I could call Superintendent McWilliams with what I knew . . . or suspected. He would ask why I didn't tell him earlier. I wouldn't have an answer, but it would be better than getting in any deeper. He could handle it from here on in. I knew that was what I should do. But I wasn't going to do that. I had been on St. Pierre for almost five years without incident. I loved my new home and wanted to remain on the island. I knew what I was planning might jeopardize my citizenship, but I didn't care. I felt a certain obligation to take care of this myself. And on some primal level I very much looked forward to it.

I drove back to the Sporting Place. Tubby was behind the bar, talking to Garnett Evans, who was on a stool nursing a beer. They both looked at me when I walked in.

"I hear Mr. Grainey someone beat he bad," Tubby said. "Is that where you go? You knew?" He stared at me suspiciously.

"I didn't know," I said, being as truthful as I could be. I didn't want anyone else to have any idea what I was thinking. I didn't want to bring anyone else into this. This was for me to handle alone.

"Where you go?" Tubby inquired, his eyes still on me.

"I needed to check on my house," I lied. "I forgot to leave food and water for the dogs."

Tubby hissed through his teeth and shook his head. He was putting clean glasses into the cabinet below the bar. He knew me well enough to know I was bullshitting him, and it wasn't making him happy. But I didn't care. I wasn't bringing him in on this.

"Ferguson come in here while you gone and tell us they find the body of Ricky Sagee in the lagoon," Garnett said.

"Sagee?" Ricky Sagee was a local small-time hustler who worked the beaches and cruise port, selling ganja, hallucinogenic herbs, Viagra, sex, and anything else perceived as exotic to tourists.

"Gunshot," Garnett added, pointing his finger to his forehead and pulling the trigger. "Executed what Ferguson say."

And McWilliams said nothing about that to me, I thought to myself. So we were keeping information from each other.

I quickly thought of the dark figure running down the hill earlier in the day. The one who put the breadfruits on my bar counter. Was it Sagee? I had no evidence. I didn't know for sure. I was what they called surmising.

"What that man say to you earlier? The skinny man with the hair," Tubby asked, looking me in the eye. "He tell you something about all this? About Grainey or Sagee?" He was demanding answers. I wasn't giving any.

"No, he didn't tell me anything about any of that," I responded truthfully, looking back into his eyes.

But Tubby didn't believe me, as I knew he wouldn't. He stormed out of the bar, grumbling loudly about "a crock of shit."

I could have told him that the man just talked to me about breadfruit, Captain Bligh, and the mutiny on the *Bounty,* but Tubby would have read that as an insult to his intelligence; that I was busting his balls while withholding information. So though I wanted to tell him all, to confess what I knew, I said nothing. It was better he knew nothing, even if it potentially destroyed our relationship.

One of the four televisions was on, this one to ESPN Caribbean. There was a rugby match from the U.K. playing. I turned it off and began shutting everything down.

"Garnett, I'm closing up," I told Johns. "You should go home now."

He slowly got off the stool, took one last drink from his beer, and put the empty bottle on the bar. "Okay, but why you make Tubby so angry?" he asked. He waited a moment for an answer but, knowing he wasn't going to get one, made his way to the door without looking back.

I was probably closer to Tubby Levett than anyone else on St. Pierre. I met him within a month of my arrival on the island. The first time was when he drove me up to look at the house I would eventually buy on the east coast, overlooking the Atlantic and the island's rocky bluffs. He was filling in for a friend who owned the minibus he was driving, which was also used as a taxi. The next time I saw him, a few days later, he was working behind the bar of the Garrison Yacht Club, where I was to meet a real estate man about the property I was interested in purchasing where I would eventually build my sports bar. He remembered me immediately. "Mr. Len," he said, smiling broadly.

"Call me Len," I tried to correct him, but he wasn't listening.

"You bought that little house on East Road," he said.

"How did you know that?" I asked. He just shrugged. The longer I stayed on St. Pierre, the more I realized that everyone pretty much knew everything about everybody on the small island.

"What are you drinking, Mr. Len?" he asked, his smile wide and generous. "You know I make the best rum punch on de island."

"Oh yeah? Well, let me be the judge of that," I said. After a month on the island I was becoming an expert in rum punches. They say the recipe is "one part sour, two parts sweet, three parts strong, four parts weak." Tubby made it differently. I took one sip and immediately was overpowered by the rum.

"Damn, Tubby! You got the strong and the weak mixed up. Not that I'm complaining." I laughed.

He laughed with me when he saw my reaction. "I don't believe dat old recipe. A true rum punch should be 'one parts sour, two parts sweet, three parts weak, and four parts strong, and if you finish it, you'll know that you belong.'" He grinned. "At least that's what we say here in St. Pierre."

I did finish it, but even after drinking many more of Tubby's special rum punches over the years, I still wasn't sure if I belonged.

A few days after meeting him in the Yacht Club, I ran into Tubby again. I had decided to go for a dive on St. Pierre's acclaimed Purple Reef, a protected underwater site where the coral gave off a purplish glow and the variety of tropical fish supposedly was unsurpassed at any other dive sites around the island. To my surprise, it was Tubby who would accompany me on the dive.

"You drive a taxi, make a mean rum punch, and now you're gonna go on a dive with me?" I asked him as we sat in the boat in our wetsuits. I was bewildered by his work ethic. "What don't you do?"

He just laughed softly at my question. "Well, Mr. Len, I don't play the piano. But I really wish I could."

After purchasing the land where I planned to build the Sporting Place and hiring a local construction crew, I was having trouble communicating exactly what I wanted done. It wasn't that the crew chief and I didn't literally understand each other; there were subtle things I couldn't convey. I needed someone local as a go-between —a liaison between myself and the crew. I thought of Tubby immediately.

I tracked him down at a high school where he was refereeing a cricket match. I sat in the grandstand in the hot sun for almost three hours while the crowd clapped and cheered at action on the field I couldn't follow. A batsman swatted the ball with the flat end of the bat and then ran to a post and back. Sometimes another runner would run while a different batsman hit. Fielders would try to stop a ball from getting through to what looked like an outfield, and the pitchers, or what I learned were the "bowlers," threw with as much velocity as some hard-throwing baseball major leaguers. Sitting there, I had no idea who was winning and how the game was scored, but when the small crowd began to get up and leave, I guessed the match was finally over.

I met him on the field and offered to buy him a beer. We got together at a picnic table near the field out of the sun and I laid out my proposal. I wanted him to work for me. To help me get the Sporting Place off the ground. I told him he could work part-time and continue his other gigs, or I could use him full-time with the promise of continuing once the bar was done as its manager and main bartender. He didn't hesitate. He told me he would take the job even before I told him how much I would pay him for his services. "You pay me fair, Mr. Len, I'm sure of that," he said while looking me in the eye. "I don't want to have to fill in driving Murvin's minibus or working at the Yacht Club only when they call. It's time I do one thing good, not many."

Tubby became more than just an employee. He was really a partner. And he was a friend. The best friend I had on St. Pierre. The Sporting Place was as much his as mine. Despite how close we had become, how much I trusted him, I wasn't going to bring him in on what was potentially a very dangerous affair. After I hired him he got married, and now, with three young girls and his wife pregnant with a fourth child, there was no chance I would risk getting him involved.

I put the two breadfruits on top of the bar exactly where I found them earlier in the day. I reached under the bar and pulled out the cutlass I kept there for whenever Tubby or I needed to crack open a coconut. I slowly sliced through the top of one of the breadfruits. It came apart easily—its center had been hollowed of flesh and seeds. As it split in half, the tinted brown plastic packets filled with white powder spilled out onto my mahogany bar. I stared at them for a moment. I did the same to the other breadfruit. More brown packets fell out.

All of the Caribbean islands were ripe for smuggling, but St. Pierre had a reputation as being mostly immune to hard drugs and drug smuggling. The island did have its share of ganja, and occasionally there would be a big bust in the waters around the island or at customs at the port or airstrip, but for whatever reason, the hard stuff and what followed was kept out.

I continued to stare at the plastic packets of powder. I knew where I could reach Superintendent Keith McWilliams. He was who I should have called. But I remembered what I felt when I saw the flashing lights of the ambulance in front of Adolphus Grainey's house. What the man took from them to protect his neighbor —from something I gave to him. I reached into the back pocket of my jeans and took out the card I was given earlier by Mr. Arjoon. I turned on my cell phone and punched in the numbers that were on the card.

"Mr. Buonfiglio," he answered. I could hear the satisfaction in his voice. "How did I know I would get your call?"

The sound of his voice made me cringe. "I don't know. I guess you have skills others don't."

He laughed. "I think not, just business instincts. That's all. And you are calling to tell me you have what I need to conduct my business?"

"Yeah, I've got them at my place. I can meet you there in an hour."

There was a pause on the line. "I hope you use good sense, Mr. Buonfiglio. It would be bad for all if there were a lapse in your judgment. I know a bit about you. As I said, I think it's good business to understand what motivates potential partners."

"You don't know a thing about me," I grumbled. "I'll see you in an hour." I cut off the line and sat for a moment. What I did in New York was public record. Why I did it I knew, wasn't.

I quickly turned off all the lights in the bar and headed out to my jeep. I was moving on pure instinct now. There were no deep thoughts and introspection about what I really should do. I was just letting my mind follow my body, rather than the opposite. The same feeling I had on that morning in June. I know now I should have handled things differently then. Doing what I did on that day changed my life. On that day for those people, they had no choice; their lives, their futures were not in their hands. But mine was. And my family's. I had a choice then, and I had a choice now. Or did I really?

An hour later I was sitting alone in the semidarkness of the Sporting Place. The only lights on were the lighting under the bar and behind the bottle display; they gave off a dim greenish glow. You couldn't see much in the bar overall, but when Arjoon arrived, the two breadfruits on the bar would be easily visible.

I was sitting at one of the tables. I had thought about keeping the cutlass close by, but then decided against it. The cutlass was what I had always known as a machete, a tool for cutting away brush. But since moving to St. Pierre, I had adapted the Caribbean term for the tool. It was a household staple on the island. You could see them dangling from the hands and even belts of men walking to work in the mornings. There was almost no gun violence on St. Pierre. Gun laws were strict, and firearms were illegal without a series of hard-to-obtain permits and expensive tariffs. Attempts at gun smuggling, and there had been a few since I had lived on the island, were dealt with harshly. As an alternative, the cutlass was often a cause of violence and crime. And when it occurred, it wasn't pretty. Thankfully those instances were also rare. But whoever put a bullet in Ricky Sagee's head had a gun. It very likely could have been Arjoon. The cutlass, even if I were skilled in using it, would do me no good if Arjoon had a gun. What would? I really had no idea.

I had left the door to the bar open, and as I peered from my seat at one of the tables, I could see the approaching headlights of the black Lexus make their way toward the Sporting Place. The headlights shone into the doorway as the car turned into the three-car parking lot in front of the bar.

I heard two car doors open and then close and then Arjoon was at the doorway, followed by a very large light-brown-skinned man with a curly Mohawk and a thick black beard. Arjoon grinned as he looked at me, revealing those crooked teeth.

"Mr. . . . Buon . . . fig . . . lio," he said, drawing out my name with intended drama. "Very good of you to invite us here at this late hour. It has been a long day and I'm tired. I expected to be asleep by now in one of LuJean's comfortable beds and dreaming about her famous breakfast."

I kept my eye on the big man as Arjoon walked past me to the bar.

He glanced at the bar, staring at the breadfruits there. "I came to St. Pierre bearing breadfruit, a carton of twelve. I have accounted for ten—two went missing. Are those my missing breadfruits?"

I didn't answer. "You didn't have to do what you did to Mr. Grainey," I said instead. Arjoon turned back to face me. I looked back at him.

"Oh, but we did. He had something that belonged to me and would not tell me where it was. We . . . well, not we, really, but my associate Parker here did his best to get him to tell us where we could find my property, but the old man just wasn't much of a talker." Arjoon was studying me—trying to read my expression. "I know you gave him what was mine. The poor man suffered because of what you did. But how would you know? You shouldn't really blame yourself. It wasn't your fault at all."

His smile returned, and I felt my mouth go dry. I sensed the big man behind me. I wanted to get up from my chair. It took all I had to stay put.

"I'm hoping our business can conclude without more violence," he said, again turning to the breadfruits on the bar. "I would very much like that. I would very much like to collect what is mine and leave this island. It was a mistake to come here, and I take full responsibility for that."

He leaned against the bar and picked up one of the breadfruits, weighing it in his hand. He looked back at me. His smile was gone. He pulled out a knife from his pocket and opened it, the blade glinting from the lighting behind the bar. He slit the breadfruit open with the knife. Pulp and seeds spilled onto the bar. He quickly cut open the other — again just pulp and seeds. He shook his head as he looked at me and then glanced at the big man behind me.

Before I knew it I was lifted up off my chair and thrown hard against the side of the bar. I felt the air whoosh out of me. I tried to get onto my feet, but the big man, Parker, had me again; this time his fist was driving hard into my chest, knocking me back again.

I slowly tried to stand. Parker was moving toward me again. I needed to get to my feet. I had to get up. Arjoon moved in front of me and held out his palm, keeping Parker away from me. "This is no game, Mr. Buonfiglio," he said, bending over me so close I could see the blackheads on his pockmarked face and smell the curry he ate for dinner on his breath. "Where is my property?"

I stood straight up now. My chest felt as if it had been hit by a sledgehammer. I kept my eyes on Arjoon. "You shouldn't have hurt that man," I whispered to him.

Arjoon just shook his head and pulled his hand back. Parker moved to me again. This time I set myself so I had one leg in front of the other, leaning back a bit on my rear, right leg. It had been a long time since I had done this. I hadn't trained at all since I left New York. I never had the desire. That was part of my past; St. Pierre was my future, whatever was left of it. I didn't think there would be a need for anything like this, but now there was. I flexed the ball of my left leg and, opening up my back right leg, swung up my left leg, whipping it around as fast and straight as I could, my shin driving hard into Parker's neck, the roundhouse kick sending him backward and down onto one of the bar's few tables, shattering it.

The kick stunned me as well; my leg was throbbing and the many nerves in my back buzzing like high-voltage jolts of electrical shocks. Parker was down, but the kick was not forceful enough to put him out. He got up surprisingly quickly and grabbed hold of me. He pinned my left arm against my chest tightly as he delivered jabs to my neck and jaw, but there wasn't enough behind them to take me out. Still, each blow was like a shovel to my head. I wasn't sure how much more I could take. He was much younger. He was much bigger. And my window was closing fast. He had his left arm tight around my own left arm and chest, holding me firm as he delivered his blows, but he had left my hips and legs free. Again, trying to draw on my training from years ago, I quickly swiveled, and almost leaving my feet, I drew the fist and elbow of my right arm up in a rapid motion, spinning it around at full force and driving it through Parker's temple, just above his eye. The diagonal elbow strike stunned Parker, and his arms went lifeless now as they fell from my body. He went down again. I turned, poised now in a fighting position. But this time he didn't get up.

The pain from the blow to Parker's head shot through my elbow down my arm and back up to my neck. It was a numbing tingle that made my legs sway. I was about to turn to Arjoon when I felt the cold gun muzzle against the back of my head. "Put your head on the bar," he commanded. I did as he said. "Very impressive, Mr. Buonfiglio. But now it's over. I have no more time for any of this. I will kill you. And though I liked meeting and chatting with you earlier, now I don't like you at all and will take enormous pleasure in seeing your brains splattered on your shiny bar. So one last time before I take my leave from this backwater island: where is my property?"

With my head pressed to the bar, I heard his words, but I wasn't thinking about them. They were just fading background noise. Instead I thought about how heavy the smoke was and how it singed my throat as I made my way up those stairs on that June morning. I was as close to death then as I was now. But I kept moving. I survived and helped others survive. I didn't do it to be a hero. I had my own selfish—dishonorable—reasons. But they said I was a hero. And that was my curse. I survived that day and many times wished I hadn't. Did I want to survive this one? I wasn't sure.

"Okay now." I heard him grunt and then I heard what sounded like a shot. I expected pain. But all I felt was the force of his body on top of mine.

I pulled myself out from under him. The back of his head was caved in; even that unsightly male hair bun was matted with blood and indented into his skull.

I slowly turned around. Tubby was there. In his hand was a cricket bat, the blood from Arjoon's skull discoloring its wooden finish. I fell back onto one of the barstools. My body was a painful throb that wouldn't stop.

"I see a move like that on TV once," he said. "Muay Thai?" His eyes were on me in a combination of awe and pity.

I looked at him but didn't answer. I could hear my heart pounding in my chest. I was too tired to talk.

"You go to my ma's house and take her breadfruit," Tubby said to me, his eyes on the beat-up mess in front of him. "Next time ask me and I bring the breadfruit to you. Next time you'll know better than to hide de stuff from your partner."

Next time? There better not be a next time, I thought to myself. I gave him a weary nod. "Yeah, Tubby, I will," I mumbled while I continued to try to suck air back into my lungs.

When my heart slowed enough for me to speak more clearly, I pointed to the door to the back. "Tubby, go out to the smoker," I said. "There's a big jar in it. Bring it here."

He put down the bloody cricket bat. I stared at it while I waited. A few moments later he returned, holding a half-gallon jar filled with the brown packets of powder. "Dis what dat man come for? He bring it in the breadfruit?" He laughed to himself and shook his head. "Dem think of everything."

The sound of McWilliams's police car siren was slowly getting louder as it made its way up the hill.

"One more favor, Tubby," I asked, looking up at him. I still couldn't move from where I was.

He put the jar on the bar next to the split breadfruits and looked at me, waiting to see what it was I wanted.

"Make me one of those rum punches of yours."

A small smile began to form on his face. "'One parts sour, two parts sweet," he rhymed. "Three parts weak . . . and four parts . . . strong."

I was able to finally smile.

He kept his eyes on me and continued the rhyme as he went behind the bar and ducked under to grab a bottle of rum. "Drink it all . . ." He stood back up and pulled a glass from the drainer. ". . . and you'll know that you belong."

I drank it all.

Contributors' Notes

In the words of the *New York Times*, **Louis Bayard** "reinvigorates historical fiction," rendering the past "as if he'd witnessed it firsthand." Bayard's affinity for bygone eras can be felt in both his recent young adult novel, the highly praised *Lucky Strikes* (named one of Amazon's top 2017 titles), and his string of critically acclaimed adult historical thrillers: *Roosevelt's Beast, The School of Night, The Black Tower, The Pale Blue Eye,* and *Mr. Timothy.*

A *New York Times* Notable author, he has been nominated for both the Edgar and the Dagger Award. He is also a nationally recognized essayist and critic whose articles have appeared in the *New York Times,* the *Washington Post,* and *Salon.* An instructor at George Washington University, he is on the faculty of the Yale Writers' Conference and was the author of the popular *Downton Abbey* recaps for the *New York Times.*

• How did I go from writing about history to writing about the imminent future? It goes back to the day my mother asked me about my father.

By then Dad had been dead for three years, and my own memories of him were colored by the Alzheimer's that in his final days had swallowed him whole. Mom's dementia, by contrast, was gentler and more incremental, and if she sometimes blanked on the names of her grandchildren or forgot something that had happened to us when we were kids, she was able to find some other memory to cling to, even create new ones here and there.

So when she began quizzing me about my dad, I took it at first for minor fact-checking. But then the questions began to run deeper. What did he do for a living? What did he look like? What did he sound like? What was *he* like? The man with whom she'd spent half a century, the man she'd grieved for so wantonly three years earlier, had simply vanished.

From that realization, a new kind of grief—and, perhaps by way of understanding, a pair of thought experiments.

#1: Imagine learning on unimpeachable authority that from here on out your life will be a continuous cognitive decline. You will go from forgetting people's names to forgetting people. The smiles and faces dearest to you in the world will, sooner or later, be utterly lost to you, and there will be no reversal, no appeal, no reprieve. Do you get out now? While the going's good? I suspect most of us wouldn't. Living is a hard habit to kick, after all, so we would probably muddle along, congratulating ourselves on what we were still able to recall, and by the time the shadows had well and truly descended, it would be too late. We would no longer even be able to mourn our losses, because we would have no memory of what we'd lost.

#2: Now imagine that someone offers to make the call for you—gauge the exact moment when you have slipped into oblivion and afford you the release you no longer have the capacity or awareness to effect for yourself. Do you take them up on it? Knowing that you won't recall having made the transaction? If so, what will your criterion be? The point beyond which you will not suffer yourself to slip?

Those are the end-of-life questions that haunt "Banana Triangle Six." It goes without saying that they haunt me too.

Andrew Bourelle is the author of the novel *Heavy Metal* and coauthor with James Patterson of *Texas Ranger*. His short stories have been published widely in literary journals and fiction anthologies. This is his second story selected for inclusion in a volume of *The Best American Mystery Stories*. Bourelle lives in Albuquerque with his wife, Tiffany, and two children, Ben and Aubrey. He teaches writing at the University of New Mexico.

• Rhonda Parrish asked me to contribute to an anthology she was editing titled *D Is for Dinosaur*. Each author was assigned a letter of the alphabet and was asked to write a story about dinosaurs using that letter. I looked up dinosaurs whose names began with *Y* and came across the Yangchuanosaurus, otherwise known as the Yangchuan Lizard. I kicked around some ideas for a few months, but I couldn't think of anything that I was in love with. Then, as the deadline loomed, I had a strange dream that provided the premise for the story. I can't remember much of the original dream. It certainly wasn't as coherent as the story turned out to be. But the dream gave me my idea: a drug made of dinosaur bones. I wrote the first draft in a rush. It was one of those magical writing experiences where you have just the seed of an idea and the rest of the story grows during the act of writing.

I'm indebted to Rhonda Parrish for publishing the story and for her helpful edits. And thanks to Otto Penzler and Louise Penny for including "Y Is for Yangchuan Lizard" in this volume of *The Best American Mystery Stories*.

T. C. Boyle is the author of twenty-eight books of fiction, including, most recently, *The Relive Box and Other Stories* (2017), *The Terranauts* (2016), and the forthcoming novel *Outside Looking In.* He has published his collected stories in two volumes, *T. C. Boyle Stories* (1998) and *T. C. Boyle Stories II* (2013), and was the recipient of the PEN/Malamud Award in Short Fiction in 1999 and the Rea Award for the Short Story in 2014. He is a member of the American Academy of Arts and Letters.

• Over the course of my career I've taken it as a challenge to inhabit the points of view of characters of diverse ethnicity, gender, and age, attempting, like most artists, to examine the human condition from every angle possible. Early on, when I wasn't nearly so close in age as I am now to Mason Alimonti, I got a letter from my grad-school mentor praising me for my insight into the worldview of the elderly in my stories and novels, and that praise meant as much to me as any prize or blue ribbon. I figured I must have been doing something right, because he was old and I was young, and if anybody knew how the elderly perceive things, he certainly did. But then for me, for all of us, it's an act of imaginative projection to enter that limbic world of the aged—barring accident or disease we will all someday get there, and when we do there will be predators like Graham Shovelin awaiting us.

I received a letter very similar to the one Mason did—in fact, I even lifted certain phrases from it for the sake of authenticity. It was so obviously a fraud I was amazed that anyone could be taken in by it, but then the news is chock-full of stories about people who have been. I didn't have to look too far. A friend of mine fell for a similar scheme, which cost him everything he had—his business, his family, his friends—and no amount of evidence or reasoning could ever persuade him that he'd been taken. Once you invest—financially, yes, but emotionally, in the deepest repository of hope and expectation—you're hooked. And once you're hooked, you're going to be landed, just like Mason.

Michael Bracken is the author of eleven books, including the private-eye novel *All White Girls,* and more than twelve hundred short stories in several genres. His short crime fiction has appeared in *Alfred Hitchcock Mystery Magazine, Black Cat Mystery Magazine, Ellery Queen Mystery Magazine, Espionage Magazine, Mike Shayne Mystery Magazine,* and in many other anthologies and periodicals. A recipient of the Edward D. Hoch Memorial Golden Derringer Award for lifetime achievement in short mystery fiction, Bracken has won two Derringer Awards and been shortlisted for a third, and he has received numerous awards for advertising copywriting. Additionally, Bracken has edited six crime fiction anthologies, including the three-volume *Fedora* series and the forthcoming *The Eyes of Texas.* He lives, writes, and eats barbecue with his wife, Temple, in Central Texas.

• Each time we visit my wife's parents, we spend much of the three-hour drive brainstorming story ideas while Temple notes them on a legal pad. Shortly before one such trip, I read the submission call for *Noir at the Salad*

Bar, which sought stories that "feature food or drink, restaurants, bars or the culinary arts," and during that trip my wife filled two handwritten pages with every food-related story idea we could imagine.

Then she suggested barbecue.

By the time we arrived at her parents' home, I knew the story's setting and primary characters. While Temple visited with family, I filled several more pages of the legal pad with notes, and I created a rough outline. But after inspiration comes perspiration, and the story required several drafts before becoming "Smoked."

James Lee Burke is the author of thirty-six novels and two collections of short stories. He and his wife, Pearl, live in western Montana.

• I wrote "The Wild Side of Life" in part as a tribute to Jimmie Heap, the man who recorded the original of the most famous song in the history of country music. The postwar era marked our entry into neocolonialism and the building of a petrochemical empire, but the vision of those who worked in oil exploration was confined to coastal swamps dotted with cypress and gum trees and live oaks strung with Spanish moss, and beer joints and honky-tonk bands on the levee and jukebox music that played until two in the morning.

People who used to pick cotton and break corn now worked on drilling rigs and strung pipe, and had money and felt an independence they'd never experienced. The southern oligarchy had been broken. Unfortunately, an equally dark reality lay just beyond our ken. Oil companies don't pick fights, but they don't take prisoners either. The bombing I describe took place in South America in 1956.

I've never gotten Jimmie Heap out of my head. Or Kitty Wells, who sang the rebuttal to Jimmie's lament. It was a grand time to be around. Anyone who says otherwise has no idea what he's talking about.

Previously a television director, theater technician, and law student, **Lee Child** is the author of the globally best-selling Jack Reacher series, evaluated by *Forbes* magazine as the strongest brand in contemporary fiction. He was born in Britain and lives in New York City.

• My U.S. publisher wanted to do a collected edition of all the Jack Reacher short stories and asked for a new story to anchor the volume. I wasn't keen—I was in the middle of writing my next novel and didn't have much time. But ironically I ended up very happy with "Too Much Time" —as a concise piece of work I thought it was one of the best things I had ever done.

Michael Connelly has published thirty-one novels, most of which have been about the exploits of LAPD detective Harry Bosch or the Lincoln lawyer Mickey Haller. He is a past president of the Mystery Writers of America.

He splits his time between the Los Angeles he writes about and the Florida where he grew up.

• In "The Third Panel" I got the chance to write about the painter who has had a great influence on me and my books, Hieronymus Bosch. I studied this fifteenth-century artist while in college, and what I found is that there are many different interpretations of his paintings, particularly his masterpiece, *The Garden of Earthly Delights*. I have always been drawn to the third panel, because it depicts the wages of sin and in many ways is similar to a macabre crime scene. Though Harry Bosch does not appear in this story, his name and perhaps grim outlook are drawn from this panel. This is the world where he dwells. I enjoyed writing about it.

John M. Floyd's work has appeared in more than 250 different publications, including *Alfred Hitchcock Mystery Magazine, Ellery Queen Mystery Magazine, Strand Magazine,* the *Saturday Evening Post, Mississippi Noir,* and *The Best American Mystery Stories 2015.* A former air force captain and IBM systems engineer, he is also an Edgar Award nominee and a three-time Derringer Award winner. John's seventh book, *The Barrens,* is scheduled for release in 2018. He and his wife, Carolyn, live in Mississippi.

• As soon as I received the invitation to submit a story to the *Coast to Coast: Private Eyes* anthology, I knew what kind of tale I wanted to tell. Back in 2013 I'd published a long story called "Redemption," about a former gunfighter turned Pinkerton's agent who quit both careers to open a private-investigation office with his brother in San Francisco in the 1880s, and I had for some time been considering doing a sequel to that story. After all, I'd grown up watching westerns and reading about private detectives, and I've always been fascinated by stories/novels/movies about reluctant gunfighters in the Old West — *Shane, Unforgiven, Open Range,* etc. And since I already had a main character I knew well, my only task was to give him a challenging new case and come up with some twists and turns. I finished "Gun Work" several weeks later, sent it in, and was pleased to find that the *C2C:PI* editors, Andrew McAleer and Paul D. Marks, liked it. Now I'm even *more* glad they did . . .

David Edgerley Gates is the author of the Cold War thrillers *Black Traffic* and *The Bone Harvest* and the companion novella *Viper.* His latest book is *Exit Wounds;* the next is *Absolute Zero.* His short stories have been nominated for the Edgar, Shamus, Derringer, and International Thriller Writers Awards. Gates blogs regularly at www.sleuthsayers.org; his website is www.davidedgerleygates.com.

• "Cabin Fever" is one of those stories that started in my head with the weather, something ominous building on the horizon, and picked up momentum from there. It's the fourth of my stories to feature Hector and Katie, and like the others, it's much about physical landscape. Here's a curious thing. I'd already written "Cabin Fever" when I happened on the Craig Johnson novel *Hell Is Empty*, which I hadn't read before. Craig's book has Walt Longmire in pursuit of an escaped con deep in the woods, trapped in a blizzard. Ideas gather shape in their execution. Two different guys pluck a similar situation out of the zeitgeist, independently, and then take off at right angles to each other. It's a little odd, but there it is.

Charlaine Harris is a true daughter of the South. Born in Mississippi, she has lived in Tennessee, South Carolina, Arkansas, and Texas. Her career as a novelist began in 1981 with her first book, a conventional mystery. Since then she's written urban fantasy, science fiction, and horror. In addition to over thirty full-length books, she has written numerous short stories and three graphic novels in collaboration with Christopher Golden. She has been featured on bestseller lists many times, and her works have been adapted for three television shows. Charlaine now lives at the top of a cliff on the Brazos River with her husband and two rescue dogs. She has three children and two grandchildren.

• I've written about Anne DeWitt several times, and it's always fun to see what she's up to. High school principals always seem extremely powerful to the staff and students, but Anne takes this several steps further; she's a survival expert who's trained clandestine operatives, and she's intensely goal-oriented. Travis High is going to be the best high school in North Carolina . . . or else. "Small Signs" is about Anne's past rising up to bite her and how she reacts to the threat.

Rob Hart is the author of five novels: *Potter's Field, The Woman from Prague* (selected as one of the best reads of summer 2017 by *Publishers Weekly*), *South Village* (a best-of-2016 pick by the *Boston Globe*), *City of Rose,* and *New Yorked* (nominated for an Anthony Award for best first novel). He also cowrote *Scott Free* with James Patterson. His short stories have appeared in such publications as *Thuglit, Needle, Joyland,* and *Shotgun Honey.* Nonfiction articles have appeared at *Salon,* the *Daily Beast, Literary Hub, Nailed,* and *Electric Literature.* He is the publisher at MysteriousPress.com and the online writing workshop director at LitReactor. Find him online at @robwhart and www.robwhart.com.

• Someone else noticed before I did: over the course of a few months I had published short stories involving a bagel maker defending his storefront, warring food trucks, and a restaurant scam. A friend asked when my collection of food-noir stories was coming out. When he said that, I was working on a story about the murder of a bouncer at a popular pastry shop. I was writing to a theme without knowing it. Which, in retrospect, is not surprising. I like crime fiction and I like food. And they're both great vehicles for storytelling. Crime is a measure of people at their worst, and food speaks to a wide range of cultural and personal attributes. It turned into a challenge: how many food-noir stories could I write? This is my tenth. I knew I wanted to set a story in Chinatown, and I knew I wanted it to involve enigmatic deliveries. I've always loved walking into Chinatown restaurants and bodegas and feeling completely lost in the city where I grew up. Those vague notions percolated for months until I ran across a news story about a gambling parlor busted above a restaurant in Chinatown. The story clicked immediately.

David H. Hendrickson's first novel, *Cracking the Ice,* was praised by *Booklist* as "a gripping account of a courageous young man rising above evil." He has since published five additional novels, including *Offside,* which has been adopted for high school student required reading. He is at work on a new suspense series, scheduled to release in early 2019. His short fiction has appeared in *Ellery Queen Mystery Magazine* and numerous anthologies, including multiple issues of *Fiction River.* He has published over fifteen hundred works of nonfiction and been honored with the Joe Concannon Hockey East Media Award and the Murray Kramer Scarlet Quill Award. Visit him online at www.hendricksonwriter.com.

• During my family's trip-of-a-lifetime to Africa, I was amazed at the breathtaking wonders of the Serengeti, from the stunning diversity of life in the Ngorongoro Crater to the hundreds of thousands of wildebeests and zebras gathered near the Mara River, where crocodiles awaited, including one giant beast estimated to be eighteen feet long and weighing over a ton.

At the same time I was saddened to hear stories about poachers and their impact, especially devastating on the rhinoceros population. In fact, during our entire trip our group spotted only a single rhino, and that one only barely discernible in the distance through the strongest of binoculars.

That trip inspired my novel *No Defense* (a seemingly oxymoronic combination of a hockey romance and Africa) as well as several short stories. When I heard that *Fiction River: Pulse Pounders Adrenaline* would consist of short thrillers, going back to Africa was the ultimate of no-brainers. If my imagination doesn't make many more return trips to the Serengeti, I'll be very disappointed.

Andrew Klavan is the author of such internationally best-selling crime novels as *True Crime,* filmed by Clint Eastwood; *Don't Say a Word,* filmed starring Michael Douglas; and *Empire of Lies.* He has been nominated for the Mystery Writers of America's Edgar Award five times and has won twice. He wrote the screenplays to *A Shock to the System,* which starred Michael Caine, and *One Missed Call,* which starred Edward Burns. His political satire videos have been viewed by tens of millions of people, and he currently does a popular podcast, "The Andrew Klavan Show," at the *Daily Wire.* His most recent book is a memoir of his religious journey, *The Great Good Thing: A*

Secular Jew Comes to Faith in Christ. His most recent fiction is the fantasy-suspense podcast "Another Kingdom."

• The idea for "All Our Yesterdays" came to me more than twenty years ago, when I was living in London. I had meant to come to the city for a year but fell in love with the place and ended up staying for seven. Part of what I loved about London—and about the U.K. in general—was the deep presence of the past. Something about walking on ground the ancient Romans had trod gave me a peaceful feeling of being part of the great sweep of history. The notion that the love of the past might have a dark side as well led to the idea. I thought it would make a good movie and have pitched it many times without success. But now, with an increasing awareness of "time's wingèd chariot hurrying near," I feel the urge to get as many of my best ideas as possible down on whatever passes for paper. I'm delighted to find myself once again included in this anthology.

Martin Limón spent twenty years in the U.S. Army, ten of them stationed in South Korea. While still on active duty he began writing, typing on a Smith Corona portable typewriter (purchased in the PX) at his on-base quarters. After four years of trying, he published the first of what have now become over fifty short stories. His debut novel, *Jade Lady Burning,* featured 8th Army criminal investigation agents George Sueño and Ernie Bascom. It was published in 1992, shortly after he left the service, and it was selected as a New York Times Notable Book of the Year. Since then George and Ernie have appeared in twelve more novels in addition to *Nightmare Range,* a short story collection. The most recent novel in the series, *The Line,* concerns a murder at the Joint Security Area on the Korean DMZ and is scheduled for publication in the fall of 2018.

• Juliet Grames at Soho Press challenged me to write a Christmas-themed story for inclusion in their collection *The Usual Santas.* At first I balked. Christmas stories seemed to be mostly set in quaint little towns in cozy little bungalows with plenty of snow outside and warm fires inside.

I write about military bases. And military crime.

But then I realized that even at overseas military bases, Christmas —inevitably—comes and goes. And what did commanders worry about most during those holidays? One word leapt immediately to mind: suicide. The military suicide rate rises before, after, and during the Christmas holidays, despite the army's best efforts to keep it down. Back in the early seventies, at the 8th Army Headquarters in Seoul, the commanders also worried about an increasing holiday rate of black market activity. That is, soldiers and their dependents buying duty-free consumer goods in the PX or commissary and then reselling them on the Korean economy. Profit margins were two or three times what the GI shelled out in the first place.

I threw these two issues together, posed a problem for my intrepid investigators, backed them up with a few other characters who I hoped would be interesting, and came up with "PX Christmas." It's not a story for the faint of heart, but I hope that the reader might come to realize that Christmas gifts come in all sorts of packages, even a few wrapped in horror and still dripping with blood.

Paul D. Marks won a Shamus Award for his novel *White Heat,* a mystery-thriller set in Los Angeles during the 1992 Rodney King riots. His story "Ghosts of Bunker Hill" (*EQMM,* December 2016) was voted number one in *Ellery Queen Mystery Magazine*'s 2016 Readers Choice Awards and was nominated for a Macavity Award for Best Short Story. "Howling at the Moon" (*EQMM,* November 2014) was shortlisted for the Anthony and Macavity Awards for best short story in 2015 and came in seventh in *Ellery Queen*'s Readers Choice Awards. His short fiction also has been published in Akashic's Noir series (St. Louis), *Alfred Hitchcock Mystery Magazine, Crimestalker Casebook,* Dave Zeltserman's *Hardluck Stories* magazine, Gary Lovisi's *Hardboiled Magazine, Weber — The Contemporary West,* various anthologies, and many more. He is coeditor of the Coast to Coast: Sea to Shining Sea mystery anthologies. His novella, *Vortex,* was released in 2015. *White Heat* has been reissued and the sequel, *Broken Windows,* is due out in fall 2018.

Paul also has the distinction, dubious though it might be, of being the last person to have shot a film on the fabled MGM back lot before it bit the dust to make way for condos. According to Steven Bingen, one of the authors of the well-received book *MGM: Hollywood's Greatest Backlot,* "That 40 page chronological list I mentioned of films shot at the studio ends with his [Paul D. Marks's] name on it."

Paul has served on the boards of the Los Angeles chapters of Sisters in Crime and Mystery Writers of America. Visit his website at www. PaulDMarks.com.

• Much of my work is inspired by Los Angeles, which I like to think of as another character in my stories. Growing up here, I've always had a fascination with Venice (where I lived for a time as a child and which I visited a lot as a teenager and over the years), both its history and the current carnival-like atmosphere that permeates every inch of it. Venice started as developer Abbot Kinney's fever dream of creating an elegant resort mimicking the romance of Italy's Venice, complete with canals and gondoliers. He wanted his Venice-by-the-Sea to be a cultural mecca. That didn't last long. Neither did most of the canals, many of which were gone by 1929. Over the years the culture and glamour wore off, leaving behind a kitschy and slightly rundown beach town of leftover canals. By the 1950s it was a slum. In the 1960s it was a hangout for Jim Morrison and the Doors. In the '70s and '80s it was a haven for hippies and gangs. Today it's a mix of free spirits, skateboarders, tourists, and gentrifying locals. That contrast between elegant and seedy, glamorous and gauche, old and new, trendy and trashy, rich and poor, intrigues me.

And despite its past-its-prime appearance, Venice has become the number one tourist destination in Los Angeles, at least according to some.

Most everyone knows the famous Venice boardwalk that runs along the shore, but one of my favorite spots is Windward Avenue, a street known for its long, arched colonnade that runs perpendicular to the shore and dead-ends into it. Windward doubled as a Tijuana street in Orson Welles's great film noir *Touch of Evil*, and Venice's oil wells of that time (the late 1950s) were where the oil-field scenes in *Touch of Evil* were filmed.

Venice is a little piece of the exotic on the edge of Los Angeles. That got me thinking about setting my story there and showcasing the colorful and sometimes dangerous streets of Venice Beach in my story "Windward" for *Coast to Coast: Private Eyes from Sea to Shining Sea*. So I gave Jack Lassen, my PI, an office (complete with 1950s bomb shelter) amid the old-world columns and archways of Windward. With a setting like that I needed a crime that would be equally intriguing, and what better fodder for crime than the façade of the movie business, where nothing is what it appears to be and a hero onscreen might be a monster offscreen?

Ultimately Venice is more a state of mind than a location. But either way, a great setting for a story.

Joyce Carol Oates is the author most recently of the story collections *Dis Mem Ber* and *Beautiful Days*. She is visiting professor in the English Department at UC Berkeley (spring 2018) and visiting distinguished writer in the Graduate Writing Program at New York University (fall 2018). Stories of hers have appeared previously in *The Best American Mystery Stories* and in *Pushcart Prize: Best of the Small Presses*. She is the 2017 recipient of the International Festival of Literature and Art with Humor Award (Bilbao, Spain) and was inducted in 2017 into the American Philosophical Society.

• "Still she haunts me, phantomwise"—this line from a poem by Lewis Carroll about his great devotion to Alice Liddell, the seven-year-old daughter of Oxford University friends to whom he'd told the original story of *Alice in Wonderland*, has also haunted me for years. Indeed, the very word *phantomwise* is unique to this poem; I have never encountered it elsewhere.

In my story "Phantomwise: 1972" a nineteen-year-old named Alyce, a sophomore at an upstate New York university, finds herself the object of devotion of an older, much-acclaimed poet with an obsessive interest in the original "Alice in Wonderland" at the same time that she is, less benignly, an object of revulsion on the part of a young philosophy professor who has exploited her naiveté and regrets his involvement with her as a threat to his professional career. The story follows Alyce's adventures in a wonderland, or perhaps a looking-glass world, in which she is simultaneously loved sincerely by one man and detested by the other; a world in which she is simultaneously treasured by one man (who wants to marry her) and an impediment to the other (who wants to annihilate her). Which Alyce prevails? The reader is welcome to decide.

Alan Orloff's debut mystery, *Diamonds for the Dead,* was a best first novel Agatha Award finalist, and his eighth novel, *Pray for the Innocent,* was released earlier this year. His short fiction has appeared in numerous publications, including *Jewish Noir, Alfred Hitchcock Mystery Magazine, Mystery Weekly, Black Cat Mystery Magazine, Snowbound: Best New England Crime Stories 2017,* and *The Night of the Flood.* Alan lives in northern Virginia and teaches fiction writing at the Writer's Center (Bethesda, MD). He loves cake and arugula, but not together. www.alanorloff.com.

• In "Rule Number One," I tried to weave two threads together. First I wanted to explore the honor-among-thieves notion. Was it a workable trope? Or a bunch of tripe? In this story a crook gets involved in a heist with his aging mentor. Which proves stronger, the "criminal drive" or that special bond between student and teacher? Where does a crook's loyalty really lie? With the profession itself, where ripping people off is admired? Or with his criminal partners?

The second thread was born from my fascination with the double-cross, the double agent, the *Mission Impossible* pull-off-the-latex-mask deception where nothing is as it seems. That dark place where morals are murky and shifting allegiances are standard operating procedure.

Which begat the question, how many double-crosses and switchbacks could I shoehorn into one story without things getting ridiculous?

(FYI, nine double-crosses is too many.)

William Dylan Powell is an award-winning author who writes funny and sometimes dark crime stories set in Texas. Powell's short fiction has been featured in *Ellery Queen Mystery Magazine, Alfred Hitchcock Mystery Magazine,* and other publications. He's also the author of *Untimely Demise: A Miscellany of Murder.* He lives in Houston.

• I've always been fascinated with the intersection of nature and urban living—which can seem so fundamentally unnatural. When I first heard about the one hundred–plus vehicles submerged in the murky water of Houston's bayous, I couldn't help but wonder about the story behind each. At the same time, cheap oil was eviscerating the energy-based Houston economy, which had for the most part shrugged at the downturn felt by the rest of the country. I wanted to write a story bringing these two very Houston phenomena together.

Texas EquuSearch, a volunteer force that helps find missing persons via horseback, initially discovered the vehicles while using sonar equipment in the course of their work. After "The Apex Predator" was published (though not because of it), the Harris County Flood Control District, together with the City of Houston and Harris County Precinct 2 commissioner Jack Morman, initiated the Submerged Vehicle Recovery Project.

Working in phases, the project removed more than seventy vehicles from Houston bayous. Most of the vehicles had been stolen, one during an aggravated robbery and another during a home invasion. Seventeen were too deteriorated for identification, and many simply fell apart. Unlike in my story, nothing of investigative interest was found in any of the vehicles. The project was completed in mid-August 2017. Hurricane Harvey hit on August 29, 2017.

Scott Loring Sanders is the author of two novels, a short story collection, and an essay collection called *Surviving Jersey: Danger & Insanity in the Garden State*. A previous story of his appeared in *The Best American Mystery Stories 2014*, and he's also had work noted in *The Best American Essays 2015*. The piece selected for this year's anthology was first published in his collection *Shooting Creek and Other Stories*. He is a frequent contributor to *Ellery Queen Mystery Magazine*, and his work has appeared in a wide array of journals, ranging in scope from *Creative Nonfiction* to *North American Review* to *Sweet*, among many others. He's been the writer in residence at the Camargo Foundation in Cassis, France, and most recently was a fellow at the Edward F. Albee Foundation in Montauk, NY, where he began work on a new literary suspense novel. He teaches creative writing (including mystery writing) at Emerson College and Lesley University.

• The evolution and actual creation of this story, like all of my work, is more or less a complete mystery (pun intended.) I do know that at the time I was teaching a story by Larry Brown called "Big Bad Love," which has nothing to do with crime or mystery at all. But I've always loved that protagonist's voice, and so, using my own little spin, I tried to mimic some of that with my main character, Steven. Except where Larry Brown's protagonist was a bit of a sexist, drunken dimwit, I wanted Steven to be much more savvy and complex than the way most people perceived him on first blush. In fact, I wanted him to use that misperception to his advantage. I believe the saying that best describes him goes something like, "Oh, he's dumb all right. Dumb like a fox."

I often set my stories in the Blue Ridge Mountains of Virginia, where I lived for twenty-five years. I love those mountains, as well as the people who hail from them. For several years I worked on Christmas tree farms in the area and always knew that one day I'd probably write about the experience, because it's such a rich and unique environment. It's tough, brutal work (far more difficult than sitting at a desk and punching keys on a keyboard) but also gratifying and a great way to experience the outdoors through all four seasons, with each period offering its own particular challenges and rewards. During my time on the farms I met some of the hardest-working people I've ever known, as well as some of the most down-to-earth and caring, but I was always bothered by how certain groups were clearly treated differently than others. Perhaps, in my own little way, this sheds some light on that. But mostly it's just a story full of twists and turns and surprises to keep readers thinking and on their toes. I hope I was able to accomplish that with "Waiting on Joe" while creating a bit of an homage to the late, great Larry Brown. And yeah, I once had a dog exactly like Erick—smelly rabbit fetus, leather footballs, dirty diapers, and all. But his name was Kafka, swear to God.

Brian Silverman has been a professional writer for over thirty years. The diverse subjects he has covered over those years include food, travel, music, and sports. His travel and food writing has appeared in publications such as *Islands, Caribbean Travel & Life,* and *Saveur.* He served as senior writer for Frommer's Travel Guides for ten years and was the author of that brand's New York City guidebook series. His sports background includes, most notably, editing *Going, Going, Gone: The History, Lore and Mystique of the Home Run* and, in a collaboration with his father, Al Silverman, *The Twentieth Century Treasury of Sports.* A lifelong love of mystery literature and the works of Elmore Leonard, Robert B. Parker, Walter Mosley, and Charles Willeford, to name just a few, inspired him to write his debut mystery story, "Breadfruit." He lives in New York with his wife of twenty years, his two sons, and a dog named Milton.

• As a travel writer I've visited most every Caribbean island and some more than a few times. I covered the region mainly from a cultural perspective; I would write about the music, the food, festivals, and the people rather than about the all-inclusive hotels or the cruise-boat lines that frequent the Caribbean. I came to love many of the islands, especially the smaller, more remote ones that were still somewhat immune to the encroachment of big-time tourism and all that entails. I wrote a short story not long ago with the main character, an ex–New Yorker, who settles on one of those small remote islands, a fish out of water who starts a business on the island and slowly comes to learn the sometimes strange ways of the island. The story, "Pane di Casa," was not a traditional mystery, though you could, I guess, call it a mystery of the heart. I wrote another with the same character and on the same fictional island, which I named St. Pierre, and then, thanks to the persistent prodding of my wife, who knew of my love of the works of Lawrence Block, Chester Himes, Michael Connelly, and others, encouraged me to try something similar to what I was reading and had read almost all my life. Taking the characters and the fictional island I created in the other stories, I turned the main character into someone who, whether he wants to or not, begins to solve crimes and other problems; who becomes involved in a deeper way in the lives of the islanders. The first of those stories is "Breadfruit."

Other Distinguished Mystery Stories of 2017

LEE, M. C.
Angel Face. *Ellery Queen Mystery Magazine*, May-June

MALLORY, MICHAEL
Aramis and the Worm. *Alfred Hitchcock Mystery Magazine*, September-October

McCAULEY, TERRENCE
The Solitary Man. *Down & Out: The Magazine*, vol. 1, no. 1, ed. by Rick Ollerman

McGEE, KAREN
Something of Value. *Dark City Crime and Mystery Magazine*, April

McMAHAN, ALISON
The Drive-By. *Busted! Arresting Stories from the Beat*, ed. by Verena Rose, Harriette Sackler, and Shawn Reilly Simmons, Level Best

PARKER, ALESIA
Ma'am. *Atlanta Noir*, ed. by Tayari Jones, Akashic

PETRIN, JAS. R.
Money Maker. *Alfred Hitchcock Mystery Magazine*, May-June

PLUCK, THOMAS
Deadbeat. *Down & Out: The Magazine*, vol. 1, no. 1, ed. by Rick Ollerman

ROZAN, S. J.
Chin Yong-Yun Stays Home. *Alfred Hitchcock Mystery Magazine*, January-February

RUSS-COMBS, DOMINIC
Manglevine. *Ellery Queen Mystery Magazine*, November-December

SOLDAN, WILLIAM R.
Houses Burn. *Mystery Tribune*, Spring

SOOS, TROY
Family Tradition. *Mystery Weekly Magazine*, February

STRONG, SARAH PEMBERTON
Callback. *New Haven Noir*, ed. by Amy Bloom, Akashic

TUCHER, ALBERT
Sensitivity Training. *Busted! Arresting Stories from the Beat*, ed. by Verena Rose, Harriette Sackler, and Shawn Reilly Simmons, Level Best

VASICEK, RENE GEORG
Vera Musilova. *Bellevue Literary Review*, vol. 17, no. 2

WALKER, JOSEPH S.
Awaiting the Hour. *Day of the Dark: Stories of Eclipse*, ed. by Kaye George, Wildside

WARSH, SYLVIA MAULTASH
The Ranchero's Daughter. *13 Claws*, ed. by Donna Carrick, Carrick

THE BEST AMERICAN SERIES®

FIRST, BEST, AND BEST-SELLING

The Best American Comics

The Best American Essays

The Best American Food Writing

The Best American Mystery Stories

The Best American Nonrequired Reading

The Best American Science and Nature Writing

The Best American Science Fiction and Fantasy

The Best American Short Stories

The Best American Sports Writing

The Best American Travel Writing

Available in print and e-book wherever books are sold.

hmhco.com/bestamerican